LORD OF FIRE

Also by Gaelen Foley

The Duke
Lord of Fire
Lord of Ice
Lady of Desire
Devil Takes a Bride
One Night of Sin

LORD OF FIRE

Gaelen Foley

All the characters in this book are fictitious and any resemblance to real persons, living or dead, is entirely coincidental.

First published in Great Britain in 2005 by
Piatkus Books Ltd of
5 Windmill Street, London W1T 2JA
email: info@piatkus.co.uk

This edition published 2005

First published in the United States in 2001 by
The Random House Publishing Group

A catalogue record for this book is available from the British Library

ISBN 0 7499 0768 1

Set in Times by
Phoenix Photosetting, Chatham, Kent

Printed and bound in Great Britain by
Mackays Ltd, Chatham, Kent

To my favorite feisty heroine, Aunt Yi,
and her lovable tough-guy hero, Uncle Gene,
in honor of their fortieth wedding anniversary.
May there be many, many more—
Love always,
G

Georgiana's Brood: THE KNIGHT MIS

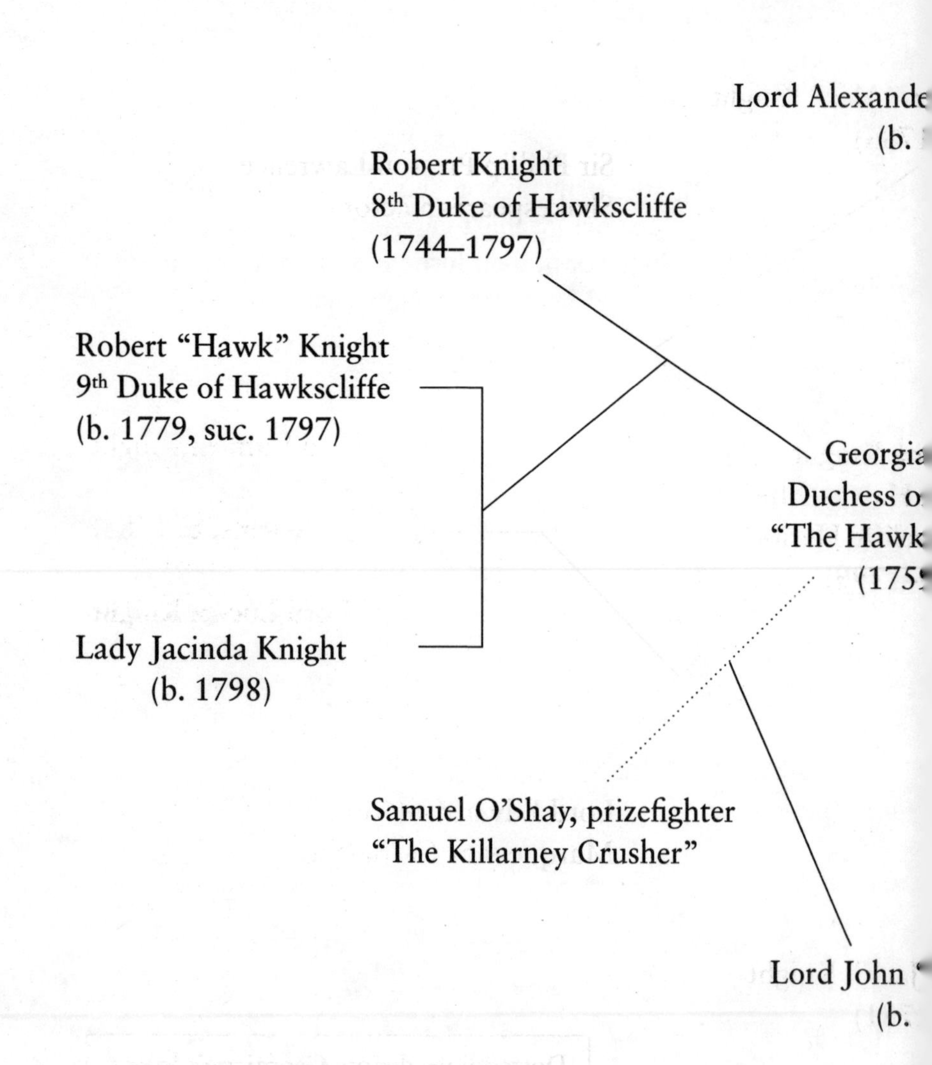

CELLANY

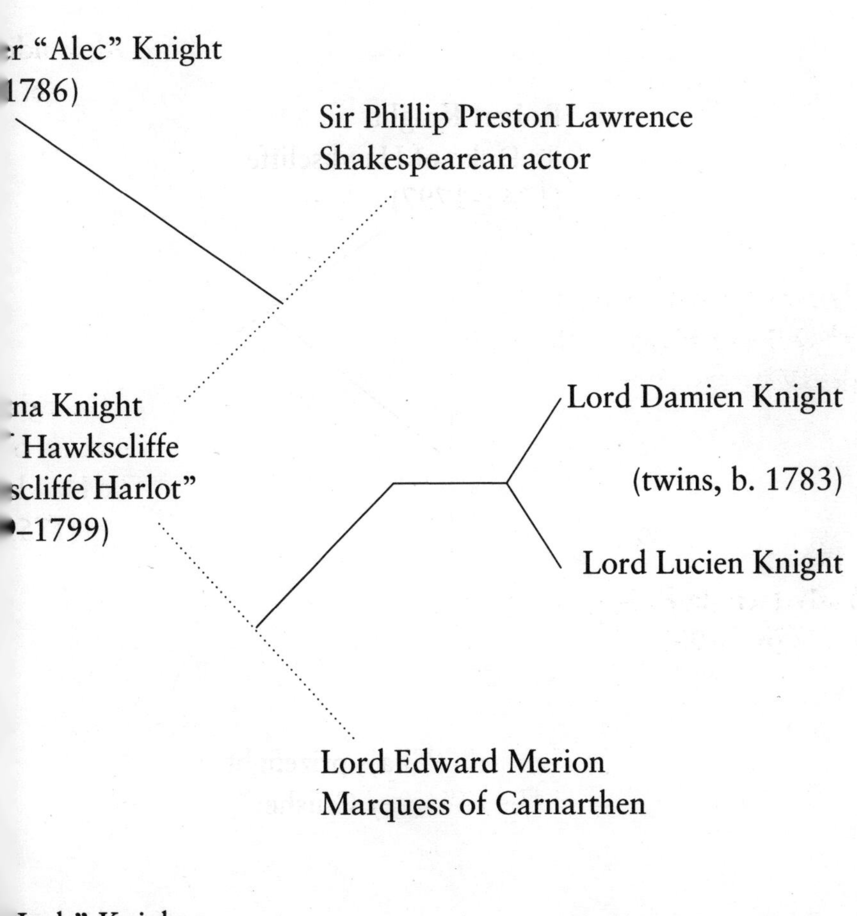

Jack" Knight
781)

Dotted lines denote Georgiana's lovers

Something wicked this way comes.

—SHAKESPEARE

CHAPTER ONE

London, 1814

Shadows sculpted his sharp profile as he watched the crowded ballroom from the dim, high balcony; in the oscillating glow of the draft-buffeted wall candle, he seemed to flicker in and out of materiality like some tall, elegant phantom. Its shifting radiance glimmered over his raven-black hair and caught the Machiavellian glint of cunning in his quicksilver-colored eyes. *Patience.* Everything was in order.

Preparation was all, and he had been meticulous. With a musing expression, Lord Lucien Knight lifted his crystal goblet of burgundy to his lips, pausing to inhale its mellow bouquet before he drank. He did not yet know his enemies' names or faces, but he could feel them inching closer like so many jackals. *No matter.* He was ready. He had laid his trap and baited it well, with all manner of sin and sex and the siren's whisper of subversive political activity that no spy could resist.

There was nothing left to do now but watch and wait.

Twenty years of war had ceased this past spring with Napoleon's defeat, abdication, and exile to the Mediterranean island of Elba. It was autumn now, and the leaders of Europe had gathered in Vienna to draw up the peace accord; *but any man with half a brain could see that until Bonaparte was moved to a more secure location farther out in the Atlantic,* Lucien thought dryly, *the war was not necessarily over.* Elba was but a stone's throw from the Italian mainland, and there were those who opposed the peace—who saw no profit for themselves in the Bourbon King Louis XVIII's return to the throne of France and who wanted Napoleon back. As one of the British Crown's most skilled secret agents, Lucien had orders from the foreign secretary, Viscount Castlereagh, to stand as the watcher at the gate, as it were, until the peace had been ratified—his mission, to stop these shadowy powers from stirring up trouble on English soil.

He took another sip of his wine, his silvery eyes gleaming with mayhem. *Let them come.* When they did, he would find them, snare them, catch and destroy them, just as he had so many others. Indeed, he would make them come to him.

Suddenly, a round of cheers broke out in the ballroom below and rippled through the crowd. *Well, well, the conquering hero.* Lucien leaned forward and rested his elbows on the railing of the balcony, watching with a cynical smirk as his identical twin brother, Colonel Lord Damien Knight, marched into the assembly rooms, resplendent in his scarlet uniform with the stern, high dignity of the Archangel Michael just back from slaying the dragon. The glitter of his dress sword and gold epaulets seemed to throw off a shining halo around him, but the famed colonel's unsmiling demeanor did not discourage the swarm of smitten women, eager aides-de-camp, junior officers, and assorted hero-worshiping toadies who instantly surrounded him. Damien had always been the favorite of the gods.

Lucien shook his head to himself. Though his lips curved in wry amusement, pain flickered behind his haughty stare. If it weren't enough that the colonel had captured the popular imagination with his gallant exploits in battle, as the elder twin, Damien would soon be made an earl by a rather convoluted accident of lineage. It was not jealousy that stung Lucien, however, but an almost childlike sense of having been abandoned by his staunchest ally. Damien was the only person who had ever really understood him. For most of their thirty-one years, the Knight twins had been inseparable. In their rakish youth, their friends had dubbed them Lucifer and Demon, while the alarmed mothers of Society debutantes had warned their daughters about "that pair of devils." But those carefree days of laughter and camaraderie were gone, for Lucien had transgressed his brother's soldierly code.

Damien had never quite accepted Lucien's decision to leave the army a little over two years ago for the secret service branch of the Diplomatic Corps. Officers of the line, as a rule, deemed espionage dishonorable, ungentlemanly. To Damien and his ilk, spies were no better than snakes. Damien was a born warrior, to be sure. Anyone who had ever seen him in battle, his face streaked with black powder and blood, knew there was no question of that. But there would not have been quite so many victories without the constant stream of intelligence that Lucien had sent him—against regulation, at the risk of his life—on the enemy's position, strength, numbers, and likeliest plan of attack. How it surely chafed the great commander's pride to know that the fullness of his glory would not have been possible without his spy brother's help.

No matter, Lucien thought cynically. *He still knew better than anyone how to prick the war hero's titanic ego.*

"Lucien!" a breathy voice suddenly called from behind him.

He turned around and saw Caro's voluptuous silhouette framed in the doorway. "Why, my dear Lady Glenwood," he purred, holding out his hand to her with a dark smile. *Wasn't Damien going to be cross about this?*

"I've been looking everywhere for you!" Her doll-like side curls swung against her rouged cheeks as she flounced over to him in a rustle of black satin. She smiled slyly, revealing the fetching little gap between her two front teeth as she took his hand and let him pull her up close against his body. "Damien's here—"

"Who?" he murmured, skimming her lips with his own.

She groaned softly under his kiss and melted against him, the black satin of her gown sliding sensually against the white brocade of his formal waistcoat. Last night it had been skin to skin.

Though the twenty-seven-year-old baroness wore mourning for her late husband, Lucien doubted she had shed a tear. A husband, to a woman like Caro, was merely an impediment to her pursuit of pleasure. Her ebony gown had a tiny bodice that barely contained her burgeoning cleavage. The midnight fabric made her skin look like alabaster, while her crimson lips matched the roses that adorned her upswept, chocolate-brown hair. After a moment, Caro made an effort to end their kiss, bracing her gloved hands on his chest.

When she pulled back slightly, he saw that she was gloating, her cheeks flushed, her raisin-dark eyes glowing with amorous triumph. Lucien masked his insolent smile as Caro coyly lowered her lashes and stroked the lapels of his formal black tailcoat. To be sure, she believed she had done the impossible, what none of her rivals had ever achieved—that she alone had snared *both* Knight twins as her conquests and could now play them off each other for her own vanity. Alas, the lady had a large surprise in store.

He was a bad man, he knew, but he could not resist toying with her a bit. He licked his lips as he stared at her, then glanced suggestively at the nearby wall, cloaked in shadows. "No one can see us up here, my love. Are you game?"

She let out one of her throaty laughs. "You wicked devil, I'll give you more later. Right now I want us to go see Damien."

Lucien lifted one eyebrow, playing along with consummate skill. "Together?"

"Yes. I don't want him to think we have anything to hide." She gave him a crafty glance from beneath her lashes and smoothed his white silk cravat. "We must act naturally."

"I'll try, *ma chérie*," he murmured.

"Good. Now, come." She slipped her gloved hand through the crook of his elbow and propelled him toward the small spiral staircase that led down to the ballroom. He went along amiably, which ought to have warned her that he was up to something. "You swear you didn't tell him?"

"*Mon ange,* I would never say a word." He did not see fit to add that such was the bond between identical twins that they hardly required *words* for the exchange of information. A glance, a laugh, a look spoke volumes. Appalling, really, to think that this wanton little schemer, for all her beauty, was on the verge of snaring Damien in marriage. Lucky for the war hero, his snake of a spy brother had come to his rescue again with the crucial information: Caro had not passed the test.

Lucien bent his head near her ear. "I trust you are still coming with me to Revell Court this weekend?"

She slipped him a nervous glance. "Actually, darling, I'm . . . not sure."

"What?" He stopped and turned to her with a scowl. "Why not? I want you there."

Her lips parted slightly, and she looked like she might climax on the spot in response to his demand. "Lucien."

"Caro," he retorted. It was hardly a lover's devotion that inspired his insistence, but the simple fact that a beautiful woman was a useful thing to have on hand when trying to catch enemy spies.

"You don't understand!" she said with a pout. "I *want* to go. It's just that I received a letter today from Goody Two-Shoes. She said—"

"From whom?" he demanded, cutting her off with a dubious look. If he recalled correctly, it was a character in a classic children's story by Oliver Goldsmith.

"Alice, my sister-in-law," she said, waving off the name in irritation. "I may have to go home to Glenwood Park. She says my baby might be getting sick. If I don't go home and help take care of Harry, Alice will have my head. Not that *I* know what to do with the little creature." She sniffed. "All he does for me is scream."

"Well, he's got a nurse, hasn't he?" he asked in disgust. He knew that Caro had a three-year-old son by her late husband, though most of the time *she* seemed to forget the fact. The child was one of the reasons why Damien was so interested in marrying the woman. Aside from some bizarre fatherly impulse toward a child he had never even seen, Damien wanted a wife with a proven ability to bear him sons. An earl, after all, needed heirs. Unfortunately, Caro had not proved worthy, surrendering wholeheartedly to Lucien's seduction. Damien was going to fume at the blow to his pride, but Lucien refused to allow his brother to marry any woman who did not love him to distraction. Any woman worthy of Damien would have refused Lucien's silken trap.

"Of course he has a nurse, but Alice says he needs, well . . . me," Caro said in dismay.

"But *I* need you, *chérie.*" He slipped her a coaxing little smile, wondering if his own late mother had occasionally suffered similar pangs of conscience. What a piece of work she had been, the scandalous duchess of Hawkscliffe, making conquests of half the men she met. Indeed, the twins' own father had not been their mother's husband, but her devoted lover of many years, the powerful and mysterious marquess of Carnarthen. The marquess had died recently, leaving Lucien the bulk of his fortune and his infamous villa, Revell Court, situated a dozen miles southwest of Bath.

As Lucien stared at Caro, he realized why he felt so strongly about stopping Damien from marrying her. He could hardly let his brother end up with a wife who was just like their mother. Turning away abruptly, he began walking down the hallway, leaving Caro where she stood. "Never mind, woman. Go home to your brat," he muttered. "I'll find someone else to amuse me."

"But, Lucien, I want to come!" she protested, hurrying to catch up in a rustle of satin.

He stared straight ahead as he stalked down the hallway. "Your boy needs you and you know it."

"No, he doesn't." Her tone was so bleak that Lucien looked askance at her. "He doesn't even know me. He only loves Alice."

"Is that what you think?"

"It's the truth. I am an incompetent mother."

He shook his head with a vexed sigh. What was it to him if she wanted to lie to herself? "Come along, then. Damien is waiting." Tucking her hand in the crook of his arm, he led her to the ballroom to face her fate.

Under the bright glow of the balloon-cut chandeliers, the ballroom looked like a civilized place to those who did not know better; but to Lucien, not for nothing was the marble floor laid out in black and white squares like a giant chessboard. Carefully watching the crowd from behind the facade of the decadent, self-indulged persona he had created, he kept all his senses sharply attuned, on the lookout for anyone or anything that set his instincts jangling. Nothing was ever obvious, which was why he had cultivated an enlightened paranoia and trusted no one. In his experience, it was the most average, ordinary-looking people who harbored the most dangerous treacheries. The strange characters were usually harmless; indeed, he had a fondness for all creatures who refused to be crushed by the iron mold of conformity. This preference was borne out in his acquaintance as, here and there, disreputable persons, odd fellows, outsiders, assorted voluptuaries, rebels, disheveled scientific geniuses from the Royal Society, and freakish eccentrics of every stripe nodded to him, furtively offering their respects.

Ah, his minions were eager to return to Revell Court for the festivities, he thought in jaded amusement, accepting their subtle homage with a narrow smile. He cast a wink to a painted lady who greeted him from behind her spread fan.

"Your Unholiness," she whispered, giving him a come-hither look.

He bowed his head. *"Bon soir, madame."* From the corner of his eye, he noticed Caro staring at him in fascination, her lips slightly parted. "What is it, my dear?"

She glanced at the velvet-clad scoundrels who bowed to him, then met his gaze with a sly look. "I was just wondering how Miss Goody Two-Shoes would fare with you around. It would be such fun to watch you corrupt her."

"Drop her by sometime. I'll do my best."

She smirked. "She'd probably faint if you even looked at her, the little prude."

"Young?"

"Not very. She's twenty-one." Caro paused. "Actually, I doubt that even *you* could scale her ivory tower, if you take my meaning."

He frowned askance at her. "Please."

Caro shrugged, a mocking smile tugging at her lips. "I don't know, Lucien. It wouldn't be easy. Alice is as *good* as you are *bad*."

He lifted his eyebrow and dwelled on this for a moment, then pursued the matter, his curiosity piqued. "Is she really such a paragon?"

"Ugh, she turns my stomach," Caro replied under her breath, nodding to people here and there as they ambled through the crowd. "She won't gossip. She doesn't lie.

She doesn't laugh when I make a perfectly witty remark about some woman's ridiculous dress. She cannot be induced to vanity. She never even misses church!"

"My God, you have my sympathies for having to live with such a monster. What did you say her name was again?" he asked mildly.

"Alice."

"Montague?"

"Yes. She's my poor Glenwood's little sister."

"Alice Montague," he echoed in a musing tone. *A baron's daughter,* he thought. Virtuous. Available. Good with the brat. Sounded like a perfect candidate for Damien's bride. "Is she fair?"

"Tolerable," Caro said flatly, avoiding his gaze.

"Mm-hmm." He passed a scrutinizing glance over her face, and his eyes began to dance at the jealousy stamped on the baroness's fine features. "How tolerable, exactly?"

She gave him a quelling look and refused to answer.

"Come, tell me."

"Forget about her!"

"I'm only curious. What color are her eyes?"

She ignored him, nodding to a lady in a feathered turban.

"Oh, Caro," he murmured playfully. "Are you jealous of little luscious twenty-one?"

"Don't be absurd!"

"Then where's the harm?" he insisted, goading her. "Tell me what color Alice's eyes are."

"Blue," she snapped, "but they are lackluster."

"And her hair?"

"Blond. Red. I don't know. What does it signify?"

"Indulge me."

"You are an utter pest! Alice's hair is her crowning glory, if you must know. It hangs to her waist, and I suppose you call the color of it strawberry blond," she said peevishly, "but it is always filled with the crumbs of whatever kind of muffin the baby ate for breakfast. Quite disgusting. I have told her a hundred times that long, cascading Rapunzel hair is entirely out of fashion, but Alice ignores me. She likes it. Now are you satisfied?"

"She sounds delicious," Lucien whispered in her ear. "Might I bring her to Revell Court instead of you?"

Caro pulled back and smacked him with her black lace fan.

Lucien was still laughing at her ire as they sauntered into the knot of red-coated soldiers. "Ah, look, Lady Glenwood," he said in bright irony. "It is my dear brother. Evening, Demon. I've brought someone to see you." Sliding his hands into the pockets of his black trousers, he rocked idly on his heels, a cynical smile sporting at his lips as he waited to watch the show unfold.

Damien's fellow officers looked disparagingly at Lucien, muttered farewells to their colonel, and predictably walked away, lest their honor be tainted by contagion, he thought dryly. With a war-hardened visage and lionlike decorum, Damien pressed away from the wide pillar where he had been leaning and gave Caro a stiff bow.

"Lady Glenwood. It is a pleasure to see you again," he clipped out in a low, brusque monotone. *Damien's manner was so grave that he might have been laying out battle plans for his captains instead of greeting the damsel of his choice,* Lucien thought. Indeed, after serving in nearly every major action in the war, Damien had come home with a deadened, icy look in his eyes that rather worried Lucien, but there was nothing he could do to help when his brother would barely talk to him.

"I trust you find the evening's entertainments to your liking, my lady," he said gravely to the baroness.

Caro smiled at him in an odd mix of patience and lust, while Lucien suppressed the urge to roll his eyes at his brother's tense formality. Damien could lop off an enemy's head with one blow of his sword, but put him in the vicinity of a beautiful woman, and the steely-eyed colonel turned as shy and uncertain as an overgrown schoolboy. The ladies of the ton were such sugar-spun confections that he seemed to fear that if he touched them he might break them. The hardy lasses who worked St. James's Park at night put the war hero much more at ease.

Ah, well, Lucien thought, shaking his head to himself, *it was comforting to know that his exalted brother had his foibles.* He looked on in amusement as Damien cast about haphazardly for something to say and suddenly seized on a topic.

"How's Harry?"

Lucien shut his eyes briefly and pinched the bridge of his nose in irritation at his brother's dim-wittedness with the opposite sex. Could he have made it any more obvious that he only wanted a highborn broodmare? No pretty compliments, no requests for a dance. It was a wonder women bothered with the great brute at all.

Even Caro looked uneasy with his choice of subjects, as though to admit that she had borne a child was to admit she was beyond the first blush of her youth. She glossed over her reply, not bothering to mention the boy's illness, then quickly steered the conversation to other matters. Watching them, Lucien could tell that it cost his brother an intense effort to pay attention to Caro's empty prattle.

"What a monstrous dull Little Season, don't you think? All the *best* society has gone home to the country for the hunt, or to Paris or Vienna—"

Bored in seconds, Lucien suddenly slipped his hand around Caro's waist and yanked her to him. "What do you think of this pretty wench, eh, Demon?"

She fell against his chest with a coy squeal. "Lucien!"

"Does she not tempt you? I find she tempts me quite to the breaking point," he murmured meaningfully, tracing the curve of her side with a slow, wicked caress.

Damien looked at him in shock. *What the hell are you doing?* his scowl demanded, but perhaps he sensed the note of deviltry in his twin's smooth voice, for he delayed judgment for a moment, regarding Lucien warily. He knew better than anyone that with Lucien, things were never as they seemed.

"Doesn't she look ravishing this evening? You should tell her so."

Damien glanced at Caro, then at him. "Indeed." The single, ominous word rumbled like far-off thunder from the depths of his chest. He studied the woman, as though trying to penetrate her nervous, sugary smile, for he had not been born with Lucien's gift of seeing past pretense in a glance.

"Let go of me, Lucien. People are staring," Caro murmured uneasily, brushing her shoulder against his chest as she tried to squirm free.

"What's wrong, *mon ange*? You only want my touch in secret?" he asked, his tone silky-smooth, though his grip on her body tightened ruthlessly.

She froze and stared at him in shock, her brown eyes looking even darker as her face turned white.

"Time to confess, love. You've been trying to manipulate me and my brother, but it's not going to work. Tell Damien where you were last night."

"I don't know what you are talking about," she forced out.

With a look that could have turned her to a pillar of ice, Damien cursed under his breath and turned away. Lucien laughed softly and allowed Caro to shove free of his embrace.

"Damien, don't listen to him—you know he is a liar!"

"You would bat your lashes at me after you've lain with my brother?" he whispered fiercely shoving off her clutching hands.

"But, I—it's not my fault, it's his!"

"You are brazen, madam. Moreover, you are a fool."

She whirled to Lucien with a frantic look. "Did you hear what he called me? You can't let him speak to me like that!"

But Lucien's only answer was a small, rather sinister laugh. He took another drink of his wine.

"What is going on here?" she demanded in a shaky voice.

"Caro, my heart, the man's not a fool. There is something I neglected to tell you last night. Damien has been meaning to propose to you."

Her jaw dropped. For a moment, she looked as though she couldn't draw in a breath past the tight stays that pressed up the splendid globes of her breasts; then her stricken gaze flew to Damien's. "Is this true?"

"I am sure there is no need to discuss it," he growled.

"Is it?" she cried.

"I merely thought it would be helpful to give your child a father, since he lost his own." Damien's frosty glance swept her body, lingering at her hips. "Pity you are unable to temper your wantonness with a little discipline." His angry gaze swung to Lucien. "A word with you, sir."

"As you wish, brother."

"Lucien—you can't leave me!" She clutched at his arm quite without shame.

"Caro, my pet." He lifted her hand and kissed it, then let it trail from his grasp as he moved away from her. "He's right. I'm afraid you failed the test."

"Test?" Understanding flashed in her eyes, then rage. "You *fiend*! Bastard! Both of you! That's what you are! A pair of bastards!"

"Why, everyone knows that, *ma chérie*," Lucien said with smile. "Our mother was an even greater slut than you."

With a wordless cry of fury, Caro hurled her empty wineglass at him, but he caught it out of the air with catlike reflexes, placed it gently on the tray of a passing waiter, and blew her a kiss from his white-gloved hand. Offering her a smooth, mocking bow, he turned and followed his brother out of the ballroom.

Despite their estrangement, the Knight twins fell naturally in stride with each other as they crossed the adjoining lounge and descended the grand staircase to the ground floor. People stared as they passed, but the twins were used to that reaction. They passed several of the luxuriously appointed refreshment salons, coming at last to the billiard room tucked away in the corner. When they stepped into this dim, oak-paneled male sanctuary, Damien cleared the room with a glower. Lucien held the door sardonically for the gentlemen who put out their cigars and hastened out, leaving a miasmic cloud of smoke drifting over the three pool tables.

Nodding to the last man to leave, Lucien glanced out the door and saw that Caro had followed them as far as the hallway. It seemed she didn't dare come any closer. Her gloved fists were clenched at her sides. Her dark eyes snapped sparks. She pursed her red lips like she was trying not to scream obscenities at him. He laughed under his breath and shut the door more or less in her face. The most amusing thing about Lady Glenwood was that when he was done here, he had no doubt he could go back out and smooth things over with a few soft words and bring her to his villa for the party this weekend, just as they had previously planned—sick child or no. Caro was determined, after all, to find out if his gatherings at Revell Court were every bit as wicked as she had heard.

Turning, he found Damien studying him, his shiny Hessian boots planted wide, his arms folded across his chest. The formidable colonel stroked his chin with a brooding air. On his guard, Lucien sauntered over to the nearest pool table, reaching across its green velvet surface to toy with the glossy black eight ball. He spun it like a top and watched it whirl under his white-gloved fingertip, like God in a sadistic mood, toying with the earth. *Where shall I send a famine, a plague?*

"Didn't we make a pact once never to let a woman come between us?" Damien asked.

"Why, yes, on our eighteenth birthday. I remember it well."

"Do you?"

Damien waited for an explanation; Lucien let him wait.

"Well?"

"Well, what?" He looked innocently at his brother. "Oh, come, you can't be serious."

"You're damned right I'm serious!"

Damien's roars could make whole regiments quake in their boots, but Lucien merely sent him a long-suffering, rather bored look. "I cannot apologize when I am not sorry."

Damien's eyes narrowed to steel-gray slits. "Sometimes I think you are an evil man."

Lucien laughed mildly.

"What kind of game are you playing now?" He took a step closer. "You're up to something, and I want to know what it is. Give me a plain answer for once or I'll flatten you. Damn it, Lucien, if you weren't my brother, I would kill you for this."

"Over Caro Montague?" he asked dubiously.

"You deliberately humiliated me."

"I *saved* you from humiliation. You should be thanking me," he retorted. "Now at least you know what your angel is made of. Jesus, I was trying to do you a favor."

Damien snorted. "Admit it. You seduced Caro to get back at me. To even the score."

Lucien paused, cast him a veiled look of warning. "Score?"

"You know exactly what I'm talking about. The title."

"I don't want your bloody title." Lucien's eyes flickered with gathering fire, but Damien ignored his words and charged on.

"You have no reason to resent me. Your fortunes are

set now since Carnarthen left you the unentailed property. Frankly, I don't fancy living on half pay for the rest of my days. I am accepting this earldom, and you're just going to have to learn to live with it. Incidentally . . ." When he stopped mere inches from Lucien and stared coolly at him, it was like looking into a hostile mirror—the same black hair, the same haunted gray eyes. Both men were too hard and proud to admit that in their own separate ways, each had been left shattered by his experience of war.

"Yes?" Lucien asked prosaically.

"I hope you don't plan on seducing every woman I take an interest in, because I won't brush off an insult like this twice. Not even from you."

For a long moment, Lucien stared at him, incredulous. "Did you just threaten me?"

Damien held his stare in granite stillness. Stunned, Lucien turned away in amazement. He ran his hand through his hair for a moment, at a loss, then began laughing, low and bitterly. "You glory-hound! I should have let you marry the slut and watched her cuckold you all over Town. Are we through here?"

Damien shrugged.

"Good." With a lightninglike movement, Lucien rolled the eight ball at the other billiard balls. It struck them with a savage crack and sent them scattering, pell-mell, over the table, colored and striped, some crashing down into the pockets. He pivoted and stalked toward the door.

How fitting, that this was what his life had come to, he thought acidly as he crossed the billiard room. For the past two and a half years, he had worked alone, changing identities like a shape-shifter each time he had moved on to a new assignment, drifting in and out of countless people's lives like a ghost, never quite connecting. Now not even his twin brother knew him anymore—did not know him and did not want to know him, for he was a spy, a deceiver, a man without honor. A man who knew the rules of gentlemanly conduct and ignored them. Self-loathing pulsed through him, and despair. If Damien did not give a damn about him anymore, who ever would? *No one,* he realized, with an empty, sinking feeling in the pit of his stomach. *He was utterly alone.*

"One more thing," Damien called after him.

Lucien turned in formidable, elegant hauteur. "Yes?"

Damien lifted his chin. "I've been hearing odd rumors about you. Bizarre things."

"Do tell."

"People are saying you've resurrected our father's old secret society. There is talk of . . . indecent goings-on at Revell Court. Strange rites."

"You don't say," he uttered blandly.

Damien searched his face. "Most people seem to think you're merely having wild parties, but a few claim you're involved in some kind of . . . pagan cult, along the lines of the old Hellfire Club."

"How very interesting," he purred.

"Is it true?"

Lucien merely slipped him a dark, jaded smile, turned, and strolled out of the room.

Morning sunlight gilded the Hampshire countryside with the mellow glow of autumn and streamed through the French windows of the cozy parlor at Glenwood Park. Alice Montague picked a crumb of Harry's breakfast muffin out of her hair with a slight frown and went on singing softly to the toddler, rocking him in her arms. She glanced restlessly out the bow window each time she paced across the room, for she expected Caro's carriage any minute now. At least she hoped.

All week Harry had been uncharacteristically whiny and tired. Yesterday he had fallen asleep on the parlor floor with his thumb in his mouth and his blanket wrapped around him, while Alice had sat intently sewing a new suit for the dashing Mr. Wembley, Harry's jointed wooden doll. This morning at dawn, however, his old nurse's warnings had proved correct. The diminutive Baron Glenwood had awakened the entire household with a wail of lordly ire—one fevered, angry, miserable little boy, covered in chicken pox.

Having itched and fussed and cried since breakfast, he dozed at last in Alice's arms with an air of defeat, his rose-petal cheek resting on her shoulder.

"Mama," he bleated wearily, just as he had been doing all morning.

"She's coming, my love," Alice whispered, hugging him. "She's on her way. I promise."

"Bumps."

"Yes, I know you've got the bumps, lambkin. Everyone gets them. I had them too when I was your age." Unfortunately, it was going to get worse before it got better.

"Three."

"Yes, you are three. Such a clever boy." She squeezed him gently, ignoring the strain in her back. He was too big for her to be carrying around like an infant; but he reverted to babyish ways when he was sick, and she couldn't bear to watch him suffer without doing what she could to comfort him.

"Look!" Harry said suddenly, lifting his peach-fuzzed head and pointing over her shoulder at the window.

"What is it?"

"Mama!"

"Can it be?" she asked doubtfully. Walking over to the window, Alice shifted him onto her hip and pushed the damask curtain aside.

Harry pointed his tiny finger in excitement, then looked into her eyes with his first wide smile of the day, showing his little white teeth. To Alice, his smile was like the sun breaking out from behind the clouds. She gazed lovingly into his sky-blue eyes, ignoring the approaching carriage for the moment. When Harry smiled, he looked so much like her brother, Phillip, that it brought tears to her eyes.

"Mama! Mama!" he began shouting, kicking his legs violently as he craned his neck to look at the distant carriage.

"Didn't I tell you she was coming?" she teased, hiding her relief, for the baroness was not the most dependable creature. Caro had a way of popping in and out of her child's life as the whim struck her, but Alice had written to her three days ago warning her the boy was coming down with something.

"I go!" Harry squirmed out of her arms and went careening out of the room with small pattering steps, trailing his blanket from his tiny, clenched fist. "Mama! Mama!"

For a moment, Alice listened to her nephew's hollers trailing down the hallway, and his nurse Peg Tate's hearty exclamation as the big, sturdy woman intercepted him.

His rambunctious excitement at the prospect of seeing the glamorous stranger, his mother, nearly broke her heart. He wanted so badly to get to know the baroness, but every time Caro visited, she would leave again just when Harry was starting to get used to her. It left the child confused and angry—and played havoc with Alice's future. She sighed quietly, turned, and took a long look at the bright, airy room where she spent most of her time. Her gaze traveled from the large, intricate cage of white-painted cane that she had fashioned to house her pet canary, to the round table where she idled away the serene country hours of her life at Glenwood Park, absorbed in her various crafts, all very suitable for a quiet-tempered young lady. Yet she couldn't help but feel she was living in a dream here while life was passing her by.

She was haunted by a hunger for she knew not what, sometimes so intensely that it kept her awake at night. She was torn between her devotion to her nephew and the running of Glenwood Park, and her own need to *find* her life. But the overriding fact was that Harry needed someone he could depend on to be there for him all the time, not just when the whim struck her. Since it was a duty his mother had abdicated, that person was Alice. She slipped her hands into her apron pockets and stood very still, the sunlight warming her skin, glistening upon her bright, reddish-gold hair. She tensed her body tightly, trying to get rid of the well-hidden tension that plagued her, then forced her shoulders to relax and took deliberate pleasure in gazing upon the vase of dried hydrangeas that she had arranged just yesterday. The flowers graced the center of the table. Beside them lay the elegant silk purses she was sewing as Christmas gifts for a few of her London friends, and her delicate japanning tools, perched well out of Harry's reach. Her latest piece, an intricate jewel box, sat in a middle stage of completion. All of her hobbies ran in an artistic vein, but in her heart, she knew in a sense they were merely distractions, her way of trying to burn off her restlessness.

Hearing the baroness's carriage rumble to a halt outside the manor house, Alice moved dutifully to the window to wave hello, but when she looked out, her eyes widened in appalled shock. It was not Caro's fashionable yellow barouche.

It was the mail coach. She paled and pressed her hand to her mouth, realizing instantly what this meant. A letter. A paltry letter! *She isn't coming. She simply doesn't care.* The realization dazed and then enraged her.

Her dark blue eyes narrowed, and her pale, oval reflection in the window filled with an untapped depth of passionate fury that reached down for fathoms below her placid surface. Overwhelming anger seized her, but very little surprise. She shook her head in silence. *No,* she thought fiercely. *Not this time, Caro. I will not let you do this to that child. This is the last straw.*

She straightened up from the window, pivoted, and left the parlor, walking out to the entrance hall. At the front door, she paid the postman and glanced at the folded letter, then exchanged a worried look with Peg, who had ambled into the entrance hall, wiping her large, capable hands on her apron.

Peg Tate, Harry's nurse, had been Phillip and Alice's nurse when they were children. Alice thought of her more as a family member than a servant. Kind-hearted as she was, even Peg was skeptical when it came to Lady Glenwood. "This ought to be a good one," she grumbled.

"It's not from Caro," Alice said tautly, examining the letter. "It's from Mr. Hattersley." Hattersley was their

London butler, who ran the Montagues' elegant townhouse in Upper Brooke Street off Grosvenor Square.

"Oh, dear, I hope nothing's wrong," Peg murmured, her wrinkled brow creasing more deeply with worry.

A premonition prickled along Alice's spine. She had long feared that her sister-in-law's reckless pursuit of pleasure would end in disaster.

"Where's Harry?" she asked uneasily.

"Nellie's washin' him up to see his mother."

Alice nodded and cracked the seal. " 'Dear Miss Montague,' " she read out quietly, " 'received your letter day before last. Regret to inform you Lady G. left Town yesterday in the company of Lord Lucien Knight.' " She stopped and looked at Peg in astonishment. "*Lucien* Knight? But I thought it was Lord *Damien* . . . Oh, *Caro*!" She groaned, grasping at once what the feckless creature had done. Just when the woman had finally managed to pick a decent man—a man who would have made a perfect stepfather for Harry—she had gone and ruined it by running off with his brother!

She still recalled the conversation she had had with her sister-in-law weeks ago, when Caro had first bragged about catching the eye of the national hero. She had mentioned that Lord Damien had an identical twin brother, Lord Lucien, who was in the Diplomatic Corps. Demon and Lucifer, Caro had called them. Alice remembered it clearly because the baroness had shivered with a strange look of fascination in her eyes. *I would never get involved with Lucien Knight,* she had said. *He scares me.* Nobody scared the flamboyant Lady Glenwood.

"What else does Mr. Hattersley say?" Peg asked in trepidation.

"Lord, I hardly dare look." Alice lifted the letter and read on. " 'They were bound for the gentleman's country house, Revell Court, which I was able to learn lies about a dozen miles southwest of Bath. Her Ladyship is not expected back until next week. As the baroness ordered me not to tell you anything, I do not wish to cause any awkwardness. Please advise. Your servant, et cetera, J. Hattersley.' "

Peg scratched her cheek in stumped silence.

For a long moment, Alice stared at the floor, shaking her head in rising anger. She looked over broodingly and found the old woman watching her in patient, stoic concern. She gazed at Peg for a long moment, narrowed her eyes as her exasperation climbed, then suddenly handed Peg the letter and stalked past her toward the stairs.

"I'm going after her."

"Oh, dearie, you mustn't!" Peg exclaimed.

"I have to. This flagrant behavior must stop. Now."

"But this man is a stranger and a scoundrel, I fear! If Her Ladyship sees fit to act like a hoyden, that is her concern."

"And mine, as well. Did I not promise Phillip on his deathbed that I would take care of them—both of them? Harry needs his mother, and Caro needs to come home. Do you really think this man cares about her?"

Peg shrugged skeptically.

"Neither do I. I daresay this time she has gone and got herself caught in the middle of some petty sibling rivalry." Alice paused. "Besides, you know if it turns into a full-blown scandal, it will taint my reputation, as well."

"But Bath is so far, dear."

"Only a day's travel from here. I know the journey

well. I have been there often enough." She glanced toward the French windows, dainty and white, like the intricate bars of her canary's cage. Dared she fly free out into the large and dangerous world?

She knew how Phillip would have answered—with a resounding no. Her brother would have called it unthinkable for a gently bred young lady to venture halfway across England without benefit of a male relative's protection or the chaperonage of a married lady at the very least, but at the moment, Alice had neither. Besides, acting swiftly might be the only way to prevent Caro's reckless affair from blossoming into an ugly scandal.

She turned back to her worried old nurse. "The weather is fine. If I leave right away, I can be there by tonight and have Caro home by tomorrow evening. All will be well," she insisted with more self-assurance than she felt. "Mitchell will drive the coach, and Nellie will attend me."

"Oh, but my dear," Peg said sadly, "you and I both know she'll only get in the way. We can tend him better by ourselves."

Just then, Harry came barreling out of the hallway that led from the kitchen and hurtled against Peg's skirts, clinging to her. He peered up the stairs at Alice. "Where my mama?"

Alice gazed at him in pained love. "Lost, lambkin." She exchanged a meaningful glance with Peg. "But I know where to find her, and I am going to bring her home to you straightaway. I promise."

"I come!"

"No."

"Don't scratch," Peg chided, pulling his hand away

from his scalp. He fussed and growled at her like an annoyed kitten.

Watching the scowl on his poor, red-spotted face, Alice felt torn in two. She could not bear to leave the child at a time like this, even for the purpose of fetching his errant mother, but she knew Caro would not come home unless she showed up in person to browbeat her into doing the right thing. She knew that with Peg on hand, she needn't fear for Harry's safety. Peg Tate had shepherded scores of children through the chicken pox and worse in her sixty-odd years and knew more about the whole matter than the arrogant local physician.

"Well, then," the old woman said as she smoothed Harry's rumpled hair, "the sooner you go, the sooner you'll be back. I'll tell Mitchell to ready the horses." She bent down and scooped the lad up, bouncing him in her fleshy arms and distracting him from his itches with a teasing little song.

Alice held up her skirts as she ran up the stairs to her bedroom. With brisk efficiency, she packed a satchel for her overnight stay, then took off her apron and morning gown and changed into her smart carriage dress of dark blue broadcloth. It had long, tight sleeves with a puff at the shoulder and pretty ribbon trimming along the hem.

Going to stand before the mirror, she neatly buttoned up the high-necked bodice, frowning at the slight tremble in her hands. In truth, she was unaccustomed to traveling alone, and Caro's shadowy seducer did sound a wee bit intimidating. He was not going to like it one bit, she supposed, that she would soon arrive at Revell Court to snatch her sister-in-law out of his arms. Alice was not a particularly bold creature, but she knew she could stand up to anyone for Harry's sake.

Pulling on her prim white gloves, she stared hard into the looking glass and squared her shoulders, ready to do battle. *Enjoy your escapades, Lady Glenwood, for they are about to come to an end. As for you, Lord Lucien Knight, whoever you are, you, sir, are in a great deal of trouble with me.* With that, she picked up her satchel and marched out of her room.

CHAPTER TWO

A thousand hours later, or so it felt, Alice sat tensely in her jostling carriage, steadying herself with a cold-sweating grip on the leather hand loop. They still had not found the place. The full moon led them along the bumpy, winding road through the moors like a sly links-boy with his lantern—one of those dubious London street urchins who, for a coin, would convey a pedestrian homeward through the city after dark, but who were just as likely to deliver one into the hands of thieves.

She glanced constantly out the windows, certain that she and her two servants were going to be set upon by highwaymen in this desolate waste. They were hopelessly lost in the Mendip Hills, far from any sign of civilization: up another slope through woods of oak and beech, to a rough, wind-blown heath like the one they now traversed; down again, into the plunging combes and gorges, up and down, again and again. The weary horses strained and stumbled in their traces; the night air wrapped them in a clammy, vaporous chill; and it was anyone's guess how much longer they might be on the road. The only thing, in fact, that Alice knew for certain was that she was going to wring Caro's neck for this.

She exchanged a taut look with her frightened maid, Nellie, but neither spoke aloud what both women were thinking: *We should have stayed the night in Bath.*

Alice was beginning to wonder if the *maitre d'* at the elegant Pump Room, where they had stopped for tea, had deliberately lied to her when he had said that Revell Court was only fifteen miles to the southwest. Perhaps it had only been her imagination, but she thought she had detected a faint, disapproving sneer in his countenance when she'd asked for directions to the place. Given the urgency of their quest, and confident that they could cover the distance within two hours, Nellie, Mitchell, and she had unanimously agreed to press on in spite of the fact that the October sun had already set.

Now, with the night growing blacker by the minute, she realized uneasily that if they ever succeeded in finding Revell Court, they were going to have to spend the night there, accepting Lucien Knight's hospitality—provided, of course, that he offered it. Who could say for certain what to expect from a man who seduced his brother's chosen lady? She only prayed he was not heathen enough to turn travelers away in the dead of night, for she and her servants were ravenous, bone-tired, and full of aches and pains from being battered and bounced over the coaching roads of England all day.

Looking back over the day's journey, she shook her head. There had been the queerest traffic on the roads since they had left Bath. Nearly twenty carriages—some flashy, some gaudy, some elegant—had passed them at breakneck speeds, but the passengers had all seemed either mad or intoxicated. Adults—male and female—had actually pulled faces at them like rotten children as the carriages went careening by, sticking out their tongues, yelling taunting abuses. She shook her head to herself, still puzzled.

Gazing out the window as the road descended into the gloom of another hidden valley, she studied the trees raking the indigo sky with their stark, brushy silhouettes. Moonlight polished the eerie, majestic limestone outcrops until they gleamed bone-white, while the road floated precariously above the forest, a sheer, high pass that hugged the mountain on one side. On the other yawned a gulf of empty darkness. She moved to the edge of her seat and stared down over the dizzying drop into the wooded ravine. You could throw a stone and it would fall forever, she thought. As her gaze pierced the deepest recesses of the black abysmal forest, suddenly she saw it—a distant flicker of fire.

"There's a light! Nellie, do you see it? There, in the valley!" She pointed in excitement. "There!"

"Yes, I see it!" her maid cried, clapping her hands. "Oh, Miss Alice, at last, it's Revell Court! It must be!"

Suddenly animated, both women called to Mitchell, the coachman, who was slumped down in dejection on the driver's box. He let out a cheer when he, too, saw the bonfire burning like a beacon in the valley.

"By Jove, we'll be there in ten minutes!" he boomed.

Even the horses picked up their pace, perhaps smelling the distant stable. Alice felt new life rushing into her veins. She hastily dug in her reticule for her combs and began trying to put her hair into presentable order. "Oh, how I long for a warm bed," she said ardently. "I could sleep until noon!"

"Bed, pshaw! I've had to use the w.c. for the past two hours," her maid retorted in a whisper as she buttoned up her pelisse over her plump bosom.

Alice chuckled. As they came down to the bottom of the valley, the carriage clattered across a stout wooden bridge that straddled a small, lively river. She was taken aback to notice how the cascade spurted straight out of the living rock. Falling in rills and milk-white spume, the little river glistened in the moonlight, churning and eddying in countless miniature gullies beneath the bridge.

"There's the house," Nellie exclaimed suddenly, pointing out the other window.

Alice peered out eagerly. In the foreground loomed tall wrought-iron gates whose formidable pillars were topped with rearing stone horses. Beyond them, the courtyard bustled with activity as servants in maroon-and-buff livery hurried about, tending to the dozen or so carriages lined up there. It seemed their host was entertaining, Alice thought uneasily, half certain that she recognized some of those carriages from on the road today. The house was an ivy-covered, red-brick Tudor mansion built in a U shape around the courtyard, with two large gabled wings that jutted forward symmetrically from the sides, their banks of mullioned windows reflecting the glint of the great iron torch stand that towered in the center of the cobblestone courtyard.

This was the wheel of fire that had beckoned to them from the distance, she realized, and as she gazed at the dancing flames, writhing and reaching for the black velvet sky, she was filled with the strangest intuition that the unknown object that her heart had yearned for in secret was very near. Then her bemusement turned to dread as half a dozen armed guards—big, menacing men in long black coats—materialized out of the shadows and began marching toward her carriage, each with a rifle under his arm. They yelled roughly at her driver to halt.

Mitchell had not expected armed guards any more than she had, but when Lord Lucien's men continued shouting at him, telling him he must turn the coach around and leave, Alice's fury soon overtook her fear. She jumped out of the carriage without warning, her long, fur-trimmed cloak swinging around her as she angrily marched over, going to her driver's defense. She was too incensed, hungry, and irritable from the day's exertions to accept this sort of insolent trifling from servants. Ignoring their requests—veiled orders—for her to get back in the coach, she stood arguing with them in the cold for a quarter hour. It seemed there was a written guest list, and her name, of course, was not on it. But that was only the beginning. When they told her she must give the password if she wanted to go in, she scoffed outright.

"You listen here," she scolded sharply, hands on her hips, "I have no truck with such things as passwords and secret handshakes. For heaven's sake, I am here to fetch Lady Glenwood for the urgent reason that her child is seriously ill. Allow me to be very blunt—Lady Glenwood is Lord Lucien's mistress. If you do not allow me in to collect her—if you turn me away—she is going to be furious. She will blame your master, and Lord Lucien, in turn, will blame you. Is that what you want? I've heard he is a man not to be crossed."

"Aye, ma'am, that is our worry exactly. Come 'ere, lads," the leader mumbled to the others. Grumbling in disgust, the gatekeepers walked away to confer on the matter.

Alice could feel Mitchell and Nellie staring anxiously at her, but all her attention was focused on the men as she attempted to eavesdrop on their argument. She was not leaving here without Caro, she thought, her firm chin stubbornly set.

"Wee spunky thing, ain't she?" the first gatekeeper muttered.

"She ain't one of 'em. I never seen her 'ere before," another said.

"Course you 'aven't. Look at her. She's harmless," muttered one big fellow with a scar on his face. "I say we let her in."

"He'll kill us if we let 'er in without knowin' the password!" another whispered harshly.

"But she says she's related to his mistress! He'll kill us for embarrassment if we turn the lass away."

"That devil," the scarred one muttered. "We're damned if we do and damned if we don't, with 'im."

Clearly, Lord Lucien's men held their master in awe, but it was their terror of getting him into trouble with his mistress that finally persuaded them to allow Alice and her servants through the gates. She was displeased when Nellie and Mitchell were separated from her and hurried off to the servants' quarters, but she dared not complain for fear of being turned away again. The big, scarred gatekeeper showed her into the manor house and entrusted her to the care of the austere, gray-haired butler, Mr. Godfrey.

While the guard gave the butler some instructions pertaining to her in a low, secretive tone, she glanced into the dark, empty rooms adjoining the richly carved entrance hall and promptly found herself more puzzled still.

Where were all the guests? The first floor was eerily silent, and barely a candle burned in the cavernous rooms. *Something very strange was going on here,* she mused. She had seen the carriages and the army of servants, and had personally run up against the exclusive guest list, so she *knew* that Lord Lucien was having a party tonight; but there was no sign of life in the house. Then she overheard a bit of the conversation between the butler and the guard that piqued her curiosity even more keenly.

"See that she stays in 'er room. She is not to go down to the Grotto."

"I understand. We will inform His Lordship of the young lady's presence in the morning."

Alice looked over quickly, glancing from one man to the other. As though noticing her furtive study, Mr. Godfrey bowed to her.

"This way, Miss Montague," he said cordially. "I will show you to your room." Lifting a candle branch from the wall holder, he picked up her satchel and led her up the dark oaken stairs, which had wood-carved statues of knights and saints serving as stair posts. A large portrait of a nobleman in sixteenth-century doublet and ruff peered down haughtily from the landing where the stairs turned. He had piercing, steel-gray eyes, a pointed black beard, and a sly smirk of a smile. He seemed to watch her as she passed.

"Who is that?" she asked, eyeing the portrait in trepidation.

"That is the first marquess of Carnarthen, ma'am. He built this house as his hunting lodge." Mr. Godfrey gave a heavy, troubled sigh, but offered nothing more.

Peering everywhere around her into the shadows, Alice followed him up the creaking stairs and down a dim corridor. They ascended another, more modest flight of stairs to the third floor and wove through a labyrinth of turns, finally stopping in the hallway, whereupon Mr. Godfrey took out his massive keyring, unlocked a door, and opened it for her.

"Your quarters, ma'am. Would you care for supper?"

"Oh, yes, thank you. I'm famished."

The chamber had a thick Persian carpet, a canopied bed, and a fine Renaissance plastered ceiling. A low fire already burned in the hearth as though someone had been expecting her. As Mr. Godfrey moved about the chamber lighting the candles for her, a hulking Elizabethan wardrobe emerged from the gloom. She glanced at it, then looked at the butler again, unable to resist her curiosity.

"Mr. Godfrey, has Lady Glenwood gone to the Grotto?" she asked innocently.

Lighting the pair of spidery candelabra over the mantel, he glanced over his shoulder at her in wary surprise. "Why, yes, miss, some time ago."

"Is she with Lord Lucien there?"

"I imagine so."

She gave him a winning smile. "May I go there, too?"

"My humblest apologies, miss, but I'm afraid it is not possible."

She dropped her gaze, unsurprised by his refusal, but she had always been a persistent creature. "Why not?" she asked brightly.

"It would displease the master. The, er, guest list is highly exclusive."

"I see. Then will you send for Lady Glenwood to come to me?"

"I will try, but his lordship's guests generally do not wish to be disturbed in the Grotto."

"Why is that?"

"I do not know," he said blandly.

Alice gave him a wry smile, for he really was the best sort of butler, discreet and loyal to his master. "Thank you, Mr. Godfrey."

Relief darted over his lined face. "Very good, miss. One of the staff shall return shortly with your supper and wine. Here is the bellpull if you require anything else in the meantime. Good evening." He bowed out, pulling the door shut.

When he had gone, Alice took a turn around the room, exploring its shadowy regions. *What a curious place!* she mused. Her weariness from the day's travel fell away in youthful curiosity. Furtively padding over to the great wardrobe, she undid the latch with a careful twist. The wooden door creaked loudly in the stillness when she pulled it open. Peeking inside, she found a single piece of clothing hung there. Unsure what it was, she reached out and touched the coarse brown wool, puzzling over it; then curiosity got the best of her. She pulled the shapeless garment out and held it up before the fire, examining it.

It was a domino, a robe like a monk or medieval friar would have worn, only quite new and clean. It had wide voluminous sleeves and a large hood that hung down the back. A length of cording cinched the waist. She suddenly heard a burst of laughter as a few people passed in the hallway beyond her door. *Aha, not* all *the guests had vanished,* she thought. Hearing the voices pass by, she hurried over to the door, opened it a crack, and peered out. Several figures wearing long, hooded robes like the one in the wardrobe glided by. When they had disappeared down the dim hallway, she closed the door again silently, gnawing her lip in thought. *So, that's what the robe is for.* Apparently, Lord Lucien's soiree was some kind of costume ball. It was late October, after all, and nearly Hallowe'en. A bit of a sulk passed over her face to think that, as usual, she had to miss out while Caro got to have all the fun.

With a huff at the unfairness of it, she changed out of her carriage dress and slipped on her comfortable morning gown from earlier. Then she took down her hair and brushed it out. The maid soon came with her supper tray, and Alice sat down to a feast of almond soup and warm bread, a fillet of beef with mushrooms, and an apricot pudding for dessert, the lot washed down with an excellent glass of burgundy. Later she reclined lazily on the massive bed and dozed, her long hair strewn around her, a cozy warmth in her body from the wine. She rested her head back on her arm, gazing into the flickering hearth fire, waiting with growing impatience for Mr. Godfrey to bring Caro to her.

She was beginning to worry. Maybe the butler had forgotten about her request or had chosen to ignore it. Alice knew her sister-in-law. If Caro was at a costume ball, she would drink too much and have too sore a head to leave tomorrow morning at the crack of dawn, as they must if they were to make it back to Hampshire by nightfall, as promised. Well, she thought, pushing up to a seated position with a determined look, if Lord Lucien's servants were not going to fetch Caro for her, she would simply go to the masque and collect the baroness herself. Clad in an unadorned morning gown, with her hair flowing freely over her shoulders, she knew she was not dressed for any sort of gathering, but the domino would hide that fact. Besides, she would only go for a few minutes, she reasoned, just long enough to find Caro.

Moments later, she slipped out of her room, her blue eyes glowing from the shadowy depths of the hooded brown robe. In perfect anonymity, she stole silently down the hallway in the direction the other guests had gone, her heart pounding with the fun of her adventure, leavened a bit by the wine. She wished her friend, Kitty Patterson, were with her, for they would have laughed like errant schoolgirls every step of the way, and truthfully, the mazelike house was rather eerie.

Venturing on alone, she explored the web of dim corridors, making several wrong turns before she found the second, smaller staircase that Mr. Godfrey had led her up earlier. She went down the steps and peered into several hallways until she spied the grand staircase of dark-colored oak, where the marquess's painting hung over the landing. He seemed to wink at her in sly complicity as she crept down the staircase, biting her lip to hold back a nervous giggle. She couldn't believe she was doing this. *I'm never going to find my way back.* In the entrance hall at the bottom of the stairs, a footman in maroon-and-buff livery looked at her attentively. She withdrew deeper into the voluminous hood, shielding her face.

"The Grotto, ma'am?" he asked politely, failing to recognize her.

She nodded. He pointed a white-gloved finger toward the hallway on the left. Spying Mr. Godfrey chastising one of the servants in the adjoining salon, she hurried on before her escape from her room was discovered. Another footman waited at the end of the next hallway and again pointed the way. The third footman she came to opened a modest-looking wooden door for her and gestured to the darkness within.

"This way, ma'am."

Nervously, Alice approached the pitch-black vault. She looked at the footman in doubt. Surely he was jesting, but his obliging smile did not waver. Alice peered in.

Beyond the door, a narrow staircase led down into what she surmised were the wine cellars beneath Revell Court. Then a few hollow snatches of laughter echoed up to her from the bowels of the house and she realized this was indeed the way to the Grotto. Lord, this was getting stranger and stranger. A small voice in her head warned her to turn back, but she was determined to find Caro. She braced herself and stepped inside.

Instantly, the dank chill in the air licked at her skin like the clammy kiss of a frog prince. Holding onto the banister, Alice descended into the ebony gloom. She had only gone down a few steps when she became aware of a constant, soughing whisper like soft breathing; the sound was familiar, but she could not distinguish it. By the time she reached the packed-earth floor of the cellar, there was no sign of the laughing people she had heard, only another obliging footman in livery posted beside the yawning mouth of a cave. He bowed to her and swept a gesture toward the cave's mouth.

She paused with prickling chills running down her spine. Just what kind of man had her sister-in-law become involved with? she wondered in growing uneasiness. Caro had described Lucien Knight as a worldly, sophisticated, dangerously cunning *chargé d'affaires* of the Foreign Office who spoke six or seven languages, but what sort of man kept armed guards posted around his house, required a password at his gates, and held a party in an underground cave? She knew she should turn back, yet the soft, whispering sound drew her onward. Her heart pounding, she slowly walked into the cave.

Torches jutted from the walls, illuminating the glistening stalactites here and there like great dragon's teeth. As she ventured deeper into the cave, the mysterious sound grew louder; then she smelled the bracing scent of freshwater and suddenly realized what it was—an underground river. She had seen the cascade flowing out of the rock when her carriage had crossed the little wooden bridge. Her guess was confirmed when she rounded a bend in the tunnel and came to the river itself. At last, she saw people. Here the footmen were assisting the robed guests into fanciful gondolas. On the bow of each playfully shaped boat, a torch burned, reflecting the glossy onyx surface of the subterranean river. One of the servants beckoned Alice over.

"Hurry, please, madam. We can fit you aboard this one," he called briskly.

Alice hesitated, her heart pounding wildly. If she got on that gondola, she knew she might not get another chance to back out—but then the people in the boat began yelling at her, as rowdy and impatient as they had been on the road.

"Hurry up!"

"Are you daft, woman?"

"Don't just stand there. We're already late!"

Simple, obstinate pride barred her from fleeing like a coward in front of so many people. Not daring to think what her dear brother would have had to say about this, she hurried forward and accepted the servant's hand, climbing aboard the gondola. After she had taken a seat, the boatman shoved off with his pole, slowly ferrying the passengers deeper into the limestone caves. She tucked her slippered feet under her and folded her hands primly in her lap.

"Now we're going to be even later," someone grumbled in the seat behind her.

Alice glanced anxiously over her shoulder. She was beginning to feel jumpy and scared, but it was too late now.

"Don't mind them," the portly drunkard seated next to her slurred. Short and balding, he looked like Friar Tuck from the Robin Hood tales, his sloppy brown robe pulled taut over his potbelly. "We've probably missed the service, but personally, I only come for the party."

Service? she wondered, eyeing him in trepidation.

He smiled at her, his eyelids sagging with intoxication. "What about you?" he prodded. "Lady of pleasure or a true believer?"

Alice just looked at him warily, edging away from him in her seat while the gondola glided gracefully through the ink-black water. She did not talk to strangers, especially leering, drunken males. Besides, she had no wish to reveal the fact that she had no idea what he was talking about.

He studied her with a shrewd sparkle in his small, brown eyes. "You can call me Orpheus."

He spoke with the hard *r*'s and exaggerated vowels of an American, which seemed odd, since England and America were at war. The newspapers had reported that British ships were still blockading the bay at New Orleans, just as they had off and on since 1812. Just then, the fluttering of some bats above distracted her. She quickly looked up and wrapped her arms around herself with a grimace, only to realize she should have been more worried about Orpheus, who sidled ever closer to her with a slight, lewd grin.

"You're new, aren't you? Shy little thing. Young, too," he whispered, laying his hand on her thigh.

The violence with which she recoiled from him rocked the boat. "Sir!"

Orpheus withdrew his hand, laughing at her. "Never fear, little one, I know the rules. Draco gets first crack at you." He pulled a flask out of the inside of his robe and uncorked it. "To Draco, Argus, Prospero—Master of Illusion and Lord of Lies," he said cynically. "No doubt he will enjoy you."

Alice stared at the man in shock. "Who?" she blurted out.

"Why, Lucifer, my dear. Who else?"

She gulped. Her heart was pounding hard and fast as the ferryman brought them drifting to a halt on a gently sloped landing. It seemed highly imprudent to get out of the boat, yet her fellow passengers were disembarking in high spirits. They tumbled out of the gondola and trekked merrily up the shallow steps carved into the limestone toward a low, rounded door.

"Come, come, little one. Don't dawdle!" Orpheus grabbed her wrist and tugged her along with them.

She winced in distaste when she saw the carving that adorned the arched door—the jolly, gnomelike figure of Priapus, the Celtic fertility god, who wore nothing but a wide grin and a ludicrously outsized erection. Priapus was depicted with his finger laid over his lips, as though binding to secrecy all those who entered this door.

"He rather looks like me, don't you think?" Orpheus asked with a chuckle; then a man ahead of them hauled the door open.

At once, a rush of sound, music, and the low roar of many voices poured out from the subterranean cavern beyond, engulfing them. The music startled her, part plainchant, part war drums, punctuated by the shimmering clash of cymbals and the deep, buzzing drone of exotic Turkish instruments. The smell of frankincense wafted out from the soupy blackness beyond the open door.

"Come on, blue eyes," Orpheus said jovially.

Alice knew it was a foolish idea to follow him into that darkness. She sensed danger here, but knowing that her sister-in-law was somewhere in that darkness, she *had* to go. Whatever Caro had gotten herself into, Alice knew it was up to her, as usual, to get her out of it. Keeping her face well shadowed in the depths of her hood, she held tightly to her courage and followed the portly American through the arched door.

What Alice saw inside froze her motionless. She could only stare—stricken, amazed. It was a moment she would remember for the rest of her life, clipping her history neatly in two: her naive existence before Revell Court, and after; the moment her eyes were opened to the existence of another world, a world of secrets.

Lucien's world.

The smell of frankincense filled her nostrils. Candles burned everywhere amid the serenely dripping stalactites. She struggled for clarity against the shock of the grotesque, orgiastic scene that sprawled out in the vast cavern below her, like a Hieronymous Bosch painting come to life. The mesmerizing music wove its snake-like spell over her, lulling her senses, numbing her astonished mind.

One thing, at least, was clear, she thought. This was no costume ball.

"Come on," Orpheus said eagerly, leading the way down the steps chiseled out of the porous limestone, descending into a vast subterranean cavern that seethed with a throng of robed people who all were facing, as in homage, the huge carving in the limestone of a hideous, fanged dragon. Every scale was intricately carved; the monster was posed in a reptilian crouch. Braziers of red-glowing coals gleamed in the carved hollows of its eyes. The open mouth alone was as tall as a man, and from its black recesses, a bubbling hot springs flowed into the great cave. The steam from the naturally heated water puffed in spirals through the dragon's nostrils, as though, at any moment, it might breathe a blast of fire. The hot springs ran down a shallow four-foot channel into a crystalline pool like the one at Bath. It was adorned with tiled mosaics and free-standing Corinthian columns that might well have been put there by the ancient Romans.

Alice had never seen so much naked flesh in her life. Perhaps it was due to her passion for art, particularly for portraiture, but she was surprised at how quickly her shock and moral indignation evaporated in sheer artistic interest. Though many people sported in the waters nude, most were still clothed, their identities shadowed by their hooded brown robes. Some wore masks for extra anonymity, but all appeared engrossed in the drama unfolding on the stagelike platform that was hewn into the serpent's back, cleverly carved to resemble a saddle. The chief feature on the stage was a stone altar, behind which a pale young man stood, his priestly robes draping his tall, lanky frame. Holding up his hands at his sides, he chanted in some unknown language—probably nonsense—with a clear, reedy voice. The people answered at regular intervals in a mockery of a church service. Alice shuddered uneasily.

When they reached the bottom of the stairs, Orpheus immediately began pushing his way into the thick of the swaying crowd. She tapped him on the shoulder.

"I have to find Lady Glenwood," she yelled over the thunderous beat of the drums. "Do you know her?"

"No names, chit!" Scowling at her, he glanced about as though to make sure no one had heard, then lowered his head close to hers. She noticed abruptly that he did not seem at all drunk anymore. "Never speak anyone's real name here," he said sharply. "God, you are new, aren't you? No, I don't know the woman. Now, just follow me and don't talk to anyone, or you're going to get yourself into a lot of trouble."

Chastened, Alice obeyed and filed after Orpheus as he moved through the crowd, which she estimated to be over a hundred people. She searched the sea of faces around her for Caro while Orpheus chose a position in the middle of the crowd. They stopped and turned toward the stage. The reedy voice of the pale young man carried louder. The people answered in unison; she did not understand their words but could feel their anticipation building. Pronouncing a few more bizarre incantations, the pale man turned once more to the people, holding out his arms. The speed of his incomprehensible words and the pitch of his nasally tenor rose steadily with excitement. "Vee-nee-ay mil-sit dren-sa-il *Draco*!"

Cymbals clashed at the sound of the name. Fires flared

in the braziers on the ends of the stage as the priest's assistants doused the coals with lamp oil. The choir and drones fell silent, but the drums continued more softly and all around her the people began a low chanting: "*Draco, Draco.*"

A pair of doors flew open at the end of the stage. Alice stared, riveted, as a tall, powerful figure swept out of the open doors and stalked across the stage, his face concealed by the deep hood of his robe, which was of black silk. It billowed out behind him with each determined stride as he prowled to the center of the stage with the grace of a massive black leopard. The sheen of the material reflected the flickering fires that seemed to caress him as he passed. The robe hung open down the front, revealing his black trousers and boots and his loose, white shirt with a deep, fringed V that partly bared his bronzed, sculpted chest. Alice gazed at him in wonder. Draco stopped and turned toward the crowd. White lace cuffs dripped below the sleeves of his robe as he stretched forth his large, murderously elegant hands. She could not tear her gaze away.

Though his eyes and the upper half of his face were shrouded by his hood, she stared in fascination at his square, chiseled jaw and strong chin. Then he spoke, and his deep, mesmerizing voice rolled over the crowd in natural command, filling the cavern. "*Brothers and sisters!*"

The people roared in adoration.

"Tonight we come together to welcome two new initiates into our most vile and ignominious company." The throng cheered wildly at his insults; a small, mocking smile flitted briefly over his beguiling lips. "They have been tested—and tasted—by the Elders, as you all have," he purred, "and they have been found worthy. Initiates, come forward and receive the final rite." He pulled back his hood, unveiling a face of burning, satanic, male beauty.

Alice held her breath, enthralled, feeling the resounding slam of some fateful premonition. *Lucien Knight.* One look erased any lingering doubt in her mind who he was. He had the bold, patrician features of a dashing adventurer and silver eyes that glittered like diamonds. The glossy jet of his hair set off his sun-bronzed complexion and the wicked, white gleam of his smile.

Then she gasped as two naked women crawled up onto the stage and went to him on their hands and knees. *Oh, God, don't let that be Caro.* The women crouched at his feet, and Alice nearly fainted with relief to realize neither was her sister-in-law. "Draco" laid a hand on each one's head and began making incantations over them in the same incoherent language the pale young man had used. The women moaned, caressing him all the while. Alice watched their hands travel over his hard, lean body as if they could not get enough of him, and the writhing sensuality of the Grotto began to penetrate her naive awareness. She could not stop staring in fascination at Caro's beautiful, evil lover. *No wonder they called him Lord Lucifer,* she thought. *He was made for temptation.*

Concluding his prayer a moment later, he leaned down and kissed each woman gently on the forehead. They sought his mouth, but with a cruel, delicious little smile, he denied them; then the pale young man wrapped the women in white robes and led them away. Draco's faithful began growing restless. Alice glanced in rising uneasiness as the people all around her began mingling into pairs and more exotic combinations. Here and there, they were embracing, kissing, beginning to slither out of their brown robes. The service seemed to be drawing to a close.

Orpheus suddenly grabbed her arm, startling her. "Give us a kiss, blue eyes." He grunted, a bead of sweat trickling down his round, ruddy face.

She jerked back. "Let go of me!"

"What are you, a virgin?"

"Get away from me!"

They struggled for a moment and he tried again to kiss her, but Alice shoved him away as hard as she could. Muttering a rude epithet, Orpheus angrily withdrew and moved off into the crowd, leaving her alone.

Shaken, Alice brushed a few strands of her hair back, her hand trembling slightly, then glanced around and stood on tiptoe, trying to spy Caro. She began making her way through the crowd, looking for the prodigal baroness everywhere. The pipers started up again on their drones, making dizzying, undulant music that seemed to coil and twist through her body. With every step, she heard various languages being spoken in the crowd. She realized there were people there from all over Europe—and they were beginning to let loose the fullness of their depravity. The robes were coming off. The great pool was filling up with laughing nymphs and satyrs, as were the small, dark lovers' nooks carved into the cave walls. Erotic wonders bloomed around her like otherworldly flowers. She saw a masked lady flogging a man who was tied to one of the Corinthian columns, his hands bound above his head; each time she struck his bare back with her riding whip, his body jerked and he cried out with pleasure while other people watched. A few steps farther on, she saw two women locked in a passionate kiss. She stared at them as she passed by, amazed and entirely confused. On every hand, people were doing things to one another that she never could have imagined. She was so overwhelmed by it all that she knew she would have to try to absorb it later. For now, she could only focus on her task—finding Caro, bringing her home to Harry.

The thought of her nephew cleared her head and bolstered her determination. For his sake, she began pushing her way more aggressively through the crowd, ignoring the sex acts, both natural and unnatural, and the score of obscene propositions that strangers made to her as she passed, until at last she came to the edge of the great pool.

The steam rising from the hot spring dampened the tendrils of her hair around her face as she searched the swimmers' faces in the dim half-light, but after a couple of minutes, her heart sank as she realized her sister-in-law was not among them. She pressed her hand to her forehead. *Oh, God, what if she is off somewhere making love with Lucien Knight?* She glanced at the stage. The fair-haired man was still there, but "Draco" had disappeared.

Alice scowled and dropped her hand to her side again, longing to be spared the unthinkable prospect of having to interrupt her sister-in-law's liaison with her demon lover. No matter, she told herself. She would throw Caro's clothes on her and march her home by her ear, if necessary. Resolved to search the nooks and crannies that lined the cave, Alice pivoted—and crashed right into a man's bare, muscled chest.

Right at her eye level, his loose white shirt hung open, revealing a deep V of velvety skin. At this close range, she could see every sculpted ridge of his stomach, every hard plane of his magnificent chest; could practically taste the salty, vibrant sheen of sweat that glowed on his skin. Her heart leaped into her throat with instant recognition; her wits scattered like chickens with a fox in the henhouse.

Oh, no, she thought, choking on her gasp.

Slowly lifting her gaze, Alice tilted her head back and looked into the silvery, mocking eyes of Lucien Knight.

CHAPTER THREE

Moments earlier, Lucien had been sauntering through the crowd, watching everything, his senses on full alert behind his air of nonchalance. He had a staff of five roguish young agents-in-training who assisted him in the operation. Four of them each worked a quadrant of the Grotto, while Talbert, the fifth, used his flair for showmanship and flummery to play their "priest." Six ravishing courtesans were on Lucien's payroll, as well, and each one knew her duty—to ply the foreign agents with wine, offer her favors, and seduce information out of them. Blending easily into the crowd, the lads and the girls alike would learn all they could and report back to him at the end of the night. For his part, Lucien strolled freely through the Grotto, overseeing everything and staying sharply attuned for any hint of information regarding his enemies.

A man, however, could not be all business. The unbridled sexuality all around him made his blood hot. He needed a woman, and soon. Not Caro—he had bored of her at some indefinable moment during the long carriage ride from London to Revell Court. He had been considering one of his obedient new initiates—or both, perhaps—when he had noticed the girl.

She still had all her clothes on. That was the first thing that had snagged his attention. It didn't seem quite right. With her hood hiding her face, it was impossible to tell who she was, yet somehow he instantly knew that she didn't belong.

But that was impossible, he thought. He knew everyone and everything that happened in the Grotto. His control was absolute. No mere chit could have breached his security.

Then he had noticed that she was alone, and the full, fierce spear of his awareness had homed in on her. He had watched her carefully picking her way through the crowd, slim and stealthy. She set his instincts jangling. The only question was, which instincts?

Intent on a closer look, he had begun following her casually through the crowd while his pulse took up a deep, primal drumming. His craving for a fiery coupling, skin on skin, twisted through his veins. It was the best he could hope for in the bitter knowledge that what he really needed did not exist, not in his world. Like anything else, however, love could be simulated. He wanted to be held like the last man on earth; he wanted to fuck until he was drenched in sweat, to lose himself in adoring a woman's body and perhaps, for an instant, drive back the isolation that engulfed him.

Closing the distance between them, he had savored the modest allure of her walk and felt his body respond to the graceful sway of her hips as they approached the pool. He had envisioned her taking off her robe and showing him her slender nakedness, but instead, she had just stood there, as though searching for someone. It skipped through his mind that when he caught up to the girl, he would either apprehend or ravish her. He still wasn't sure which it would be as he stood before her, blocking her escape with a dark, slight smile.

As she peered up at him fearfully from the shadowed folds of her hood, he found himself staring into the bluest eyes he had ever seen. He had only encountered that deep, dream-spun shade of cobalt once in his life before, in the stained glass windows of Chartres Cathedral. His awareness of the crowd around them dimmed in the ocean-blue depths of her eyes. *Who are you?* He did not say a word nor ask her permission. With the smooth self-assurance of a man who has access to every woman in the room, he captured her chin in a firm but gentle grip. She jumped when he touched her, panic flashing in her eyes.

His hard stare softened slightly in amusement at that, but then his faint smile faded, for her skin was silken beneath his fingertips. With one hand, he lifted her face toward the dim torchlight, while the other softly brushed back her hood. Then Lucien faltered, faced with a beauty the likes of which he had never seen.

His very soul grew hushed with reverence as he gazed at her, holding his breath for fear the vision would dissolve, a figment of his overactive brain. With her bright tresses gleaming the flame-gold of dawn and her large, frightened eyes of that shining, ethereal blue, he was so sure for a moment that she was a lost angel that he half expected to see silvery, feathered wings folded demurely beneath her coarse brown robe. She appeared somewhere between the ages of eighteen and twenty-two—a wholesome, nay, a virginal beauty of trembling purity. He instantly *knew* that she was utterly untouched, impossible as that seemed in this place.

Her face was proud and wary. Her satiny skin glowed in the candlelight, pale and fine, but her soft, luscious lips shot off an effervescent champagne-pop of desire that fizzed more sweetly in his veins than anything he'd felt since his adolescence, which had taken place, if he recalled correctly, some time during the Dark Ages. There was intelligence and valor in her delicate face, courage, and a quivering vulnerability that made him ache with anguish for the doom of all innocent things.

A noble youth, a questing youth, he thought, and if she had come to slay dragons, she had already pierced him in his black, fiery heart with the lance of her heaven-blue gaze. He felt as though she saw through him in a glance, the same way he saw through everyone else. It frightened him even as it held him riveted. If only . . .

It was then, as his initial amazement passed, that reality struck him. He did not know her. He had never seen this girl before, let alone approved her.

Good God, he thought in sudden horror, *she was just the sort of weapon Fouché would send against him!*

He instantly tightened his grip on her face to a shade short of cruelty, for innocence, too, could be counterfeited. He saw terror fill her eyes. He didn't care. "Well, well," he snarled, "what have we here? You're very pretty, aren't you, my pet?"

"Let go of me!"

He laughed nastily at her struggles. She wrapped her hands around his wrist and tried to dislodge his relentless grip. *Wings, ha!* he thought in self-disgust, baffled by his moment of irrationality—gawking at her like some love-struck youth! The only thing this wench was likely hiding under her robe was a dagger that Fouché had sent her to stick between his ribs!

He was enraged that she had nearly duped him in his own game even for a second, but he did not want to make too much of a scene with so many foreign operatives present. His visitors hailed from the Habsburg court, Naples, Moscow—he had even seen the detestable, barrel-bellied, American double agent Rollo Greene in the crowd. Fortunately, Lucien specialized in hiding the truth in plain view. He had to get her alone, learn who she was, and find out who she was working for.

Certain that she was hiding a weapon of some kind beneath her robe, he stopped her from reaching for it by catching her wrists up roughly behind her back, clenching her against his body. The little hellcat fought him, squirming and twisting, bucking against his body.

"Let me go, I say!"

He let out a lusty laugh as her hip chafed his groin. "Mm, I like that," he purred, holding her slender body against him.

"You, horrible—stop it!" she yelled. "You're hurting me!"

"Good." He lowered his face toward hers and looked into her eyes with a menacing glower. "Now, then, my beauty, why don't you and I go somewhere private?"

She stopped fighting suddenly, her blue eyes widening, her lovely face going from flushed to pale.

Without warning, he lifted her off her feet and threw her over his shoulder, still gripping her wrists with one hand while he clapped the other firmly on her backside to hold her in place.

Her high-pitched shriek went unheard amid the lusty cheers of the people all around them as Lucien carried her off, barbarian-style, to his private observation room behind the glowing red eyes of the dragon.

* * *

His wide shoulder was as hard as iron under her stomach, and his whole body gave off angry heat like a furnace. If Alice's notion of reality had been skewed by the decadence of Revell Court, her wits were absolutely routed by being carried off by the demonic master of the place. The people clapping for Lucien Knight and cheering for him seemed to think that he had singled her out for one reason only. Alice was terrified that they were right.

Her protests, threats, and begging went unheeded, drowned out by the throbbing music and drums. Her kicks and flailing punches when she finally wrenched her hands free had not the slightest effect on him. She even tried pulling his wavy black hair in her wild scramble to free herself, but it only brought his hand down on her backside in a hearty spank.

"How dare you?" she gasped, her body going rigid, her eyes smarting at the sting, though the blow hurt her pride more than her flesh.

"Quit pulling my hair or next time it'll be your bare arse."

At his crude threat, her courage blasted up in a geyser of fury and indignation. For a man who supposedly spoke seven languages, he was a master of the vulgar tongue! She did not think she had ever been so angry in her entire life. She felt helpless, hefted in his powerful arms, and she hated it—more specifically, she hated him. Oh, how she wished her brother were still alive! Phillip would have put a bullet in him if he could have seen this—first Caro, now her!

Nevertheless, as "Draco" stalked toward the great

carved dragon, Alice stopped fighting temporarily, knowing she was overpowered physically and had best regroup before they arrived wherever he was taking her. She was going to need her wits about her if she had any hope of stopping the fiend from ravishing her.

A guard in a long black coat opened a door for him behind the dragon's elbow. Lord Lucien strode through it. It closed behind them, muffling the echoing roar of the music and the crowd. She braced her hands on the curve of his lower back and tried to twist around to see ahead.

"Where are you taking me?" she demanded in a shaky voice.

"Wouldn't you like to know?" he replied in a nasty tone.

She winced at his mockery, bounced against his rock-hard body as he began marching up a narrow spiral staircase hewn into the stone. His stride was tireless. At the top of the steps, another guard opened yet another door for them. With Alice still dangling over his shoulder quite bereft of her dignity, Lucien marched into a small domelike room, dim and overheated. It had a couch, a wooden table with a couple of chairs, and two oval windows of scarlet stained glass that overlooked the Grotto and the great pool. She was startled to realize they were inside the skull of the dragon.

He leaned down and set her on her feet. "Don't move."

The order was futile. She was already in motion, instinctively backing away from him as she would from the wildest of predators.

He reached into his shirt and pulled out a pistol, which he coolly leveled between her eyes. "I said don't move, love."

She froze in place, staring in astonishment down the barrel of the gun. Her stomach plummeted with terror.

"Hand over your weapon."

"What?" she whispered, her shocked gaze swinging from the pistol's barrel to the ruthless beauty of his face. The lurid red glow from the dragon's stained-glass eyes bathed the harmonious planes of his cheeks and forehead, contoured the sharp angles of his princely nose and square, determined chin. His sable hair was blacker than night in the underworld, spun from silken shadows. His silvery eyes gleamed with anarchy as he stalked toward her.

"You're not going to cooperate, are you?" he chided in velvet menace. "Very well, *chérie*. If you'd rather have me search you, I am more than willing. Take off your robe."

"My lord!"

He gestured with the gun. "Take it off."

She looked into his steely eyes and promptly decided she wasn't about to argue with a madman holding a pistol. With shaking fingers, Alice untied the cinched cord of her belt, then lifted the brown robe off over her head, revealing the demure cotton morning gown that she had changed into before leaving her chamber.

His gaze traveled over her with slow, scorching heat. "Throw it on the floor."

She obeyed.

"Place your hands behind your head."

"Please—you're making a mistake—"

When he narrowed his eyes at her in warning, she shut her mouth and quickly linked her fingers behind her head. He thrust his weapon back into the discreet leather holster inside of his shirt and closed the space between them, putting his hands firmly on her waist. He patted her sides, then circled behind her and began searching every inch of her body with his deft, deadly hands. With a small cry, she jerked her arms down and squirmed her hips away from his touch, but he captured her wrists and thrust them up behind her head again.

"I suggest you cooperate, *mademoiselle*."

"This is absurd! I am not armed!" she protested with a scarlet blush.

"Be quiet and stand still, or I shall strip you of every stitch of your clothing, and richly enjoy doing so."

She nearly choked. Good God, what had she gotten herself into? If only she had stayed in her room! She held her tongue and did her best not to flinch and twitch as his large, roaming hands explored her.

"You are very tempting, you know," he said in a musing tone, "but I'm a little insulted that they should send such an amateur. Were they trying to get you killed?"

"I—I don't know what you're talking about."

"Ah, of course, you don't. Darling, you had better think fast about how you want to play your hand, because I know your kind all too well. I know why they sent you, of course—to lie with me, then stab me in my sleep."

She gasped at his words.

"And yet—" His lips hovered by her ear as he ran his hands slowly up her belly. "—I could almost believe a night with you would have been worth it." He lifted her breasts in his palms. She jerked back with a small cry into the hard wall of his chest right behind her, her heart pumping in a tumult of confusion, arousal, and fear.

Her chest heaved, thrusting her breasts more fully into

his hands, but her breath had formed a tangled knot in her throat. She could not speak, could only feel the heat of his hands burning through the thin muslin of her gown, igniting bewildering forces in her blood. With his powerful arms wrapped around her, she could feel every inch of his lean, iron body molded against her—the angular jut of his knees nudging the backs of her legs, the slopes of his strong thighs against her buttocks, the sculpted plane of his stomach pressing against her back, and his muscular chest pillowing her head.

"Pity," he whispered. "We fit together perfectly."

A bewildering tremor ran the length of her body at his words; then he moved on, resuming his search. Her heartbeat tripped to a frantic staccato as he lowered himself to a crouched position by her right hip and slid his hands under her skirt.

"What are you doing?" she forced out in a wobbly voice.

"Just this." He ran his touch with leisurely slowness up her stockinged leg and hooked his finger into her garter, tracing it all the way around her thigh. A traitorous shiver coursed through her. Sizzling warmth flooded her lower body, making her burn with mortification. "What's your name?" he murmured, lightly tickling the back of her knee.

Her head was spinning. Her knees were weak. She thought of lying to him or making some kind of stand, but she could barely think with his hands all over her. Her heated skin had turned maddeningly sensitive to his every caress. It was humiliating to have one's body react so to such a fiend. She shivered and jerked involuntarily, aroused and infuriated, as he took his time about his task.

"Your name, *ma chérie*."

"Alice," she replied through gritted teeth. "Get your hands off of me."

He looked up again and stared at her in sudden stillness. "Alice what?"

"Alice Montague. I've come to get Caro—to rescue her from you!"

Shock flared in his eyes. He swept to his feet and stared at her.

She tilted her head back to meet his stunned gaze, for he was over six feet tall, with shoulders twice the width of hers.

"You're Alice Montague?"

"Isn't that what I just said?"

He narrowed his silver eyes and picked up a length of her hair with a skeptical expression.

"Ow," she muttered, as his light grasp tugged her head. "Let go of my hair."

"Be quiet," he muttered. He studied the color of her hair for a very long moment, then dropped it abruptly. As it swung back down over her shoulder, he braced his hands on his waist and glared at her.

"What is it?" she asked in worry, shrinking from him.

"You're Alice," he accused her, his smooth voice gone oddly strangled.

"Yes."

"Caro's sister-in-law."

"Yes."

"The one that takes care of the baby." He fairly sneered.

"Yes! Did she mention me?"

His silver eyes narrowed like a wolf's sizing up a lamb. "Alice goddamned Montague. How the hell did you *get in my house?*" he yelled in a sudden crescendo that made her jump.

"You don't have to curse at me!"

His hands planted on his lean waist, he waited for her explanation with a quite terrifying look of brooding sarcasm.

Alice refused to show her fear. She scowled up at him, staunchly holding her ground. "I told you, I came to bring Caro home. Your gatekeepers tried to keep me out, but fortunately, I was able to make them see the urgency of my request; then your butler told me he would fetch Caro for me, but he never did, so I came myself. I thought it was a costume ball."

His left eyebrow shot up. "A costume ball?"

"Yes."

He seemed to find her blunder amusing, though his smile was far from kind. "You realize this is extremely easy to verify. All I have to do is bring Caro in here to find out if you're really who you say you are."

"I wish that you would. I have traveled three counties to fetch her," she said with a weary sigh. "Her son is very ill."

His sardonic expression sobered instantly. "Harry? What's wrong with him?"

"He has the chicken pox," she replied, startled that he knew Harry's name and that he showed even a flicker of concern. "All he's done is cry for her," she added, on her guard but relaxing by a degree or two. "It'll be worse over the next few days. He just broke out this morning."

"It was a hell of a lot of trouble for you to go to, coming here. For your information, chicken pox aren't that serious."

"They are if you're three," she said indignantly.

"Well, you've got me there," he retorted under his breath. Shaking his head, Lucien turned away and went to the table beneath the dragon's-eye windows. He pulled out one of the wooden chairs for her. "Sit," he ordered, then stalked over to the door and hauled it open. "Find Lady Glenwood and bring her to me immediately," he ordered the two big, black-clad men posted there.

"Yes, my lord."

Alice sank into the chair, overhearing his command with considerable relief. The men marched off to do his bidding. Folding her hands nervously in her lap, she tucked her feet under the chair and watched him in trepidation as he slowly closed the door. He just stood there for a moment, his head down, the red light playing over his broad back and athletic shoulders; then he turned around and leaned wearily against the door, his angular face veiled in shadows.

He slipped his hands into his trouser pockets and stared at her, keeping a wary distance. In her mind, she could still feel his hands gliding up her legs. She quickly tucked her chin, avoiding his penetrating gaze.

"Miss Goody Two-Shoes," he taunted softly.

She stiffened, sliding him a frown. "I do not appreciate being called that."

His insolent gaze traveled over her body. "I hear you're quite the little saint."

"Compared to whom? Caro?"

His cynical smirk widened to a genuine smile at her retort. "I daresay you're having a bit of an adventure tonight, aren't you?"

"An ordeal is more like it."

"Well, you seem to have come through it all in fine spirit." He pressed away from the door and sauntered toward her.

Her heart began pounding anew as he approached, and once more, she felt the inward shudder of fate as he drew near. Gooseflesh rose on her arms as though someone had walked over her grave. He stopped beside her, the lean, belted waistband of his black trousers at her eye level. She dared not meet his gaze, but felt the throbbing heat that radiated from his body, smelled the musky male scent of him; then she noticed the great cylindrical bulge in his trousers. It was right in front of her eyes, after all, and too astonishingly large to miss. She tore her gaze away from that region and cursed herself for looking, but now that she had noticed his most manly attribute, she could not seem to forget about it.

She jumped when he captured one of her long tresses again and ran the length of it slowly between his fingers like a satin ribbon. Resenting the galling forwardness of his touch, she glanced up at him angrily only to be captivated by his smoldering, hypnotic stare.

When he spoke, his voice was an intimate murmur that could have coaxed the deepest secrets from her heart. "Virginal Alice Montague. Tell me, what do you think of what you've seen here tonight?"

She shook her head and looked away, blushing. "I do not know."

He lifted her chin, forcing her to meet his gaze, diamond-sharp, crystal-clear. "Does it arouse you?"

Her eyes flared with shock. She could not find her voice even to tell him that she had no intention of answering such a question, but he cut her off before she could speak.

"Don't lie," he chided in a velvet whisper, holding her chin between his fingertips so she could not look away. He gazed at her as though his keen, crystalline eyes could see into the depths of her heart, things she had never revealed to anyone—the unruliness of her passions, the hunger in the core of her. His gaze seemed to accept it all with dark, satin gentleness. "Tell me," he breathed. "Let me remember how it felt to be as innocent as you." He paused, though she did not reply. "Have you never seen people making love before?"

Wide-eyed, her heart in her throat, she gathered her courage and shook her head after a long moment. His expression softened. He gazed down almost tenderly at her. She had never seen such hunger in a man's eyes before, such stark, hurting loneliness. She quivered in response to it, flooded with the strangest, tingling feelings as he picked up her hand and lifted it to his lips.

He placed a gentle kiss in her palm, then pressed her hand to his chiseled midriff. A soft gasp escaped her lips, not merely that he should do such a thing, but at the feel of his bare skin beneath her palm. It electrified her.

She looked up at him, helpless, trembling. Her voice was a strangled whisper, the weakest of protests. "My lord—"

"Shh, Alice, I can see it in your eyes. Go on. I won't bite. All is allowed in this place. Your curiosity is . . . quite natural," he finished hoarsely.

Hesitantly, she glanced at her hand, so pale and delicate looking against the sun-bronzed iron of his body. She bit her lip, knowing she was playing with fire, but truly, he was as beautiful as a god. His body was like a fine classical sculpture, while his broody, quicksilver sensitivity registered a thousand different emotions in his chiseled face, or hid them all. Though she didn't dare move even a finger to explore him, she didn't pull her hand away, either. She noticed in fascination the fierce rhythm of his pounding pulse.

"Your heart is racing," she said, sweeping her gaze up to his face.

His eyes burned like stars; his face was shadowed. He stroked her neck, his fingertips coming to rest on her artery. "So is yours."

Oh, God, she wanted him to kiss her. She closed her eyes, savoring the power of his large, deadly hand on her throat even though she knew that every second of this indulgence was extremely dangerous. It was madness to encourage him, but his touch was so irresistibly gentle.

When she dragged her eyes open again, the concentrated need in his angular face had intensified near the point of agony. As her gaze drifted downward over his heaving chest and lean waist, she saw the clear outline of his massive erection through his snug black trousers. His eyes pleaded with her to touch him while he caressed her arm all the way down to her fingertips. Her pulse escalated to an even wilder rhythm as she realized in shock that she wanted to. She swept her gaze back up to meet his. They stared at each other. Her breathing deepened with a savage rhythm as he began inching her hand lower, making her feel every exquisite plane and muscled ridge of his belly.

All of a sudden, a knock sounded at the door, breaking the spell just as her hand reached his waist. The sound snapped Alice back violently to her senses. Good Lord, what was she doing? With a gasp, she yanked her hand out of his light hold as though she had been burned. "You are bold, sir!"

"And you are blushing." He slipped her a narrow, charming little smile and went to answer the door.

Anger and confusion thudded in her temples as she tucked her still-tingling hand in her lap. She scowled, furious at her own bewildering state of arousal. She had never felt such things before. Wet and aching between her legs, she squeezed her knees together firmly under her skirts, trying to remind her body that her head and her morals were in charge. Lucien Knight was not. Lust was hardly a sentiment to which she aspired. She slid a furtive glance his way, wondering why he had not yet opened the door. He just stood there, one hand on the doorknob, his head down. Then she realized he was struggling to bring his magnificent body under control.

As though he felt her gaze on his powerful, V-shaped back and lean, muscled derriere, he slowly looked over his shoulder and met her stare in raw longing. Neither of them spoke for a moment, swept up in a totally unexpected, unsought, unwanted attraction of dizzying power.

"Shall I come to you tonight?" he asked very quietly.

She gasped and tore her gaze away, her heart pounding. "No!"

Heaven above, the sooner she collected her sister-in-law and left this wicked place, the better. First thing in the morning, she would race home to Glenwood Park and forget everything she had seen here tonight—including him. Especially him.

She heard his vexed, long-suffering sigh, then a *snick* as he turned the lock.

The minute he opened the door, Caro launched into the room and threw her arms around his neck. "Darling!"

Alice's eyebrows shot upward at the sight of the haughty baroness, tipsy and disheveled, her hair wet from the pool, her brown robe falling over one bare, white shoulder. She clung to Lucien, unaware of Alice standing at the other end of the room.

"Did you miss me? Did you need me, my bad boy?" She thrust her hand between his legs, caressing him where Alice had not dared to. "Were you jealous? You should be," she chided with a drunken laugh. "I've been coming my brains out down there. I'm quite addicted! But I have a plan, you see. I've been building up slowly, saving the best for last. That's you."

Alice's greeting wilted on her tongue. Shocked, she watched her sister-in-law rubbing against him, riding her leg up the side of his thigh. Caro slipped her hand inside his open shirt and pulled him closer.

"Take me, Lucien," she panted, biting his earlobe.

Alice clapped her hand over her mouth. Good Lord! No wonder Lucien had scoffed when she had said that she had come to rescue Caro from him. What a sickening display! If anything, Lucien needed rescuing before the baroness devoured *him*.

He cleared his throat and plucked her roaming hands gingerly off his body. "Er, Lady Glenwood, there's someone here to see you." He turned and gestured toward Alice with the detached interest of a spectator at a polo match, as though merely curious to see what would happen.

Caro followed his gaze and discovered Alice standing there. The lusty mirth drained instantly from her face, which took on a waxy pallor. With a stricken look, she lifted her hand automatically to smooth her damp, tangled hair. "Alice! W-whatever are you doing here?" the baroness stammered weakly.

Unable to meet her sister-in-law's gaze, Alice looked at Lucien in misery, wishing the ground would open up and swallow her. A flicker of some guarded emotion flitted through his deep gray eyes, but he offered not a word to ease the excruciating silence. He did not care about all this, she realized. What was left of her family was being finally destroyed before his very eyes, and he probably found it amusing. How she wished she had stayed home with Harry and held onto her willful ignorance about the full extent of Caro's debauchery. Clearly, it had been a mistake to come.

"Harry has the chicken pox," she replied at last in a leaden voice. "You must come home. We leave at dawn."

Caro gazed helplessly at her, her façade ripped away as though, through Alice's eyes, she had peered into the most painfully truthful of mirrors. She turned to Lucien, at a loss. He rested his hands on his waist and just looked at her.

There was a long, hollow, excruciating silence.

Then, without warning, Caro lashed out at them in explosive rage. *"How dare you come here?"* she screamed at Alice, her face twisting with fury. She started toward Alice like she wanted to claw her eyes out, but Lucien grabbed her arm, holding her back. "Get her out of here, Lucien! How could you let her come in here? I swear to you, Alice, if you say *one word* to me, I'll throw you out of Glenwood Park! You'll never see Harry again!"

"Calm yourself," Lucien ordered curtly.

"Let go of me!" Caro called him a dozen filthy names as he pulled her roughly back to the door and handed her over to the guards.

"Lady Glenwood has had too much to drink. Escort

her back to her room and lock her in," he ordered them curtly.

"You bastard! Fiend! Let go of me, you swine!" she raged at the guards. "Don't you dare smirk at me, you little witch!" she screamed at Alice, fighting her guards as they tried to bring her under control. "Do you think you're so pure? He made me do it—and he can make you do it, too! Then you'll see you're no better than me! Show her, Lucien! Do what you do best! At least you can do one thing as well as Damien!"

Lucien slammed the door in her face so hard that it shuddered on its hinges.

Alice pressed her hand to her forehead, shaken. The room was too hot, and it was altogether possible that she might cry.

Lucien, too, was silent. His back was to her, but she could feel the fury that thrummed through every taut line of his powerful body. "She's drunk. Don't listen to her. She spoke only from shame." When Alice said nothing, he turned around and slid her a guarded look. "Are you all right?"

"I don't even know why I came," she whispered, her chin trembling with the threat of tears. She fought them for all she was worth.

"Why did you come?" he asked in a low voice.

She did not want to tell him, but the words rushed out as shocked, angry tears flooded her eyes. "Because I promised my brother on his deathbed that I would look out for Harry and for her—and this is my thanks! She is ruining my life! I love my nephew, but—" Abruptly cutting off her impassioned words, she spun around, turning her back to him as the tears spilled down her cheeks. She wiped them away with shaking hands, then pivoted back to him, for this was all his fault. "What did you do to her?" she demanded in shaken ire. "She said you did something to her. What did you do?"

He lifted his chin, giving her a hard look. "She did it to herself."

"Why did you have to go and ruin everything between her and your brother? Why?"

"Isn't it obvious? You saw how she behaved. I did it to protect him."

"Lord Damien is a grown man!"

"He's no good with women."

"And you are?"

"Sometimes."

"Then where's your wife, Lucien? Where's the person who loves you?" she flung out.

His face fell, and for a moment, she glimpsed him exactly as he was behind his many masks—lost, scarred. Desperate for someone to reach him. He held her in a stark stare, then dropped his gaze. "Why, I don't have one, Alice," he said with only a remnant of his former sarcasm.

"My point exactly." Exasperated by the twinge of guilt she felt to see how her sharp words had struck their mark, she quickly wiped her tears away and attempted to soften her tone. Lost soul that he was, perhaps he simply did not *know* any better. "Love changes people, Lucien. That's what it *does*. If you had let them be, perhaps Lord Damien could have helped Caro change for the better. And then maybe Harry would have had a bit more security in life, a father to teach him how to become a man in time."

His sharp, angular face suddenly flushed with angry guilt. "That's not my problem! For one thing, Lord

Damien's head is in shambles and for another—God!" He laughed scathingly at her. "Do you really presume to lecture me on love? What do you know of the matter? I'd wager my house that you've never even been properly kissed! *Damn* it!" Without warning, he closed the distance between them in two strides, yanked her roughly into his arms, and claimed her mouth before she even had time to gasp.

The first, harsh, scorching contact of his lips obliterated her girlish visions of idyllic kisses from gentle swains. His left hand tangled roughly in her hair while the right crushed her to him. He kissed her like he would consume her, his hot, hungry tongue thrusting her lips apart. It was an act of possession, suffocating her with his fiery demand. She pushed weakly against his chest; he nudged her feet wider apart and moved his knee slightly between her legs, while his hands moved up and down her back. Stiff and bewildered, she clung to him merely to keep from swooning, engulfed in the radiating warmth of his lean, muscled body. She tried to turn away, to refuse the dangerous pleasure he wanted to make her taste, but as he ran his hands up and down her back, her response was difficult to hide, impossible to fight.

Trembling and uncertain, she ceased struggling by degrees and opened her mouth wider, slowly, hesitantly met his tongue with her own. Lucien groaned low in his throat, his forceful embrace softening at once. His kiss deepened and slowed, and she melted into his arms.

He went still after a long moment and ended the kiss, but his fine mouth still lingered near hers. He rested his forehead against hers, his chest heaving against her breasts. She could feel the soft warmth of his heavy breathing against her moist lips, while his palms grazed along the length of her arms.

"What about you, Alice?" he whispered raggedly. "Who loves you?"

She lifted her lashes, meeting his tempestuous stare uncertainly. "A—a lot of people."

"Who?" he demanded roughly.

"It's none of your business—"

"I gave you my answer; now give me yours."

"There's my nephew—Harry," she stammered.

"He's a child."

"He's someone!"

"Let me come to you tonight."

"Are you mad? Let go of me!" She wrenched out of his arms and backed away, wiping his kiss off her mouth with the back of her hand.

When he saw her wipe his kiss away, hellfire leaped into his eyes. He looked so outraged that for a moment she did not know what he would do to her. For a moment, he bristled like an angry wolf, frightening her with the intensity in his angular face and the sheer need burning in the depths of his luminous eyes; then he stalked past her to the door and snapped his fingers rudely at the guard posted outside.

"See Miss Montague safely to her chamber."

"Yes, my lord," the guard said with a short bow. "Miss, if you will follow me."

Alice looked uneasily at Lucien. He was watching her with a glitter of hostile lust in his eyes that did not worry her half so much as the sly, rather bitter half-smile that crept across his lips.

"Good-*bye*, my lord," she forced out in bravado. With

any luck, she would flee this place tomorrow morning without having to face him again.

He slid his hands in his pockets and leaned his shoulder against the door frame, watching her every move. "Good*night*, *chérie*."

She turned away, feeling his burning gaze on her body as she followed the guard across the anteroom. When the black-coated man started down the narrow spiral stairs, she glanced back over her shoulder one last time at Lucien. He was still standing there, his tall, powerful figure cloaked in shadows, a gleam of calculation in his light-tricked eyes.

Rollo Greene of Philadelphia, known in the Grotto as Orpheus, blotted the sweat from his bald pate, his chest heaving with too much wine and excitement. He'd be lucky if his heart didn't fail on him in the roasting, humid heat of the Grotto, he thought. He tore his stare away from the nude dancing girl nearby as Lucien Knight came back out from his secret headquarters inside the carved dragon. He had seen Lucien carry off the lovely young blue-eyed nymph a short while ago, just as Orpheus had warned her he would.

That was quick, he thought with a smirk, watching their host return to mingle among his guests, moving easily through the crowd. Rollo did not fret over his own failed attempt to coax a kiss from the girl. He could hardly compete with a man of Lucien Knight's looks and charm when it came to women, but he liked to think that at least he was his equal in craft and cunning.

They had a wary professional understanding between them, Lucien Knight and he, though they were on opposite sides of the war. Rollo was one of the few people who knew that the indulged, worldly diplomat, Lord Lucien Knight, was also the ruthless British agent whose code name, Argus, made foreign government ministers tremble and even caused Fouché, Napoleon's spymaster, to blanch.

Rollo and Lucien could not be called enemies, for they had swapped information several times in the past, but they were far from being friends. Rollo knew that Lucien held him in distaste for his mercenary ways and his lack of lordly polish, while for his part, Rollo resented the Englishman's physical and intellectual superiority, not to mention his arrogance. Tonight, however, Rollo savored the fact that he knew something that the omniscient Lord Lucifer did not.

Something big.

And he, Rollo Greene, was right in the middle of it all, making everything ready. Perhaps he wasn't tough and mean enough to outplay the likes of Lucien Knight, but he was preparing the way for someone who was every inch Lucien's equal, and possibly even a bit more terrifying.

The thought of the man who was coming fell like a cold shadow over Rollo's heart, forcing him to tear his leer away from the sweat-covered dancing girl. There was work to be done. Scanning the crowd, his gaze homed in on the highborn young rogue he had come to hire.

The Honorable Ethan Stafford was a younger son of an earl and ideal for their purposes. With a boyishly handsome face and guinea-gold curls, he was a well-bred, fashionable young rake who knew everyone in the ton. The ton, however, did not know Ethan Stafford's secret—that he had ruined himself gambling.

Cut off by his wealthy father, Stafford had avoided

debtor's prison and public knowledge of his bankruptcy only by carrying out dubious deeds for shadowy underworld figures like the cutthroat moneylender who had told Rollo about the lad.

Fortunately, young Mr. Stafford was not overly drunk when Rollo shuffled over and nudged into the crowd beside him. Stafford stood with half a dozen other young bucks, watching in absorption as the masked lady with the whip disciplined her next willing slave.

"Pardon me, sir!" Rollo got Stafford's attention, then lowered his voice. "I hear you might be interested in a bit of work."

The young man's sideward glance sharpened. Rollo nodded encouragingly. Warily, Stafford joined him. They walked away from the others.

"I'm told you are reliable. You made a few deliveries for a friend of mine."

"Right," Stafford said cautiously.

Poor little rich boy, Rollo thought. *Can't live without the niceties.*

"What do you need done?" Stafford demanded in a low tone, lifting his square chin haughtily.

"A good friend of mine will be visiting from Prussia in a week or so. He will need some introductions into Society. Someone to show him around Town."

"That's all?" Stafford asked dubiously.

Rollo boomed a cheerful laugh. "Yes, m' boy, that's all!"

"How much will you pay?"

"Three hundred pounds. No questions asked. Not a ha'penny more."

"Three hundred pounds?" Stafford echoed. "What's the catch?"

"There is no catch," he said cheerfully. "My friend is very rich and very determined to make a good impression on London Society. I'll be in contact with you when the time comes and remember . . . *shhh.*" Rollo laid his finger over his lips like the carving of Priapus on the outer door, binding the young man to secrecy.

Stafford nodded and returned to his friends. As Rollo turned away, he saw Lucien talking with a cluster of people a few feet ahead. He tried to sneak away, but Lucien saw him, passing an amused glance over him.

"You are looking industrious this evening," he drawled in his low, lilting voice. "Keeping your ear to the ground?"

"I only come for the women, old boy," he said with a harmless chuckle. "Your parties are the only place I can get laid for free."

Lucien laughed and moved on. "Happy hunting, Orpheus."

"Same to you." Rollo watched him saunter on, greeting more of his adoring guests.

He let out a long exhalation, feeling like a picnicker who had just been sniffed over by a wolf and miraculously left unscathed. His business done, Rollo downed his glass of wine and looked around for any female drunk enough to have him.

It was nearly dawn when Lucien's men cleared the Grotto of the last stragglers. The black-coated guards picked up the drunken fools who had passed out here and there and carried them back to their quarters, while Lucien met in his observation room with his staff of shrewd young rogues and savvy whores. They drank coffee and lounged about on the couch and chairs as they discussed the night's gleanings and bandied about the information that they had collected.

Lucien leaned by the red-glassed window, his arms folded over his chest, and listened to each one's report in turn, but it was difficult to concentrate when his thoughts kept wandering back to Alice Montague in mingled desire and irritation.

How dare she wipe away his kiss? Who did she think she was? And why, for God's sake, couldn't he get her out of his mind? It was absurd. He, Lucien Knight, was madly attracted to a doe-eyed little virgin. The girl was a prig. No wonder she drove Caro mad with her prudery. Her patronizing words still chafed him. *That's what love is, Lucien. That's what it does.* Love, he thought with a snort of disdain, and yet, an illogical part of him was wary, even a bit afraid of Alice Montague. Her clear gaze and transparent emotions unsettled his cynical nature. She was real in a way he had not been for years.

She was dangerous, that's what she was, he thought. A threat to his hard-won understanding of the world, in all its ruthlessness. Life had stripped him of his ideals and illusions—and yet, he would have paid any price to find someone who could make him believe again.

But was she really so virtuous? he scoffed inwardly. *Was anyone?* The girl had stung him, and he had half a mind to repay her for the insult by showing her that, deep down, she was not the paragon she seemed to fancy herself. He did not want to hurt her, but he was not above giving her a good scare to prove his point—that Miss Goody Two-Shoes was just as fallible as everyone else. Her air of purity snagged at his conscience, but it was so much easier to knock her down a peg than to try, futilely, to lift himself up to her lofty realm.

A disturbing thought flitted through his mind. *What if you test her and she doesn't fail? What if she proves you wrong?*

A burst of laughter in the room drew him from his brooding; then Marc handed him the list of the various agents who had come tonight. England's allied nations were well represented—Russia, Austria, Prussia, Portugal, and others. Lucien studied it absently, chasing Alice Montague out of his mind for the moment by a heave of effort.

In simplest terms, the so-called Order of the Dragon was a counterespionage tool that had evolved since the days of Queen Elizabeth and her sinister mastermind, Walsingham, who had been the very father of espionage in England and a personal friend of the original marquess of Carnarthen. The robes and all the mystical mumbo jumbo existed as part of the age-old correlation between espionage and the occult. The occult nonsense drew the rebels, adventurers, and malcontents of a society; these people, in turn, drew the spies. Smart agents knew to look for sympathetic allies among the outcasts and the dissatisfied, unsuspecting souls who could be used in their schemes—dupes who would lend them money or who could introduce them into the circles they wished to infiltrate.

Lucien's protégés, affectionately known as North, South, East, West, and, of course, Talbert, playacted this very role. They were in their mid-twenties, all of them fairly well-born. The young men were planted in the crowd not only to keep watch over their respective quadrants of the Grotto, but also to play the part of the type of restless, hotheaded rogues that a wise agent looked for when arranging some plot.

The lads were imminently useful to Lucien, and since there was no formal training for the Crown's agents, he had made it his postwar project to teach them what he knew, just as his father, the marquess, had taught him. They were young and still idealistic enough not to care when he warned them that it was an utterly thankless job. They were in it for the adventure and the thrill of living constantly on the edge. As their meeting wound down with little of value gained, the girls and boys began eyeing each other with recreation in mind now that their work was done.

"One more thing," Marc Skipton, who worked the west quadrant, said.

Lucien stifled a yawn. "Yes?"

"I overheard one of the czar's agents—what's his name?"

"Leonidovich?"

"Yes, him. I heard him telling one of the Austrians that Claude Bardou is alive and working for the Americans."

Lucien stared at him, feeling his blood run cold. His face went ashen, and it was altogether possible that his heart stopped beating for a moment. "Alive?" he forced out in an agonized effort to sound casual. "How can this be?"

"Leonidovich said he did not know if there was any substance to the rumor," Marc replied with an idle shrug, "but the word is that Bardou set the fire in Paris himself. Staged his own death, then escaped to America."

Oh, God. The news hit Lucien like a physical blow. At once, Patrick Kelley's weathered, Irish face rushed up before his mind's eye, haunting him like a ghost. He quickly dropped his gaze, rested his hands on his hips, and turned away to hide his stunned, horror-stricken reaction.

Damn it, he had heard that Bardou was dead—had not survived Napoleon's fall from power. When he had learned about that fire in Paris, Lucien had toasted the monster's demise with the finest port he owned. His only regret had been that he, himself, had not been the one to slay Bardou.

Behind him, Stewart Kyle of the eastern quadrant gave a low whistle. "Bardou is a legend. If he's turned mercenary and is hiring out his services to the Americans . . ." The lad shuddered.

"Remember the story about that merchant family he butchered in Westphalia for a suspected conspiracy against King Jerome?" Marc added grimly. "He's the bleedin' spawn of the devil."

"Enough," Talbert ordered them crisply. "There are ladies present."

Marc and Kyle quickly muttered apologizes to the uneasy girls, but Lucien paid them no mind. A knot had formed in the pit of his stomach, and a cold sweat had broken out over his body. He wiped his sweating palms on his thighs, pacing restlessly as he tried to think.

Claude Bardou, the French agent known as Triton, was the spymaster Fouché's top man, his secret weapon. Unbeknownst to the young people in the room, Lucien and he had a bit of a history between them.

A bloody one.

Lucien had never told Damien, nor Castlereagh, nor any living soul of his capture and torture at the hands of enemy operatives a year and a half ago, in the spring of 1813. He had killed all of Bardou's men during his escape; now the only two people alive who knew of his hellish ordeal were Bardou, who had inflicted the pain, and Lucien, who had endured it.

Though he had later found out that Bardou had been under orders from Fouché not to leave any visible scars on Lucien's body, the brute had succeeded all too well in engraving the pain upon the deepest layers of his mind. Lucien had thought he had put it behind him, especially after the news of Bardou's death, but it was there in an instant, just beneath the surface, a nightmare rising up for him to face again. In seconds it brought him back to the instinctual, almost feral state in which he had lived those last days before his escape, like an animal at bay. A surge of hatred-soaked memories poured through his veins like acid, like poison. *By God, Patrick,* he thought grimly, trying to keep hold of his control, *if that Frog bastard is indeed alive, I will avenge you yet.*

It was not implausible that the Frenchman could be working for the Americans, he thought, rubbing the back of his neck as he paced in jittery agitation. War had raged since 1812 on the shores of the former Colonies. Diplomats from both sides had been arguing for nearly two years in the Netherlands city of Ghent, but had achieved little. The fighting continued, as did the blockade. Meanwhile, Napoleon's downfall had left French spies like Bardou displaced, unable to return to France where the restored Bourbon monarchy regarded them as traitors, unwelcome throughout the victorious whole of allied Europe.

America was probably the only place where Napoleon's scattered spies could find asylum, or for true fanatics like Bardou, the place where they could go if they hungered to fight on against the British. President Madison's besieged administration in Washington—or what was left of America's new capital city, after British occupation forces had burned it nearly to the ground two months ago—would surely welcome men of Bardou's formidable skills.

Lucien turned back to his men, his face a hard, marble mask. When he began firing out orders, his voice was little more than a low snarl. "First we must verify it. Kyle, go to the guest wing and get me Rollo Greene. If something is afoot among the Americans, he'll know what it is. He'll talk, for a price."

"Rollo Greene is already gone—left hours ago. I looked at the exit list," Robert Jenkins of the south quadrant spoke up.

Lucien let out an oath. Wise agents were like skittish alley cats that had to be lured out of their hiding places. They could vanish into thin air if they did not wish to be found. This was especially true of double agents like Rollo Greene, who lived in constant fear of reprisal from someone they had sold out.

"Do you want us to ride out and try to catch up with him? I'd wager he's on the Bath Road, headed back to London," Marc offered.

Lucien brooded on it for a long moment. "Do it. Talbert, you'll stay behind and question Leonidovich with me. You four, ride up out of the valley, but if you don't find him by the time you reach the Wells Road, come back to Revell Court. It could be a trick."

"A trick?" Marc echoed in bafflement.

"You may think yourselves invincible, but if Bardou is somewhere on hand, you must not attempt to engage him. In any case, we'll move the next party up to one week from now. If you don't find Greene, I'm sure he'll be back. Till then, we'll press our other sources for information about Bardou's alleged resurrection. Now, go."

Dismissing the girls as well, he sent Talbert to fetch Leonidovich, then waited in the observation room, alone with his demons. *Bloody goddamned Claude Bardou.*

With a lost look, he expelled a heavy sigh and sat down to wait for Talbert to bring Leonidovich. Resting his elbow on the crude wooden table, he pressed his eyes with his fingertips. God, how he wanted to forget it had happened, but when he closed his eyes, he could still see the cell where he had been kept in darkness and solitude for so many weeks, starved and beaten. He could still taste the blood in his mouth from Bardou's most imaginative torture—strapping him down and extracting a couple of his molars to punish him for refusing to talk. But the physical pain had been nothing compared the shame of knowing that Bardou had succeeded at last in getting a name out of him: Patrick Kelley.

Lucien shuddered with agonized guilt that felt as though it had been carved in a deep harrow down the center of his soul. Though his father, the marquess, had inducted Lucien into the nuances of diplomacy, it was Kelley, the stout-hearted Irishman, who had taught him his field skills as a spy. Tortured to the point of mindless, semiconscious blathering, Lucien had finally gasped out Kelley's whereabouts. By the time he had managed to escape his prison hole, he had been too late to warn the Irishman that the French were coming after him. Kelley had already disappeared. He was never seen or heard from again.

"My lord?"

He flicked his eyes open with a fractured gaze, which he tried to hide as he glanced inquiringly over his shoulder. Lily, the most beautiful of his hired courtesans, was leaning against the wall in an inviting pose.

"Is there something you require?" he forced out coolly.

"You seem troubled. I thought you might do with some company." She held him in a siren's stare, running her fingertips along the frilled neckline of her gown. Pressing away from the wall, she moved toward him languidly.

His gaze traveled over her with a hunger that was fathoms deeper than her kind could ever satisfy. "Lily, you little temptress," he said in studied idleness, "you know I do not mix business and pleasure."

He tensed when she laid her hand on his shoulder and came around to the front of his chair. He scanned her face, in a dangerous mood.

She draped her arms around his neck. "Like you always say, my lord, rules were made to be broken."

"Not when they're *my* rules, pet."

"Whatever is wrong, I can make you feel better. All you need do is lie back and let me please you. Take me to your bed when you are through here." She kissed his cheek and whispered, "It would be for free."

He sat there in stony unresponsiveness as she began kissing his neck, caressing him. Wavering, he closed his eyes. A shudder of need ran through him, but it was Alice Montague who filled his mind. *That's what love is, Lucien. That's what it does.* Who the hell ever talked about love these days, or even believed in it? he thought, while the smell of the harlot filled his nostrils, her musky odor of sweat covered up with sickening sweet perfume. He understood all too well the willingness to cheapen oneself merely to be held in someone's arms through the night, but he refused to hunger for what did not exist. Love was for poets, and hope was for fools. When Lily grasped him through his breeches with an expert caress, his body responded instantly, but his mind despaired. *God, help me,* he thought, drowning in the sheer emptiness of this meaningless ritual. He could not do it anymore. Suddenly, this was no longer enough.

Clutching her forearms, he pushed her hands away and set her aside. He rose from the chair and walked away from her to the red-glassed windows, turning his back on her. "I brought my mistress from London."

Lily did not reply, though he could feel her angry dismay. A moment later, he heard her rise and leave the room—the rustle of her skirts, the pattering of her silk slippers—and then he was alone again. He gazed sorrowfully through the red-glass window at the graceful pillars and the trickling pool. The waters were said to have healing powers, but they had never done anything for him. He folded his arms over his chest, dropped his chin, and mentally scraped himself back into order, for the night's work was not yet done. But if he could have shared a bed with any woman tonight, it would have been Alice Montague, the only one with the imminent good sense to turn him down. *Who loves you, Lucien?* she had asked. What a dismal question. *Nobody, Alice.* His heavy sigh hung upon the silence. *No one even knows me.*

When Talbert returned, they questioned Leonidovich and learned nothing. As they were finishing their interrogation, Marc and the other lads returned empty-handed. Rollo Greene had evaded their search. Their duties done, they parted ways near dawn, the lads returning to their military-style bunker by the stable complex, while Lucien, exhausted, left the Grotto at last and went back up to the silent, sleeping house.

A short while later, he walked into his large, elegant bedchamber and crossed before the bank of eastern windows, lifting his shirt off over his head. Undressing in the pearl-gray half-light, he crawled onto his bed, too tired to bother with the covers. He was determined to get at least a couple hours' sleep before the day began, but the moment he closed his eyes, Claude Bardou's ugly face was there, or sometimes Patrick Kelley's laughing one. He drove both torturous images away by losing himself in thoughts of young, delicious Alice Montague. Her shy, skeptical smile, so reluctantly given and therefore so much more precious, charmed him even now. There was a wholeness, a simplicity in her that eased him. He began to relax at last as he savored the memory of touching her, the silken tenderness of her thighs under his hands, the delectable softness of her breasts. The wonder in her response as he had tasted her warm, virginal mouth. *So innocent,* he thought. It pleased him deeply to know that he had touched her where no one ever had, that he had been the first to kiss her.

As he lay in bed, a diabolical inspiration took shape in his mind, emerging more clearly by the second. His eyes widened as he stared up at the ceiling; then he sat up abruptly, his heart pounding at the notion.

No. It was wrong. A bad, outrageous scheme—but hardly his first. Could a starving man walk away from a feast?

He would never get another chance with Alice Montague. This much he knew, as surely as he knew that a woman like her could change everything for him. If he ever saw her in Town, she would cut him dead like any proper young miss. For God's sake, she knew him only as "Draco," the leader of a pagan cult. Even if he tried calling on her, respectable-fashion, Caro, her jealous chaperon, would never let him near the girl. Not after tonight. Worse, he realized, in London Alice would eventually cross paths with Damien and he would look even worse by comparison. He did not think he could bear it.

Rather dazed by the force with which his outrageous notion had struck him, he sank back down onto the mattress and folded his arms behind his head, searching the darkness for answers. Dared he try it?

She would be angry. She wouldn't like it, but it was her own fault, his wicked side reasoned. She was the one who had willfully trespassed where she didn't belong. She had barged into his house, into his life, and now she was not getting out of it until he was satisfied. He knew she was planning on leaving first thing in the morning, but there was no way he was letting her go. Maybe the mysterious thread of connection he felt toward her was nothing, but maybe it was the answer to everything.

Turning his face pensively on his pillow, he gazed through his bedroom window at the distant glimmer of dawn along the horizon. He fancied the flame-gold sunrise the very color of her hair.

CHAPTER FOUR

Alice slept like a woman drugged—long, deep, and dreamlessly. Even when she awoke a dozen hours later, she lay peacefully in the bed that smelled of lavender, letting awareness drift back to her by degrees, the gentle morning light filtering through her lashes. When she opened her eyes, her gaze fell upon an unfamiliar room. It startled her up onto her elbows. For a second, she forgot where she was—then it all came back to her. With a groan, she lay back down and buried her face in her pillow.

Lucien. He was the first thing on her mind, but she shoved the thought of the silver-eyed devil away with a vengeance. She did not wish to think of him, or last night, or the depravity of the Grotto *ever* again. Today she would flee home to Glenwood Park and forget such things existed, but Lord, she was not looking forward to this day, she thought. The prospect of spending the next fifteen hours in the close confines of the carriage with her malicious sister-in-law made her shudder.

Hearing a loud clattering outside her chamber window, she sat up, slid down from the high bed, and went to investigate. Peeking through the curtains, she saw a few of the guests' carriages storming away from Revell Court in a noisy cavalcade.

She whirled to face the room. *What time is it?* she thought frantically. If the debauchees of the Grotto were already up and about, it must already be midmorning! The mantel clock affirmed her realization. *Eleven o'clock!* she read with a groan. Now, she, Caro, and the servants would be forced to get a late start on the road. Once more, they would have to travel the last leg of their journey in the dark, but at least the way home was more familiar than the hills of Somerset.

She hurried over to the chest of drawers, where she poured water from the pitcher into the porcelain wash-bowl, thoughts of Lucien continuously plaguing her. Splashing the fresh, bracingly cold water on her skin, she resolved to forget him. He was tricky, dangerous, and bad. She could not begin to figure him out, but he was hardly the lackadaisical diplomat she had been led to expect. He was as fierce as a tiger, as quick as an adder, and as wily as a fox, and when he wanted to, she thought as a few droplets of water rolled sensuously down her throat into the valley between her breasts, he could be totally, irresistibly charming.

She shivered and kept moving, toweling her face and chest dry. She slipped into the fresh chemise and clean stockings she had stashed in her satchel. Rolling the thin, white stockings up and fastening them to her garters, she ignored the little thrilling flashes of memory of his hands skimming so expertly up her thighs. Such thoughts! She did her best to keep her mind fixed on poor little Harry, who was waiting for her to come home.

Rising briskly to don her dark blue carriage gown

once more, she prayed that she would never cross paths with Lucien in Society—especially not this Season, for by then, she would have turned twenty-two, which was practically at a woman's last prayer. That meant it was time to choose once and for all which of her longtime suitors she would accept for her husband.

Blast! she thought suddenly, pausing with a scowl. She had forgotten all about her suitors last night when Lucien had turned her own pointed question upon her, asking who loved her. Unfortunately, she knew why she had forgotten they existed in that moment—because they paled into invisibility next to him. She batted away this vexing realization like a badminton shuttlecock. "Draco" was beyond redemption. If any woman ever agreed to marry him, Alice felt sorry for her.

All three of her suitors were agreeable, sincere young gentlemen of good family and fine prospects; all had courted her chivalrously "by the book" for the past four Seasons since her debut. Roger was clever; Tom was brave; Freddie was amusing. Only, in her heart of hearts, Alice wanted a man who was clever, brave, and amusing all in one person, and so much more. Bless them, they had been so patient with her, waiting for so long for her to make up her mind, for all the good it had done them. But her tepid reaction to her suitors was not the only problem.

Larger still loomed the fact that she could not possibly leave Harry with Caro acting such a thoughtless and irresponsible mother. She could never simply abandon her nephew to the care of servants, no matter how good and capable Peg and the others were. A person needed family around them to grow properly—her own experience had shown her that. If Caro did not start acting like a mother to her son, Alice was never going to be able to leave Glenwood Park and marry. She would end up on the shelf, never having a child of her own to love. With a frustrated sigh, she plunked down on the stool before the mirror, pinning her hair up in a sleek topknot with a few curls dusting her neck.

Just then, a knock sounded on the door. She glanced toward the door in the reflection. "Come in!"

At her call, the door opened and a plump, cheerful maid carried in her breakfast tray. Removing the silver lid, Alice discovered an assortment of mouth-watering pastries and toast with various jams and honey, fruit, and a slab of the local Cheddar Gorge cheese, but her eyes widened with intrigued delight to see the pink rose laid carefully alongside her silverware. Resting under its thorny stem was a small piece of fine linen paper folded in thirds and sealed with a drop of red wax.

She reached for it at once while the maid poured her tea. She cracked the seal and unfolded it with a slight tremble in her hands; then she read, hearing his deep, smoothly modulated voice in her mind, so casually seductive:

Good morning, Alice. Come to me in the library at your earliest convenience.

Your servant, etc.
L.X.K.

An order! Well, she should have known. His high-handedness made her indignant, but the thought of seeing him again made her slightly light-headed. She read the note five times over, her heart pumping with fear and thrill. *What did he want with her now?* she wondered, trying to summon a proper annoyance. *Should she even heed the summons?*

There was no possibility of eating much after that. The maid carefully presented her with her teacup, but Alice's hands shook so that a few drops sloshed onto the saucer and nearly onto her gown. All she could force past her lips was a single slice of toast and jam. Admittedly, she was highly curious to see him one last time. She had hoped to slip away from Revell Court without having to clash with him again, but she should have known the man was too perverse to make it so easy on her. Perhaps he wished to apologize for his shocking advances he had made on her last night—or perhaps, she mused with a slight, wry smile, he merely wanted to try again. She decided that it could not hurt to indulge him briefly, since she was on her way out, in any case. After all, it was beneath her pride to hide from him like a coward.

As soon as she had finished eating and had quickly scrubbed her teeth, she stole a nervous glance in the mirror, frowned at the high blush of anticipation in her cheeks, and smoothed her hair, then asked the maid to conduct her to the library.

A few minutes later, she traipsed through the maze of hallways on the upper floor until they reached the main staircase, where the first marquess of Carnarthen spied down from his portrait upon the bickering knot of guests who bustled about in the entrance hall, taking their leave. Mr. Godfrey and a half dozen footmen dodged hither and thither, trying to pacify the guests' last-minute demands, while two of the brawny armed guards in black coats stood like brooding pillars in opposing corners, watching over all.

Draco's faithful appeared to have recovered a modicum of shame, shading their faces from one another under the brims of top hats and bonnets. Some of the ladies had even draped veils over their bonnets to more thoroughly conceal their faces, but the portrait of the marquess smirked down at them from the landing; his sly smile seemed to say that, hide as they may, he knew all of their nasty little secrets.

The guests' frayed, fretful bickering faded as Alice followed the maid down a quiet corridor. By the light of day, the Elizabethan splendors of Revell Court dazzled her. She peeked into the various rooms they passed—soaring, oak-timbered spaces with creamy plaster walls, imposing Renaissance chimneys, and colorful, age-faded carpets covering the taupe-colored granite flagstones of the floors. Sunlight streamed in through the diamond-shaped panes of the mullioned windows, danced over the square, heavy furniture with its mellow patina of age, and warmed the rich, old tapestries depicting stag hunts and scenes of falconry.

The austere, manly atmosphere of the place was a world away from the relaxed, airy lightness of Glenwood Park, with its pastel rooms and cozy scroll couches, but the sturdiness of Lucien's house was comforting. She liked the way it smelled—of leather, of beeswax polish for all that gleaming dark wood, and of a faint, piquant trace of a gentleman's tobacco pipe. The maid stopped before a closed door at the end of the main corridor.

"The library, miss," she murmured with a quick curtsey.

"Thank you." With a nod, Alice reached for the doorknob, but having learned her lesson last night about walking in on places where she had not been invited, she gathered her courage and knocked.

Her heart skipped a beat as Lucien's strong voice answered, "Come in!"

She squared her shoulders and opened the door. She saw him at once on the far end of the room. Leaning idly against a bookcase by the window, he was reading a slim, leather-bound volume, the morning sunlight gleaming on his jet-black hair, which was slicked back, she noted, still damp from his morning ablutions. Staring at him, she took two cautious steps into the room, dazzled by the transformation in his appearance. This morning he was dressed with the casual elegance of a country lord at his leisure. His morning coat was a rich shade of burgundy, worn over a single-breasted silk waistcoat with a high standing collar and fawn twill trousers. With his head bent over the open book, he did not look up at her arrival. She was momentarily distracted by the way he held the book in his hands, his fingertips subtly caressing the kid-leather binding. He had princely hands; they were large and manly, full of strength, yet ineffably elegant. She routed a shivery-sweet memory of those smooth, warm hands gliding up under her skirts.

"You wished to see me, my lord?" she asked in a studiedly formal tone, one hand still on the door latch.

" 'Come live with me and be my love,
And we will some new pleasures prove,
Of golden sands and crystal brooks,
With silken lines and silver hooks.' "

Alice blinked with surprise. "I beg your pardon?"

He slid her a disarming, rather wily smile and continued in a low, magical singsong:

" 'There will the river whispering run,
Warmed by thine eyes more than the sun.
And there the enamored fish will stay,
Begging themselves they may betray.

When thou wilt swim in that live bath,
Each fish, which every channel hath,
Will amorously to thee swim,
Gladder to catch thee, than thou him.' "

A blush crept into her cheeks as pink as the rose he had sent her, but she gave him an arch look. Did the cad really expect her to fall for this?

"Shut the door, Alice."

She obeyed with an arch smirk, then clasped her hands behind her back and began strolling cautiously toward him while he resumed reading:

" 'If thou, to be so seen, beest loath,
By sun or moon, thou darkenest both;
And if myself have leave to see,
I need not their light, having thee.' "

"Andrew Marvell?"

"No."

"Christopher Marlowe?"

"Ignorant girl, it is John Donne, 'The Bait.' May I?" he asked with feigned annoyance.

"By all means," she replied with equally feigned gravity. He was a scoundrel and a cad, but he really was rather amusing, in his way.

" 'Let others freeze with angling reeds,
And cut their legs with shells and weeds,
Or treacherously poor fish beset
With strangling snare or windowy net.' "

"Windowy net," he echoed, shaking his head. "That is superb."

"It is good," she admitted. Sidling up next to him, Alice looked down at the text and read the next verse aloud:

" 'Let coarse bold hand from slimy nest
The bedded fish in banks out-wrest,
Or curious traitors, sleave-silk flies,
Bewitch poor fishes' wandering eyes.' "

" 'For thee,

He interrupted her with a chiding glance askance.

" 'thou needest no such deceit,
For thou thyself art thine own bait;
That fish that is not catched thereby,
Alas, is wiser far than I.' "

With a smile, she looked from the page to him and found him gazing at her, his gray eyes sparkling like the surface of a lake stirred by a breeze. She held his stare, heedless that she was standing much too close to him—

so close that she could feel the vital warmth of his body and the full force of his overwhelming magnetism. So close that for a moment, she thought that he would lower his head and kiss her again. She had not realized she was holding her breath until he snapped the book of poetry shut, startling her with the noise.

He captured her hand, lifting it to place a debonair kiss on her knuckles.

"Alice," he said, with an easy, welcoming air. "I trust you rested peacefully." Tucking her hand into the crook of his arm, he led her away from the window and toward the couch.

"Well enough, thank you." She chastened herself mentally over her racing heartbeat and her vague disappointment that he had not made another improper advance on her. "And you, my lord?"

"Lucien," he corrected her with an intimate little smile. "I trust we are past the formalities. Sit?"

"Thank you." It did not seem worth the bother to point out that it was not at all proper for him to address her by her Christian name. She wasn't staying long enough for it to matter, and God willing, she would never see him again.

The thought made her oddly desolate.

She lowered herself to perch nervously on the edge of the couch while he brushed out the tails of his morning coat and took his seat across from her. He leaned his head back wearily against the high leather back of his chair and studied her. She looked away, reminded anew that she was alone with a dangerous man—no chaperon, no maid, not even Caro to keep an eye out for her. In Town, girls had been ruined for less, but clearly, she was in Lucien's world now, where the normal rules no longer applied.

"You wished to see me?" she attempted.

"Yes." He rested his chin on his fist and smiled at her.

She waited primly for him to state the purpose of the meeting, but he just stared at her.

"Well?"

No answer. He merely smiled back at her, two fingers obscuring his beguiling mouth as he rested his elbow on the chair arm. His gaze unnerved her. She quickly looked away, her heart skipping a beat. What a rude beast he was.

"Ahem, very well." Wringing her hands in her lap, Alice tried to look interested in the elegantly appointed room. The library was long and narrow, with shelf-lined walls and windows that stretched nearly from floor to ceiling at regular intervals, deep window seats tucked behind the dark ruby curtains. The bronze busts atop the bookcases seemed to watch her and Lucien together like the spying gossips of the ton. She shrugged some of the tension out of her shoulders as her gaze wandered over the various oil paintings on the walls, over the tapestry and the linen-fold paneling; all the while, Lucien studied her. She regarded the chess table, where the ebony and ivory pieces had been abandoned midgame, then inspected the Paisley whorls of the carpet until she could no longer stand it. "My lord, you are staring."

"Forgive me." Languidly stretching his long legs out in front of him, he crossed his booted heels. "Somehow you are even more lusciously tempting than I remembered."

She stiffened, her chin rising to a prim angle as a hot blush rushed into her cheeks. "What is it you wished to see me about, please? If you will forgive me, I am in a bit of a hurry."

"I find myself curious about you, Alice. I am eager to further our acquaintance."

Her heart quaked. She stared at him, then lowered her head. "Respectfully, sir, it is not possible."

"Cruel lady!" he exclaimed mildly, sounding not the least bit surprised. "Why ever not?"

She gave him a quelling look. "Do you really have to ask?"

"Are you going to deny that we are extremely attracted to each other?"

His brazen question, so casually delivered, left her nigh speechless. "Do you really imagine you can succeed with me after you seduced my sister-in-law?"

"Do you really think you can resist?" he countered, his gray eyes flashing wickedly.

Her nostrils flaring with her sharp inhalation, she jumped to her feet intent on making a grand exit, but his hand shot out and captured her wrist. She turned to him in rebuke. "Let go of me! Just when I think you might be an agreeable man, you shock me again like a very lightning bolt! You, sir, are beyond the pale! The things you say—the way you choose to live your life—you are scandalous, outrageous and . . . bad!"

"I know, I know. Can't you see I need help, *mon ange*? Clearly, it may take the strictest Goody Two-Shoes in the realm to reclaim me."

"Reclaim yourself! If you brought me down here just to toy with me, allow me to inform you that I want nothing to do with you. Indeed—" She gave her hand a jerk, but the harder she tugged, the more tenaciously he clung on. "—if ever I have the misfortune to cross paths with you in public, I shall cut you entirely!"

"You threaten me with the severest of penalties," he said gravely, his eyes sparkling like diamonds. "Clearly, I must reform, but how? Wait—I have an idea."

"Why does that not surprise me?" she retorted.

He sat forward with an upward gaze of angelic sincerity. "Maybe your goodness could rub off on me. Maybe your influence could help me change. What was that you said last night? About love?"

"I should have known you would not be above throwing my own words in my face."

"They were true, weren't they? Don't you want to save me, Alice? Women are always trying to save me—of course, none of them have had much success so far. I was hoping you'd care to give it a go."

She looked flatly at him. "That is some very fine and, might I add, original flattery, Lord Lucifer, but I am not a fool. You have no wish to change, and as for love, the swans on the lake and the wolves in the forest know more of it than you ever will, for all your cleverness. Now, if you will excuse me—"

"I would change for you, if you could make me believe, if you could show me the reason why to be good at all." He pressed her hand to his clean-shaved cheek. "Teach me, Alice. I have an open mind. Do you?"

She held his stare, wavering dangerously. "You are cruel to toy with me so," she forced out.

"I am in earnest." The intensity in his gaze was beginning to frighten her. She tried to pull her hand away, but his grip turned implacable. He turned his face just enough to press a kiss into her palm, closing his long-lashed eyes for a moment. "Do not think I come to you empty-handed. I so want to help you, Alice." He opened his eyes and gazed tenderly at her. "You're too young to realize it yet, but I know what is going to happen to you."

"You do?" she whispered, staring uneasily into his deep, crystalline eyes.

"I've seen it a thousand times. They're going to make you just like everybody else, but I can protect you, your bright, beautiful soul. You're in a cage and you don't even know it, but I can free you. Let me take you under my wing. I can teach you how to outwit them if you'll let me. I won't let them turn you into another pretty, empty shell in ribbons and French silk. You are too good for that fate."

His softly uttered words staggered her. It was as though he had looked into her soul and read her very heart. She stared at him, mesmerized. "What do you want of me?"

"The same thing you want, sweet," he said as he stroked her hand in gentle reassurance. "Both of us, we just want someone to accept us for who we really are."

"Who *are* you, Lucien?" she asked in a trembling whisper.

"Stay with me and find out."

"Well, I daresay!" a rude voice broke in on them from the doorway. "Are we announcing the banns? Have we picked out the flowers? The church?"

"Caro!" Alice yanked her hand out of Lucien's light grasp, feeling her cheeks fill with a scarlet blush. She glanced at him in chaos, her heart pounding.

He was watching her calmly.

"Oh, dear, I was summoned—but I do hope I'm not interrupting," Caro said spitefully. Not a hair out of place, the baroness was perfectly coiffed and elegantly attired as she sauntered into the library. Her eyes, however, were bloodshot, and the excessive rouge on her cheeks could not conceal the pallor of her skin. "I would come back after you've finished your little tête-à-tête, but my son is waiting. Alice, are you ready to leave?"

"Coming—"

"Not so fast, my dear." Lucien stood, the emotion in his face smoothly vanishing behind a mask of arrogance and worldly aplomb. His silver eyes became like mirrors, completely concealing his thoughts. "Lady Glenwood, come and sit down. I called you both here on a serious matter."

He had indeed summoned Caro to the library as well? Alice wondered, turning to watch him as he stalked past her to the baroness.

"Oh, yes, it looked terribly serious to me," she muttered.

"You will keep a civil tongue in your head, madam." He grasped the baroness's elbow and propelled her over to a chair across from the couch.

As she sat down, Caro sent Alice a haughty warning glance. She rested her elbow on the chair arm and braced her forehead with her fingertips, the very sketch of a person suffering the aftereffects of intemperance. *Serves you right,* Alice thought, sending her an answering look that flashed with rebellion.

"Miss Montague, please be seated." Between them, Lucien stood tall, his shoulders squared, his chin high. "I am aware of the urgency of your departure. Thus, I will be brief." Diabolical amusement danced on his lips. He turned away and sauntered idly to the nearby chess table. "I find myself in the mood for company of late," he said. "I have considered the matter at some length and have arrived at a decision."

Tilting his head, he studied the board, then moved the

black knight, trouncing the white queen. He removed the ivory piece from the board, looked at Caro, then at Alice, and said smoothly, "I am only letting one of you leave."

Both women stared at him without comprehension.

"Pardon?" Caro drawled as though suddenly finding her voice.

Alice sat stock-still, staring at him with a terrible premonition. "What do you mean, you are only letting one of us leave?"

He looked at her with bland cordiality, not batting an eye. "One may go; the other shall stay for a while as my companion, provide me with a pleasant diversion—it grows so dull here in the country, don't you know, but I leave it to you to decide, Alice. Who will go home to Harry and who will remain here at Revell Court . . . with me?"

The look on her face was priceless, but Lucien managed not to crack a smile. He kept his expression calm, his eyes unreadable, but God, he wanted her. He did not care that what he was doing was outrageous. He had made up his mind and was not backing down. He needed this too much.

Her lovely face had paled; she appeared to be in shock. Lucien suppressed a dark smile. The moment had come to find out if his good girl was really so noble and true. He knew exactly how to trap her—through her deathbed promise to her brother, which she had foolishly revealed to him last night, and her devotion to her nephew.

He was testing her, of course, making her walk the very knife-edge of decision. It was the one sure way to discover what kind of woman she really was at her very core, under duress. If she chose selfishly, freeing herself at the expense of little Harry's need for his mama, if she proved a fraud, then her mysterious hold over him would be instantly broken with no great loss. His mind and heart would be released at once from her spell, and he would let both women leave without further argument.

Ah, but if she chose unselfishly, in spite of all the dire possible consequences, at the cost of her reputation and the perilous risk of her virtue, then he would have her here by his side to revere her and to learn the secret of her innocence. Either way, he won. It was, in fact, the perfect plan, and he was deuced pleased with himself for thinking of it.

Both women were still staring at him, dumbfounded.

"Oh, you are a devil," Caro whispered at last in awe. "No. You are *the* devil."

He glanced indifferently at her, then returned his hungry stare to the girl. "So, who shall it be, Alice, Caro or you?"

Her eyes were huge and deep, dark blue as she gazed up at him, at a loss. Her severe chignon accented her aristocratic bone structure—her smooth forehead and high cheekbones, that feisty chin, and her long, graceful neck. Lucien gave her a look to suggest that, if she stayed, his intentions toward her were purely sexual. *That ought to scare the truth out of her,* he thought, fear and need and terrifying hope making him ruthless.

"Surely, my lord, you are jesting," Alice forced out.

"He is in earnest," Caro breathed, shaking her head. "I know that gleam in his eyes. He has some perverse devil flying around in his head and won't be satisfied until he has gotten what he's after."

"Well?" he asked.

"This is absurd!" Alice shot to her feet in haughty indignation, but her eyes were indigo with fright; her ivory skin had paled. "Come, Caro. We are getting out of here."

"Sit down, Miss Montague," Lucien clipped out sternly. "You will not run away from this choice. You should be grateful I am willing to let one of you leave, for I am tempted to keep you both—but then, who would comfort poor little Harry?"

"Lucien, stop this." Caro rose abruptly and scanned his face, trying to read him. "My child is sick. I must go to him."

"Now you care?" He shook his head at her in contempt. "Speak to Alice. It is in her power to release you."

"So, it is *her* you're after. Lucien, she is a virgin."

"And so she will remain, if she chooses."

The lady in question let out a little gasp of alarm. "This conversation is most unseemly! My lord, you know full well you cannot keep either of us here against our will. It is practically kidnapping! We could have you arrested!"

"Oh, I wouldn't be too alarmed, my dear." Caro folded her arms over her chest and looked askance at her. "Lord Lucien is merely testing you. You're not the first, and you won't be the last. I daresay he wants to see if he can debauch you. This is what the fiend enjoys—poking, prodding people, trying to find out their weaknesses. He won't go out of his way to harm you, but if you stumble, you are lost."

"Now, now, my lady, aren't you being a bit harsh?" he chided.

"I know why you are doing this," Alice said in a shaky tone, taking a defiant step toward him. "To punish me for trespassing in the Grotto—but I'm not going to tell anyone about your filthy cult! Whom would I tell? I'd be ashamed even to mention it!"

"Why, I would never punish you for anything, Alice," he replied in a reasonable tone. "Who am I to punish you? Your parent? Your husband?"

She blanched at the word. "You can't make me stay here! Harry needs—"

"His mother." He cut her off.

"He needs me, too!" She struggled visibly for calm. "My lord, if you are so fixed on a friendship, then, very well, you may call on me in London in the spring. . . ." Her voice trailed off at his dark, low laughter.

"That is hardly what I had in mind, *ma chérie.*"

"But I will be ruined!" she wailed.

"Now, now, my dear, there is no need to be melodramatic. Nobody is going to ruin you. I can boast a certain expertise in keeping secrets," he said modestly. "No one will ever know you're here. I give you my word."

"Your word—Draco? Don't make me laugh!" She pointed toward the door. "Those people in the hallway saw me. What if they go back to London and tell the whole world I'm here?"

"For one thing, they are not going back to London. They're going their separate ways, back to their country houses—you know the ton is largely dispersed for the autumn. Secondly, even if they did recognize you, they don't want their names mentioned any more than you do. We believe in secrecy here at Revell Court. You have nothing to fear."

"Don't do this, Lucien. I beg of you. You know it is impossible!"

"Why? Do you think I give a damn for Society's strictures?" he asked sharply, suddenly losing patience as her obvious rejection cut through his facade. "Life is too bloody short to play by their rules. I take what I want, and I want you here. Now choose, damn it."

She stood staring at him in shock. A helpless, bewildered look passed over her classical features.

He held her stare fiercely, willing her to remember how she had melted in his arms, how she had opened to his kiss. How she had tapped into her own fiery passion when she had begun kissing him back in sweet, aching need.

She turned away, pale and shaken, and marched toward the door. "I am going home to Harry, and you can't stop me. Lady Glenwood, do please come along."

"My men have their orders," Lucien called after her, his body tensed with excitement. "They won't let you pass without my permission."

Caro remained where she stood, studying him. Lucien merely flicked her a glance then followed his quarry out into the hallway. In truth, he could scarcely believe she had not yet said no. She had not refused outright nor immediately passed the task on to Caro, as he had half expected. Instead, Alice was fighting to avoid making any decision at all, as though, deep down, she knew that her own nature would compel her to do the honorable thing. In guarded fascination, he watched her slim figure as she strode down the flagged, shadowy corridor ahead of him toward the entrance hall. He restrained his pace to a casual saunter, trailing after her.

Alice, meanwhile, promptly found herself blocked at the front door by two of his black-coated guardsmen. "Let me out of here!" she yelled at them, but the men didn't blink.

"Convinced?" Lucien inquired, joining her by the bottom of the staircase.

She spun around and glared at him, her fists balled at her sides. "If my brother were alive, he would call you out for this."

"Life is for the living, *chérie*."

She looked into his eyes. "Why are you doing this to me?"

He tensed, feeling naked in her stare. It was unnerving how she seemed to pierce into the very core of him and take his measure. He deflected her searching gaze with his most arrogant smile. "Because it amuses me. Quit dodging the question, Alice. Caro or you?" He took out his fob watch and glanced at it; it was time to raise the stakes. "If I don't have an answer in ten seconds, I shall keep you both and poor little Harry will have to suffer alone."

"Go to the devil! I don't have to listen to you!" She stalked down the other corridor, but once again, her way was blocked by his menacing guards. She turned around in wrath. "Call them off, Lucien."

"No."

"You can't do this!"

"If you wanted the good twin, you should've gone to Damien's house. Ten. Nine. Eight."

"Caro!" Alice turned to her sister-in-law, who now joined them in the hallway. "The man is mad! He will not listen to reason! You must stay with him!"

Ah, here it comes, Lucien thought with a pang of disappointment behind his smirk.

"But you know Harry needs me, Alice. Isn't that the reason you came here? I am his mother, and I should be with him."

"*Now* you finally choose to care about him?" she cried.

"How dare you? I love my son! You're the problem, Alice. You're always coming between us!"

"Seven. Six," he counted on, standing a small distance away.

Alice stared at the baroness in open-mouthed fury. "That's rubbish! You run off and forget he exists. If it weren't for me, that child would have no one but the servants."

"Five, four . . ." *If only someone had dared have this conversation with* his *mother when he was Harry's age,* Lucien mused sardonically. He and his brothers might have turned out so differently.

"It is disgraceful how you treat that child," Alice went on. "Do you know how confused he is for days after you leave? If he starts crying, that's when you run—but don't you see, you're the thing he's crying for?" Her face tautened, as though she realized the significance of her words only as she uttered them.

Mesmerized by the play of warring emotions in her delicate face, Lucien slowed his counting. "Three . . ."

Caro stared at Alice, as well, then lowered her head and turned away. "Let me have my child to myself for once, and this time will be different, I promise you."

"You promise me," Alice echoed bitterly.

"Yes."

"Two . . ."

There was a long pause as Alice held her sister-in-law in a penetrating stare.

"One." As Lucien snapped his fob watch closed, the small *snick* rang like a cannon's boom in the palpable silence that had fallen over the corridor.

Lucien held his breath.

"Very well, then," Alice said barely audibly. "I will be the one to stay." With a tempestuous stare, she turned to him so suddenly that he hardly managed to hide his incredulity. "But if you lay a hand on me against my will, I will not hesitate to have you arrested and I *shall* press charges against you. If it is scandal that you crave, my lord, you shall have it."

He shook himself out of his stunned astonishment as a dark, rich smile spread slowly across his face. His world had just been turned upside down, but his heart soared wildly like a Congreve rocket. Truly, he had found himself a worthy opponent. "I consider myself duly warned."

"He does not fear the law," Caro remarked, passing a scathing glance over him. "No, if he harms you, we won't waste our breath telling the constable, my dear. We'll tell Damien."

The mention of his honor-bound brother brought him up short. Lucien shot Caro a bristling scowl. An image of Damien's hard, honest face flashed in his mind. He could almost hear his brother's voice in his head. *Don't you dare keep that girl. You've proved your point; now let her go.* Lucien knew that the imaginary order from his brother was the only decent thing to do. He might masquerade as "Draco," but he knew right from wrong as well as Damien did. Yet the thought of losing Alice suddenly panicked him. How could he possibly let her go now that he knew she was the genuine article? The words to release her would not form on his tongue. He floundered, torn, his heart hammering in his chest.

Alice Montague was that rarest of flowers, a beautiful woman of integrity. Someone he might even be able to trust, in time. He had searched the world for such a creature. He had her in his grasp. How could he possibly let her slip through his fingers?

He could not. He could not help himself. By God, he was not letting her go. Exultation surged through his veins, but he had no idea what the hell he thought he was doing. *This is foolishness,* his better sense rebuked him. He had a job to do. Was not Claude Bardou alive and at large? She would only be a distraction.

But it was the news of Bardou's resurrection and the horror of his own excruciating memories that had weakened Lucien, made him reach for the girl. He could no longer face it alone. From the moment he had looked into her heaven-blue eyes, he had been possessed by a burning neediness for something pure and good and clean. The only desperation that even came close to it had been the thirst he had suffered when Bardou's men had denied him water for two days in that black hellhole.

He was no prisoner now. He was free to act, to save himself by whatever means availed—even if it meant damning himself, throwing what remained of his honor into the flames. Winning her, body and soul, would be worth it.

To assuage his conscience, he decided that if he could not do it in a week, he would let her go then. He was, of course, a shrewd enough negotiator to ask for much more than he really expected to get. "I will send her home in my carriage after a fortnight, quite unharmed."

"Two weeks!" Alice gasped in horror. "Absolutely not! One day at the most!"

Lucien turned to her. "Ten days."

"Two!"

"Oh, come. It will be fun, *chérie*. Stay for eight days."

"Three, not an hour more!" she cried in fright.

"One week, then—and I won't try very hard to seduce you," he offered with a wicked half smile.

"A week?" Alice echoed, gazing at him in despair.

"You'd best take it, dear. When he puts his mind to it . . ." Caro sighed meaningfully.

Apparently incensed by her glib tone, Alice turned on her. "You find this all very amusing, don't you?"

She shrugged. "I didn't ask you to come here. You shouldn't have done it."

Alice stared at her, clearly incredulous. "I came to help you!" she exclaimed in shock.

"Well, you only managed to embarrass us both."

"How can you let him do this to me? You should be the one to stay!"

"Perhaps." Caro glanced at the ceiling, as though choosing her words with care. "But frankly, Alice, as your elder and your chaperon, I find you lack a proper respect for me. It is extremely irritating, and I cannot think of a better person to teach you your place than Lucien Knight. I'm sick to death of you walking around putting on airs like some kind of plaster saint. You think you're so much better than me, but we'll see how high and mighty you are by the time he is through with you."

"You—I—you're worse than he is!"

"Am I? Well," Caro said blandly, "let's not forget who puts a roof over your head and food on your plate, sweet." She glanced at Lucien. "As for you, darling, tinkering with people's lives is one matter, but let us get one thing perfectly clear."

"What is that, *ma chérie*?" he asked, turning to her with an expansive smile.

"If you send her back pregnant, you *will* marry her."

His smile faded. His heartbeat roared in his ears. He stared intensely at Caro for a heartbeat, holding on hard to his facade of jaded nonchalance. "Fair enough," he replied.

His lack of hesitation shocked him and apparently horrified Alice.

She gasped so hard he worried she'd faint. When he glanced cautiously at her, she spun around, picked up her skirts, and fled him, pounding up the stairs past the smirking portrait of the marquess, whose gray eyes, so like his own, seemed to dance with devilish congratulation, as if to say, *Well done, my boy.*

Lucien couldn't have agreed with him more. Caro gave him a disparaging look and walked away, calling her carriage, but Lucien slid his hands into his trouser pockets and peered uncertainly up the staircase in the direction Alice had gone, discreetly jubilant at his triumph and rather amazed, in all, that he had gotten away with it.

CHAPTER FIVE

Running all the way back to her room, Alice slammed the door, locked it, then further barricaded it with a wooden chair. Her heart thumping, she ran her hands through her hair and paced in agitation. *This can't be happening! What am I going to do?*

"Damnation!" she cried, hot tears of fury rushing into her eyes. She stalked to her pillow and punched it in most unladylike wrath, half wishing it was Lucien Knight's smug, handsome face. *Cruel, ruthless, wicked man!* Pacing a few times back and forth across the room, she finally stopped and rested her forehead against one of the bedposts, struggling for equilibrium. *How could he do something so scandalous?* But what else should she have expected from "Draco"? A thousand questions whirled through her mind. *If you send her home pregnant, you will marry her. . . . Marry her . . .* The dire words re-echoed in her mind like her death knell. *Fair enough,* he had dared to say. *Fair enough! To whom?* she thought furiously. She wanted to have a child someday, yes, but not with the prince of the underworld!

Hearing a carriage rattling over the cobbles below a few minutes later, she lifted her head and ran to the window, bracing her hands on the sill. With a stricken expression, she watched her carriage rolling away through the iron gates of Revell Court. Her driver, Mitchell, looked over his shoulder with a worried frown as he drove off. Alice tried waving to flag his attention, but he returned his gaze to the road before him. She could only wonder what fairy story that the traitor, Caro, would tell the servants to account for her absence.

She stared out the window in distress until the carriage had crossed the wooden bridge over the river and started up the hill, disappearing from view among the trees. When it had gone, she still stood there, slowly becoming aware of the profound silence of Revell Court, alone in its hidden valley. The guests had gone. The halls were quiet. The efficient army of servants moved soundlessly throughout the Tudor manor. Now it was only Lord Lucifer and her. A tremor ran through her. She looked around uneasily, rubbing her folded arms. How she missed Harry's babbling. Even her nephew's worst temper tantrum was preferable to this eerie stillness. She went over to the bed and sat down, leaning against the headboard. Drawing her knees up, she wrapped her arms around her bent legs, resolved to stay in her room until that silver-eyed devil lost interest. With any luck, she could find some way to escape.

A sudden noise in the corridor made her gaze zoom to the door of her bedchamber. Her heart skipped a beat. Heavy footfalls pierced the deafening silence in a swift, relentless rhythm, approaching from down the hallway. *So soon he comes.* She knew she could not lock him out forever. She eased silently off of the bed, casting about for a weapon with which to defend her virtue, if need be. She tiptoed over to the hearth and picked up the fire poker, brandishing it, then crept over to the furniture-barred door as the footsteps drew nearer. She held her breath as he rapped softly on the door.

"Oh, Alice, my pet, come out and play," he called urbanely.

She clutched the fire poker harder in her sweating hands. "Go away! I don't want to see you!"

"Tut, tut, my dear, I know you are cross, but—"

"Cross?" she cried, taking an angry step toward the door, emboldened by the fact that he could not get to her, or if he did somehow, she would brain the cad. "Cross does not begin to describe my sentiments, Lucien Knight! What am I to think of you? One minute you are pointing a gun at me, the next you are reading me poetry!"

"But I thought you liked the poetry."

"You know full well that is not the point. You usurp control of my life and expect me to swoon at your feet?"

"Why, swooning would be perfectly acceptable—"

"How dare you make a joke of this?" she roared, her face turning red with fury.

A pause.

She heard his vexed sigh. "Are you going to hide in there like a coward for the next week?" he inquired in a tone gone suddenly flat with boredom.

"I don't care what you say, you odious cad. I am not staying here for a week."

"I see. Well, if you are going to insult me, darling, in addition to breaking your oath, at least come out here and say it to my face."

"Ha!" she retorted. "Do you think I'm fool enough to fall for that trick? I know exactly what you want of me. If I open this door, you'll ravish me!"

"Now, look here," he said crossly. "I have never touched a woman against her will in all my life—or is that what you're afraid of? That it won't be against your will? That you'll want me?" he suggested in a silken tone through the door.

"You are shocking, sir! You must know I *despise* you."

He laughed idly and let out a sigh. "Ah, well. Be that as it may, have pity on me, Alice. Come out. I'm not going to bite you. Better yet, let me in."

"In here?" She gasped. The two of them, together, in a bedroom? How could he even suggest such a thing? What did he take her for? She did not allow her suitors even to touch her bare hands. She decided on the spot that she would not have permitted Lucien Knight to court her if he begged on his hands and knees.

"Come out to me, sweeting. I promise I'll be good," he cajoled her through the sturdy oaken door. She glared at it. "Walk with me on the grounds. There won't be many days as warm and fine as this before the cold sets in. Have you looked outside? The leaves are ablaze, the grass is emerald, and the sky is as blue as your eyes. Does it not beckon to you?"

Not like your voice does, she thought with a small quiver, for his satin murmur was pure temptation.

"We are free here, Alice. Totally free."

Free? she wondered. *What is that?* She fought the dangerous magic of his charm and glanced behind her at the window, then had a sudden inspiration. "Perhaps if you have a horse for me we could ride?"

"Very crafty, my dear," he chided with a soft, rich laugh. "If I put you up on a horse, you'll be racing back to Hampshire like a jockey in the Royal Ascot."

The corners of her mouth strained to frown, but she could not help but smile at the image. She shook her head in dismay at her own traitorous desire, for a part of her actually wanted to be with him. She clung to her resistance. "You know," she said in defiance, "there is something I have been meaning to tell you regarding our conversation of last night."

"Oh?"

"Yes. We were discussing the people who care for us. Do you recall?"

"Ah, yes—or the lack thereof."

She rested the poker, tip down, on the wooden chair, her eyes gleaming. "For your information, I have a number of beaux who are entirely smitten."

There was a pause.

"I'm sure you do, *ma chérie,*" he said, his tone gone bland and superior.

She smiled heartily, glad to have made a dent in his arrogance. At last, it was her turn to taunt him! "First, there's Roger Manners, a nephew of the duke of Rutland. He has proposed to me on three separate occasions. His excellences of character are too many to name and he has such beautiful dark eyes—they quite melt me. Then there's Freddie Foxham, who is a tulip of fashion and terribly droll, and a very close friend of Beau Brummell—"

"Now, there's something to brag about."

"And Tom de Vere, who wins the brush at nearly every foxhunt he attends. My suitors have been faithful to me since the night of my debut. *They* are perfect gentlemen. *They* would never kidnap me."

"Then they don't want you as much as I do," he growled hotly into the crack of the door.

Her eyes widened; her heart skipped a beat. "At least their offers have been respectable!"

"Oh? Then why haven't you accepted any of them yet?"

As she stared at the door, trying to think of a tart rejoinder, his voice softened, beguiling her, weakening her. "I know why. Because you want more. You sense that these men fail to grasp your true worth. Any man who realized what a rare, exquisite jewel you are would not hesitate to do what I did today—aye, even to kidnap you, as you call it—if it was the only way to have you. Do not ask me to repent of it, Alice, for I never shall. Come out to me, Alice. I swear I'll be good."

He paused, and she eased down onto the wooden chair that she had used to block the door. She rested her elbow on the chair back and laid her cheek in her hand, gazing out the window at the picture-perfect autumn day, feeling torn. *Free . . .*

"You wrong yourself and me by assuming my interest in you is purely physical," he went on. "I told you I am eager to further our acquaintance. I want to know what you think about things. What you want out of life. What you dream." He hesitated. "Alice, I would have your trust."

"How am I to give it, when you have so thoroughly compromised me?"

"I would not hurt you, nor allow you to be hurt because of me. I know what I'm doing."

"You are selfish."

"Yes, yes, that has already been established," he said impatiently. "But if you knew me—if you gave me a chance—you might understand why I did it."

She lowered her head, silent for a moment. "I do not want to know you," she said quietly. Even as she uttered the words, she knew it was a lie—a cold, defensive lie.

"I see."

She winced at the crisp, mocking hurt that came through so eloquently in his voice. The memory of his outraged face flashed through her mind from last night, when she had wiped away his kiss; she had not merely angered him, she knew, but wounded him. It seemed she had done it again. The pang of remorse she felt was vexing, but she could not bring herself to say she had not meant it.

Truly, what was she doing, hiding in here? she thought, pressing her hand wearily to her forehead. Nothing was going to be solved by cowardice. She was not being fair to him—she was not even being entirely truthful. There were butterflies in her stomach, but they were not born entirely of anger and mistrust, as they should have been. She cursed herself for it, but a small, traitorous portion of her thrilled to the prospect of sparring with him again. She doubted she could match him in strategy, but she was his equal in pride—and in loneliness.

She rose from the chair and began pacing, wringing her hands in distress. *Had she brought this on herself, encouraged him somehow?* she wondered. She had certainly succumbed last night to his kiss.

"Alice?"

She spun toward the door, her skirts whirling softly. "Yes?" she forced out.

"Do you know what I am holding in my hand?"

"No."

"Care to guess?"

"A pitchfork?" she asked in a stilted attempt at levity, hoping to invoke his earlier, playful mood.

"No, my dear," he answered drily. "A key to your room."

"*What?*" she breathed, aghast.

"I should hate to have to use it."

"You have a key to this room?"

"Mm-hmm."

She took a step toward the door, panic rising up in her throat. "You're bluffing!"

"Do you wish me to prove it?"

"No!" Heaven help her. Her back was to the wall. She would have to do as he said—but he *had* sworn that he would not lay a hand on her. Though she did not trust him for an instant, she had no choice but to take the blackguard at his word. The only way to keep her dignity intact was to come out willingly and face him, eye to eye. Her whole body tingled with wayward, hostile excitement as she slid the chair aside, stepped up to the door, and laid hold of the latch.

Resolute as she was on concealing her fear of him, she was even more determined to hide her intense physical attraction to him. She refused to give him the satisfaction. Gathering all her bravado, she threw open the door and glared at him.

Leaning against the wall by her door, he gave her a charming smile. "There she is, my fair, young guest. Mind you wear your mantle, dear. The weather in these parts is changeable."

"You want to go for a walk?" she demanded, her eyes narrowing to angry slits. "Let's walk—by all means! Anything you desire, my lord. You've only got a few days. I suggest you enjoy them, because when they are over, you will never see me again." She shoved the great, muscled hulk out of her path and stalked past him down the dim hallway.

"Anything I want, truly?" he called after her in a roguish tone.

She rolled her eyes and kept going.

When he caught up to her a moment later, he was carrying her fur-trimmed pelisse. She stopped long enough to let him hold it for her while she slipped her arms into the sleeves, and though she continued to glower at him, he merely gave her a knowing little smile and said nothing.

Lucien had not owned Revell Court long enough to have undertaken the task of reclaiming the gardens from nature, let alone keeping the surrounding woods properly groomed and tended. It had been enough of a task to bring the stables back into working order. Both the gardens and the woods had run wild for the past two or three years, their upkeep falling by the wayside as the marquess of Carnarthen's health had slowly crumbled, for he had run the estate himself, not trusting an estate manager with so peculiar a property.

They crossed the terrace where weeds, ivy, and goldenrod had run amuck in the flowerbeds that lined the weather-beaten stone balustrade. Mounds of blue hydrangeas nearly as tall as Lucien crowded the three mossy steps that led down into the formal garden. He went down them, and Alice followed him toward the circular fountain. As they approached, two doves that had perched on the stately stone fountain urn fluttered away, cooing. Alice stopped beside the fountain pool and gazed down with a faraway expression at the lily pads, driven with dreamlike slowness over the surface of the shallow water like tiny sailing vessels. She studied the scene as though memorizing it, while Lucien gazed at her, watching the wind toy with her clothes and the tendrils of her hair that it had worked free from her neat coif.

Her waving red-gold hair, blue eyes, and ivory skin, and the chaste, faraway serenity of her face, put him in mind of Botticelli's Venus, rising from the sea upon her scallop shell.

"Shall we?" he murmured.

She turned absently from her contemplative study of the lily pads. "Your garden is beautiful."

He shrugged and glanced around at it. "It is overgrown."

"Yes, but it has a lost, eerie beauty that quite pleases me. I wish I had my watercolor set."

Lucien lifted his eyebrows. "Ah, are you an artistic young lady, Miss Montague?"

She smiled reluctantly. "I have been known to dabble."

He laughed softly, tickled by the revelation. *An artist. Of course.* Those beautiful hands. That penetrating gaze. The seething passion under her cool, demure surface. "What sort of work do you most enjoy?" he asked as they sauntered past rows of once-conical yews that had grown into huge, dark green lumps.

"Sketching faces."

"Really?"

"Portraits in charcoal are my forte, but I love watercolors and all sorts of crafts. Japanning, fancy embroidery."

He turned to her suddenly. "Do you enjoy landscapes? There is a spectacular view of the valley that will delight your artist's eye, but it is a bit of a walk—about a mile and a half each way. Do you feel up to it?"

She nodded with interest. "I am accustomed to taking a daily constitutional."

"Good! Come, then. I'll show you the way." Trying to restrain his enthusiasm, he led her toward the opening in the overgrown boxwood hedge where a pair of musk rose bushes formed a thorny turnstile, marking the exit from the garden to the fallow fields and woods beyond. They stopped to take deep, lung-filling inhalations of the musk roses' delicious, honeylike perfume. Exclaiming with unaffected joy at the roses' late-blooming beauty, Alice cupped one of the creamy white blossoms gracefully in her gloved hand. He picked one, pulled off the thorns, and offered it to her. She took it in silence, searching his face warily, then turned away and walked on. Lucien just stood there watching her, praying he wouldn't do anything wrong.

They ambled across the meadow and watched the breeze ripple through the high, golden grasses, serenaded all the while by larks and pipits on the wing; then they followed the twisting footpath into the whispering woods. Birds swooped from branch to branch, following them. Wind-eddied leaves flew before him like the little whirling frisson of delight he felt watching Alice negotiate her way over a stream, daintily stepping from rock to mossy rock.

As they trekked through the woods, the minutes fell away in inexorable succession like toppling dominoes, and time began to skate. Its acceleration dizzied him like the smoky, metamorphosing clouds, ceaselessly shifting as they chased across the late afternoon sky, but slowly, slowly, she began warming up to him.

She smiled at him more frequently as they chatted about nothing in particular, pointing out various flowers and the occasional woodland animal to each other. They saw plump squirrels in the trees, pheasants in the brush, and a horned stag and his shy, delicate does gliding soundlessly through the shadows.

On three separate occasions, he caught her gazing at him longer than she should. He felt distracted, entranced, and painfully alive as he watched her in the mellow autumn afternoon, dazzled by the coppery richness of her golden hair. Her innocence captivated him, and her guileless simplicity healed him somehow. He felt like a man whose fever had broken, flush with the euphoria of the first, tenuous return of strength—still weak, but buoyant with the hope of an eventual return to wholeness. The sickness in his soul, however, laid a jealous claim on him. Just as often and as quickly, the cold, dense cloud shadows would come, flying wraith-like overhead,molding the landscape and casting Alice in a gray half-light so that he wanted to draw her up close in his arms, shelter her until they passed—but he did not. It was too soon. She would pull back. He knew full well that he had only succeeded in luring her out of her room by resorting to the threat of unlocking her door himself. He could not risk scaring her away again.

All the while, the sun rolled west like a miser's dropped coin. The day was dying; the year, as well. The smell of fallen leaves reminded him of this fact, wafting gently from under his every step as he followed Alice up the steep, twisting forest path. Determined to make her trust him, he hid his impatience behind an amiable smile as she glanced over her shoulder at him.

"Are you coming, lazy?" she asked pertly, her cheeks rosy from the brisk cold and the climb.

"Lazy?" he retorted.

"Well, what are you doing back there?" she asked. "Counting the rocks beneath your feet?" Turning away again to continue her climb, she lifted the hem of her skirts, unconsciously affording him a glimpse of her pretty calves.

"Merely enjoying the view," he said, savoring the maidenly sway of her hips. But when his perusal led to dangerously tempting thoughts, he brushed past her and took the lead in determination, his black wool greatcoat swinging with his strides. "You'd best keep up, boots. If you fall behind, you'll lose your rations."

"Boots?"

"Army slang for a fresh recruit. Hurry, we're almost there. We'll be just in time to watch the sunset."

"You were in the army?" she exclaimed, hurrying after him.

"Five years."

"You're jesting!"

"No," he said with a sigh. "Would that I were."

"You, in the army!" She laughed. "I find that hard to imagine."

"So do I."

"You don't strike me as the sort to follow orders. What was your regiment?"

"The Hundred and Thirty-sixth Foot."

"Oh," she said with a dubious glance.

"I know—not a very fashionable regiment." He gave her his hand and pulled her up over a tree root that formed a steep step in the path. "We were going to join the Blues, but Damien actually wanted to *fight* in the war rather than lounge around London in a smart uniform, which, I assure you, would have been perfectly acceptable to me."

"You and he joined the army together?"

He nodded. "We saw our first action in Denmark under Cathcart, then went to the Peninsula."

She laughed as though she could not believe it. "What rank did you attain?"

"Captain."

"Captain Lord Lucien!" she echoed, laughing harder. "Did you buy it or earn it?"

Taken aback, he laughed in mingled surprise and indignation. "What impertinence! Earned it, I assure you. For your information, Damien and I captained our regiment's elite flank companies. I was—"

"No, don't tell me! Let me guess." Eyeing him in amusement, she tapped her lip in thought. "You're no grenadier. Grenadiers are big, stalwart souls, the first into battle, or so I've been told."

He raised his eyebrow at her, unsure if he was being insulted.

"No," she concluded, "you must have been captain of the light infantry company. The quick-witted ones, the sharpshooters."

"How ever did you guess?"

"I know these things," she said with a sage look, then turned away and walked on, entirely pleased with herself.

Lucien gazed after her with a smile on his face. God help him, he was utterly charmed. "How do you know about the workings of a regiment?"

"From my brother, of course. He was in the Forty-third," she added proudly.

"The Glorious Forty-third," Lucien admitted, impressed. "I heard about Lord Glenwood's gallantry at Vittoria. He was a brave man and a distinguished officer."

"And a good brother," she added more softly. "Were you at Vittoria, Lucien?"

"No, I left the previous year, after Badajoz."

"Badajoz," she murmured, her expression turning grave. "Phillip said it was the most dreadful battle of the war."

Lucien was not sure how much her brother had told her. When she laid her hand gently on his arm a moment later, he looked down at it in silence, realizing it was the first time she had touched him of her own accord.

"Captain Lucien, you look so grim suddenly," she murmured. "Was the battle very difficult for you?"

"It was difficult for everyone," he countered with a shrug and looked away, irritated with his own habitual evasiveness. He stared into the shadowy woods, routing from his mind the memory of billowing black smoke that parted just long enough to reveal a glimpse of well over a thousand scarlet-uniformed bodies piled against the sun-baked walls of the old Spanish citadel. The British army had battered the French-sympathizing town into submission. "It was not so much the siege itself, but . . . afterwards," he forced out. He looked at her, searching her face. "Did your brother tell you anything about it?"

Alice held him in a somber gaze. "Some."

"It is not the sort of thing one normally tells a young lady. . . . But I promised I would not shelter you from the true workings of the world, didn't I?"

She nodded. "I want to know."

"By the time the town fell, we had suffered so many casualties that the troops were beyond rage. They were frenzied. They were our men—Englishmen—but they turned into animals. They sacked the town. Looted, raped, murdered civilians. It took us officers three days to bring them under control again." He watched her face. She seemed to be taking it in stride. Her expression was troubled, but by no means hysterical, and for his part, he needed to speak of it. "We erected a gallows and hanged the worst offenders. After that, I left the army—I thought surely there had to be a better way."

"You joined the Diplomatic Corps instead?"

He nodded.

She studied him with a thoughtful pause. "I admire you for it," she declared suddenly. "I'm sure many of your comrades disparaged the choice, but diplomacy is ever more civilized than war. What great strength of will you must have, to have defied the majority's opinion. I wish my brother had chosen as you did, or better still, had possessed the same strength of will. . . . May I tell you why Phillip went to war?"

"You can tell me anything," he replied, inwardly dodging the pang of guilt at her misled compliment. His role in the Diplomatic Corps had been anything but peaceful, but of course he could not tell her his true role as spy. He shuddered at the thought. If she knew the truth, it would surely drive her away, as it had driven Damien away. He could not take that chance. Besides, it was dangerous information. It was safer for her to keep her in ignorance.

"Caro made remarks that called my brother's manhood into question," she said, fleeting bitterness passing over her delicate features. "But she merely wanted him out of the way so that she could misbehave in London without her husband looking over her shoulder. Unfortunately, Phillip did not see through her ploy. He took her words to heart—and off he went."

Lucien shook his head. "Men do foolish things in the name of pride," he said in regret.

"He was invalided home with terrible saber wounds that had become infected. Peg and I—she's our old nurse, who minds Harry now—we tended him day and night, but we knew he wouldn't recover. Phillip knew it, too, but at least he got to see Harry again and we got to say good-bye."

"Were you close?"

She nodded. "Losing our parents at a young age drew us together."

Lucien tensed, scanning her face.

She looked away. "He lingered for three weeks before he died. He was twenty-nine."

"I'm sorry," he whispered.

She gazed at him for a long moment as though sizing him up while the wind riffled through their hair and clothes. Then she smiled wryly. "Don't be. If Phillip were alive, he would have challenged you to a duel and shot you dead for all of this."

"Ah," he said in chagrin as she turned away with a chiding smile and walked on.

Feeling rather penitent, Lucien caught up to her a moment later, then forged ahead to the crest of the path where he searched out his visual marker: a dead, gnarled tree trunk, hollow and gray. Going past it, he stepped out onto the limestone outcrop that was their destination. It jutted out from the hill, affording a stunning view of the valley in all its jewel-toned, October glory, lit up by the fireball of the sun, which had just begun to set.

The shot of wind that rushed up the cliff face lifted his hair and ran riot through his long black wool greatcoat so that it billowed behind him as he stood on the edge.

"Behold, madam," he said with a sweeping gesture full of theatrical grandeur as she appeared a moment later, rosy-cheeked with exertion. "The legacy of my ancestors."

He turned and offered her his hand. She glanced nervously at the precipice, but took his hand and came slowly to him. He drew her to his side and they stood together.

"Oh, Lucien, it is magnificent," she said softly, her gaze drinking in the vista of the hills clad in amber, maroon, rusty orange, and scarlet.

"Indeed," he murmured, gazing at her delicate profile and her milky skin illumined by the dazzling light. Then he glanced at the valley again, lest she catch him staring. "How I ever wound up with all this to my name is beyond my comprehension, but it does keep one in comfort."

She visored her eyes against the sun. "I did not know the marquesses of Carnarthen were related to your family and the dukes of Hawkscliffe."

"They're not," he said drily. "To be specific, the lords of Carnarthen no longer exist. They are a lost breed, alas. The title went defunct when the legitimate line died out with the death of the tenth marquess."

"There is an illegitimate line?"

He held his arms up at his sides. "You're looking at it."

Her eyes widened, and her fingertips flew to her lips. "Oh! I'm so sorry—"

"Not at all," he said frankly, amused at her discomfiture. "My father was Edward Merion, the last marquess of Carnarthen, a rum chap, and I am proud to be of his blood, bar sinister or otherwise. Carnarthen's ancestral pile in Wales and two other large holdings reverted to the Crown upon his death, but luckily for me, there was no entail on Revell Court, so he was able to leave this property to whomever he chose. You look shocked."

"Well . . . yes! I thought the duke of Hawkscliffe was your father!"

"That's what it says on my birth certificate," he replied with a shrug. "Of course, it is a lie."

"You are telling me you are a . . . *bastard,*" She whispered the last word.

He grinned. "Aye, what of it? It's as good a family as any to belong to. The clan issues from the area around Mount Snowdon. The Carnarthen lords even boast their own bit of ancient Welsh lore. My father told me we are descended from warlocks and berserker warriors. What do you think of that?"

She gave him a dubious look. "I think that is more of your foolery."

"As I stand here, it's true. He told my mother that Damien and I are the final flowering of our line. Twins, you know, are magical beings."

She scoffed halfheartedly, eyeing him as though she knew not what to believe.

"I tell you, it's true. Damien and I always had this superstitious notion—which we conceived of when we were quite small—that as a pair, we were invincible, that nothing could ever harm us if the other was close by. That's the only reason I joined the army. I was sure that Damien would get killed if I weren't on hand. But, then, even after I left, he proved more than able to fend for himself," he added with a wistful laugh, as though his estrangement from his twin were not one of the greatest thorns in his heart.

She appeared uncertain of whether he was teasing her or not. "So, which one are you, warlock or warrior?"

"Why, it's just an old peasants' tale, *ma chérie,*" he said with a coy smile and lifted her hand to his lips, placing a breezy kiss on her knuckles. "Still, it's strange to think that one night my mother went to the Grotto, met my father, and voilà—"

Her gasp interrupted him. She yanked her hand out of his grasp. When he looked at her again, her eyes were as round as china-blue saucers. "Your mother went to the Grotto?"

"I'm afraid so. On the other hand, if she hadn't, I wouldn't exist, and then where would I be? The Duchess Georgiana was a wild, flamboyant hussy, God rest her soul, but she spoke her mind and was true to herself. She was an original, I'll give her that. You still look shocked."

She stared at him in perplexity.

He leaned closer and lowered his voice to a conspiratorial tone. "All right, my dear Miss Montague, I will let you in on the family secret, though I really thought everyone in the ton already knew. Only my eldest brother, Robert, the present duke of Hawkscliffe, and my little sister, Lady Jacinda, are of the true blood. The rest of us are, as they say, cuckoos in the nest. Georgiana's husband only claimed us as his own to avoid the humiliation of having been cuckolded yet again by his wife."

She stared at him intensely for a long moment, absorbing this with a scandalized look, then turned away. "I believe," she said gravely, "that it is time for tea."

His smile faded. He thrust his gloved hands into the deep, voluminous pockets of his greatcoat and looked down at the toes of his polished black boots. "You think less of me because of my parentage."

"No—"

"Yes, you do. I can see it in your face."

"No, Lucien, it isn't that. I am . . . embarrassed."

He studied her warily.

"I don't know what to make of you," she said simply, shaking her head. "Surely this causes you pain and has caused you pain all your life, and yet you laugh. I don't understand. And I am not accustomed to speaking so intimately, especially with a man I barely know."

"Alice." He turned to her and stared into her eyes, willing himself to keep his hands in his pockets, though he longed to take her into his arms. Her questioning gaze was so serious, so vulnerable. "Pray, do not be embarrassed. That was not my intention. I like talking to you."

She smiled uncertainly, the wind playing with wispy tendrils of her hair.

He returned her smile, drew his hand slowly out of his pocket, and gently brushed her hair out of her face. Her smile widened, and a blush filled her cheeks.

"Who can account for it?" he murmured. "There are some people that we know all our lives and yet never really feel we know them at all. But there are other people—" Unable to resist the temptation, he ran a feather-light caress down the curve of her cheek with one leather-sheathed knuckle. The cobalt depths of her eyes flickered with response, but she said nothing, heeding his every word. "—people we meet in a day, and instantly, it feels as though we've known them all our lives."

Holding his stare, she turned her cheek away from his touch. "How many women have you said this to?"

He flinched and drew his eyebrows together in sudden anger, though he knew he deserved it. "I am not toying with you," he said, his tone low and hard. "Perhaps there was a time when I would have, but I am not a boy anymore. I have seen too much death and too much pain and now all I want is—" His words broke off.

"What, Lucien? What do you want?" she whispered.

His fractured gaze dropped to her lips. His touch slipped down from her cheek to her jaw, tilting her head back. He took a step toward her, closing the distance between them. He caught a glimpse of the desire and confusion swirling in the blue depths of her eyes before he closed his and lowered his head, caressing her mouth with his own. He pulled her carefully into his arms, trembling at that magic moment when he felt her graceful body melt receptively against him. She parted her lips and let him slip his tongue into the warm, honeyed sweetness of her mouth. Blissful longing racked him. He held her face between his leather-gloved hands and drank of her kiss, savoring her with a tenderness that came from his knowledge of her innocence. She clung to him, there on the precipice.

"Please," she moaned, trying to turn her face away. Her cheeks were rose-red, her eyes feverish blue beneath her sandy lashes.

"Look at me." He cupped her jaw and made her meet his hungry stare. "I'm not going to hurt you." She peered uncertainly into his eyes. "I would never hurt you," he whispered. "I'd rather die."

"Why must you kiss me?"

"Because I cannot bear waiting for you to kiss *me*."

If she had been poised to continue bewailing her fate, his blunt answer visibly caught her off guard. "You actually expect *me* to kiss you?" she retorted in breathless indignation.

"Expect it? No. Desire it? Yes." He gave her a lazy half smile. "With every fiber of my being."

She stared at him with a quizzical expression somewhere between thrill and alarm. "But . . . I don't know how."

"Oh, yes, you do," he whispered.

She did not pull away. Blushing helplessly, she flicked her gaze downward to his mouth, then back up to his eyes. He drew nearer, offering himself. He tilted his head, so close he could feel her soft breath on his lips, warm and soft against the wind's sharp cold.

A second later, she mirrored his movement, tilting her head in the opposite direction. She lowered her lashes as her lips danced a mere sliver of an inch away. "I don't know how," she protested again barely audibly, then rested her hands on his shoulders and closed her eyes, kissing him as softly as an angel.

Lucien held perfectly still, filled with such pleasure that he wanted to die rather than ever to let it end. She slid her arms around his neck and kissed him again, more firmly this time. Her slender body trembled against him as he wrapped his arms around her waist. She was tentative, careful, but her breasts heaved against his chest and her eyes had turned a sensuous shade of midnight blue when her gaze met his. Her lashes drifted closed, and he lost awareness of everything in the world but her as she pulled him down to her and skimmed the tip of her tongue past his lips into his mouth.

Shocked and entranced, he surrendered to her will, wanting nothing more than to fulfill her every whim. She groaned as she tasted him more deeply, raking her fingers through his hair. She ran her hands along his jaw, his throat, tracing the edge of his cravat, demolishing his capacity for reason—then she suddenly stopped and pulled back.

When he tried to reach for her again, she braced her hand against his chest, firmly holding him at arm's length. "No." Her eyes blazed with cobalt fire, warning him back. Her lips were wet and bee-stung, her cheeks rosy. "That's enough," she panted, her bosom rising and falling rapidly.

His famous cunning fled. His Machiavellian mind was blank with lust. Drunk with the taste of her, his silver tongue was left devoid of one coherent line with which to coax her back to him. She lowered her hand from his chest and marched unsteadily away.

"Alice," he panted.

She kept going, returning to the path in the shady woods. He paused and pinched the bridge of his nose for a moment, trying to weave together the tatters of his sanity. He dragged his hand through his hair and surrendered to a quiet, utterly intoxicated laugh. Good God, he had *not* seen that coming. He strode after her into the woods, where gray dusk had already arrived. She had a lead of several yards on him, and she was all but running back to the house.

"Alice!"

No response. She didn't even pause.

"Wait!"

She brushed off his call with an annoyed shrug. He had to jog to catch up, but when he reached her side, she ignored his questioning gaze, her dark blue skirts luffing like sails in the breeze as she marched on relentlessly.

"Alice?" he asked gingerly.

"Stay away from me."

He noticed the scarlet blush in her cheeks and realized she was mortified by her lusty response to him. A rakish grin spread over his face. "My darling, there is no reason to be embarrassed—"

"You are making me break my promise to my brother that I would take care of Harry. Do you realize that? Do you even care?"

He grabbed her arm and stopped her. She whirled to him.

"Stop it," he ordered quietly, but he saw fear darting through her eyes, not of him, but of her own feelings. She was not prepared to accept her passion—at least not her passion for him.

"This is not who I am! I am not your plaything—"

"Don't say that again. I know you're not. Alice, I told you I'm being sincere. I've never been more earnest in my life. Or is that what frightens you?"

"*You* frighten me! You, Lucien—Draco—whoever you are! All you care about is yourself—your pleasure! Do you even realize how selfish you are? Are you able to see it?" She wrenched her arm out of his grasp. "If not, let me remind you that you are holding me here against my will. You forced me into this. I don't want to be here, and I am *not* getting involved with a . . . a jaded scoundrel whose only wish is to debauch me!" She tore the white musk rose he had given her out of her buttonhole, threw it on the ground, and started to stride away.

"I am alone, Alice."

His sharp words took even him by surprise and stopped her as she reached the meadow. She paused and looked warily over her shoulder, her long shadow stretching over the faded grasses. His body was rigid, and his glare was fierce as he stood there staring at her. He felt naked before her—impatient, frustrated—but he could not stop himself. Somehow he had to make her understand.

"Don't you see?" He checked the dark note of pleading in his voice, but he could not expunge the tone of quiet despair. "I need . . . I don't know what I need. All I know is that I am alone. Entirely . . . alone."

There. The words were out.

He held her stare, his entire soul at her mercy. He saw the tremor that shook her, saw her battle with herself, but she was an ivory tower of virtue; she did not break.

She passed a scathing glance over him. "I'm not surprised."

He flinched, dropped his gaze.

She turned on her heel and walked away.

CHAPTER SIX

Hours later, Lucien swept out of the gates of Revell Court astride his Andalusian stallion and rode into the black, windy night. The horse's hoofbeats thundered over the wooden bridge, its long, vigorous strides flying over the road, taking the hill in lusty exertion.

He rode low in the saddle, a taut give in the reins, the wind rippling through his hair and the stallion's mane. Around him, the blowing woodlands were alive with the creaking of branches and the rattle of dead leaves. The horse didn't like it, snorting in warning at the wind, tossing its head.

The peasants claimed that phantoms walked on nights like this, Lucien thought, his mood as sulky and dark as the sky, where no moon shone. Woolly clouds trampled the crisp elegance of the constellations as the wind herded them on like vast gray sheep. The chill of the night and the speed of his stallion's gallop helped to take the edge off the hurt and anger he was still nursing, thwarted passion burning in his veins. Alice's words had cut him, but even so, he had waited like a fool for her to come out of her room, busying himself for hours with minutiae, unable to concentrate until the maid told him that Miss had asked for supper in her room.

He had realized that she was battening down in there for a siege. He had spent enough time in the army to hate sieges with every fiber of his being. They always ended disastrously. He didn't suppose he could starve her out, but he refused to try to wheedle her out again with words. He still had the key, of course, and could win the battle in a trice, but that was hardly an honorable victory. If he simply barged in on her, she would only detest him more. He was beginning to see that he *could not* win by any of his usual methods. What the devil had he gotten himself into? He slowed his horse, sensing that the stallion's initial explosive burst of verve upon being let out of its kingly stall had been spent.

Predictably, the stallion settled into a more amenable temper. Lucien gave the horse's velvety neck a grateful pat; he understood the animal's eccentricities, and the horse understood his. Leaving the woods for the open moors, they dropped back into a leisurely canter.

After half an hour's ride, his destination came into sight perched atop the next rise—a lonely coaching inn called the George's Head. It was an assuming rectangle of stone with a slate roof and neat, narrow windows with white-painted frames. The George's Head served one of the best draught bitters in the county, but its obscure location and the reliable discretion of its innkeeper, Gus Morgan, was what had made Lucien select it as his intelligence postbox for his secret communiqués from Lord Castlereagh and messages from his far-flung contacts. His body tensed and his vigilance heightened as he neared the tavern, his sharply honed reflexes ready to reach for the sword at his side or the pistol under his coat in the blink of an eye. Ambush by enemy agents was a constant possibility, one he had learned to live with.

As he rode into the hay-strewn yard, clucking chickens scattered out from under his horse's hoofs. He scanned the area, dismounting as Morgan's teenaged son hurried over to hold his horse while he went inside. Lucien stalked toward the inn, drawing off his black riding gauntlets. His movements were smooth and unhurried, but his eyes were hard and an intensity of purpose filled his face. He heard raucous peasant laughter and smelled hearth smoke and roasting game as he reached for the door. When he opened it and walked into the warmly lit, low-ceilinged taproom, absolute silence dropped.

He swept the modest establishment with a glance. There were about twenty of the local country folk, peasants, and cottagers gathered around the tables. They knew perfectly well who he was, and they stared at him like they thought he was the devil. He pulled the door shut behind him and strode slowly across the taproom to the bar, where Gus Morgan was polishing glasses on the end of his stained apron and putting them away on the overhead rack. The innkeeper was a stalwart bull of a man with ruddy cheeks and a glow of sweat on his bald pate. He braced his powerful forearms on the bar and nodded to Lucien as he approached.

They both knew the procedure.

"Offer ye a pint, my lord?" Morgan asked on cue.

"Bitter," he answered with a nod, turning to rest his hip on the edge of a nearby stool, his body at an angle where he still had ample view of the room and the door. He rested his elbow on the bar while Morgan held the tap, pouring out his draught with a frothy head on it. After a moment, Morgan set the pewter tankard before him and Lucien lifted it to his lips, savoring the rich, mellow beer.

The peasants slowly began to breathe and move about again, though their conversations had subsided into whispers. Morgan marched back into the kitchens to give orders to the cook, returning a few minutes later. Lucien looked into his beer with a broody sigh and almost wished for a moment that he was the sort of man who could pour out his woman troubles to a sympathetic barkeep, but it was beyond his power.

Couldn't she understand that when a man lived his life knowing death lay in wait for him around every corner, he had no choice but to reach for the boon that landed in his path? Perhaps he was being unreasonable, but he wanted her to open her arms to him unconditionally, aye, even as Draco, leader of a pagan cult and the man who had made her a pampered prisoner in his house. Only if she proved that she could love the worst in him could he then trust her with the information that would put his life in her hands.

At length, he set his empty tankard down on the bar. "A fine brew, Mr. Morgan."

The square of reflected light on Morgan's bald pate moved with the man's hearty nod. "Aye, sir, best in the West Country," he said with a grin.

"What's on the bill of fare tonight?"

"Shepherd's pie, sir."

He concealed his pleasure at this response. It meant that a message had arrived for him. Usually Morgan answered, "Fish and chips, sir," which, translated, meant that there was nothing to be delivered at this time.

"Fetch you a plate, sir?"

"No, thanks." He stood, acutely aware of the furtive scrutiny of the patrons. Tossing his generous payment for the beer onto the bar, he walked slowly to the door, drawing on his gloves. He strode out into the windy night, heartened by the ale and keenly curious about the communiqué that had arrived. Crossing the inn yard to the livery stable, he slid the wooden door open and walked down the dimly lit aisle to where the wiry lad was still trying to befriend his black stallion.

"Your father's looking for you, boy," he said, offering the lad a few coins for minding his horse.

"Thank ye, sir!" The boy bowed and darted past him to return to the tavern.

Lucien patted his horse's neck and checked his girth. A moment later, he heard the stable door sliding open again and stepped out into the aisle as Morgan brought him his message.

"Damned fine brew, Mr. Morgan," he said with a smile, laying a small cloth pouch containing twenty gold sovereigns in the innkeeper's hand.

The big, bald man bowed his head. "Happy to be of service, sir."

"Thank you. That will be all."

Morgan nodded again and hurried back to his kitchens, all very neat and confidential.

Lucien held up the small folded and wax-sealed letter to the stall window. The clouds parted long enough to admit a few tenuous moonbeams, and a smile spread over his face as he caught a glimpse of the return address: *España*. The name said Sanchez, but that was only one of the many aliases of his old friend, Padre Garcia.

To this day, Lucien did not know whether or not Padre Garcia was really a priest. Some claimed the man was actually an Andalusian count by the name of Santiago, connected by marriage to the king of Ascension. All Lucien knew was that the Spaniard was one hell of a fighter.

Padre Garcia and his tough, ragged band of rebels had aided the British in their cause of driving Napoleon out of Spain. Garcia had innumerable sources, and his information was usually dead on the mark. With a wry smile at the thought of his fearless Spanish friend, Lucien slipped the letter into his breast pocket and led his horse back out into the night.

Each red-hot coal that glowed in the braziers was a crimson rose, and in her dream, the Grotto was empty but for the two of them: Lucien and she.

Silken wisps of slumber entwined Alice in her most secret fantasy while the fierce wind blew beyond the windows of her bedchamber. *His muscled thighs and lean hips felt like warm steel under her hands as she caressed him on her knees, kissing his chiseled belly, while his large, gentle hands stroked her shoulders and her hair. She felt the mystery of his rock-hard manhood brush her throat. He was swollen solid behind the barrier of his tight black breeches. He needed her, she knew, and it pleased her.* There was no sound in her dream but his urgent whisper, *Give it to me. Give it all to me.*

Yes, she thought, her body arching, *yes.*

She was naked beneath the brown robe and painfully aroused, acutely aware of the feel of coarse wool against her tender flesh. She wanted to be rid of it, but she waited patiently, weaving a wreath of careful, rosy kisses around his navel, for she knew he would sate her. When he touched her face, gently lifting her chin, she looked up and met his stare.

It was the intensity in his silvery eyes, so haunted and fierce, so demanding, even in her dream, that woke her all of a sudden. With a startled gasp, she sat bolt upright in the bed, her heart pounding. The room was dark. Her skin was fevered, and the virginal place between her thighs pulsated with want. She swallowed hard and came back by slow, shaky degrees to reality. *Oh, God,* she thought, covering her face with her hand in a flood of shame. Every wanton detail of her dream throbbed vividly in her mind. She dragged her hand through her hair and fought to reclaim control of her body.

I've got to get out of here. If she did not, very soon, she was going to do something worthy of Caro's rash recklessness.

The lavender scent of the sheets and the very softness of the coverlet snagged at her starved desire. She threw off the blanket and climbed out of the warm nest of her bed. The fire had burned down to embers in the hearth, but the chilly air soothed her agitation.

Thirsty after her long nap, she crossed to the bureau where she had left her supper tray. She ventured a sip of the cold tea left over from supper. The syrupy-sweet sugar on the bottom washed over her tongue, and a tremor moved through her as she thought of Lucien's delicious mouth.

There was no use denying it. She wanted that odious cad, body and soul, and it terrified her.

I am alone, he had said, and she had answered him heartlessly, like a liar and a coward. If it had been anyone else in the world, she never would have spoken so coldly, but when he had stood before her, offering himself with such breathtaking sincerity, asking for her to care about him, he had utterly unnerved her, aye, even more than when she found herself looking down the barrel of his pistol.

Moving with measured care, Alice set the teacup back on the tray, her lashes veiling her downward gaze. She sat down heavily in the darkness and listened to the soft, high-pitched whistle of the draft rushing through the seams of the window. The panes shook, and a wild scattering of leaves flung against the glass. A few large, silvery raindrops slashed down from the skies and struck the panes, but the dark clouds still did not release the full power of the cold autumn rain. She knew it was coming. She could feel the pressure building in the air. She hoped Lucien would not get caught in the downpour. Distress filled her eyes at the thought of him. She rested her forehead on her fingertips and squeezed her eyes shut.

Devil take it, she was more ashamed of her cruel words to him than she was of her wanton dream or even of the wild kiss she had given him out there on the lookout rock. She had accused him of toying with her, but she knew full well that his silent stare asked for something deeper than the pleasure of her body. He was needy for something she did not understand, no more than she comprehended her own need to give it to him.

She drew her knees up to her chest and wrapped her arms around them, gazing pensively into the embers of the fire, no longer sure of right and wrong. She could not help feeling that she owed him an apology, but that was absurd. She owed him nothing. The man had kept her here against her will. Yet all she could do was sigh at the knee-jerk indignation that Society and even pride told her was the proper reaction. It was not at all what she really felt.

What she really felt was remorse for hurting his raw, exposed feelings and for being dishonest about her own. She was drawn to Lucien Knight, deeply drawn.

Thunder rumbled in the distance, and the rain began falling in earnest. Rising from her chair, she moved restlessly around the dim room, stopping to prod the fire with the poker until small flames of gold, orange, blue, and green began to dance along the top of the log. Just then, she heard clattering hoofbeats in the courtyard. Abandoning the fire poker, she stole over to the window and looked out as Lucien swept through the gates astride a large black horse.

The flaming torch stand lit the courtyard, defying the rain that sought to quench it. She stared in hushed admiration as it bathed him and his horse in its lurid glow. He was dressed in black, his expression fierce and forlorn in the stormy night. Unaware of her study, he swung down off his horse, handed off the reins to a groom, and paused to wrap his arm affectionately around the animal's muzzle in a gesture of masterly thanks. It tugged at Alice's heart. The rain fell harder, pounding the cobblestones. He quickly turned, waved off the umbrella a servant offered him, and dashed into the house.

When he had disappeared from view, she leaned against the windowpanes with a lingering flutter of infatuation in her belly. She watched the groom lead Lucien's horse away, her sigh misting the glass; then she turned back to face the hearth fire.

Now that he had come home, she supposed it was time to start worrying again about whether or not he would use his key to enter her room during the night. On the other hand, she doubted he wanted anything to do with her just now, after her cruel words. Blast it, why was she hiding again in her room? It was Saturday night, and she wanted to be with him. He was right—she was not free, for somehow she didn't dare do what she wished. She was afraid of what might happen—what she might allow to happen. She was afraid of what he made her want. With the night's velvet darkness, the intimate whisper of rain, and the sensuous spell of his charm, she did not trust either of them to behave respectably. Her own longings made her want to run, to find some means of escape, though he had an army of watchful servants and black-clad guards posted around the property. He was so very dangerous—and yet Lucien Knight made her heart sing as no other man ever had. How could she reject that simply because he had sidestepped the conventional procedures of courtship? Conventional men had left her entirely uninspired.

Oh, very well, she thought impatiently, relenting against her better sense. *I will give him a chance.* She would start afresh in the morning, for even a silver-eyed devil ought to be good on a Sunday. Marching back to bed, she climbed in under the covers only to lie awake, gazing at the rain and waiting, wide-eyed, for tomorrow to come.

Lucien rode through the gates of Revell Court minutes before the few plump raindrops that had slapped at him and his horse during the journey home turned into a deluge. Ducking his head against the rain, he held his greatcoat closed to protect Garcia's letter in the breast pocket of his waistcoat from the elements. The door swept open before him as he strode into his house.

Shrugging off his dripping greatcoat presently, he left it in the hands of his butler. "I shall be in my office, Mr. Godfrey. I am not to be disturbed."

"Yes, my lord," the butler said, bowing his head.

Lucien bounded up the steps two at a time, wove through the maze of hallways in the upper floor, then climbed another staircase, narrow and wooden, that led up, up into the attic of Revell Court.

In the dark, the rain drummed on the roof just above him and the wind whistled through the eaves. He had claimed one small section of this dusty, lugubrious region above the servants' quarters for his private working space. He unlocked his office door and felt around for a tinderbox and candle, which he lit. As the small flame rose, he closed the door behind him and locked it again. Due to the covert nature of his work, no one besides himself, not even Mr. Godfrey, was allowed into the hallowed space of Lucien's office for any reason, not even to dust the bookshelves, which needed dusting badly. He sat down at his desk, pulled out Garcia's letter, and coolly cracked the seal.

Glancing over the paper, he smirked in amusement at his friend's contrivance. Garcia had disguised the coded message as a fictional hotel keeper's bill of unpaid charges. Below the señor's irate note, the three columns of numbers bore the secret burden of the coded message. Every date, quantity, and charge listed corresponded with a numbered page of the Catholic Bible that Garcia had given him to use as their handbook. Each number referred to a page in the Bible, a particular line, and the correct word within the specified line. Proper names of key figures and active agents were distinguished from the other numbers by being circled. A circled number one, for example, stood for the pope; two, for Napoleon; three, for King George; four, for the prince regent; five, for the czar; and so on.

Scanning down the list of charges, he paled to note a circled number seventy-seven. Every known, active agent had a code number—Lucien's own was twenty-one. Though he didn't know every agent's number by memory, he knew that seventy-seven signified Claude Bardou.

While "Sanchez" railed at him for the items he had broken, eaten, or otherwise consumed during his imaginary stay at a Spanish *pensione*, Lucien dipped his quill in ink and began flipping through the pages of the Bible as the numbers directed him. Swiftly and meticulously, he reconstructed Garcia's message. When he had written down the words that matched the numbers, all that remained was to translate it from the Bible's Latin.

Greetings, my friend. I hope this letter finds you well. I am writing to warn you that Claude Bardou is alive and at large. We have learned he has assembled a small band of loyalists. As to their mission, my sources conflict. One says Bardou means to attack the Congress of Vienna. The other claims he is organizing a rescue mission to free Napoleon from Elba. We must prepare for either possibility. God keep you. Garcia.

Lucien sat back in his chair, stroking his jaw. His gaze had hardened. His slow, firm exhalation made the candle flicker. Garcia mentioned nothing about the possibility that Leonidovich had presented, that Bardou might be working for the Americans. *So much for third-hand rumors,* he thought. He picked up his pen and immediately began writing to his colleagues stationed in Italy and Austria. The thought of Napoleon being smuggled off of the island Elba and back into France was galling, but the threat to the Congress unsettled him even more deeply, because four members of his family were there.

His eldest brother, Robert, the duke of Hawkscliffe, had been appointed as one of Castlereagh's assisting delegates to the Congress. Robert had taken his new bride, Bel, with him to enjoy the glamorous festivities surrounding the Congress, as well as their little sister, Lady Jacinda, and her companion, Lizzie Carlisle, who was Robert's ward and was like a second sister to the Knight brothers. His heart pounded with dread as he wrote to Robert and to Castlereagh, sans code, warning them in the strongest possible terms of the threat.

When his letters were finished and sealed, he brooded on the possibility of contacting Sophia Voznesensky to see if she knew anything about Bardou's new mission or his current whereabouts. The dark beauty was one of Czar Alexander's deadliest creatures, a Russian agent whose past missions had included seducing Bardou to gain information about his orders.

Bardou and Sophia had worked together since the Treaty of Tilsit, throughout Russia's five-year-long alliance with France. Though the two nations had become enemies again, Sophia had captured Bardou's fancy in a powerful way. Tough and ruthless as Sophia was, she had never been quite able to escape from the claim Bardou had staked on her. Lucien knew this because he, too, had once had a brief affair with her. Shaking his head, he decided not to seek her out. It was too dangerous for her. Bardou was insanely possessive of the woman. Besides, Lucien had never entirely trusted her.

With bitter memories tormenting his mind, he thought of going to Alice, seeking comfort in her arms. *How he longed to bathe his spirit in her light, her innocence, her steadying softness. But that girl had cut him to ribbons today,* he thought, staring into the small flame of his candle. *A man had his pride. Next time, by God, she would come to him.*

Swirling arms of fog wrapped London's crowded skyline in a damp shroud as Rollo Greene waited nervously across the river on the Lambeth coal wharf, just downstream from Westminster Bridge. He could see a boat's lantern coming through the fog, casting a feeble beam of light over the glossy onyx surface of the Thames.

Right on schedule.

He pulled his top hat lower over his eyes, glad of the blade concealed inside his walking stick. The surrounding warehouses, breweries, and timber yards were dark and silent. His carriage waited in the shadows nearby. As the boat crept nearer, moving slowly against the current, he made out the masts and hanging nets of a fishing skiff. As the crew brought the boat up to the dock, he wet his lips, hid his jittery uneasiness, and put on his big, easy, American grin.

It faded somewhat as an enormous, hulking silhouette emerged from the lantern-lit mist. Standing at the bow of the boat, a cigar clamped between his teeth, the man must have been six-foot-five, seventeen, eighteen stone. *Holy Jesus.* The tip of his cigar glowed red in the darkness. Then the whole fishing boat rocked as the monster stepped up onto the rail and jumped off the bulwark, landing with terrifying agility on the dock. He shrugged his haversack up higher onto his boulderlike shoulder.

Rollo gulped silently as the blond, square-faced giant came marching relentlessly toward him, a slight limp in his stride. Somehow Rollo shook himself into action, drawing up his diminutive height as he went toward the Frenchman, his cheerful grin held in place by sheer fright. "Monsieur Bardou, I presume?"

The giant flicked a derisive glance over him. His eyes were pale blue, deadened, and mean. Rollo offered him a bow. "Name's Rollo Greene, sir. I've been assigned by our esteemed friends in Virginia to assist you."

Bardou eyed Rollo's walking stick as though he knew at once that it concealed a weapon. He did not look particularly concerned of the fact. He removed his cigar from between his teeth, exhaled a stream of smoke, then tossed the butt onto the dock.

"Do you have my papers?" he asked in a gritty, flat-toned voice. His French accent was thicker than Rollo had expected.

He had heard that Bardou was of peasant stock, but had managed to rise in the midst of France's turmoil and had gotten himself passably well-educated. Enough so, Rollo hoped, to ape the manners of a gentleman—particularly a German gentleman. The English aristocracy was gullible enough to be fooled, especially if one claimed kinship to the old Prussian warhorse, General Blücher.

"Everything is in order, sir. If you'll step into the carriage, I will take you to your hotel. I've arranged a suite for you at the Pulteney—finest in the city. The czar even stayed there during his state visit this past summer."

Bardou looked at him in mistrust, then studied the carriage closely and peered inside before getting in.

"It is a strange feeling, is it not, being on enemy ground?" Rollo commented to him in fluent French as the carriage rolled into motion. He pulled out a bottle of wine and two glasses, then poured carefully, offering one to Bardou. "From your homeland. I brought it in your honor. Go on," he urged him with a smile. "Our friends in Virginia would hardly appreciate my poisoning you, Mr. Bardou. I am at your service."

Bardou took it from him skeptically and waited for him to drink first. "You have arranged for my cover?"

"Yes, indeed, sir. You will be meeting London society in the guise of Baron Karl von Dannecker of Prussia. I've found a well-connected young gentleman who is willing to introduce you into the highest circles."

"Funds?"

"In the account. It has all been arranged."

For a long moment, Bardou gazed out the carriage window as they crossed Westminster Bridge. "And my Sophia," he asked more softly, "is she still in London?"

"I saw her at Vauxhall a week ago. Beautiful as ever." Rollo sighed.

"What is this Vauxhall?" Bardou asked gravely.

"Pleasure gardens on the river. It has a theater, dancing, fireworks. I'll show it to you. Most diverting."

"I will need Sophia," he said. "She is always . . . useful."

Rollo furrowed his brow. Claude Bardou had been hired by a powerful group of enraged gentlemen-planters, friends of President Madison, who wanted revenge on the redcoats for the burning of Washington. Though America's gold coffers were empty thanks to the British blockade, the pride of the Southern gentlemen had been so incensed at the humiliation of having their shiny new capitol burned that they were paying for Bardou's services out of their own personal fortunes, which they had built on the backs of their African slaves. Rollo did not know how the Virginians would feel about Bardou's bringing in outside help.

"Mr. Bardou, with all respect, your fee has already been negotiated. Do you really think Madam Voznesensky will agree to help?"

"Sophia will do as I tell her." Bardou met his gaze, needing no words to suggest that Rollo had best do the same. He took another sip of his wine.

Rollo blanched at the deadened look in the man's pale blue eyes. A change of subject was most definitely in order. "Where did you learn to speak German?" he asked awkwardly.

"Westphalia. I was in charge of protecting King Jerome for a while."

"Ah, Napoleon's baby brother, correct?"

Bardou nodded. "Do you know a Lord Lucien Knight, Mr. Greene?"

Rollo did not know what prompted him to lie, but when his gut told him to do something, he did it. He shook his head. "Heard of him, don't know him. Why do you ask?"

Bardou just looked at him, his face brutal in the fleeting glow of a street lamp that the carriage passed.

There was another awkward pause. Rollo cleared his throat, getting the message clearly enough that he was not to ask too many questions. He liked it not. He forced himself to gather his nerve. "Mr. Bardou, when will I be allowed to know your plan exactly?"

Bardou considered his question, gazing out the window as they drove past Westminster Abbey. "Fifteen years of service," he murmured, "and now I cannot go home. I would be tried and executed. I did nothing wrong. I served my country. Do you know what that is like, Mr. Greene? Defeat is a very bitter cup. These proud, arrogant English must taste it."

"Er, yes." *Well, that was neatly evaded,* he thought. He, Rollo, had no real ill feeling toward the English. He had been stationed in London for two years, and though he was a patriot and was angry as any American about the blockade and the burning of Washington, he had developed an affection for the English people in spite of himself. His own ancestors, after all, had been hard-working Cornishmen. He liked their food, their women, and their ale.

Bardou took another sip of his wine. "Your first assignment will be to find me a manufacturer of explosives. You will say that you are an engineer with a rotted bridge that must be demolished before it can be built anew. You will be placing an order for saltpeter. I will tell you the quantity after I have seen the targets."

"Oh, you have already chosen the targets?" he asked in surprise. "What are they?"

Bardou just smiled coldly at him.

CHAPTER SEVEN

Alice was already awake, dressed, and eager to start the day when the maid arrived, right on schedule, but instead of bringing her breakfast tray, the plump servant bore the news that His Lordship had ordered Miss was not to be served anymore in her rooms. *Ah, so he has resorted to starving me out,* Alice thought with a low laugh. She could barely wait to see how shocked he would be by her obliging mood.

They went downstairs into the entrance hall, where the maid handed her over to the liveried hall porter posted by the door.

"I will take you to His Lordship, miss." The manservant bowed to Alice and opened the front door. "This way."

"He's outside?"

"His Lordship is training in his studio, as he does every morning," he said politely. "Shall I fetch your wrap?"

"Is it a far walk?"

"No, miss."

"Then lead on."

With a nod, he escorted her outside. The morning was bright and chilly and full of promise. She rubbed her arms, a puff of steam misting from her lips when she spoke. "What sort of studio is it exactly?"

"An athletic studio, miss. My lord practices his swordsmanship there, as well as his boxing."

"Boxing! My goodness, I am sure it is not proper for me to go there!" A young lady did not enter the very temple of masculine prowess. It was Sunday morning—she should have been going to church, not to a bachelor's private boxing studio!

The footman slid her a glum look of sympathy. "Nevertheless, miss, it is where he has ordered your breakfast to be served."

Indeed, he was once more throwing down the gauntlet, luring her like the mouse she was toward scandalous freedom with a bit of cheese. With a shrug of annoyance at herself, she acknowledged her curiosity to see a world that other young ladies would never glimpse and followed the footman without further comment. He led her across the graveled courtyard and along the drive that wound around the house. The gardeners were hard at work, pruning the sculpted bushes that adorned the house and trimming back the ivy that clung to the red brick walls. They tipped their hats to her as she followed the footman away from the house and down the sloping drive that curved through green meadows dotted with horses and acres of harvested alfalfa fields where towering golden hayricks stood like fortresses. Beyond the fields, the trees at the edge of the woods stood sunning their luxuriant autumn colors.

The earthy stable smells carried to her on the breeze as Alice hurried after the footman, her anticipation building as they neared the impressive stable complex, built of the same red brick as the house. The main building had a small, elegant cupola gracing the roof; a few of Lucien's pampered horses had stuck their fine heads out of their carved stall windows, as if to have a look at what was going on in the world this day. Chewing mouthfuls of hay with comical expressions of friendly equine curiosity, they watched Alice pass.

She paused to admire the king of the horses when they came to the paddock and saw a groom exercising the magnificent black stallion on a lunge line. Rippling with velvety muscle, the black seemed to float with every dream-smooth stride. Awed by the animal's noble grandeur, she reluctantly left her spot by the white-fenced paddock and followed the footman toward another square outbuilding of medium size, with high windows. Even before the servant opened the door to Lucien's studio, Alice heard the fierce, metallic clash of swords.

A foreign-accented male voice punctuated the morning stillness, firing out regular, sharp calls. The footman opened the door and held it for her. Alice hesitated, but when she peeked around the door, her gaze fell at once upon the table laden with pastries and a gleaming silver tea service. Ah—the bait! Her sense of decorum wailed for her not to go in, but she was determined to overcome her timidity, which people like Caro mistook for pristine virtue. Lucien had been the first to see through her. Bracing herself, Alice walked into the studio, trying to appear as nonchalant as though she were walking into a milliner's shop.

The swarthy swordmaster and the five, aristocratic young rakes training with Lucien barely flicked a glance her way, as though they had been warned in advance that she would be joining them and that they were to ignore her. Nor did her entrance break Lucien's deadly concentration. She caught a glimpse of his face and saw his fierce silver eyes, brilliant as diamonds afire, while the morning sunlight flashed on his sword.

Keeping well out of the way, she edged self-consciously around the perimeter of the studio to the table where her breakfast waited. An attendant pulled a chair over to the table for her while Alice poured herself a cup of tea from the spigoted urn. She did her best to appear perfectly cool-nerved, as though butterflies were not dancing in her stomach. If only she could control her blushes! Spooning some sugar into her tea, she stilled the trembling of her hand by dint of will and picked up her saucer and teacup, turning to watch the gentlemen with a polite expression; but at the sight of Lucien, she sank down onto the wooden chair a moment later, feeling a trifle weak-kneed.

If this was the savagery he brought to his practice, she never wanted to see him fight in earnest, she thought as the metallic staccato of clashing blades rang out through the studio. The swarthy Spanish fencing master stood off to the side, giving instructions and curt orders. Lucien's angular face was fixed in deadly concentration as he danced through the positions of the master's wheel in elegant violence, pushing himself to the limit. The five young men training with him were posted at regular spaces around the outer circle. Lucien kept each of them on the defensive, engaging each one smoothly, weaving back and forth between opponents with dazzling speed, seeming never to have his back turned to any of them.

He was dripping with sweat, his snug black breeches hugging every line of his athletic legs and disappearing into his smart black boots. He wore a protective leather vest over his loose white shirt. The straps molded over his powerful shoulders and cinched at the sides of his lean waist. Alice didn't realize she had been holding her breath, but she exhaled at last when the drill was done.

Lucien saluted his opponents carelessly and handed off his weapon, his chest heaving. The sword master congratulated him on an excellent performance. Alice waited for him in anticipation, but instead of coming toward her, he walked over to a bench on the other side of the athletic studio, sat on the end of it, and picked up a large iron dumbbell, curling his right hand up again and again while he braced his elbow against his inner thigh.

Oh, my, she thought in admiration. When he let the dumbbell clatter to the floor again, she watched him reach his arms over his head, stretching his shoulders with the luxurious ease of a great cat. After working his left arm in turn, he pressed up lightly from the bench and accepted a small towel from the waiting servant, blotting his face with it while he received a few instructional remarks from the sword master. He towered over the man by half a foot, she noticed.

Alice waited with growing impatience, wondering if he meant to ignore her entirely. But why would he force her to join him here if he was still too angry to speak to her for her cold words yesterday? Realizing she was openly staring, she tore her gaze away and turned her attention to the five young men. They, too, were lifting weights and doing various exercises, though in much more leisurely fashion, joking with each other as they worked. She wondered who they were. A couple of them looked vaguely familiar; she wondered if she knew them from Town or if she had merely seen them in the Grotto. When three of them furtively glanced her way and lowered their voices, she realized they were discussing her.

She quickly looked away, hoping in belated mortification that they did not mistake her curious glance at them for immodest gawking.

Just when she was beginning to despair that he was indifferent to her presence, Lucien nodded his thanks to the sword master and crossed the studio to her, patting his neck with the towel before tossing it over his shoulder. Alice let her gaze travel over him as he swaggered toward her with a guarded look and lustrous fire in his eyes.

"Miss Montague, what an unexpected pleasure." Another attendant handed him a water canteen as he passed the man.

"And a most impressive display," she answered with an arch smile as he joined her.

"Thanks." He pulled out the cork and took a swallow, tilting his head back. Even his throat gleamed with sweat, his Adam's apple moving up and down rhythmically as he drank. She watched it in fascination until he finished and licked his wet lips.

"I would like," he said, "for you to visit someone with me today."

"Whom?"

"Wise old man," he said with a faint twinkle in his silvery eyes. "I have another half hour before I'm through here. You will stay and watch so I can make sure you're not getting into trouble. Agreed?"

Alice said nothing, dismayed by the pleasure she took in his order. He untied the straps holding his protective leather vest in place and lifted it off over his head. She bit her lip and tried to look away as he handed off the vest to the attendant. The sight of his thin white shirt clinging to his sweat-dampened skin, the musky, overwhelmingly male scent of him stirred something primal in her blood. He cast her a wink and turned away, returning to his men for the next phase of their regimen.

The sword master was replaced with a squat, tough, grumpy-looking man who proved to be the boxing coach, a veteran pugilist. *Oh, dear,* she thought with a wince. Fencing practice was one matter, but she wasn't sure she could bear to watch Lucien and his men bruising and beating and pounding each other senseless. Then Lucien peeled off his shirt and her mind went blank.

With an artist's fascination and a woman's desire, she stared, mesmerized by the play of bronzed muscle across his back. His arms were huge, his chest smooth, sculpted, gleaming. He began winding a length of leather around and around his knuckles to dull the impact of his fists.

It occurred to her that, for all her art lessons, she had never had the opportunity to sketch that most classical of subjects, the male nude. Before she had come to Revell Court, the very thought would have made her reach for her smelling salts, but ever since she had met Lucien Knight, anything seemed possible.

As their boxing drills started, she flinched at the violence, but it did little good to look away, for the sounds were inescapable and somehow worse—the hard thud of leather-wrapped knuckles connecting with flesh; the low, rough grunt of a man taking a blow to the belly; the Cockney accent of the old fighter ruthlessly urging the youngbloods on. Lucien flattened "West" with a neat clip in the chin. Though the lad got up grinning, she vowed she would never let Harry try his "morleys" in this sport when he grew up, no more than she would ever allow him to join the army.

The red-haired lad they called South was the next contender. He charged into the square and managed to land a blow on Lucien's cheek before he, in turn, was on the floor. This was repeated several times before Alice could no longer stand it.

She jumped to her feet. "Stop!"

Every man went motionless and looked over at her in perplexity.

"You really should stop before someone gets hurt," she said awkwardly, turning red.

Lucien exchanged a mirthful look with the old prizefighter as the boys cleared their throats and swallowed their chuckles. He walked toward her, brushing the sweat off his brow with his forearm. She could not help but let her gaze travel down his gleaming chest. She turned even redder.

"No one's going to get hurt, love. It's just a sport," he said, catching his breath.

"It's brutal."

"But a man must do it so he may stand and defend his lady's honor," he said, his eyes sparkling. "I am touched beyond words that you should fear for my safety."

"I'm more worried about them," she retorted, nodding toward the lads, who were openly eavesdropping on their exchange. They grinned when she looked over at them.

"Nonsense, you should worry about me," he said indignantly. "I'm outnumbered five to one, and those hellborn babes are all at least five years younger than I. I believe that gives all the advantage to them."

"Well, I don't want to see them thrash you, either!"

He smiled roguishly. "You see? You do care. I think you are beginning to like me in spite of yourself. Now sit down and try to enter into the spirit of the game, girl." He slammed his fisted knuckles together and pivoted, swaggering back to his companions. "She says you're not to hit me in the face, lads. She especially asks that you take care not to bruise my lips."

The young bucks laughed and pretended to be scandalized by her supposed request, while Alice scowled, fighting a smile. *He really was the most provoking man,* she thought. A little sigh escaped her.

Lucien did not know what angel had visited Alice in the middle of the night to plead his cause with her. It seemed some miracle had taken place, for she was actually being nice to him today. This changed matters. If she could find it within herself to take a step toward him, then he was eagerly willing to meet her halfway. Compromise was not a natural part of his makeup, but perhaps it had been a little unreasonable of him to expect the girl to accept him as "Draco" in all his evil glory. He had decided to provide her with a character reference.

After a hasty but thorough bath and a change into fresh clothes, he led her through the woods on the same path they had trod yesterday. It was a good deal muddier after the rain. They were bound for the tiny hamlet of cottages in the valley to visit his elderly, boyhood tutor, Seymour Whitby.

If Lucien's pace was slower today, it was because every muscle in his body was already feeling the extra effort he had put into his training. Knowing that Bardou was out there somewhere had driven him to push himself to the limit—and of course, *she* had been watching. He had been aware of her gaze clamped on him from the second she had tiptoed into his studio. He had been sure she would lock herself in her chamber and pout all day, but he had managed to hide his exultation at her arrival. The ruse had worked.

The hungry admiration in her stare had filled him with lusty pleasure. *It was shameless how he craved her attention,* he thought, *but there seemed no remedy for it.* He had wanted to treat her with a certain distance today, but one look into her Chartres-blue eyes had dissolved all his resolution. Merely being near her helped to ease the knot in his stomach about Bardou.

As they marched through the woods in companionable silence, he slung the leather bag of books up higher onto his sore left shoulder. It contained the latest tomes he had ordered for Mr. Whitby from his favorite London bookseller. Alice, meanwhile, carried the basket containing half a dozen muffins and a sponge cake, as well as a jar of the mineral waters from the hot springs beneath Revell Court. Mr. Whitby was a firm believer in taking the waters. Its medicinal effects, he said, worked wonders for his arthritis.

They stopped briefly at the limestone outcropping, as they had yesterday, to enjoy the view. The sky had turned overcast. It looked like rain. As they gazed at the valley, side by side, he sensed her nervousness, as though standing on this spot reminded her afresh of how passionately she had kissed him.

He slid a hopeful, sideward glance at her, more than willing to endure another, but if she felt his gaze, she did not turn to him. He smiled to himself, studying her in soft delight. Such graceful, long lashes. Her lips were the color of a dewy pink rose. Seized with the desire to sweep her into his arms once again, he quickly reined himself in, keeping a firm grip on his impulses, for he was determined not to do anything wrong. Today he was bent on showing her what a very good boy he could be when he chose.

She turned and walked back to the path. He followed obediently.

"Lucien?" she asked in a thoughtful tone.

The sound of his name on her tongue swept him with shivery sensations of pleasure like the tickling breeze. "Yes?"

"May I ask you something?"

"Yes," he cautiously agreed, steadying her by her dainty gloved hand as she stepped up onto a fallen log that barred their path.

She hopped off it, the basket swinging in her grasp. "I'm curious. Why did your father leave Revell Court to you and nothing to Lord Damien?"

"Actually, Damien is to be made an earl by virtue of our father's bloodlines."

"Really?" she exclaimed.

"Yes. As I mentioned, Carnarthen had no legitimate heir. He was so devoted to my illustrious mother, Georgiana, that he never married—four-hundred-year-old lineage be damned. She was the love of his life. He refused to marry another. At any rate, he had a great many friends in the House of Lords who saw his situation and said to themselves, "There but for the grace of God, go I." They rallied together after his death to petition the Crown that a new title be created to ensure that even if the name of Carnarthen would be lost, the ancient bloodlines would not. As Damien is older than me by twelve minutes, the title will go to him. Of course, the decision was influenced by Damien's fame as a decorated war hero and his reputation for courage and integrity—not to mention his private assurance to the prime minister that he and his descendants can be counted upon to vote Tory for three generations."

"I see. Lord Carnarthen must have been mad over your mother to forsake his heritage for love," Alice said in a tone of awe.

"He was. He had met her when she was a young girl, before she wed the duke of Hawkscliffe, but he overlooked her. He told me the story when he was dying last year."

"Oh, I'm sorry."

"Thank you. It was for the best. He was very ill."

"It's good that you were with him. Was Damien by his bedside, too?"

"No, Damien could not leave the Peninsula. Besides, Damien prefers to ignore our true parentage and simply pretend that he is really Hawkscliffe's son."

She gave him a sympathetic wince.

"I prefer the truth. Would you like to hear their story?"

"Yes, very much."

"Georgiana had a year at the Sorbonne to finish her education before her debut. Edward—that was Carnarthen's name—was a twenty-one-year-old dandy on Grand Tour. He first saw my mother one sunny afternoon when she was taking an art lesson with her classmates in the garden at Versailles."

"How romantic," she murmured with a smile.

"Yes, but unfortunately, he paid her little attention, too busy chasing French courtesans. The next time he saw her, she was a fast young Society wife. He realized he had made the mistake of his life, letting her get away. They were meant to be together, but of course it was too late." He did not mention aloud the exhortation that Carnarthen had given him at the crux of this conversation: *When you find the one, my lad, grab her up in your arms and never let her go. You may never get another chance.* "He begged her to divorce Hawkscliffe," Lucien continued, "but she would not because she knew the duke would have kept her children. She had Robert and Jack at that point. At any rate, Damien and I were born. Hawkscliffe had his various mistresses; Georgiana had Carnarthen. Things continued quietly that way until Damien and I were four years old."

"What happened then?"

"Carnarthen was a high-ranking navy man, you see. He had to go off to sea from time to time for long periods. When I was four, he came back to find that my mother had comforted herself in his absence with—"

Alice gasped. "Her husband, the duke?"

"No. No, that would have been much too tame for Georgiana," he said drily. "This time, it was Sir Phillip Preston Lawrence of Drury Lane, a Shakespearean actor renowned for his looks more than his talent. Once more, Georgiana was in the family way."

"Gracious!" she said, blushing.

"Do you know my younger brother, Lord Alec?"

"Of course," Alice said. "Everyone does. My friend, Freddie Foxham, does not buy a waistcoat until he finds out whether or not Lord Alec approves of the tailor."

"Yes, that's Alec. It is that showman's blood," he said with a chuckle. "You would do well to warn your friend never to let Alec beguile him into sitting down with him at cards. Alec is a cardsharp with the devil's own luck."

"I will," she answered with a smile. "You have an interesting family. But I wonder, does it bother you at all that Lord Damien will be made an earl and you won't?"

"Not at all," he said at once. "He deserves it. Besides, I'm quite used to being in Damien's shadow. I don't really mind it."

"Lucien," she protested. "I'm sure you're not at all in his shadow."

"Of course I am. You're just being polite. I always have been." He stopped to wait for her as she negotiated her way around a slippery patch of mud.

"Lucien, really."

"It's true. Ask anyone. There's Damien and 'the other one.' I'm 'the other one.' I don't really mind—only, I admit, it does render one a bit redundant."

With a soft, tender laugh, she caught up to him and laid her hand on his back, caressing him as she came up beside him. "I don't think you are at all redundant. If it's any consolation, to me, Damien will always be the other one."

"Why, it is, Miss Montague." He flashed her a rueful grin. "It is a very great consolation, indeed."

"Good." She gave him a pert smile, the dappled shadows of the leaves playing over her smooth ivory skin, then walked on ahead of him. "Now, come along."

"What about you?"

"What about me?"

"Tell me something no one else knows about Alice Montague."

She cast him a wry look. "You mean a deep dark secret?"

"Yes, exactly!"

"Sorry, I don't have one."

Lucien smiled and marched on, swallowing the remark before he uttered it that he had more than enough for them both.

"Tell me something good, then. Tell me the best day you ever had."

"That's easy. My tenth birthday party. My father gave me my first horse—not a pony—which meant I was terribly grown up. Everyone was there."

"Everyone?"

"Mother, Papa, Phillip, Nanny Peg." She shrugged. "It was my last birthday before my mother got sick."

Sensing the carefully controlled grief in her voice, he snapped his head up. "What happened to her?"

When she glanced at him, her sad, faraway smile twisted his heart. "She was a vibrant, active, beautiful woman, thirty-six years old, but one day, she got a cough that grew worse and worse, until a few months later, she couldn't even walk up a flight of stairs without gasping for breath. The doctors did not know what to make of it. First they thought it was consumption, then pleurisy, though she had none of the other symptoms of either disease. Finally, they discovered it was a concealed tumor in the breast that had spread into her lungs. There was nothing they could do. They gave her hemlock for the pain. It only made her sicker."

"I am so very sorry, Alice," he said softly, stricken.

"Me, too. She was a woman of humor and grace to the very end. I still remember sitting on her bedside, reading the Society column of the *Morning Post* to her. She would make jokes about the ton and tell me how grand I would be when I made my debut." She paused. "My father died two years later in a fall from a horse he should not have been riding, over a jump he should not have attempted, especially after drinking an entire bottle of blue ruin."

Lucien stopped and stared at her. She flicked a hesitant glance over him, as though uncertain whether or not to say more.

"Go on," he urged her softly.

"Papa fell apart after she died. They had been very much in love. I think he was glad to go. I miss them so." She looked away. "I can still see all of them when I look at Harry—in his eyes. I am so glad I have him, Lucien. I would do anything for him." Her voice broke on her final words, and tears welled in her eyes.

"I know you would," he whispered, pulling her brusquely into his arms. He held her hard for a long moment while the brown, dead leaves scattered around them on the breeze. Closing his eyes, he pressed a fervent kiss to her hair.

Something profound changed inside him at that moment, as he held her. He wasn't sure what it was. One second he was praying for some way to take away her pain, and the next he felt as though a sledgehammer had just knocked a gaping hole in the biggest, thickest wall that he had built around his heart. Light poured through—aching, nourishing light.

He pulled back from her a small space and captured her delicate face between his hands, lifting her gaze to his. With his thumbs, he wiped away the tears that had rolled down her cheeks.

"If you ever need anything, anything at all," he whispered fiercely, "I want you to come to me. Do you understand?"

"Oh, Lucien—" she started, trying to pull away.

He held her in a firm, gentle grip. "I mean it. You don't have to be alone. I am your friend, and I will always be there for you. And Harry."

"Why?" she whispered with a shaky trace of defiance. "What do you care?"

Her question reminded him anew that she was still nowhere near trusting him. He shook his head, his slick eloquence failing him once again with her. "Because I like you," he said simply.

"You barely know me."

"I know enough. You don't have to believe me right now, Alice. In time you'll see it's true. Come," he said gruffly, forcing himself to release her from his embrace after a moment's awkward pause. He was shaken by the ferocity of his desire to protect her from all harm. "We're almost there."

Still reeling with his astonishing vow, Alice followed a moment later. Lucien marched ahead of her down the path—broad-shouldered, masterful, an air of command in his long strides. His focus on her was apparently intensifying, and she did not know whether to be terrified or overjoyed. She wouldn't have believed his oath of loyalty at all, except for the fact that he had extended his protectiveness to include Harry. That, she had not expected.

They came out of the woods onto a dirt road that curved toward a cluster of five or six cottages a short distance away. The smell of a welcoming hearth fire carried to them on the wind, which had picked up and went whisking through the branches. They had been shielded from it in the woods, she thought. Holding down the checked cloth that covered the basket to prevent it from blowing away, she glanced at the leaden clouds rolling in from the west, then noticed the restlessness of the crows that flapped across the sky, which had turned a bleak whitish-gray.

"We shan't stay long," Lucien murmured. "It looks like rain."

She nodded. Arriving in the quaint hamlet, Lucien led her to a charming wattle-and-daub cottage with a thick thatched roof and neat white shutters. He let her in through the waist-high gate and escorted her up the walkway lined with chrysanthemums. He knocked on the door but did not wait to be admitted. Instead, he opened it and leaned in, glancing inside. "Mr. Whitby?"

"Ah, young Master Lucien," said a weak, wobbly, and very proper old voice from within. "In here! Do forgive me, I must have dozed off."

Trying to peek in behind him, Alice could see little past the breadth of his shoulders.

"I am sorry to wake you," he said fondly.

"Not at all, dear boy, not at all."

"Your books have arrived, and," Lucien announced, "I have brought someone to meet you."

"Oh?"

He opened the door wider and stepped aside, passing an elegant gesture before him, inviting Alice into the house. Full of curious anticipation, she stepped past him into the cottage and promptly found herself in the shrewd, bespectacled gaze of a frail old man hunched down in a cushioned armchair.

"Mr. Whitby, may I present Miss Alice Montague, the daughter of Baron Glenwood. Miss Montague, it gives me great pleasure to present to you the hero of my wretched boyhood," Lucien said sardonically, "my most esteemed tutor, Mr. Seymour Whitby."

Alice curtseyed to him. "How do you do, sir?"

Through a grave effort, leaning on his cane, Mr. Whitby doddered to his feet. Alice started to protest at his taking the trouble to rise at her entrance, but Lucien touched her arm and shook his head. Her heart clenched as she realized—a gentleman always remained a gentleman, even if he did appear to be a hundred years old. She walked over to the old man and steadied him on the pretext of shaking his hand. He squeezed her hand, leaning on her.

"I am so pleased to meet you, sir," she said warmly.

He lifted his chin and peered sharply at her through his spectacles. The flat line of his mouth slowly pulled into a heartfelt smile. "La, child, you are as kind as you are pretty. May I offer you some tea? I am afraid at the moment my housekeeper is at church, but I think we can manage—I say, do shut the door, Master Lucien."

"Sorry," he mumbled with a boyish smile, shoving the door closed.

"I have been trying to teach the lad that for twenty-five years," Mr. Whitby told Alice, his blue eyes twinkling. "Calculus, Greek—these, he masters in a glance, but the boy cannot learn to shut the door."

Alice chuckled and cast Lucien a smile, quite beguiled. The old gentleman adjusted his gnarled fingers over the head of his cane.

"Mr. Whitby had the unenviable position of tutoring me and all of my brothers before we went off to school," Lucien said.

"What a task that must have been!" she exclaimed.

"Hercules had his twelve labors; I, my five young Knights."

She laughed, charmed. "Well, I shall be most keenly interested to hear some of your tales, but do please sit down. I think some tea would be lovely. You must allow me to prepare it. I insist. We've brought muffins and a sponge cake to tempt you with, and your pupil has brought you some books. Here, why don't you take a pillow, Mr. Whitby? Lucien, hand me that cushion from the couch." He quickly did so. She put the pillow behind the old man's back as he eased down once more into his chair. "Are you near enough to the fire? Lucien, move his chair."

"Oh, dear, I'm sure I don't wish to be any trouble," Mr. Whitby protested, clearly delighted by her fussing over him.

"Not at all," she scolded gently.

Lucien caught her gaze for a second and sent her a deep, soulful look of appreciation before moving to do her bidding. He slid his old tutor's armchair nearer to the fire, then pulled the cushioned ottoman closer and sat down on it, shuffling out the books. As the men began to discuss the books, Alice made her way to Mr. Whitby's kitchen and found the large water cauldron standing over the very low fire, just as she would have expected a capable housekeeper to leave it. She found the kitchen bellows nearby and stoked the fire to get the water boiling again. Caro would have considered the task impossibly beneath her station, but Alice did not mind. She enjoyed taking care of others.

"Wasn't that wind fierce last night?" Lucien asked the old man as she came back out into the parlor to fetch the tea caddy.

"Why, it blew one of my shutters off the house," Mr. Whitby declared.

"It did? Where?"

"Right there, off the parlor. Mrs. Malone leaned it against the side of the house this morning."

Lucien stood. "I'll go rehang it."

Mr. Whitby protested at his offer, but Lucien waved him off.

Alice smiled at him in approval. "Tea will be ready soon."

"I'll be back in a trice." He sent her an answering smile over his shoulder that warmed her to the core, then closed the door firmly as he went out. She became aware of the blush in her cheeks and the faint smile on her lips only when she noticed Mr. Whitby studying her.

"Well, this is all very curious," the old man said, peering over the rim of his spectacles at her.

"What is, sir?" Trying to hide her embarrassment, she busied herself with the task of laying out the sponge cake and muffins.

"Master Lucien has never brought a young lady to meet me before." He lifted his bushy white eyebrows and regarded her expectantly. "Has he asked you yet?"

"Pardon, sir?"

"Has he offered yet? Proposed, my girl?"

Alice stared at him, taken aback. A jolt of tingling wonder shot through her body. With a tremble, she dropped her gaze, her blush deepening. She dared not explain the strange circumstances that had brought her into Lucien's company. "Mr. Whitby, Lord Lucien and I are little more than friends."

He snorted. "Then you haven't noticed how he looks

at you. Miss Montague. Surely you have not allowed his wily ways to confuse you?"

She looked at him, then smiled with a reluctant sigh. "Everything he does confuses me."

"I will concede the lad has difficulty being straightforward at times, but that is only because he has never been quite sure of his welcome in the world. It is this old business of comparing himself to Master Damien," he said in answer to her questioning look. "He never quite felt up to par, especially having been so ill as a boy, while Damien enjoyed perfect health."

"Lucien was ill?" she asked, taken aback.

"Why, yes, he's lucky to be alive. Did he not tell you?"

She shook her head, wide-eyed.

"Dear, me. He would call me a meddling old fool for speaking of it, but between you and me, he was afflicted with childhood asthma. For much of his early years, it prevented him from keeping up with Damien and the others. He spent a good deal of his time alone—or, in any case, with me. He never learned quite how to fit in, at least not comfortably. But I'll tell you one thing—he got a jolly lot of reading done as a result. He was three years ahead of his classmates in his studies by the time he went off to Eton. Damien may have the muscle, but Lucien's got the brains," he told her with a conspiratorial smile.

She stared at him, quite shocked. "He does not still suffer, does he?"

"No, no. He had outgrown it by the time he reached his teens, thanks to God." He shook his head sadly. "By then, however, certain patterns had been set. Damien had long since appointed himself Lucien's protector—the twins have always been quite devoted to each other—but, as you may imagine, this was rather damaging to

Lucien's pride. Ever since he got well, in all his activities, especially in sports, he has pushed himself relentlessly. It's not enough for him to be equal to other men, no, indeed; for his pride's sake, he must exceed them."

"To prove himself?" she murmured.

"Precisely. So, you see, my dear, you must be very gentle with him and very patient, but I promise you, he will be worth it. He doesn't take to many people, doesn't give his affection easily, but when he does, he is unswerving. Each of my young masters is dear to me, but I admit, Lucien was always my favorite. Heaven knows—" He sighed. "—he needed to be somebody's favorite."

She was still pondering this a moment later when the door opened and Lucien returned, bringing in a gust of wind with him.

"Note that I am shutting the door," he announced, closing it firmly behind him. "Your shutter is fixed, sir. Unfortunately, the weather is turning steadily more foul." He took off his greatcoat and tossed it on the couch.

Alice picked up the tea caddy and hurried back into the kitchen, where the cauldron had come to a low boil. She warmed the china teapot with hot water, then measured out four teaspoonfuls of Ceylon tea, one for each guest and one for the pot. While the tea steeped, she poked around in the unfamiliar kitchen until she found teacups, small plates and spoons, sugar, and milk. In short order, she returned to the parlor, bringing out the tea tray.

Suddenly struck shy, she could not meet Lucien's gaze as she handed him his tea on a saucer. The old man smiled knowingly as he watched them together. Alice sat down and inhaled the steam from her tea, looking on politely as the men discussed the books, but inwardly, she continued mulling over Mr. Whitby's description of Lucien's lonely childhood. Her hands shook slightly with the overwhelming emotion that Mr. Whitby's revelations had roused in her. Realizing now how deeply Lucien had meant those words, *I am alone,* she lifted her gaze slowly from the unknown fortune in the tea leaves to his chiseled face.

He was smiling warmly as he argued with the old man about some theory of Hippocrates's. It did not seem possible, but how much more plainly did she need him to say it? This beautiful, charming man was desperate for someone to love him.

She suddenly felt a lump rise in her throat of sheer remorse for having hurt him yesterday. Now she knew how hard it was for him to reach out to anyone; he had chosen her and what had she done? Deliberately cut him, in her cowardice. It was all she could do to sit still by the fire, fighting the impulse to rush over and hug him for all she was worth. He looked at her suddenly, taking her off guard, for her soul was in her eyes.

"We had better go if we're to stay ahead of the weather." He glanced meaningfully out the window. Blushing, Alice followed his gaze and saw that the day had indeed darkened.

She nodded mutely, doing her best to hide the turmoil of her emotions as they bid Mr. Whitby farewell. Lucien threw another log onto the fire for him; Alice felt moved to give the grandfatherly old fellow a kiss on his papery-thin cheek.

When they stepped outside, Lucien shrugged deeper into his greatcoat and looked uneasily at the sky. "The temperature's dropped. We could be in for a storm. Maybe we should wait it out here."

"Mr. Whitby is tired from our visit, Lucien. I'm sure it's only a bit of rain."

He gave her a brooding look, nodded, and hurried her down the garden path to Mr. Whitby's front gate, where they met Mrs. Malone, the housekeeper, coming back from church. They greeted the woman and left the property, striding down the dirt road side by side.

In the distance, the bells from the country parish church were chiming in restless agitation. The gale was high, carrying in mysterious changes, as though it had come to blow away the old life Alice had known. She turned her face into the fierce, cleansing wind and watched as a crow blew by, screeching and pumping its wings against the current. Then the first raindrops began to pelt them sporadically. They glanced at each other in surprise.

"Come on." Unburdened by books or basket, Lucien took her hand, the wind rippling through his black hair. As the rain began falling faster, they raced hand in hand down the road to the path, then plunged into the darkened woods.

CHAPTER EIGHT

"Come on, come on," he said, pulling her along by her hand. They dashed through the woods, leaping over a fallen log, rushing past the limestone formations that jutted out from the hillside. "Climb!" he urged her, helping her up the steep grade of the path from behind.

The canopy of the trees shaded them at first from the light drizzle. Leaves rushed around her on chilly spirals of air that blasted her in spurts from all directions. The woods turned dark, and as the wind mounted, everything began moving. Trees were blowing, leaves scattering, branches snapping. Alice kept looking at Lucien for reassurance. He strode through the woods with an unflinching stare and an air of power, his black greatcoat billowing behind him. There was something almost supernatural about his self-possession, as though he had summoned the storm himself.

An image flashed through her mind of him as a dauntless soldier, marching into battle amid clouds of black smoke. It comforted her to remind herself that light infantrymen were experts in using the terrain. One of their chief functions was to scout out the land ahead of the regiment's marching columns, discerning safe routes and possible dangers ahead. Clearly, no mere foul weather was going to scare Captain Lucien, but as thunder rumbled in the distance, Alice could not say the same for herself. Growing ever more nervous, she stayed close to him, close enough to feel his body heat. The sky, she noticed, glimpsing it through a parting of the swaying trees above her, had turned the leaden color of his eyes.

They had gone almost half the way to Revell Court when suddenly, without warning, the drizzle turned into a heavy shower. They ran, drenched in minutes by the frigid downpour. It pounded the forest's carpet of leaves with a deafening babel and turned the steep uphill path into a river of mud, up which they went slogging. Alice could not believe they had at least another mile to go before they reached shelter. She was already soaked to the skin, her fur-trimmed coat, her gown, her gloves and boots all thoroughly ruined—as she herself would be if anyone ever found out she had been staying at Lucien Knight's house without a chaperon, she thought grimly. Then a deafening thunderclap exploded right overhead. With a small cry of fright, she lurched instinctively against Lucien.

He put his arm around her, steadying her. "It's all right."

She clung to him, but could barely hear his soft reassurance over the din of wind and thunder. She looked up at him, her face ashen. "Let's hurry!"

He nodded and grasped her hand firmly. The ground leveled out; the path twisted this way and that. On and on, they ran. The wind assailed them like a horde of devils chasing them through the darkened woods, throwing leaves and bits of bark and twigs at them, sending branches crashing onto the path around them. They slowed as they approached the next upward grade, which was as steep as any staircase, stepped with large rocks here and there like islands amid the stream of mud.

Lucien led the way. He climbed the hill ahead of her, turning every few steps to pull her up by the hand. Alice pressed on, clumsy with fear, her teeth chattering in the cold, her face flecked with mud, her knees shaky beneath her. The storm roared through the valley like the bellow of a warlock trapped within the mountain. When a bolt of lightning stabbed down out of the sky at them with a thunderclap that seemed to smash the world in one blow, Alice let out a small scream and jerked sharply in terror, slipping in the slick mud. She felt herself lose her footing and screamed Lucien's name.

Just out of arm's reach ahead of her, he whirled around as she lost her balance. She caught only a glimpse of his horrified expression as she fell backwards and crashed down the hill, rolling through the mud. She felt her knee bump a rock, but what stopped her fall was a slender tree trunk on the side of the path. Her left shoulder rammed it with a jolt that knocked the breath out of her.

Lucien was there in an instant, scrambling down to her with astonishing agility as she lay crumpled on her side, the rain pounding her stunned face.

"Alice!" He dropped to his knees beside her. The instant he touched her, she was able to breathe again.

She sucked in a sharp gulp of air and looked at him in a mix of fear and abject humiliation. His face was white, his expression fierce.

"Don't move. Just breathe," he said in forced calm.

Her next inhalation trembled with the threat of tears.

She pushed herself up to a seated position, looking around in revulsion at the mud and slimy leaves that stuck to her.

"Don't sit up—"

"I'm *filthy*!"

"Thank God you didn't break your neck," he whispered. "Did you hit your head?"

"No, my shoulder," she said, her lips trembling. She reached over and grasped her left shoulder, massaging it.

"Let me check to see if it's broken," he ordered curtly.

She whimpered a little as he palpated her shoulder joint and collarbone up to the base of her neck with intense concentration on the task. His hard face streamed with rain, and his breath misted in a cloud. Alice watched him in a state of misery. She felt like such a fool. She was covered in mud from head to toe.

Relief slowly eased the taut set of his mouth. "Where else does it hurt?"

"My knee."

She was too shaken to object when he pulled her skirt up over her knees. His lips pursed, and Alice looked at him in fear upon seeing the bloody stain that had seeped through her white stocking at her right knee.

"Can you move it?"

She gingerly bent her knee a few times, then nodded at him.

"You must have just given it a good bang." Looking up from her limb, Lucien met her gaze and saw the tears in her eyes. His expression instantly softened. "Sweeting," he whispered, gathering her into his arms. "Shh, don't cry." As he held her, sheltering her from the rain and storm, she could feel his heart pounding. "Lord, you gave me such a fright." Pulling back, he produced a soggy handkerchief from inside of his waistcoat. He wiped away the mud that streaked her face while she gazed somberly at him. She felt his hand trembling slightly as he dabbed the rain out of her eyes. "Put your arms around me," he ordered gruffly.

By his tone and the way he avoided her gaze, Alice wondered if he was disgusted or angry at her for her ineptitude, but was too chagrined to ask. She obeyed without argument. He lifted her into his arms and stood. Narrowing his eyes with a look of resolution, he studied the ascent for a moment, then began carrying her up the hill, climbing with sure strides and tireless strength. At first, she was nervous, though she doubted she could have managed the hill with her knee so badly bruised and cut; in moments, she realized that she was in good hands. She stared in wonder as the ground passed swiftly beneath her. Lucien bowed his head against the rain, but she felt the supple power of his muscled body working all around her, bearing her safely through the wind and storm.

She stared at him in grateful awe. His cheeks were flushed with the cold, and his black hair was soaked. At the top of the hill, he paused for a moment, catching his breath; then, squinting his eyes against the rain, he continued the march with renewed vigor. With her arms wrapped around his neck, she rested her head against his broad shoulder and nestled against him a little closer with each thunderclap. At last, they reached the lookout rock. Alice furrowed her brow as he walked toward it.

"Lucien, I would really rather not admire the view just now—"

"Hush. Be still."

The rain needled her as it blew across the face of the hill. She knew the wet limestone was surely slick beneath his feet as he stalked out onto the outcropping. Before she could ask what he was doing, he started down a precarious little track that wrapped around the lookout rock. She had not noticed it before. The grade was almost vertical. Her eyes widened and she clung around his neck, for below them was the dropoff into the valley. She glanced over the edge in dizzying fear, able now to see the landing nestled beneath the lookout rock, which was apparently their destination. *Shelter, yes,* she thought, *but dear God, if he slipped, if he made one false move, they would both be dead.* Alone, perhaps he could have stopped his fall, but with her in his arms, they would both be lost over the precipice.

Lucien seemed unconcerned. She held her breath for two or three more hair-raising moments, until he had braced his foot on a rock and eased down onto the landing.

When he set her down gently on her feet in the safety of the landing, Alice glared up at him, too scared after their brush with death even to scold him.

"Look," he said, gesturing to a spot behind her, his silvery eyes shining, his face flecked with mud.

She turned around and saw that the landing gave way to the drafty mouth of a cave. The lookout rock formed its overhanging roof.

"It connects with Revell Court by way of the Grotto," Lucien explained, breathing heavily. "It's dark as the grave, God knows, but at least it will keep us out of the elements. How's the shoulder feeling?"

"Sore."

He frowned at her, then ducked into the mouth of the cave and lit a waiting lantern while she stood shivering, soaked through to the skin. He lifted the lantern in one hand and held out his other hand to her.

"Do you think you can walk, or shall I carry you?"

"I can walk. My knee doesn't hurt too badly."

"Lean on me if you need me. It'll be about twenty minutes more."

"It's so dark," Alice murmured, slipping her arm through his as she peered into the hollow limestone corridor. The dim glow of his lantern barely provided a foot's visibility ahead.

"Don't be frightened," he whispered. As an afterthought, he took off his greatcoat and wrapped it around her.

"Lucien, you need your coat," she protested. "You'll catch your death—"

"Hush. Your teeth are chattering. Let's go. Stay close."

She obeyed, savoring his body heat that still clung to the heavy woolen coat.

"Watch your step," he said, lifting the lantern higher.

They disappeared into the hole in the earth as though the mountain had swallowed them. They forged on, laboring along through the damp, slimy recesses of the cave. Alice cringed against him when she heard creatures fluttering aloft. She did not need to ask what they were.

"What is your favorite song?" Lucien asked cheerfully, sensing her uneasiness.

"Er, I don't know. Why?"

"Well, to the best of my knowledge, every young lady of breeding must have at least one good song in her repertoire for showing off her musical talents at dinner parties. I'm sure you've been put through that ordeal at some point, Miss Montague."

Alice managed a smile. "I assure you, when there is a call for such drawing room entertainments, I flee."

"You can't be worse than me. I'm tone-deaf."

"I don't believe that!"

"Very well—I'm lying," he admitted with a roguish half smile. "Truly, you dislike singing?"

"I have nothing against singing or music of any kind. All I object to is public humiliation."

He laughed, and she smiled at the sound. It bounced off the pressing walls of the cave and rolled down the lightless corridor ahead of them with a jolly echo.

"Or private humiliation," she added in chagrin, glancing up at his face, warm gold in the lantern light. "Such as tumbling down the hill like Jack and Jill."

He chuckled and put his arm around her shoulders. "There, there, poor dear," he murmured, giving her a gentle caress. "I'm just thankful you weren't seriously hurt. Sing me a song to pass the time."

"Absolutely not. One humiliation in front of you is quite galling enough. Lucien, how many bats do you think live in this cave? Hundreds?" She swallowed hard as something black and screeching swooped just over their heads. "Thousands?"

Instead of answering, he began to sing softly to her. His voice was low and as rich as a warm mug of chocolate. It was the sweetest song she had ever heard, with a wistful melody and lyrics about a troubadour-knight returning from the Crusades to his ladylove. She listened, enchanted, soon forgetting all about the darkness and bats, the bone-chilling cold, and even her throbbing shoulder. He sang the last verse and came to the end, the tender strains echoing down the tunnel in a whisper.

Alice gazed at him by the light of the lantern. After a moment, he stole a sideward glance at her full of an almost boyish uncertainty, but when he read the adoring look in her smile, his eyes danced.

She clasped his hand between hers. "Sing me another."

"I would, my dear, but we're here."

She tore her gaze from his handsome face to the darkness ahead. As he raised the lantern, she saw that their way was barred by a large wooden door, fitted snugly into the rock. Lucien freed his hand gently from her grasp and walked over to it. He reached up into a small natural chink in the cave wall, feeling around until he produced a key. He unlocked the door and let her inside.

A prickle of realization ran down her spine as it occurred to her abruptly that this tunnel was a possible escape route from Revell Court, should she choose to use it. When the weather cleared, perhaps tomorrow, she could sneak away while Lucien was practicing his swordsmanship in his studio with his men. Her heart pounded at the thought, which suddenly seemed traitorous. She knew she could make her way down to the Grotto from the house. From there, she could unlock the door to the tunnel, just as he had, and flee out into the world beyond. She could get help in the hamlet where Mr. Whitby's cottage lay and surely find someone who would take her to the nearest stagecoach inn, which, in turn, would convey her home to Glenwood Park and to Harry.

Sobered by the idea, she glanced furtively over her shoulder as they walked down the remainder of the tunnel toward the Grotto. Then she looked rather guiltily at him. He was studying her with a shrewd and penetrating gaze. She realized he had seen her glance back at the door. Looking into her eyes, he seemed to read her thoughts of possible escape, as if he knew exactly what she was thinking, but he said not a word.

As they stepped out into the Grotto, the memory of her erotic dream about Lucien blazed at once in her mind in all its lush, wanton detail. Blushing fiercely, Alice avoided meeting his gaze. He gave her a look of subtle reproach, then walked ahead of her, carrying the lamp toward the great carving of the dragon.

Surely he had known going into the tunnel that she would conceive of it as a possible escape route, she thought. But then she realized he had taken that risk in favor of sheltering her from the elements. With the sweet spell of his song still sliding through her veins, Alice looked around at the Grotto. Shafts of pearl-gray daylight penetrated the soaring space from small chinks in the high, rocky dome, through which the rain also leaked in thread-thin cascades. The shafts of light played upon the swirling, mistlike steam over the hot springs. The rhythmic trickle of the rain dripping in echoed softly through the vast cavern, a serene and lulling music. Though she had seen the Grotto before, it all looked, or rather *felt*, totally different to her.

It was as though, having stepped out of the subterranean tunnel, she had come out into a new world, seemingly the same, but entirely new—or perhaps she was seeing it through new eyes. This was not a den of evil, but a cave of sacred mysteries, she thought, her gaze traveling over the whimsical carving of the dragon and the tall Corinthian pillars.

She looked at Lucien, who had just finished lighting all the tapers in a tall, metal candle stand. He carried the flaming candelabra over and placed it by the bubbling hot springs.

"What are you doing?" Alice asked cautiously.

"Ahem, how shall I say this tactfully?" Turning to her, he pulled off his ruined leather gloves with a look of thought. "My dear Miss Montague, your teeth are chattering. You have been shivering for the past half hour, you hurt your shoulder, and you're covered in mud. You, my dear, are going in the water."

Her eyes widened. She glanced at the great pool in the center of the Grotto, then back at him. "That water?"

"The same."

"But Lucien—"

"Expediency, Alice. I will not argue this. These mineral waters have all the same healing properties as those at Bath. Now, doff those wet clothes before you catch your death—and see that you clean those cuts well. I will leave you in privacy to go fetch you some soap, towels, and dry clothes. I presume you brought an extra gown? The maid should know what you'll need from among your personal effects." He turned and began striding away with a look of resolve.

"But, Lucien."

When he paused and looked back at her, she could not miss the haunted look of longing in his silvery eyes. "What?" he asked impatiently.

She noticed that he, too, was shivering. "I'm not sure I should," she said in dismay.

"Be sensible, Alice. It's your choice." With that, he left her alone.

She bit her lip and glanced at the pool, battling with herself. The hot springs did look luxuriously inviting, with a white, filmy steam swirling over them. The alternative was a tepid hip bath when she returned to her bedchamber, she supposed, but that would not get the mud out of her hair. She looked down at herself with a grimace. She was bedraggled, bruised, and freezing. Mud caked her gown and boots. It might take the servants half an hour to heat the water and fill the tub and, by then, she probably *would* have the ague.

Taking off her gloves, she walked over warily to the carved stone steps that led down into the pool. She looked behind her into the dimness of the empty Grotto, as though her mother or her strict former governess might be looking on to chastise her for even considering it. Glancing at the tiled mosaics on the floor, Alice crouched down and splashed her fingertips in the pool in an exploratory testing of the waters. Relief and pleasure shot up her arm at the invigorating heat of the springs.

Well, I don't want to get sick, she reasoned. With a determined look, she undressed with furtive speed, lest Lucien should return and see more than he ought. She slipped out of his heavy black greatcoat and her fur-trimmed pelisse, then unbuttoned the bodice of her grimy carriage gown with trembling hands. Extricating her arms from her clinging, wet sleeves, she peeled her dress down over her hips and stepped out of it, rid herself of the single petticoat she had worn under it for warmth, then pulled off her much-abused kid half boots.

She examined the bloody bruise on her knee, gingerly removing her garters and stockings; then, clad only in her sleeveless white chemise, she dipped a toe in the water. *Ah, it was glorious,* she thought, giddy with creaturely comfort. Too beguiled to hesitate longer, she walked down the steps into the hot, bubbling water, slowly immersing herself in the pool's luxurious comfort. The reflection of the flames from the nearby candelabra danced over the water around the steps, but she was still wary of the darkness beyond the candles' glow.

When she came to the bottom step, the water was about four feet deep. Her shoulder and knee were instantly soothed; her entire body felt pampered, weightless, caressed. She relaxed into it. After a moment of adjusting to the vigorous heat and the sensation of bathing in the natural cauldron, she pinched her nose and ducked under the water, rinsing the mud and cold rain out of her hair.

Braver as the moments passed, she ducked beneath the surface and glided underwater. The soaring sensation of swimming in the Grotto pool was like flying. It awakened her as she burst up to the surface again to the realization that she felt breathlessly free. Aye, freer than she had ever been in her entire life. Quite without meaning to, she had flown the cage in which she had dwelled for so many years. She found her footing in the pool once more and stood in water up to her waist, musing on the realization as she made a long, reddish-gold rope out of her waist-length hair and patiently squeezed the water out of it.

It was then, in the shadows at the foot of the stairs carved into the limestone, that she saw the silver, wolf-like eyes glowing in the darkness. A man-shaped silhouette materialized amid the shadows and emerged slowly. It was Lucien. He had been watching her, but she felt no fear at the realization. Alice held very still and stared back at him as he walked toward her with slow, prowling strides.

His white-hot stare burned into her as it traveled over her body and fixed on her breasts. She glanced down and gave a low gasp to see that her filmy muslin chemise had become quite transparent. It clung to her skin, showing him every line of her body and the dusky-rose circles of her nipples. Her pulse racing, she lifted her chin again, wide-eyed, and met his starved gaze—but checked the impulse to cover herself.

Holding his stare, she let go of the coil of her hair, letting it fall softly down her back. The stark longing that hardened his angular face was tempered by such knightly reverence in his eyes that she felt no urge to shrink from him, no fear. She held perfectly still and let him look, for in that magical moment of soul-deep recognition, she realized she had never met another man like Lucien Knight, and, more importantly, never would again.

As he stared at her in hushed wonder, it was as though the world stopped. She was the most beautiful creature he had ever seen, a virginal water nymph, her tender skin flushed and glistening, the long tendrils of her strawberry-blond hair twining around her arms and slender waist, her thin muslin chemise wafting around her elegant hips like the white, delicate flowers of the lily pads she had studied so carefully in the garden. He could barely breathe for sheer worship. Yet fear surged through him in the next instant at the risk he had taken for the sake of protecting her from the storm. She knew now about the tunnel; she knew how to get away. The thought of her fleeing filled him with despair.

Forcing himself to lower his gaze, he walked slowly to the edge of the water, his expression concentrated, his every movement careful as he set down the armload of towels and clothes he had brought for her. His heart was slamming in his chest. He felt suddenly confused, unsure of what the hell he was doing. Crouching down on one knee beside the pool, he mutely offered her the bar of flower-scented soap.

She swam over with leisurely strokes, halting before him. She stood, clear, pure water streaming down her body, her eyes shining, Chartres-blue. He quivered at the warmth and moisture of her touch as she took the soap from his hand.

He wanted to ask her if her shoulder was feeling better, but he could not force out a single word. He tried to think of something charming to say to compliment her astonishing loveliness, but mere words were too cheap for the awe that he felt. His reaction shook him deeply; he no longer knew who was doing the luring and who was being lured.

"Thank you," she murmured. Slowly, sensually, she sank back into the pool with a little smile of feminine invitation. Nearly panting with desire, he watched her glide the soap up her bare, sweet arm. He longed to drink the healing waters of the spring from her lips, her skin. To lick it from the core of her womanhood. "Lucien, you're shivering."

His chest heaving, he looked at her in ravenous hunger and knew, in this moment, that he could have her.

He could do it easily. Join her in the water and slowly seduce her, overwhelm her senses with pleasure. Take her innocence and, thus, keep her here with him forever. But he thrust the option away from him in revulsion, quite to his own shock. Not that way. Not for her. Not here in the Grotto—not for her first time. She was not ready. To be sure, he could bring her pleasure the likes of which she had never known, but she would regret it as soon as the moment's fleeting bliss had passed. She would despise him. Worse, he would despise himself. As badly as he craved her, he did not want to win by trickery. It would only end in his making her as jaded as he was. If ever he was going to prove to himself that his honor still existed, though he was a snake of a spy, it had to start here, now, with Alice. His only hope of saving his soul was to put aside all his powers of seduction and manipulation and to reach out from the deepest, truest—and most vulnerable—part of himself. Perhaps then he might be worthy of her trust. He knew he did not deserve it in his present state. The ghastly moment of her fall had illumined like a blinding bolt of lightning the fact that, contrary to his earlier whim, this was no game—this was a beautiful, honorable young woman's life he was toying with. He was responsible for what became of her.

"Are you coming in?" she asked prettily, splashing a warm plume of water at him with her toe as she floated on her back.

His eyes blazed at the sight of her pale, nubile body, veiled only by water and wet, paper-thin muslin. With a great effort, he forced his answer. "No."

She smiled, her lashes starred with droplets of water. "But you're just as cold and muddy as I was. Aren't your muscles sore from all that swordplay and boxing?"

"I will wait until you're through," he ground out.

"Why?"

Straightening up from his crouched position, he just stared at her until her innocent smile faded and she went still, understanding dawning in her blue eyes. A scarlet blush rushed into her cheeks. She looked away, recovering her maiden modesty all in an instant.

He closed his eyes and prayed for strength as she dove under the water and swam away from him to finish bathing in the candlelight by the carved stone steps.

CHAPTER NINE

About an hour later, Alice was seated before the mirror in her bedchamber, rested, refreshed, dressed in the more formal of the two remaining gowns that she had brought to Revell Court. Her carriage gown was, of course, ruined. For morning dress, she had the simple, powder-blue muslin, but since it was evening, she had donned the slightly lower-cut dinner dress of dark green velvet. It was one of her favorite gowns because the velvet was soft and cozy and the skirts draped perfectly in the back. The gown had a square-cut neckline edged with ivory lace, a black satin bow that tied beneath the high waist, and long, tight sleeves with small lace ruffles at thewrists. Matching green-and-black velvet slippers warmed her feet, which swung idly over the chilly floor as she slowly brushed her hair with a dreamy, faraway gaze.

In her mind's eye, she still savored her last glimpse of Lucien undressing for his turn at bathing in the Grotto pool. He had lifted his shirt off over his head, baring the sweeping curves of his rippling back muscles, lean waist, and broad shoulders. The thought of him made her knees weak.

A knock sounded at the door to her bedchamber, stirring her from her daydreams. When she got up and went to answer it, a liveried servant bowed to her.

"Good evening, miss. His Lordship invites you to join him in the library before going in to dinner. He bade me give this to you." With both hands, he held out a small satin pillow upon which rested a key.

She furrowed her brow and picked up the key. "What does it open?"

The footman's face colored. "Er, your chamber, madam."

"Oh," she replied, blushing crimson. Her heart instantly began to pound. What did this mean? Was it another mind game like their last encounter in the library? "Did he say anything?" she asked.

"No, miss. Shall I show you to the library?"

She gave him a wry look. "I know the way by now."

When she walked into the library a few minutes later, all she could see of Lucien was his boots, crossed at the heels, and his hand hanging idly over the arm of the chair, a goblet of red wine dangling from his fingers. Horned shadows danced across the dim library, flung out by the high, spiky outline of his diabolically carved armchair as he sat before the fire. She went warily around it and looked at him.

Lounging in the big leather chair, he sat with his cheek resting on his fist, his elbow propped on the chair arm. He met her gaze but did not move or speak as she approached. The fire lit the yearning in his eyes. His lips looked tender and soft, slightly sulky, as though he were badly in need of a kiss.

"Hullo," she murmured, clasping her hands loosely behind her back as she sauntered over and stood before him.

He just looked at her.

They stared at each other for a moment.

"How is your shoulder?" he grumbled.

"Much better. Lucien?"

"Yes, Alice?" he answered wearily.

"Why did you give me the key?"

"Shall I take it back?" he demanded, then dropped his gaze with a wince of self-directed irritation and rubbed his forehead. "Because I don't want you to be afraid. Of me." From beneath the visor of his hand, he slid her a pleading look.

"I'm not afraid," she said.

He lifted his head. "I know that you know about the tunnel. Now you've got the key. If you want to escape, I shan't stop you."

She considered this in silence for a moment. "Did I displease you?"

From the fire, his gaze swung back to her with a frank look of sensual torment. "What can you possibly mean?"

"My awkwardness, falling today like a clumsy thing. I feel like such a fool—"

"It is I who am the fool, Alice. Please, do not trouble yourself. It was all my fault," he muttered, uncrossing his heels, sitting up straighter.

"How is that?"

"I should've made us wait out the storm at Whitby's cottage. I should've been holding onto you. I should never have made you stay here," he said, his voice dropping to a whisper. "But I could not help myself."

Alice took a step toward him. "I know. You are tired of being alone. You told me."

"You don't know," he said in a low, almost hostile voice. He shook his head. "I don't even know what I'm doing with you. You're not like anyone else who's in my life—" He stopped abruptly. "Did you ever drink too much wine, Alice?" He held up the glass in his hand and waggled it idly, making the ruby contents swirl.

"I'm not one to overindulge."

"No, you wouldn't be," he said wryly. "Allow me to explain, then, that the more you drink, the more thirsty you become. Not all the wine in the world can assuage the thirst for water. Water. Wine makes you merry, but a man needs water to keep him alive. Pure, clean, sweet water." He sighed, silent for a moment. He stared almost bitterly into the fire. "I am parched, Alice, scorched like a wasteland, burning like a damned soul in hell. I thirst."

"I know," she whispered. Lowering herself slowly to her knees by his chair, she took his hand and gazed up at him in youthful sincerity.

He watched her every move with firmly checked hunger. "It's all right, if you want to run. I wouldn't blame you."

"I'm not afraid."

"You should be," he said, his cynicism growing sharper as it began to fail him. "Life with me is fraught with danger. Get out while you can—"

"Shh, Lucien. Let me say something to you." She laid her fingertips over his lips until she saw in his eyes that he had put his irritation aside and was ready to listen. "I still owe you an apology from yesterday, when your heart was on your sleeve and I . . . kicked it."

His left eyebrow lifted.

She lowered her hand slowly from his lips. "I've been trying to find the right words all day to tell you how awful I feel about what I said yesterday—that I wasn't surprised that you are alone. The truth is I can't think for the life of me why some woman hasn't snatched you up yet, and to be strictly honest, Lucien—" She tucked her chin, dropping her gaze. She could feel her cheeks heating with embarrassment. "The truth is, I'm alone, too." She could feel him staring at her. Gathering her courage, she looked up at him uncertainly. "Do you hate me? I didn't even mean it—"

He suddenly leaned forward in his chair and cut off her words with a kiss, tipping her chin upward gently with his fingertips.

As their lips met, a little breathless sigh escaped her. Her eyes fluttered closed. Sliding his hand around her nape, he coaxed her lips apart. Her heart raced. She needed little urging, accepting his kiss eagerly, capturing his clean-shaved face between her fingertips. He tasted of port. She savored it, taking his tongue even more deeply into her mouth in sensuous welcome. Her hands trembled as she stroked the strong line of his jaw and ran her fingers through his silken black hair. With a low moan of desire, he slid his arms around her, shaping the natural contours of her waist below the draped vel-vet of her gown's high-waisted style, running his hands downward over her hips. She fought to keep a rein on the passion he ignited in her blood.

"I can't take this. I don't want any more games," he whispered urgently, ending the kiss a moment later. She saw genuine fear mingled with fierce passion in the crystalline depths of his eyes. "I have to know what you plan to do. Are you going to stay of your own accord, or are you going to escape through that blasted tunnel? Because if you don't want to be with me, I don't want to keep you here against your will—not after today—and if you're not interested, I don't want to let myself get attached to you." He suddenly stopped, looking shocked by his own fervent words.

"What do you want me to do?"

"Stay, of course," he said in exasperation, his cheeks flushing. "Stay the full week that we agreed upon, not because you have to, but because you want to—and because you want to know as much as I do if there really is something between us or if this is just some . . . beautiful illusion."

She gazed at him tenderly, taken aback. It had been easy enough to believe he was attracted to her when his intentions had been purely lecherous, but now, she realized in awe, astonishingly, his interest in her had turned serious. She barely dared believe it.

He looked away from her wonder-struck stare with a large sigh of self-disgust. "God, I must sound to you like a raving fool. You might as well flee. Shall I call you a carriage?"

"No!" she said quickly. Still kneeling on the floor between his legs, she slid her arms around his neck and pressed a comforting kiss to his cheek. He closed his eyes with an air of misery and leaned his head slightly into her kiss, his broad shoulders slumped. Alice grazed her lips along his cheek back to his ear. "Lucien?"

"Yes, Alice?"

Her heart was pounding, but she willed herself to muster the courage to reach out to him—unpredictable, dangerous as he was. "I think it's real."

At her soft, hesitant words, he trembled in her arms, lifted his lashes slowly, and pinned her in a tortured stare. She whispered his name as he lifted her onto his lap then kissed her in fiery intensity. If there had been any doubt in her mind as to his sincerity, the blazing need in his kiss routed it.

"God, girl, you don't know what you do to me," he breathed after a few minutes, checking his passion with a slight wince of self-restraint. He captured her face between his hands, softly stroking her cheeks with his thumbs. "I don't want to hurt you. I don't want to scare you."

"I'm not scared. I want to know you."

"Yes," he whispered, nodding slowly, enthralling her with his stare. Holding her in his arms, he eased her down to recline across his lap, her knees draped over the chair arm. He kissed her again and again, caressing her thigh through the velvet of her gown.

"How is your poor, precious knee?" he murmured at length, bending his head to kiss it gently.

Entranced by his playful sensuality, she could not find her voice to answer. He smiled knowingly and ran his hand down her shin. His hand ducked beneath the hem of her gown, lightly stroked her ankle. She blushed a bit but did not protest. She felt so close to him in this moment. She knew he felt the same. Gratitude shone in the depths of his eyes, as though she had given him a great gift in her willingness to stay at Revell Court. Little did he suspect she would not have left for the world. Not now. He slipped his finger into her velvet shoe, toying with the arch of her stockinged foot. She giggled and squirmed on his lap as he tickled her foot.

"Do you know that every inch of you is pretty, Alice Montague?" he whispered, leaning down to kiss her neck while his hand continued exploring her.

She kissed his hair as he nuzzled his way lower, his

warm, breathy kisses heating her cleavage, making her light-headed. "I could say the same for you."

"But you haven't seen every inch of me," he murmured suggestively.

"Yet."

He looked up from kissing her chest, his eyebrow lifted.

She gave him an impertinent little grin. "Perhaps I shall sketch your portrait. You could model for me, *au naturel.*"

"What . . . shocking impropriety," he murmured in silken wickedness.

"Don't tell me you are shy. I already know better."

"I make no such claim. The question is, are *you* shy, my sweet? For it so happens I've got a bit of impropriety on my mind, as well."

"You? Never."

"Oh, yes," he whispered, running the back of his fingers over her breast in gentle provocation.

A blush flooded her cheeks as her nipple hardened under his light touch through her velvet gown. Instantly, every inch of her skin became heated, sensitized. "What, ah, manner of impropriety, my lord?"

Perhaps if she had rebuked him, he would not have grown bolder, but she was enjoying it too much to stop him. He rested his fingertip directly on her nipple, teasing it with slow, circular caresses. "Giving you pleasure. Do you trust me?" he whispered, gazing into her eyes as he slipped his hand beneath her skirts, skimming it slowly up her shin.

"In what . . . sense?" she forced out, quivering as his warm hand rounded her knee and smoothly ascended to stroke her thigh.

"In the sense that you would let me touch you without fear that I might lose control of myself. I won't, you know. I want you to let go of fear entirely in my arms."

She gulped, her heartbeat escalating still faster. "I suppose, if you gave me your assurance—"

"I give you my word."

"Then I *think* that I could," she agreed faintly.

Her eyes shot open wide as he rested his hand between her thighs. A jolt of electrifying pleasure shot through her. Lucien's eyes glittered with silvery fire, but Alice did not know if she ought to be ashamed. By touching her there, he surely felt the evidence of her arousal. She drew in a breath sharply, quivering the length of her body as he skimmed his fingertips ever-so-lightly over her sex, up and down, awakening every inch of her virginal womanhood until she moaned softly with need and sank back limply against his shoulder, her chest heaving.

The heat, the delicious pressure of his touch, made her weak. Her arms were draped around his neck. She held onto him, breathless and aching. She let out a wordless exclamation of surprise and sensual relief as he dipped his finger into her teeming wetness.

"How does that feel?" he asked in a husky tone, watching her.

She could only moan softly in response. A smile curved his mouth; her answer pleased him. Then he applied some of her body's wetness like a precious oil to the tiny, throbbing point veiled within the damp curls of her womanhood. He leaned down and claimed her mouth in a deep, drugging kiss. He caressed her with tantalizing slowness until she writhed on his lap, parting her legs. He swirled the tip of his tongue around hers, panting faintly into her mouth.

"Do you want more?" he asked in a gravelly whisper.

She could only whimper in response. She shuddered and wrapped her arms more tightly around his neck, holding on for dear life as he pressed two fingers slowly into the core of her. *God, yes.* This was what she had needed. It was a thousand times better than in her dream, and yet she realized in amazement that his intoxicating touch was only a prelude to the full bliss of a man and woman's joining.

The languorous stroking of his tongue matched his hand's rhythm. She felt his hardness next to her hip, and it excited her unbearably. But he held true to his word, keeping a tight rein on his own desire. She gave herself over completely to experiencing the gift of pleasure with which he indulged her, kissing him fervently all the while. Her heart pounded like it would explode. Her head was light; her body felt weightless. Her spirit seemed to hover on the threshold of some uncharted heaven. The moment that he rested his thumb gently on her nub, his fingers still moving deeply inside her, ecstasy claimed her, engulfing her like a brilliant white light. She cried out and clung to Lucien while he whispered raggedly to her in another language, love words she could not understand.

Passion swept through her like a fire out of control, leaving her breathless, panting, spent.

"My . . . heavens," she forced out a few minutes later. She laid her head back on the arm of the chair and looked frankly at him, her bosom heaving. "That was remarkable."

He gave her a shadowy smile. "A pleasure to be of service, madam."

She came up onto her elbows. "Why *hasn't* any woman leg-shackled you yet?"

"They try. I run." He drew little stars on her midriff with his fingertip. "Maybe I've merely been waiting for you."

She studied him, mystified. "What a silver-tongued charmer you are."

"Thank you."

She smiled and blew a lock of her tousled hair out of her face. "It wasn't a compliment."

"Ah. Well, with you, I mean every word."

She shook her head. "Strange, I had no trouble believing you wanted me when I thought you were merely toying with me, but now that you're in earnest, I find myself a trifle overwhelmed."

"Actually, Alice, I've been in earnest from the start."

Her eyes widened. "Really?"

He nodded, toying with the black satin ribbon at her waist.

"I see. So you playacted the role of a rake who was only pretending to be in earnest, knowing you would come across as though you had the lowest of motives, when in fact, you were sincere?"

"Precisely."

She gave a short, wry laugh and shook her head at him. "Convoluted sir! You are a maze."

He shot her a sulky glance. "I thought you were going to say I was amazing."

"That, too," she admitted with a rueful smile, capturing his square chin between her fingertips. "Only, promise me you won't play any more games with my mind," she said softly. "We are friends now, aren't we? We must try to be open with each other."

He nodded, his gaze sobering.

"I have many questions—"

"I implore you not to ask them."

"What?"

"Just . . . don't ask. Not about the Grotto or the armed guards or . . . anything."

"But why?" she exclaimed, surprised that he had guessed exactly the subjects that worried her.

"Because I don't want to have to tell you any lies," he said.

She stared at him. He veiled his gaze coolly.

"Trust me," he whispered.

"Just . . . trust you? That's all you have to say?"

Again, close-mouthed, he nodded.

"I'm not sure that I can do that."

"Then run away, Alice," he snapped, his expression darkening in an instant. "It's your choice. I've told you how I feel." He rolled her off his lap onto the chair, rose, and stalked toward the door.

"Lucien!"

He pivoted, turning in silhouette. The firelight flickered over his tall, proud frame. "The fact is sometimes people have commitments in this world that are larger than a little girl from Hampshire can understand."

"Oh, so you think I'm stupid?" she retorted, jumping to her feet.

"Not stupid, naive. Sheltered. I like you that way. I don't want to fight with you, Alice. In my eyes, you are—" He cast about for words. "—an angel, a goddess. But these matters have nothing to do with you, nor can they. If you want to be with me, that is my only rule. Respect my privacy."

"Privacy or secrecy?"

"Call it what you will. Can you live with that—at least for a week? Can you try?"

She folded her arms over her chest and narrowed her eyes, scrutinizing him.

He heaved a sigh and looked at the wall. "Well, think it over. I'm going in to dinner. Will you join me?"

When she did not answer, only staring at him in reproach, he turned around and strode out.

She huffed to herself when he had gone. Little girl from Hampshire! Don't ask questions? He had brushed her off as though she were a child, but still, fool that she was, she had no desire to leave him. She wanted him. His keeping her here had been outrageous, but somehow, over the course of the day, she had come to view it as a delicious opportunity. She thought of Harry, sick with the chicken pox, and felt a flash of guilt, but he had his mama and Peg. Besides, what Alice had said to Lucien was true—she was alone, essentially. She had her suitors, but they did not know her and were all so self-absorbed or dull-witted that they did not even *realize* they didn't know her. They were safe choices, but they did not not make her blood burn with passion. Lucien Knight did. Perhaps in time he would trust her enough to tell her his secrets.

She stood there pondering the dilemma for a few minutes more when her stomach rumbled, rousing her to action. She started toward the dining room, but her mulling glance happened upon the chess table as she walked past it. The board had been left untouched from the previous morning when Lucien had sprung his trap on her and Caro. Alice's gaze homed in on the little carved horse head of the black knight, with which Lucien had trounced the white queen.

A sly smile curved her lips as she noticed he had left himself wide open. If only he were there to see it! She picked up an unassuming white pawn and skipped it gently over the black knight. He was right, she thought with a renewed strength and calm; she was sheltered. But her tranquil country life at Glenwood Park had taught her one virtue above all others: patience.

Through patience, her mother always used to say, any battle could be won. Even today, the dear old man, Mr. Whitby, had warned her that, with Lucien, she would need all the patience—and gentleness—that she could muster. Setting the carved piece in the palm of her hand, she gave the knight a small kiss, then set it down daintily on the side of the board and, with a foxy smile worthy of Lucien himself, went in to dine.

In the elegant suite at the Pulteney Hotel, Rollo Greene stared, aghast, as the soulless blond giant looked in the mirror and gave his white cravat a final tug, then slipped his loaded pistol into the holster concealed beneath his formal black tailcoat.

"Not on Guy Fawkes Night, Bardou, for the love of God!" Rollo choked out. "It is a festival night! The streets will be filled with civilians—children!"

"You were assigned to assist me, Greene. Do not tell me how to carry out my mission," Bardou replied coolly.

"Look here, sir, I can't speak for you French, but massacring civilians is not how we in America conduct business!"

Bardou laughed. He turned away and swaggered across the plush room to Sophia. Her arms folded over her chest, the tall Russian beauty leaned against the console table by the wall with all the sleek, wary mystery of a

Siamese cat. Rollo saw the fear and hostility that flared in her almond-shaped eyes as Bardou approached her, but she did not attempt to escape his attentions anymore, as she had earlier, resigned to having been overpowered by the man. She flinched slightly as Bardou grasped her hips and pulled her against him, burying his face in the crook of her neck.

Rollo winced and looked at the ground. He wished there was something he could do to help her, but he could not afford to oppose Bardou on his treatment of the woman when it took all his nerve to press the matter of Guy Fawkes Night. The annual bonfire festival was held throughout England every year on November the fifth, two weeks away.

Bardou was still concealing the details of his plan from him, but Rollo had begun to realize that the former Napoleonic spy had far more mischief up his sleeve than he had been hired to wreak. Clearly, Bardou's French hatred for the English ran much deeper than did the Virginia planters' grudge. They had wanted something done on a smaller scale, more specifically aimed at the British military, preferably the navy.

Rollo knew that if somebody didn't stop Bardou, innocent people were going to die; and if the world found out that a group of powerful Americans was behind the coming firestorm, there would be shame and infamy for his president, dire consequences for his country. Not to mention his own career would be ruined for having bungled his assignment.

"Bardou, I am only asking you to reconsider the timing of your attack," he wheedled him. "I am certain that the gentlemen in Virginia intended no such radical action against the populace of London—"

"Shut your mouth!" Bardou roared, turning on him, tearing himself away from his mistress.

Rollo's eyes widened as Bardou crossed the room to him in three titan-sized strides, grasped him by the lapels, and threw him up against the wall, nearly putting him through it.

"I give the orders; you follow them," he snarled. "Stay out of my way, or you are going to end up at the bottom of the river." He released him roughly. "Now, get out of here."

Rollo's heart pounded so hard with terror that he thought it would give out on him. His whole body felt bruised from being slammed against the wall. He glanced at Sophia. She just stared back at him, silent and detached as a cat; then he looked into Bardou's insane, pale blue eyes.

"I said go," the man growled.

Rollo did not need a second warning. He fled.

Claude Bardou stared for a moment at the door, which Greene had slammed behind him, then turned to Sophia. "I don't trust him."

"You don't trust anyone, Claude. You're not capable of it. Not even me."

"Especially not you," he replied with a narrow smile. "Follow him. Go. Now."

She heaved an irritated sigh. "Must I?"

"I know a rat when I smell one. If he tries to betray me, kill him."

"Claude, I cannot kill the American. He is your liaison!"

"I don't need him anymore. Just do it, Sophie. Do it

for me," he murmured, icy warning embedded in the softness of his tone.

She glared at him in simmering rebellion, pulled out her weapon and checked it, then slid the pistol back into her thigh holster, beside the sheath of her evil-looking dagger.

"Keep me informed of what is happening. And Sophia," he added, "don't try to run off."

"Never, darling." She threw her long, fur-lined cloak over her arm and strode out, giving him a dirty look as she pulled the door shut.

Only minutes after her exit, a knock sounded at the door. *How prompt these English were,* Bardou mused cynically. He placed his monocle in his right eye, smoothed his short-cropped hair, then went to answer the door, transforming himself mentally as he crossed the room into Prussian Baron Karl von Dannecker.

What Claude Bardou had not seen fit to tell his American moneymen was that he had a personal score to settle in addition to his political vengeance. For the former, he needed Ethan Stafford to introduce him into London Society. They had gone out among the ton twice already, and Bardou had made casual, preliminary inquiries about his hated enemy. Bardou had decided that the only way he could swallow the humiliation of Napoleon's defeat was by winning the private, unfinished war between him and Lucien Knight. The one man he had failed to break—his prisoner who had, incredibly, bested him.

If only he could annihilate Lucien Knight, he knew he could bear everything that had gone wrong—the failure of the cause he had devoted his life to, Bonaparte's shameful abdication, the impossibility of ever returning home to France. Lucien Knight embodied all that Bardou hated most about the English. Knight's insufferable, British stiff upper lip had barely quavered no matter what kind of tortures Bardou had put him through.

He could not live with the thought of that gallant, aristocratic gentleman-spy living a long, happy life on this puny island of the victors, when Bardou's own life and his future had been decimated. To stalk his enemy, Bardou needed Ethan Stafford to conduct him into the world of London's rich and titled so that he could learn more about Knight and how best to destroy him. Though Bardou had held him captive for five weeks, Knight had told him almost nothing. Since he had held up against physical suffering, Bardou had begun considering ways to torment his heart and mind. Unfortunately, Knight had no wife or children, but he did have four brothers, two of whom were in London.

Bardou was leery of attacking Lucien Knight's twin, the formidable Colonel Lord Damien Knight, but the rakish Lord Alec, the youngest of the Knight brothers, seemed somewhat easier prey. *It was a pity that their little sister, Lady Jacinda, was away at Vienna,* he thought as he crossed to the door. *She would have been perfect for his purposes.* Bardou had no choice but to resort to the women in Lucien Knight's life. He intended to gain an introduction tonight to his enemy's most recent mistress, Lady Glenwood.

Masking his dark thoughts behind a cool smile, he opened the door. "Good evening, Herr Stafford."

Ethan Stafford bowed to him. "Von Dannecker. Are you ready for our jaunt to Vauxhall?"

"I have been looking forward to it all day," he replied as he pulled on his greatcoat and locked his hotel door.

The young English gentleman no doubt found this whole arrangement strange, but every man had his price. If the charming Mr. Stafford had any inkling that Baron von Dannecker was not who he seemed, he was too wary—and too determined to keep his showy house and fast carriage—to ask questions.

A few minutes later, they were racing eagerly through the streets of London in Stafford's fashionable drag. With his pockets full of gold once more, the young man was in high spirits. Stafford showed off his skill at four-in-hand driving at such a reckless pace that it was no time at all before they arrived at the riverside and took the ferry across to the pleasure gardens.

Stafford showed him the lantern-lit garden paths where lovers held rendezvous when the weather was warmer, and the artificial waterfall that he said was run every night punctually at nine, to the wonder of all who beheld it. They strode into the gaudy main pavilion that throbbed with orchestral music and beamed with bright illumination. Bardou scanned the colorful crowd, ever watchful behind his studied air of high, remote, German pride.

"Ah, there's Lady Glenwood," Stafford murmured, giving him a sly look askance. "I told you she'd be here."

He followed Stafford's nod toward a scantily clad brunette with bouncy curls that framed her heart-shaped face and enormous tits. Bardou raised his eyebrow in most prurient interest. The baroness was surrounded by fawning men.

"What a body, eh?" Stafford murmured, elbowing him in the ribs.

Bardou gave him a sly look. "But I heard she is involved with someone . . . What was the name? Lucien Knight. Do you know the man?"

Stafford blinked in surprise. "Of course." He lowered his voice. "It was at one of Lord Lucien's parties that Rollo Greene first contacted me about . . . helping you."

"Oh, really?" Bardou murmured, concealing his burst of rage. *I knew it.* That little lard-ass rat had lied to him, had told him he didn't know Lucien Knight! Thank God he had sent Sophia to watch the American, he thought in disgust. Sometimes, at any rate, luck was with him.

Having parties! he thought in scorn. *These English were so arrogant, so sure of their victory.* It filled him with smug satisfaction to know that Lucien Knight was at his country house having parties rather than on his guard. As long as Bardou knew exactly where Knight was and what he was doing, then *he* was the one in control and could strike at his leisure. He had no intention of attacking Knight at his country house, for it was foolish to give the enemy the home advantage. No, Lady Glenwood might be just the means to lure Knight back to London when Bardou was fully ready for him.

"Is he in love with her?" he asked Stafford casually.

"Well, apparently, he wanted her so badly that he stole her away from his own brother. I don't know if that's love, but it's something, don't you think? Personally, I think she's toying with both of them. With a body like that, she can get away with it," he added under his breath.

Bardou murmured hearty assent as they sauntered over to the woman. Her rouged lips were moving rapidly with her prattle. As they joined her circle, Bardou frowned slightly. The woman chattered too fast for him to follow her English. He had to translate her words a bit more slowly in his mind.

"I *couldn't* stay in the country. I tried! Honestly I did,

but a child can just as easily recuperate in Town as he can in Hampshire, can't he?"

The fops were laughing and agreeing with every word she said as they stared at her chest.

"When are you going to bring that pretty sister-in-law of yours back to Town?" one asked.

"Oh, Miss Montague is very ill, the poor dear," she said, clucking her tongue in regret. "She is confined to her room at Glenwood Park. Influenza. The doctor said she won't be allowed out for at least another week—so you will have to make do with me, *mon chéri*!"

"Lady Glenwood," Stafford spoke up. "My friend here is visiting from Prussia—"

"Prussia, eh?" The slightly drunken Englishmen gathered around her hailed him with approval. "A toast to General Blücher!"

"Thank you, sirs." Bardou nodded stiffly to them. His smile thinned only slightly, but hatred churned within him as the cheerful fools lifted their glasses to the stalwart Prussian general.

Stafford laughed at their antics and nodded to Lady Glenwood with gentlemanly grace. "As I was saying, the baron has never been to our country before, and I am eager to impress him with the beauty of our English roses. I could think of none better to dazzle him than you. May I introduce you?"

"What a flatterer you are, Stafford! Of course." The woman turned her beaming smile on Bardou. Hardened as he was, he was momentarily enchanted.

She might be a hated *Anglaise*, but he knew instantly that she was his favorite type of woman. Besides, she would be very useful.

"Lady Glenwood, may I present Baron Karl von Dannecker of Berlin," he said formally. "Von Dannecker, the beautiful Lady Glenwood."

"How do you do, my lord? Welcome to our homeland," she said gaily. "I do not know that I can dazzle you as Stafford commands, but I will certainly endeavor to try."

"Lady Glenwood, you have already succeeded," Bardou replied as he bent over her hand and kissed it.

"Charming," she murmured, a gleam of aroused interest in her eyes. "You can call me Caro." Her gaze flicked brazenly across his shoulders and down the length of his body, then locked with his in instant, mutual lust. "I have always been a great admirer of the Prussians," she purred. "They are so . . . big. So . . . forceful." The thin, greasy-haired fop beside her snickered at her flirtatious tone. Caro rolled her eyes, looking askance at him. "Lord von Dannecker, allow me to present my little brother, Viscount Weymouth. Niles, this is Baron von Dannecker."

Bardou nodded to the stringy, ill-kempt fellow, who swayed on his feet. Weymouth's skin had a sickly pallor, and his small brown eyes were glazed. "How d' ye do," he mumbled, then giggled into his wineglass.

Opium, Bardou thought, masking his contemptuous sneer.

"Beau-nasty, will you behave? Pay him no mind, my lord. He is utterly foxed," Caro scolded, giving her brother's scraggly chin a fond pinch as though he were a child. "Don't befriend him or he'll only ask you for a loan." She winced in distaste as Weymouth, quite in his own world, scratched his dirty hair then examined the grimy contents beneath his fingernails.

Even Bardou was revolted. "Lady Glenwood, would you do me the honor of a dance?"

"Why, I'd love to."

"Best to do as he says, sister," Weymouth mumbled. "Mustn't trifle with those Prussians."

Bardou gave him a warning look and offered her his arm. She took it with a smile. Weymouth's tittering laugh followed them as Bardou led her toward the dance floor. She gave him a curious look as she noticed his slight limp, then stopped and turned to him.

"We needn't dance if you would rather not," she said prettily.

"But I don't wish to disappoint you," he replied in a low tone.

She cast a quick, meaningful glance below his waistline, then peered up at him through her lashes. "Oh, my dear von Dannecker," she murmured, "I don't think that would be possible."

CHAPTER TEN

Three days passed. Miraculous days. Lucien and Alice became inseparable. If the world still existed beyond the limestone pinnacles that encircled the valley, neither of them wanted to know of it. She complied with his wishes about not asking questions; he refrained from seducing her; and together they achieved a precarious joy that was artless, simple, and chaste. Their days were full of mellow autumn sunlight and country pursuits: fishing, riding, shooting at pheasant and hare. They lived off the land and feasted like the kings of the earth upon the harvest's abundance, drank much wine and talked themselves hoarse before the fireplace into the wee hours of the night. Sometimes they played chess. Sometimes they read poetry. On Tuesday it rained, so they played a jolly game of bowls in the dusty old ballroom, then explored the rambling Tudor mansion, for Lucien himself had not yet seen all the bedrooms. At other times, they merely sat holding each other in warm silence, staring into each other's eyes, each pondering the mystery of the other and of their deepening bond. *How narrowly,* Alice often thought, *they might have missed out on their chance meeting.*

She could no longer imagine how life had been before

she had known Lucien. She must have been sleeping like the princess in the fairytale, waiting for his kiss to awaken her. She felt as though he had always been a part of her—in her blood, in her heart. On Wednesday night, she reclined on the leather couch in the dim library, her head resting on his lap while he sang her to sleep, petting her hair. Her last thought before drifting off was that she had fallen irrevocably, irretrievably in love with him. The joy of it was shadowed only by the swirling undercurrent of danger she sensed in the silences of Revell Court and in its enigmatic master. *Ask me no questions and I'll tell you no lies.*

She knew Lucien cared for her, but his regard for her apparently had not dulled his appetite for depravity; preparations were taking place for another bacchanalia in the Grotto. Huge quantities of wine were delivered. In the courtyard, she saw a few of the black-coated guards cleaning their guns. The image haunted her, whispering to her that something hidden, perhaps even darker and deeper than the orgies of the Grotto, was going on at Revell Court. Something sinister—and her beloved with his eyes full of secrets was at the heart of it.

She was not sure if she suspected Lucien of criminal activities or sacrilegious ones, or for that matter, which was worse. She was afraid to ask, for fear of dashing the enchantment of their growing love, and of rousing the dangerous side of Lucien that she had faced that first night in the little room behind the dragon's eyes. He was the perfect lover, provided she did not cross him. One rule, one forbidden thing. Plagued by fears, she paced in her room while he practiced at swords in his studio with his band of hard-eyed young rogues. She had befriended them the day before, but soon discovered that trying to get information out of them was futile. She was still uncertain of their role. They were too highborn to be servants and a bit too young to be merely his friends. They seemed to be connected to the Grotto.

Devil take it, why did he have those parties at all? she wanted to yell. If only someone would trust her with the truth. Why did he squander his money and time and taint his good name with such wildness? None of it fit the man she knew.

Trust me, he had said. She reminded herself for the umpteenth time. The Lucien Knight she knew was a sensitive man of great intelligence and strength. She had to withhold judgment until he was ready of his own accord to tell her everything. If he really had wanted to deceive her, he would have made up some cock-and-bull story to explain away all her fears, she reasoned with herself, but he respected her too much to fill her ears with lies. Did that not count for something?

In any case, the end of their promised week together was drawing near. Would they part? Would they stay together? She did not see how she could stay with him unless he gave her the answers she needed. Even if he had begun to consider offering marriage, she was not prepared to spend the rest of her life in the dark about his activities. The uncertainty of her situation agonized her in dizzying counterpoint to her euphoria in his presence. She knew she should not stand for this, being kept in ignorance, but she refused to give him up. She could understand now why Caro had forsaken even Harry to be with Lucien. A woman could become as addicted to that man as an invalid was to her laudanum drops.

Hanging onto hope for all she was worth, she thrust her fears away and hurried out to join him in his studio.

Nothing routed her fears faster than his smile. Watching him at his practice, his sheer male beauty made her yearn with desire. Yet, as she watched the dazzling speed of his sword and saw the wolfish snarl on his face, she wondered why, if it was merely practice, he fought with such savagery. If only one of the boys had fought him alone, Lucien would have made mincemeat of him. Surely, here was a man struggling inwardly against something—or someone, she thought, gazing at him rather helplessly. If only he would confide in her. She knew that he suffered, but he would not speak of the cause. She had seen the hatred that blew like smoke through the depths of his eyes when he sometimes sat staring into the fire, brooding and far away. She had learned how to bring him back from that dark place inside himself by drawing him gently into the deepest, most soulful kisses she had to give. Perhaps the mystery of what troubled him was the source of all the secrets that stood like a wall between them.

Perhaps, she thought, watching him with a deep, wanton hunger, *if she gave herself freely to him, he would reciprocate—her virtue for his trust.* The recklessness of such a gamble made her shiver. She could either win him or lose everything. She looked on in silence, unable to escape the feeling that she was blindly battling to save his soul.

In the master's wheel, he won another point, wiped his brow with the back of his arm, and attacked again.

Lucien could feel Claude Bardou drawing closer. He could *feel* it. He did not know how or why he knew, but some sixth sense honed through years of moving deftly behind enemy lines assured him that the storm was coming closer. As the days with Alice passed, he felt his life separating into two disparate halves, dark and light. He had existed for so long in a gray half-world of shadows, but he sensed he would not be able to stay there much longer. Soon a choice would have to be made. He felt pulled in two directions. Her light was the only thing that kept him from embracing the darkness in order to fight Bardou's evil with evil of his own; her love was the counterforce that stopped him from going over the edge that he had walked for so long.

One thing was certain. From the depths of his being, he loathed lying to her. He longed to tell her everything, but he was terrified of how she might react. How could he risk losing her when right now she was all that was holding him together?

Every moment with her was a resplendent, fragile gift, like the beauty of sunlight beaming through a drop of dew. He wanted nothing more from life than to make her happy, but he had a formidable duty to his country and a vendetta that he owed the man whose blood was on his hands. Thus, at the same time that he was learning how to love for the first time in his life, he was dealing in ruthless treachery, clandestinely, behind her back, setting traps to snare men and women in their own vices—whatever availed to help him get to Claude Bardou.

On Thursday afternoon, he finished writing a few letters in his office high in the attics above Revell Court, then went looking for his fair companion. He found her sitting in the large, rustic salon on the first floor with his five young rogues. She was studiously making a charcoal sketch of Marc while the other young men sat around idly chatting and joking, drinking coffee, and praising her for the accuracy of the portraits she had drawn of each one of them.

Unnoticed, Lucien paused in the doorway, watching her in quiet pleasure.

"I still don't understand why you have these silly nicknames," she was musing aloud, trying futilely to charm a few secrets out of them—the little vixen. Giving Marc's wavy brown hair a bit more shading in her sketch, she finished the portrait, carefully removed the page, and presented it to her subject.

Marc's eyebrows lifted. "Miss Montague, you are most talented!"

"If only I could coax Lord Lucien to sit for me," she said with a sigh, smiling at him as he walked into the room.

"I already know what I look like. I have a twin brother, remember?" He sauntered over behind her chair and gave her shoulders a soft squeeze. She caressed his hand on her shoulder.

"But you're *you*. You're my Lucien. I don't care about that other one. Let me sketch your portrait," she insisted, resting her head on the chair's back to gaze up at him sweetly. He blushed a little at her affectionate words in front of his men, but they took up her cause.

"Go on, let her," Marc urged him with a grin, showing him his portrait. "Look at how well she drew me!"

"She even made Talbert look handsome," O'Shea remarked. "God knows that takes talent."

"Hey!" Talbert objected.

"Aye, let her make your portrait, Draco," Jenkins chimed in cheerfully. "We could use it for shooting practice."

"Ha, ha," he replied.

"Go on, humor the lady," Marc urged him, laughing.

"Yes, please, please let me!" Alice begged prettily.

Lucien balked, but there was little he could refuse her. "Oh, very well," he grumbled at last, willing to take her undivided attention however he could get it.

She clapped her hands in delight and the lads cheered. She grabbed his hand and tugged him over to sit before her. "You had better stop scowling or that is exactly how I will portray you."

Lucien sighed. He would have relented sooner, but in truth, he did not like being studied too closely in the light. Now he found himself intrigued to learn how she saw him—who he was through her eyes.

"Don't you gentlemen have work to do?"

The lads grinned knowingly and left the two of them alone, thanking her again and sliding the salon doors shut behind them.

"That's better, isn't it?" Lucien murmured.

"They are very agreeable."

"And I'm very greedy. I want you all to myself."

"Poor me," she teased demurely, seating herself on the ottoman and picking up the tools of her art. She blew the powdery dust off her charcoal and began to study him, but when she noticed his smoldering stare fixed on her, she snorted in ladylike disdain. "Do not try to tempt me, Lucifer," she ordered loftily as her hand began moving over the page. "I'm working."

He gave her a rueful smile and slung his arm over the chair's back in a leisurely position, warmed by the autumn sunlight flooding in through the mullioned windows, lulled by the soft scraping sound her charcoal made as she wisped it lightly over the paper. They sat together for a quarter-hour in companionable silence.

Letting his gaze travel possessively over her, he drank in the loveliness of her face as she sat in a ray of sunlight. *To be sure, she had a temper to match those red streaks in her golden hair,* he thought fondly. Her pale blond eyebrows were knitted in thought as she worked. She had luxurious lashes and cobalt eyes with the power to devastate him. She had a smattering of light freckles on her cheeks and fine, aristocratic features. Her breasts were perfection, and her exquisitely curved hips had been formed for bearing children. His children.

Good God, he had never planned on falling so completely under her spell. It scared him to fall so hard, so fast, but he couldn't seem to stop himself. Indeed, he wanted ever more of her.

She suddenly looked up at him, then tilted her head, assessing him closely. "Something's not right."

He tensed with instant guilt, unsure of what she meant. Alice set down her charcoal and sketch pad, wiped her hands on a rag, and walked over to him.

"What is it?" he asked uneasily.

She plucked at his cravat. "This . . . and this," she said, tugging on the sleeve of his waistcoat. "You're wearing too many clothes."

"Oh-ho," he murmured with a grin, coming to full attention.

"Do you mind taking a few things off?"

"Anything for art," he replied as his heart skipped a beat.

"Best let me do it." Sliding him a frisky look, she began untying his cravat.

He leaned back in his chair with a lazy half smile. "Do with me what you will."

"Oh, I intend to." She nudged his legs apart and stood

between them as she pulled his undone cravat slowly off his shoulders, meeting his gaze. Next she unbuttoned his waistcoat and slipped it down off his shoulders. Leaning forward to let her remove it, he brushed his face against the inner curve of her breast. She moved away from him, smoothing his waistcoat over her forearm.

Nearly panting with anticipation, he watched the sway of her hips and the elegant curves of her derriere as she bent to lay his waistcoat neatly over the arm of a nearby chair.

"Satisfied?" he asked.

"Not . . . yet." Turning, she shook her head and sauntered back to him. Without a word, she slipped between his legs again and reached down, pulling his shirt almost roughly out from the waist of his trousers.

He smiled darkly. God, she excited him.

She took her time unbuttoning it all the way down his chest and belly, then slid it off his shoulders, caressing him as she went. He stared at her, aroused, compliant. He was rock hard. She leaned down and kissed his shoulder as she finished taking his shirt off of him, then kissed her way slowly up the side of his neck. He tilted his head back, his pulse slamming in the artery where her lips lingered at his throat. She caressed his sides and his chest with her silken hands, stroked his arms, ran her fingers through his hair, enslaving him with her feverish touch.

Wrapping her soft arms around him, she held him for a moment, then kissed his forehead. "You are a beautiful man, Lucien Knight," she whispered.

Grasping her wrist, he pulled back and gazed up at her in raw yearning. "When, Alice? How much longer must I wait?"

She passed a wary glance over his face and gracefully slipped out of his hold. "That depends."

He stared at her, awaiting instruction, as she settled herself back on the ottoman where she had been sitting across from him. "You have only to name what you want."

"I am afraid if I lie with you that you will think I am like Caro."

"Good God, never!"

She veiled her gaze behind her lashes and considered this, looking impeccably demure and very, very wary. "Lucien?"

"Yes?"

"What would happen . . . if I gave in?" She swept her lashes upward and met his momentarily blank stare.

"What would happen?" he echoed, stalling for a moment or two to come up with the perfect reply. *Watch yourself—don't scare her off. For the love of God, say the right thing.*

"Yes."

He cast about, his body throbbing wildly to realize she was considering giving herself to him. "Why, you would feel a moment's pain, *ma chérie,* and then you would know great pleasure."

"*After* the pleasure!" she exclaimed, half hiding behind her sketch pad in scandalized modesty.

"Afterwards? Well . . ." He chanced a cocky little grin, but his heart pounded. "I suppose I would have to marry you."

She peered over the edge of her sketch pad. "Have to?"

"Oh, Alice," he said ruefully, softening his voice, "you know I'm mad for you."

"Are you proposing to me, then?"

He stared at her for a long moment, his heart slamming. "I reckon I am. Aye, why not?" He swallowed hard. "What do you . . . That is, er—will you?"

There was a trace of pity in her smile, but amusement danced in her eyes. "How many languages do you speak, again?"

He scowled. "You may have received dozens of proposals before—and I'm sure this one ranks as the very worst of them all—"

"Yes, definitely," she agreed, nodding.

"But it's the first one I've ever attempted, so do please bear with me, madam."

"Of course," she answered gravely, pursing her lips to chase away her taunting smile.

He narrowed his eyes. "You little vixen." He got up, crossed to her, and bent down, kissing her soundly. Then he wiped a smudge of charcoal off the tip of her nose with a doting frown. "Don't you even think about saying no. I know you are famous for it, but this is *me* you are talking to," he added, giving her a severe look.

"The wicked Lord Lucifer?"

"The same." He noticed her sketch and paused, taken aback by the likeness. "Well, hang me." He grasped the edge of the sketch pad and turned it so he could see it better, but she smacked his hand away.

"Don't look!"

"You're good," he said, thoroughly impressed.

"I'm not finished," she muttered, pulling the sketch pad up close to her body, careful not to smudge the drawing.

A smile danced on his lips. He knew he was smitten, but even when she was cross, he found her adorable. Gently, he tilted her chin upward with his fingertips and searched her eyes. "Look here, you. If we left for Scotland on Saturday after my guests have gone, we could be married by Wednesday."

Her eyes widened. "Scotland!"

"Aye, Gretna Green."

"Elope?" She pulled away from his light touch and gave him a look of revulsion.

"Of course," he replied, instantly uncertain again.

Changing like the English weather, Alice turned prim. She pointed at the chair he had abandoned. "Go back over there and sit down," she ordered him with a quelling look.

He knitted his eyebrows in defiance but did as he was told. "You are going to be a terrifying old dragon lady when you're elderly."

"And you will be a randy old goat."

"I know a special license is more fashionable, but the bishop will never grant me one," he muttered. "He thinks I am the Antichrist."

"What about the traditional way? Announcing the banns?" she asked loftily. "Or does that lack flair for you?"

He shook his head with a smirk. "It's for peasants." In truth, he shuddered at the thought of having his name publicly proclaimed throughout the parish for three weeks in a row. Claude Bardou might already be looking for him.

"I see." Alice sat back with a sigh, rested her cheek on her fist, and studied him. "I suppose there are worse fates than a Gretna wedding. Which brings me to my next question."

"Yes?"

She sat up, rested her elbows on her bent knees, and

clasped her hands loosely. Looking at the ground, her cheeks turning bright pink, she spoke slowly. "What if . . . a baby came along?"

He stared at her, taken aback. The bachelor in him went mentally running off, screaming bloody murder, hollering at him to get out while he could, but an odd, slight smile struck him out of nowhere. He studied her, mystified. "Devil take me, but I don't think that'd be half bad. Do you?"

When tears rushed into her eyes, he realized his question had struck a nerve, but something told him that they were tears of joy.

"Would you like that, Alice? A few wee ones underfoot?"

She let out a shaky, incoherent sob of a laugh and covered her lips with her hand.

"Of course you would," he whispered as understanding dawned. "You lost practically your entire family. That's what you want more than anything, isn't it? A family of your own?"

She half burst out crying. He went back over to her, unable to stay away. He knelt down by her chair and took her into his arms, closing his eyes. "You are so precious to me," he whispered.

She pulled back, quickly brushing her few tears away. "I know you like your parties. I wasn't sure if you wanted anything to do with children—"

He stopped her worried words with a light kiss, then brushed the tip of her nose with his own. "Don't you know I have to be wherever you are? If you're with our children, then that's where I'll be, too. Besides—" He glanced hesitantly into her eyes. "—I know how it feels to have a father who treats you like you don't exist. I would never do that to my own child." He paused and shook his head. "God help me, I don't believe I'm saying this."

"Do you mean it?"

"From the bottom of my heart." He stroked her arm. "I'll give you a baby every year if that would make you happy. We can start now. Where are you in your cycle?"

"Lucien!"

"Don't be embarrassed. You can tell me. I almost became a physician instead of a soldier, you know. So?"

"Oh, it's, um, coming in a day or two."

"That's a shame," he said with an intimate smile. "It's not the right time for you to conceive."

"I'm so happy you feel the same way I do."

He lifted her hand and kissed it.

"But, Lucien, there's only one problem."

"What's that, darling? Give it to me. I'll fix it," he murmured. "We're almost there."

She looked deeply into his eyes. "Would you really allow your children to be exposed to the things that go on in the Grotto?"

His confident smile faded.

"Lucien, I will not settle for a husband who is half a stranger to me. Here is my counterproposal. Do three things for me and I will marry you without a qualm. First, tell me what is going on around here. I feel that you're in some kind of trouble, or perhaps even engaged in some kind of crime."

"You think I'm a criminal?" he nearly shouted, sweeping to his feet.

"Well?"

"Alice!"

"Lucien, you have men with rifles posted all over the property! No honest man has need of so many guards—"

"God damn it!" Thirty-one years of bucking convention and thumbing his nose at conformity kicked in as he swept to his feet and stared at her defensively, flabbergasted by her meddling demands. "How dare you?" he said in lordly anger. "Do I look like I need you to run my life for me?"

She flinched, and her gaze fell. "I'm trying to help you."

"Help me? You're trying to get me under the cat's paw, but it's never going to work. If you can't accept me as I am, then maybe we are wasting our time."

"Ugh, you exasperating—! You say you are all alone, but you won't come out of your hiding place to be with me as you easily could, if you would try!"

"The guards are there because I have enemies. That doesn't make me a criminal."

"*Violent* enemies?"

He scoffed. "Do you think I spend all that time training in my studio because I enjoy it?"

"Are you in danger, Lucien?"

He heaved a sigh, relenting with a twinge of guilt when he saw how she had paled.

"Can't your family help you? Damien or Hawkscliffe—"

"Never fear, Alice, I can look after myself—and you. My family has nothing to do with this. Please, go on with the rest of your demands. I can barely wait to hear them."

She blinked rapidly, regaining her composure. "I want you to make tomorrow night the last gathering in the Grotto, then disband the group. I don't want those awful people in our children's lives if . . . we are together. And finally, I want you to have a talk with Damien to clear the air between the two of you. I know your estrangement from him breaks your heart."

"That is all very sweet—but, no."

She threw her sketch pad aside and shot to her feet, folding her arms across her chest with a cold glare. "What if I were to put my foot down? What if I were to say I will not lie with you or marry you until you close down the Grotto and swear never to have those horrid people back to Revell Court?"

There was a long silence as he absorbed her ultimatum. "I would say that was a trick worthy of Caro. The Alice Montague I love is not the kind of woman who uses her body to get what she wants."

Her eyes widened with surprise.

"What?" he asked insolently.

"Y-you just said you love me."

"And?"

She just stared at him, her lips slightly parted, but she did not say the words back. "Isn't it a bit too soon to say that?" she asked faintly instead.

A vulnerable little piece of him died at her answer. Hurt flickered in his eyes as he gazed at her. "I suppose it is." He gave her a hard look and turned away to hide his humiliated look, going to collect the clothes she had taken off of him. He tossed his white shirt over his left shoulder and stalked past her to the door. Maybe she didn't love him—undoubtedly, he did not deserve it—but when she watched him walk by, a startled expression lingering on her face, he knew full well that she desired him. At least he had that—as usual. He slammed the door behind him as he left.

* * *

Damn that woman!

Sophia Voznesensky was part she-wolf, Rollo thought. She had tracked him relentlessly all the way from London, though he had taken the most circuitous, winding course to the West Country that he could devise. After having been tracked like a fox for two days, Rollo Greene counted himself fortunate to stay one village ahead of her as he fled under churning, marble-gray skies. His fingers were red and raw, poking through his gloves as he refilled his canteen with fresh water at the local well, then went into the tavern and bought a draught of gin to warm his belly and steady his nerves. He lingered as long as he dared before heaving his poor, bruised arse back up into the creaking saddle. Urging his horse back out onto the main coaching road, he glanced nervously over his shoulder and thanked God that the tall, sloe-eyed Valkyrie was not in sight, gusting down the road after him on her leggy gray horse.

As he urged his mount into a canter, he shook his head to himself in disgust, remembering how his eyes had nearly popped out of his head when he had first feasted his gaze on Sophia's voluptuous figure. It had been several days before he had noticed the cold, dead look in her eyes. He had considered letting her catch up to him and trying to persuade her to defy Bardou with him, but she feared her French lover too much to dare try. This left Rollo no choice but to run for his life from the woman. Still, it was better than running from Bardou himself.

By now, he supposed Sophia must have guessed where he was fleeing to—Revell Court. He had quickly realized he would never reach his superiors in time with word of

Bardou's terrible plan, but he knew he had to do something. He did not want to see women and children blown to bits in the midst of the annual fire festival. In desperation, he had decided to turn to Lucien Knight. Rollo had received a note from Lucien a few days ago asking for a meeting; no doubt Lucien already knew that something was afoot. Rollo had intended to ignore the summons, but had changed his mind upon learning of the wanton destruction that Bardou had in store.

Now Lucien was his only hope. He was the only one who would listen to a ne'er-do-well like Rollo Greene. And he was the only one with the skill to stop Bardou from wreaking havoc on the city on Guy Fawkes Night. Rollo only prayed that he would reach Lucien before that Russian angel of death caught up to him.

Throwing himself upon divine providence, he spurred his tiring horse on faster.

That night, Lucien sat in his bedchamber, staring out the bank of windows at the dark horizon and the starry firmament, brooding with a mix of hurt and self-directed anger over the way he had groveled to Alice this afternoon. He had been blind to how she had taken control of their relationship over the past few days. Their whole liaison had been his whim, for his own pleasure, but now the seducer had been categorically seduced. *Did she enjoy having him on his knees?* he wondered, taking a rather bitter drink of his brandy. Emotionally, he was in her hands now, and it scared the hell out of him.

If only she had said she loved him, he thought achingly, rubbing his chest where the denial still felt vaguely like a hole there. Ah, but his little artist with her painful honesty would rather suffer the truth to wound him than soothe his feelings with a lie. He respected that about her. Yet—perhaps wishfully—he could not help feeling that she *did* care for him. He sat there warring with himself in silence until, in the next moment, he decided abruptly to find out.

He downed the rest of his brandy for an extra dose of courage, got up, and left his room, stalking through the dim maze of hallways. In the oppressive silence of Revell Court, his heart thundered in his ears as he turned down the corridor that led to her room.

He could not take this uncertainty, this inner confusion. He hated the vulnerability he felt. It went against everything the war had taught him about staying on his guard, shutting off his emotions. If she could not love him, there was no point in going through this. He had to know, he thought as he came to her door. If she did not want to be with him forever, he would not prolong his own suffering any further, but would send her home in the morning to Glenwood Park and her precious Harry.

As he stood outside her chamber, reaching for the doorknob, he knew this moment would decide their fate. He had freely given her the key, it was in her hands either to take him in or to keep him out.

A cold sweat broke out on his brow. He closed his eyes in fear-filled anguish, his heart pounding. *God, please. I need this.* It was a desperate act, a blind clutching in the darkness for her love from out of the depths of his terrible isolation. If she did not take him in, he did not think he would ever have the courage to reach out to someone again.

Steeling himself for the worst, he grasped the doorknob and tried it—then drew in his breath as the knob turned and the unlocked door creaked open into her dark, moonlit chamber.

Alice sat up when the door creaked, her heart racing. She had sensed or perhaps felt him standing outside her door and had been lying on her side, wide-eyed, barely daring to breathe as she waited to see what he would do. He stepped into her room, one foot over the threshold, and stood silhouetted in the doorway.

She could barely breathe, mesmerized by his luminous stare. It intimidated her. His face was stark, his eyes glittering in the moonlight with sensual hunger. She swept a glance over him, feeling the catch of desire in her belly. His black trousers molded every line of his long legs. He wore no waistcoat or jacket, no cravat. His white shirt was open at the throat, his sleeves rolled up. He was frightening, deadly, beautiful.

Slowly, she moved onto her knees, holding his stare. She saw his body trembling slightly. She could feel his need. She knew what he had come for, and she knew that if she turned him away, he would never be back. Her heart beat recklessly. Without a word, she held out her hand to him as though coaxing a wild wolf to take a gift of food.

He didn't move.

"Come in here," she whispered. "Come to me."

His wary stare seemed to size her up; then, after a moment, he closed the door soundlessly behind him and prowled over to her. He stood beside her bed while she knelt before him in her night rail. He kept his hands at his sides, but by the moonlight and the faint reddish glow of the smoldering hearth fire, she saw the longing in his eyes to be touched.

"I shouldn't have asked you to have blind faith in me when we both know I don't deserve it," he said tautly. "I will close the Grotto as soon as it is possible for me to do so. I can't explain. . . . Just, don't leave me."

She reached up and cupped his strong jaw. He pressed his cheek into her hand, then kissed her wrist.

"Lucien," she whispered. "I should not have pretended that my love for you was contingent upon any of those things. It's not. I'm sorry I hurt you. I love you. And I want you."

With a low, strangled moan, he pulled her into his arms, claiming her mouth in an explosive kiss full of primal possession. She surrendered completely, eager, recklessly eager, to give herself without looking back. She waited in breathless anticipation as he dragged the straps of her chemise down over her arms, baring her breasts.

She tilted her head back with an ardent sigh as he bent his head to her chest. Her skin was cool in the autumn night, but his mouth was scorching hot, sucking hungrily on her nipple. Dazed with passion, she stroked his glossy black hair, watching him.

His hand raked her thigh, then dipped between her legs, giving heat, delicious pressure. She pulled his shirt off of him, splaying her hands across his muscled back until he came up from her breasts, his skin flushed, his hair tousled. She could feel the pounding of his heart as she caressed his splendid chest, then traced the lines of his iron-sculpted arms, her fingers tingling. She skimmed her palm lower down his flat belly, her gaze following her hand. She paused at the waistline of his trousers and lifted her questioning glance to meet his smoldering gaze.

She waited, feeling his hands trembling as he unfastened his trousers and drawers beneath them. She pushed them a few inches down his hips; then a low groan escaped him when she slid her hand inside his loosened clothes and gently clasped his shaft, discovering for herself how he wanted to be touched. He closed his eyes in rapture as she stroked him. Her left arm was draped around his neck. In climbing lust, she kissed his ear, neck, and shoulders until he shuddered and quickly stopped her, grasping her shoulders.

"Lie down," he ordered in a rough, panting whisper.

Trembling with desire for him, she obeyed, bracing her hands behind her as she eased onto her back. He slid her chemise up over her hips, covered her thighs in kisses, then buried his face in her mound. She tensed, arched, shivered with disbelieving ecstasy as he kissed and licked her. She felt like she was losing her mind as he slid his clever fingers in and out of her passage, coaxing her hips to take up the sensual rhythm with him. Gasping with wanton enjoyment, she came up onto her elbows and watched him adoring her body while he pleasured himself with his other hand. God help her, she could not believe she had denied herself this for so many days. If she had known—! Her heart was thundering, and she felt as though some long pent-up storm in her was going to burst.

When he withdrew his touch and lifted his head, leaving her incomplete, she thought she was going to die. She watched him in savage need as he moved to a kneeling position between her legs. He loomed over her, then came down, planting his hands on either side of her. His face was shadowed as he held her stare, slowly lowering his body down, covering hers.

The moment of contact, his muscled weight atop her, was heaven. His chest was damp with a light sheen of sweat against her bare breasts. His face was wet as he sought her mouth and kissed her; she wrapped her arms tightly around his neck. He stroked her once again between her legs until she was utterly drunk on his touch. His drawers clung around his lean, hard hips. As she felt him push them down lower, her very mind throbbed with ecstasy, intoxicating her senses. Bare and sleek, he eased between her thighs; instinctually, she enfolded him between her legs. She felt the smooth head of his erection caress her pulsating flesh, becoming instantly slicked with her body's dew. Kissing her in soul-deep passion, Lucien caressed her cheek and her hair, cradling her head under his large, gentle hand. For a moment, he paused, gazing down at her in dark longing, his soul laid bare in his glittering eyes—no pretenses, no masks left between them. The silence was almost holy with their love.

Held powerless in his enchanter's stare, she whispered his name, her voice hoarse with need, ran her hands down his satin-smooth back and clutched his lean buttocks, pulling him to her in wild demand. With a low moan, he gave her what she wanted, slowly mounting her.

His kiss was so deep, so overwhelming, she could not even gasp as he paused, then ruptured the fragile barrier of her virginity with one quick thrust. Her shocked cry of pain was muffled by his mouth. His every muscle strained around her with his effort to be still until her pain had passed. He did not let her go or even stop kissing her, his hands stroking her face, petting her hair, his silence begging her and ordering her to wait and to be strong until her body accepted him. Gradually, he let her come up for air, his thumbs stroking her cheekbones.

"Relax," he coaxed her in a ragged whisper. "Relax for me, sweeting. Don't be afraid. It won't hurt if you relax." He kissed her again and again. "You are so beautiful, my love. There is nothing to fear. You are mine now. Forever. Everything I have is yours. My body, my heart, my name."

"Lucien, my dark angel." She cupped his face between her hands and stared into his eyes. "I want your secrets."

He stared at her for a moment, then lowered his lashes and shook his head slightly. "No, you don't," he murmured, then bent his head and kissed her.

For a moment, he merely played, sporting with her senses, lightly skimming her cheeks and her nose with his lips. When he returned to her mouth, she parted her lips hungrily for him, her tongue meeting his in the sweetest of welcomes. Her fevered body trembled beneath him.

The firelight shimmered along their joined silhouettes as he bent his head and reverently kissed her shoulders and her chest, murmuring love words that made her rigid body soften. He stroked her hair, her arms, her sides, and her belly, showering her with light, exquisite kisses, his beguiling lips tickling and soft as they nuzzled her skin. Slowly, his gentleness eased her until she felt her body yield of its own volition, taking him in by several more inches.

"Oh, God," she moaned softly, wrapping her arms around him, shocked to discover her pleasure anew, transformed now into something deep and rich and nourishing. "*Lucien.*"

"Yes," he whispered, "now you know."

Lucien gazed down at her, lost in his worship of her. He felt redeemed in her surrender. Her ivory skin was flushed, her lashes dusting her high-boned cheeks as she lay languidly enjoying his slow, patient strokes. Her strawberry-blond hair flowed, long and luxurious, over her pillow like silk spun from sunbeams. He loved her hair. He loved every inch of her.

Threading his fingers through hers, he drew her hands above her head, filling her mouth with a fiery kiss as he pressed in hotly between her legs. She moaned with pleasure and freed her hands from his light hold, caressing him. Her body was slim and elegant beneath him, her beautiful artist's hands trailing up and down over his taut arms. She ran her fingers through his hair. He checked his savage passion repeatedly and focused on attending to her every desire. He watched her firm, young breasts joggle with his rhythmic strokes as his body rocked gently between her white thighs.

Her hands moved down his sides and clutched his hips in rising insistence; he saw a fleeting grimace flit over her delicate features and smiled darkly, realizing she was ready for more. He reached down and brushed her clitoris ever so lightly with his thumb. She moaned and lifted her hips, able, at last, to fit him completely inside of her. He stayed like that for a moment, not moving, relishing the unbearable pleasure of her tightness with his eyes closed. His breathing was ragged with his effort to hold himself in check. He came down onto his elbows, cradling her against him.

She wound her arms around his neck and whispered softly in his ear, "I love you."

He gazed down at her in amazement. "Oh, sweeting," he forced out abruptly, "I love you, too."

She curled upward and kissed him. He lost all awareness of time as they made love, moving together, losing themselves in each other. He consumed her kiss while he pleasured her with quickening strokes, his hands running all over her sweet body. His heart pounding wildly, he squeezed her nipple none too gently, catching her gasp on his tongue. He took her harder, rising on his hands above her, plunging into her body, his control slipping into oblivion. She was moaning, writhing beneath him, clutching his buttocks and pulling him in to meet every greedy lift of her hips.

"Lucien, oh, God, yes, it's so—oh, please," she whimpered, her face radiant with bliss.

"That's right, angel, come for me," he panted half incoherently, watching her, utterly enslaved by her innocent throes of passion.

Straining and heaving until the bed shook and the drafty, firelit room resounded with their groans and tender cries, they climaxed together. He felt her passage contract around his manhood, squeezing him with blinding pleasure. He shuddered with profound release, feeling as though he flung his entire soul into hers. She went limp with sated pleasure as he held her close to his heart, stroking her hair, waiting for his pulse to slow back to normal.

He withdrew gingerly from her body, then gathered her once more into his arms. They lay entwined for a very long time, silent, staring at each other. She caressed his face and chest while he memorized every line of her face, twirling a lock of her golden hair around his finger.

"Gretna Green?" she whispered at length in the dark.

"Gretna Green," he assured her with a firm nod.

"Oh, Lucien, will it really be all right?"

With a sleepy smile, he leaned near and kissed her brow. "My darling, it will be wonderful."

CHAPTER ELEVEN

They slept entwined in each other's arms and woke up late to a jewel-toned autumn morning that shimmered with promise. Though late-morning sun lit the chamber brightly and there was much to be done, they tarried in bed, playing and savoring the warmth of their newfound love.

"I want us to go to Mr. Whitby's today and tell him our good news," Alice declared, lacing her fingers through Lucien's. "He'll be so happy. He knew all along."

"What? No, he didn't," Lucien scoffed, still tousled and sleepy-eyed.

"Oh, yes he did! Do you remember when you went out to fix the shutter on his house? He told me then that you were in love with me."

"What?" he cried.

She laughed and snuggled against him. "He did, I vow!"

"How did he know?"

She shrugged, gazing at him with sparkling eyes. "Don't ask me. You said he was wise."

"Blazes! I shall have to have a word with that meddling old nuisance. I thought I did a good job of hiding it."

"You fooled me," she answered roguishly, rubbing her foot up and down over his shin under the sheets, savoring the crisp, lightly haired texture of his bare legs.

He grabbed her with a playful growl and pulled her onto him. She sat up astride him, her hands planted on his shoulders.

"Well, well. Look at little Miss Goody Two-Shoes," he said, leering at her body, then rested his head back on his pillow with a grin. "Take me."

She gave him a flat look and poked him in the chest. "What time can we go see Mr. Whitby?"

"I have a lot to do today. . . ."

"Lucien!" She bent down, wrapping her arms around his neck. "You *have* to indulge my every whim today, or I shall think you the most scandalous cad."

"I'll show you scandalous," he whispered, rolling her over onto her back. She let out a peal of laughter as he eased atop her. "Scandalous," he murmured, "begins innocently enough. . . . Like this." Lifting his eyebrow, he lowered his head and kissed the valley between her breasts.

"Lucien, I'm sore enough as it is!" She grabbed his ear and pulled him up like a naughty schoolboy.

"Ow! Let go of me, you harridan!" he said, laughing.

She smiled at him.

He kissed her nose, then pulled back and glanced ruefully at her. "It's just as well, I suppose. This is going to be a hectic day." He climbed out of the bed with a sigh and walked over to his pile of cast-off clothes.

Alice jarred herself out of staring absently at his sleek, nude body. "Do you mean you'll be busy getting ready for the party?"

He nodded as he stepped into his snug black trousers and pulled them up.

"Will this be the last one?" she asked.

"I hope so." Pulling his shirt on over his head, he came back to her, leaned down, and kissed her lips, cupping her face in his hand. For a moment, he just gazed at her with a soft smile. She stared lovingly at him.

"I will never, for as long as I live, forget last night and how beautiful you were," he murmured.

She quivered at his tender words. He kissed her knuckles, reluctantly letting her hand trail from his grasp as he moved away from the bed. She held the hand he had kissed vaguely to her heart, a dreamy smile on her face as she watched him swagger over to the door. He opened it, then turned back to her.

"Get some rest," he advised. "You're going to have to get used to staying up late." He sent her a scoundrelly wink and slipped out of the room, pulling the door shut behind him.

Still blushing from his wicked innuendo, Alice sighed and fell back onto her bed, giddy with bliss. She hugged her pillow in sheer, teeming love and thanked God for the new day, the sunlight, the seasons, the world, and him. From this bright beginning, however, her day went steadily downhill.

She could feel the tension in the air mounting as the afternoon progressed. Five times Lucien said he only had one more thing to do before they could go to Mr. Whitby's. His tasks ate up more and more of the day, so that she was left alone when she was most vulnerable, most in need of reassurance from the man she had given her innocence to the previous night.

She ate a light lunch alone in her chamber, packed her things to leave for Gretna Green in the morning, took a nap, and found, when she woke up, that he was still at work. Angry now, Alice marched downstairs and tersely asked Mr. Godfrey if he knew where His Lordship could be found. Readily enough, the butler replied that Lucien was in his studio. Scowling at the reminder that he kept his fighting skills so sharply honed because he had "violent enemies," Alice put on the shapeless woolen cloak that she had borrowed from one of the servant girls after her pelisse had been ruined in the mud and rain. With the first trickle of his horrid guests already beginning to arrive, she turned her back on them and stalked down the drive and past the stables to his studio.

Her gaze swept the lowering, gray skies. *Don't you dare rain,* she advised the clouds. *I will not have muddy roads keeping those dreadful people here an hour longer than necessary, nor slowing our drive to Gretna tomorrow.*

When she reached the studio, she pulled open the door and stopped in surprise to find the room filled with his black-coated guards, the five lads who practiced with him, and most of the footmen. Lucien was standing at the front of the room, giving them their instructions for the night in a voice that rang with command.

"The second person you are to look for is a Russian—" He stopped abruptly as his sharp gaze homed in on Alice, standing uncertainly in the doorway. "What is it, my dear?" His eyes flashed with impatient warning, as if to say, *Not now.*

She hesitated. "I am going to Mr. Whitby's," she said with a meaningful look of reproach, feeling self-conscious in front of all the big, burly men.

"Very good, my dear. Give him my regards." He gave her a smile full of dutiful charm and waited for her to leave.

She glared at him, pivoted, and walked out. This was intolerable!

Why could his servants know what was really going on, when she, who was about to become the lady of the house, was not privy to his secrets? Why could those five waggish youths know? How could he trust them more than her? And why had Lucien looked at her like she was nothing but an annoyance? A wave of confusion tinged with panic hit her. Now that he had had her, was he brushing her off?

Ach, what a vexing day! She knew she was allowing her insecurities to torment her. She felt lonely and moody and unwanted, and her head was throbbing. Perhaps the imminent arrival of her woman's courses was making her overly sensitive, she thought. She just wanted him to hold her.

Disgusted with her own churlish vacillations, she started off on the long walk to Mr. Whitby's cottage. The mere thought of the dear old man comforted her. He would surely be glad for a visitor. The walk helped to clear her head a bit. She had no interest whatsoever in the gathering festivities behind her at Revell Court.

When she knocked on Mr. Whitby's door some time later, Mrs. Malone, the housekeeper, welcomed her in. The old man was seated, as before, by the crackling fireplace in the parlor, his spectacles perched on his high-bridged nose as he read from one of the ponderous tomes that Lucien had brought him.

"Miss Montague, what a delightful treat," he exclaimed as she strode over to him and bent to kiss his cheek. He glanced hopefully behind her. "Where is your shadow?"

"He did not come today," she said with a glum smile, taking off her gloves, her displeasure written plainly in her face. "His Lordship is having another party. I have hardly seen him all day."

"Oh, dear," the old man said in dismay.

"You see why I called on you. I sorely wanted the company of a civilized gentleman." She laid her cloak over the back of the sofa and sat down on the ottoman by him, took his gnarled hands in hers, and squeezed them gently. "Mr. Whitby, I have such news for you!"

"What is it, child?"

She felt her cheeks flood with bright color. "You were right—Lucien proposed."

His lined face lit up with delight, chasing her own uncertainties away with his joy. "When?"

"Yesterday! We leave tomorrow for Gretna Green."

She visited for half an hour, talking excitedly about her future life as Lady Lucien Knight. She plucked as much gossip as she could out of the old man, as well, about the members of the ducal family she was about to join. She was desperate for them to like her, though she was only the daughter of a baron.

"My dear child, you have nothing to fear," he assured her with a chuckle. "They will welcome you with open arms."

Noting his flagging strength after a while, Alice gave him a hug farewell, bundled up again in her cloak and gloves, and took her leave, hurrying back through the woods to Revell Court as the early autumn twilight deepened to full darkness.

Coming back through the garden, she brushed past the musk rose bushes and strode into the house, her cloak billowing out behind her, her face shadowed in the depths of its hood. A footman intercepted her when she came in through the door at the back of the house. At her request, he showed her up to her room by the servants' stairs, thus avoiding the debauchees who were once more flocking in through the front entrance.

"Please tell Lord Lucien I am back and I wish to see him," she ordered the footman as she swept into her room, plucking off her gloves.

"Er, I am . . . very sorry, ma'am. His Lordship has already gone down to the Grotto and gave specific orders that he was not to be disturbed. Unless it's an emergency?"

"It's not an emergency," she sighed, rolling her eyes. "Never mind."

"Begging your pardon, ma'am, he also requested that you remain in your quarters for the duration of the evening."

"Oh, did he?" She turned to the servant, folding her arms over her chest. "Devil take him, I have no desire to see that spectacle again," she muttered under breath, then addressed the servant. "I would like something to eat, please. Could you bring me a headache powder, as well?"

"Yes, ma'am," the servant said, bowing with a look of relief.

She nodded his dismissal. She knew the sort of headache that accompanied her monthly visit from "the French lady." As usual, it came right on schedule. She stifled a quiet sigh of disappointment and drifted over to the window, where she stood looking down at the drunken revelers toppling out of their carriages into the firelit courtyard, just as they had done last week when she had first arrived at this strange place.

The flames atop the iron torch stand reached high into the night, dancing across her ghostly reflection in the window.

Several hours had passed, and the proceedings in the Grotto were well under way. Lucien stood in his observation room behind the dragon's eyes, broodingly looking down upon the crowd. He was determined to learn once and for all where Claude Bardou was and what he was doing, and for that, he needed the fat little American, Rollo Greene.

The guards had sent him word when Greene had come through the gates, but somehow they had lost track of him within the winding caverns of the Grotto. Lucien bided his time, suspecting that the randy little goat had probably sneaked off with some drunken woman.

His glance swept the orgy below in distaste. Fresh from his first night of lovemaking with Alice, the anonymous couplings taking place throughout the Grotto appeared all the more meaningless and degrading. He preferred to remember Alice bathing innocently alone in the hot springs. How he wished he could have been with her instead of here tonight, he thought with a small sigh. But the sooner it was over, the sooner he could quit this work and devote himself to her entirely. She had been right, of course. His work put his life in constant danger, and he would give it up in a heartbeat rather than risk any of it touching her or the children that might one day grace their lives.

He was musing that he could continue serving the Foreign Office in a strictly diplomatic role, when suddenly, Marc and O'Shea came rushing into the observation room.

"My lord! We've found Rollo Greene!"

"Where is he?" Lucien demanded, pivoting.

"He's bloody dead!" O'Shea answered. "Facedown in the canal."

Lucien let out an oath. "How?"

"He was stabbed in the back," Marc said tensely. "The knife's still in him, steel, with a big green jewel on the hilt—Sophia Voznesensky's trademark, I believe."

"Damn it!" Lucien cursed. "She must have slipped past the gates somehow! We have to find her. Now. Bardou must have sent her to stop Rollo from talking to me." He drew a deep breath. "I want the exits sealed. Send word to the perimeter to look lively. She's done her work; now she'll try to escape. Be extremely careful with this woman. She's tall, dark-haired, dark eyes. Don't be fooled by her beauty. She'll cut your throat if you turn your back on her."

"Yes, sir."

They strode off to carry out his orders. Marching out of the observation room, Lucien made a brief inspection of the scene of Rollo Greene's death before joining the hunt for Sophia. The American was floating facedown between two moored gondolas. The red film of his blood in the water licked at the sides of the boats and the rocky basin of the landing.

He ordered the guards to bury Greene in the woods before dawn's light. He was unconcerned about the local authorities; the death of an American secret agent killed on enemy soil during wartime was not going to draw anyone's attention.

After a nerve-racking twenty-minute search, his head of security, a gruff, dauntless Scotsman named McLeish, and two of his best men brought a viciously fighting Sophia into his observation room.

"We caught her trying to escape over the wall," the burly Scot growled to Lucien as he struggled to restrain the woman.

Sophia Voznesensky was a tempestuous beauty, tall and striking. Fear darted through her dark eyes as Lucien stalked toward her. She redoubled her struggles until it took all three of the guards to restrain her.

Stepping in front of her, Lucien wrapped his hand around her lovely white throat and drove her back against the wall, staring at her, laughing tautly at her colorful Russian curses.

"Sophia, Sophia. Your manners are atrocious. You come into my house and start killing my guests. What kind of behavior is that for a lady?"

"I have nothing to say to you!"

"Has your *cher ami* Bardou lost his nerve? He sends a woman to do his dirty work?"

"Bugger yourself, Argus!" she spat, calling him by his code name. "You'll get nothing out of me! He'll kill me if I talk to you! You know he hates you more than all the rest of the English put together!"

"You're going to tell me why he had you murder Rollo Greene," he said calmly, "and you're going to tell me right now."

"You wouldn't hurt a woman," she challenged him in bravado, but as Lucien clasped her throat with a bit more pressure, he could feel her pulse beating swiftly with fear under his fingertips.

"On the contrary, my dear. I wouldn't hurt a *lady*.

You, I could drown like the rat that you are. Mr. McLeish, I trust you searched Madame Voznesensky and stripped her of her weapons?"

"Er, no, my lord," the Scotsman replied. "She fought us too hard."

"Hold her," Lucien ordered the other two. "McLeish. You may do the honors."

"Oh, Argus," Sophia pouted, rolling her shoulders back in a sensual motion that lifted her breasts for his inspection. "Won't you do it? You have such a soft touch."

"Don't even try, Sophia. You once loved Russia, but now you only serve Bardou."

"Do you think I have a choice?" she retorted sharply, lashing out at the Scotsman with the back of her fist. "Get your hands off me! If Bardou asks you to do him a favor, you do it or you die," she said to Lucien. "You're going to have to kill me, because if I betray him, I'm as good as dead!" she finished, kicking McLeish soundly in the groin.

The Scotsman fell, groaning.

"Sophia," Lucien said irritably.

"Lucien, don't let them hurt me. You search me. I'll be good. I promise," she whispered, clasping her hands atop her head, offering herself with a sultry stare.

Lucien flicked a glance over her, then looked once more into her eyes, narrowing his own. He knew full well what she was trying to do. Perhaps she hoped that their past encounter meant something to him. It did not. "Tell me what you know, and I will protect you from Bardou."

"You can't protect me from him. Nobody can."

"This is your chance to be free of him. What is he doing for the Americans? What information did Greene come here to sell me? Trust me, Sophia. I will keep you safe."

"You can't. You won't." She suddenly threw off his hands as he began patting her down. "Leave me alone, all of you! I am an agent of the czar! I demand that you convey me at once to the Russian embassy in London! I have rights!"

"You have nothing," Lucien snarled.

The interrogation that followed alternated between shouting matches in both Russian and English and Sophia's vexing attempts to save herself by seducing him. She continued to ward off his every effort to relieve her of her weapons—and God only knew how many guns and knives were concealed beneath her skirts. Lucien was afraid to push her too hard because he believed that he could tempt her back onto his side, but he grew agitated as the moments passed and all his yelling and threats did not make a dent in her obstinate refusal to cooperate.

She was so resolute in her refusal to give him even a scrap of information that he began to fear he was really going to have to do something unpleasant to the woman. He went on trying his best to intimidate her into answering.

"Why did you kill Greene? What did he know that was so important?"

"I don't know anything," she said stoically, glaring at him.

"Where is Bardou? Is he in England?"

"I don't know."

"Why are you protecting that animal?" he roared in her face.

"I'm protecting *myself*! He'll kill me!"

"What do you think I'm going to do to you, Sophie? Take a look around! Where is your lover now? He's not here to save you. There's no one here to help you, no Claude, nobody. I'm your only hope."

"You don't scare me," she snarled back at him. "You're not like him. You never were. You wouldn't do to me in anger what he does to me for fun." She closed her eyes as though suddenly exhausted, leaning her head back against the wall. "Oh, kiss me in your soft way, Lucien. I still remember that night in Prague. . . . It's been so long since anyone has given me pleasure."

"Sophia, that is low."

She lifted her lashes and laughed, a throaty, sensual sound of despair as she gave him a hollow-eyed look. "Let me go, Lucien," she said. "I'm doomed either way."

Dodging the servants, Alice stole down the corridor, her face hidden in the voluminous hood of the brown robe. Confident of every step now, unlike last week, she knew exactly where she was going and why. Had he really expected her to sit obediently in her room while he ruled as Lord Draco in the Grotto with his disgusting little initiates crawling all over him? Only a fool would idly stand by while her future husband was besieged by immoral women throwing themselves at him. There was no harm in making sure he behaved himself. Supper and the headache powder had greatly relieved her earlier fatigue and discomfort. Now she was ready to fight for her man, if necessary.

This time as she walked down the limestone stairs into the Grotto, she was not frightened by Talbert's mumbo jumbo on the stage and simply ignored the people entwined together, pursuing pleasure in fantastic contortions. She kept her face concealed within the hood of her domino and glided silently, stealthily through the crowded Grotto. She wanted to see what Lucien was doing before making her presence known. He was going to be angry at her for intruding, she realized, but perhaps if he hadn't ignored her all day, maybe she would not need to come checking up on him like a jealous wife.

Not seeing him anywhere, she made her way to the dragon carving to seek him in his observation room. The black-coated guards balked when she demanded to be allowed up to see him, but when she reminded them haughtily that she was about to become their master's wife, they had to oblige her. They could barely keep up with her as she pounded up the dim, spiraling stairs to the observation room, brushing back her hood as she ran. Even though she was peeved at Lucien for neglecting her all day, a rush of exhilaration flooded her veins to know she would be with him shortly. She heard shouting as she neared the top of the spiral steps. When she reached the antechamber, she saw that the door to the observation room was open. Her cheeks flushed with anticipation, she flung into the doorway, eager to see him—but when she did, she froze and instantly felt the very breath knocked out of her lungs to find a beautiful brunette struggling in Lucien's arms.

He was standing behind the woman, one arm wrapped around her waist, his other hand pulling at her clothing and her skirts, which were hitched up over her left thigh.

Remembering how she had gone through this exact scene with him last week, Alice's eyes glazed over with shock.

As though feeling her gaze upon him, Lucien looked over and met her stare. He stopped cold. Panic flashed in his eyes to see her standing there—as though he realized she had just caught him . . . cheating on her.

No one had time to react.

In that horrible moment when everything went still, the woman pulled a knife out from under her skirts and swung it in an arc with blinding speed, cutting Lucien's side open. With a barbaric shout, she ran straight at Alice.

CHAPTER TWELVE

"No!" Lucien roared, lunging forward.

Alice flung herself out of the way as the woman's knife swung savagely past her, missing her face by inches. The woman bolted across the antechamber and disappeared down the steps almost before Lucien's men could react; in the next instant, there was pandemonium.

"Lucien!" Alice screamed.

"He's hurt!"

"She's cut 'is Lordship!" the guard barked.

"After her!" Lucien ordered them furiously. The four young rogues and several of the guards pounded down the stairs after the woman. Lucien pushed past them and strode to Alice, holding his side. "Are you all right?"

She nodded, staring, stricken, at the blood flowing out from between his fingers, slowly staining his loose white shirt. "Oh, my God."

"What the hell are you doing here?" he yelled at her, terrifying her.

"Lucien—you're bleeding," she whispered.

"I told you to stay away! You could have been killed! Get her out of here," he curtly ordered the guard.

"I'm sorry!"

He brushed past her with a curse and hurried after his men, still holding his side.

"Lucien!" she screamed, but he ran down the steps.

Alice followed, throwing off the guard's grasp with the sharpest words she had ever uttered. Lucien was hurt. Her suspicions were forgotten. Nothing was going to keep her away from him. She rushed down the steps and back out to the Grotto. She saw him racing up the steps carved in the limestone and plunged into the crowd after him.

Lucien pounded up the steps, gritting his teeth at the burning pain in his side, then crashed through the Priapus door and crouched under the overhanging limestone as he ran along the narrow bank of rock that hugged the cavern wall. Damn it, he had been so close to breaking Sophia down when Alice had appeared! He had realized in a flash how it must have looked to her. For one instant, his attention had been jerked away from his task, and it could have easily cost him his life. Sophia could have made it a mortal blow if she had wanted to, he realized grimly as he ran up the steps from the wine cellars into the house. A wave of dizziness from loss of blood hit him as he tore down the corridor toward the entrance hall, knocking a footman out of his way, but before he reached the door, he heard one of his lads scream, "Get her! She's stabbed Lucien!"

A shot rang out. Two.

He let out a furious roar and burst out of the door. Immediately, he saw Sophia sprinting in a beeline toward the closed iron gates of Revell Court, as though she would climb over them, but even as he bellowed, "Hold your fire!" more shots followed.

She threw up her arms, sprawling forward, cut down midstride by gunfire.

"Hold your fire!" Lucien screamed again. He raced after her, flinging down onto his knees beside her. By the blazing glow of the courtyard's iron torch stand, he saw that her back was riddled with seeping wounds.

"Oh, God. Sophia." His heart was pounding, but he already knew it was beyond his skill to save her.

Her cheek lay on the cobblestones, and she stared at him, still alive, blood trickling from the corner of her mouth. Her eyes were terrified, glassy with fear. He knew she had only moments to live. He was afraid to move her for fear of making it worse.

"Argus," she panted.

"I'm here," he said softly in Russian. He touched her hair. "I'm so sorry," he choked out.

At his words, she closed her eyes as in relief. "Now I am . . . free of him, Argus."

He laid his hand atop hers. "What is he going to do, Sophie? Do this for me. Tell me. For both our countries."

She struggled, agony written over her beautiful, ashen face. "He has . . . explosives. Guy Fawkes Night, Lucien. The . . . Americans want revenge for the . . . burning of . . . Washington. I don't know where . . . he'll strike. Maybe Parliament," she gasped out.

Good God! Guy Fawkes Night was next Saturday, only eight days hence. Perhaps Bardou intended to make history repeat itself, Lucien thought grimly. In 1605, a group of Jacobite conspirators had hired military veteran, Guy Fawkes, to blow up the House of Lords with the king and the whole peerage inside, but the plot was discovered before it could be carried out—and, by the grace of God, so would Bardou's. "Has he arrived in London yet?"

She gave an almost imperceptible nod.

"Where has he set up operations?"

"Warehouse . . . by . . . the . . . river."

"Sophia, the river is lined with warehouses—"

"Be . . . careful, Argus. He is . . . coming . . . after you." Her agonized whisper ended in a pitiable moan.

"Shh, gently, gently," he whispered in her native tongue, holding her hand and stroking her hair as he realized death was upon her.

He closed his eyes at the awful rattle in her throat as she drowned in her own blood; then he bowed his head. Her dying whisper still hung upon the night's silence.

He is coming after you.

When Lucien flicked his eyes open, there were flames in them. He had a hellish inferno burning in his heart and fire in his veins. *Let him come.* His mind churned with hatred, calling forth the savage, primal beast that he had turned into after five weeks of living like an animal in a cage: starved, beaten, unwashed. Their brutality had made him cruel when he had finally managed to escape. He had stolen silently from man to man in the darkness, cutting each one's throat, not moving on to the next until he had stood and watched each one of his torturers die. But Bardou had not been there that night. He had gone to kill Patrick Kelley, using the information he had wrenched from Lucien under torture. Bardou had escaped his retribution.

This, Lucien thought darkly, *was his chance for revenge.*

As he looked up, Alice came toward him with uncertain steps. *She would have to be protected,* he thought. *If Bardou found out that she was his woman, he would strike at her and kill her without hesitation, especially now that Lucien's men had shot Sophia.* He noticed the bewilderment in her eyes as she tried to comprehend, no doubt, the murderous savagery she read in his. He dropped his gaze, not wanting her to know this part of him.

He reached down and gently closed Sophia's glazed, staring eyes.

The terrible stillness was broken only by the popping of sparks from the great torch stand. Its flames billowed against the black night, illuminating the courtyard and outlining Lucien's hair and shoulders in a golden halo as he crouched by the fallen woman's side. There was a harsh, remote look in his beautiful face and a menace in his silence that made Alice fear to speak. She stared at him, her accusations forgotten.

A pool of crimson was spreading over the cobblestones all around the woman. The guards were standing around watching uneasily, their rifles hanging from their grasps. When Lucien slowly lifted his gaze, Alice realized aghast that the woman was dead.

She covered her mouth with her hand in shock. Guilt welled through her. *This is my fault.* If she had not been filled with jealousy, she would not have been on hand to distract Lucien; then the woman would not have cut him and would not have been shot down trying to escape. Staring at the body, Alice felt light-headed with horror. Someone was dead because of her.

Lucien swept to his feet. "Who fired?" he asked in a calm, low, hellish voice that sent chills of sheer dread down her spine.

No one answered.

"Who gave you the order to open fire?"

"B-but, my lord, they told us she had stabbed you," one of the big guards offered.

"Do I look dead to you?" he screamed.

Alice flinched. The echo of his voice carried on the wind.

"N-no, sir," the guard answered, bowing his head.

Alice gathered her composure quickly and started toward him. "Lucien—"

"Get back in the house. I want a word with you. You directly defied my orders." His voice was steely. He turned to his men. "I want whoever did this gone by morning. Collect your pay from Mr. Godfrey and get out. McLeish, see to the body. Do it quickly."

"Aye, my lord."

When Lucien and she walked into the house, she saw the bloodstain spreading down his side through his white shirt. "Your wound—"

"Upstairs," he ordered, shrugging her off.

Alice pursed her lips as he climbed the stairs ahead of her. In the corridor, she ordered a maid to bring hot water, scissors, and bandages to His Lordship's bedchamber; then she hurried after him.

In his chamber, he took a medical box out of the trunk at the foot of his bed and set it on the chest of drawers. "You know, I was going to *lock* you in your room tonight to make sure you didn't interfere; but I had already given you the key, and I said to myself, no, I must trust her. That's the point of everything between us. Can I trust you or can't I, Alice? Because, at the moment, I'm not convinced." Angrily unbuttoning his shirt, he pulled back the blood-drenched cloth from his side, revealing the wound.

"Lucien—" she started, then stopped, shuddering as she looked at the four-inch horizontal slice across his ribs.

The sight of the blood and the smell of the alcohol he poured onto a clean rag from the medicine box reminded her in awful, vivid detail of tending her brother's terrible injuries. Lucien let out a stream of curses as he pressed the brandy-soaked bandage to his side. His oaths snapped her into action. The bloody-minded fool would have her help whether he wanted it or not. She pressed him back to sit on the wide, sturdy dresser before he passed out on the floor.

"Hand me the needle and thread," he growled. "I need stitches."

"I'll do it."

"The hell you will. I'm not a handkerchief for your fancy embroidery and I *don't* need you mothering me. It's just a flesh wound. I want to know what you have to say for yourself."

"Never mind that, Lucien! We have to bind your wound first. Let me help you."

"I'll do it myself."

"You can't reach that."

"Yes, I can. Now give me the blasted needle."

"Shut up and lie *down*!" she ordered fiercely.

"Alice!"

"Lucien. Who do you think took care of my brother when he came back from the battlefield covered in wounds?"

He stared at her for a moment in defiance. "All right, then," he grumbled. He winced, glanced again at his cut, took a swig from the brandy bottle, and offered no further objections. The maid brought in the items Alice had asked for, and Lucien eased back onto his elbow on the dresser, reluctantly allowing her to patch him up.

Neither of them spoke as she cleaned his wound, holding bandage after bandage against it until the bleeding slowed enough for her to make the stitches. She threaded the needle, dipped it in the brandy, and grimaced as she sewed his torn flesh closed. Forcing aside her guilt over the terrible thing she had caused and her dread at the ramifications of it, she gave her present task her single-minded concentration.

She could feel Lucien staring at her while she worked. She tied off the first stitch and snipped the thread, then glanced at him, letting out a breath. "About nineteen more to go, I should think."

He let out a rebellious snort, but did not argue. Working as quickly as possible for the next half hour, she blotted the wound often with the brandy-soaked rag, her hands covered in his blood. God, she could have lost him and it would have been all her fault. She suppressed the urge to take him into her arms and hold him tightly, knowing it would only make her emotional when she needed a clear head. She brushed the sweat from her forehead with the back of her hand, then made the next stitch in his side.

"So," he said after a moment. "You thought you'd check up on me. Was it worth it?"

She just looked at him, then rethreaded the needle for the next stitch.

"I was not cheating on you."

"Yes, I rather guessed that when she did this to you," Alice bit back, matching his sarcastic tone. "Will you please be quiet and let me work? I am already upset enough."

"I would never cheat on you. I was searching her for weapons."

"Like you searched me last week?" She slanted him a dubious look and yanked the thread a bit too quickly through his flesh.

"Ow! You did that on purpose," he muttered with a wince.

At last, she checked each neat stitch and found the whole row of twenty little knots satisfactory and secure.

"I have to bandage you now—"

"Enough, woman!" He brushed her off with all the moody impatience of a cat. Shirtless, he slid off the dresser and stalked past her, the firelight flickering over his bare chest and sculpted arms.

"Lucien." She sighed. "Now it needs to be bandaged."

He rested his hands on his lean waist and turned to her. "Henceforth, when I give you an order, I expect you to obey it. Understood?"

"No." Throwing down the towel after washing her hands, she picked up his bottle of brandy and downed a swallow straight from the bottle to bolster her frayed nerves, then set it down squarely on the dresser.

"Pardon?" His stare darkened in warning.

"I am not your puppet, Lucien." She folded her arms over her chest. "Who was she?"

"Forget you ever saw her." He walked over to the medicine box and began bandaging his side without her help.

"Forget? Lucien, that woman is dead, and it's my fault. We have to go to the authorities."

He sent an ominous look of warning over his shoulder. "We are not going to the authorities," he said slowly.

Her face drained of color as she stared at him. "I heard what you said to your men. 'Get rid of the body.' Lucien, you can't simply cover this up. We need to send for the sheriff. Whoever she is, that woman deserves a proper burial on consecrated ground, not an unmarked grave in your woods! Her family should be notified—"

"Stay out of it, Alice."

"I will not."

"Haven't you caused enough trouble already?"

With a fleeting look of pain, she took a step toward him. "And aren't you already carrying enough secrets? How far will you go to hide your activities in the Grotto? A woman just died at your party, Lucien! If you don't send for the sheriff right away and explain what happened, eventually the truth will out. It is inescapable. Then one day, when they find out how you covered up her death, it will look so suspicious that you may be held accountable for murder. Is that what you want?"

"Nobody is going to hold me accountable for murder," he said in a low warning tone, turning his back to her.

"Why wouldn't they? Because you're one of the mighty Knight brothers? You're not above the law! What's right is right."

He didn't answer. He was standing very still, staring into the fire.

Seeing that she was making no impact on his stony will, she tried another approach. "Lucien, we are leaving tomorrow morning for Scotland to be married. I don't want this death hanging over our heads as we start our lives together. . . ." She waited for him to say something, but when he remained silent, her eyes filled with tears. She clenched her hands at her sides and marched toward the door on legs that shook beneath her.

He pivoted, watching her pass with a searing stare. "Where do you think you're going?"

"If you won't do the right thing, I will," she forced out past the lump in her throat. "That woman's death was my fault—"

Lucien appeared in front of her, leaning his back against the door, blocking her exit. He stared at her with a feral glint in the depths of his wolf-gray eyes. "Stop blaming yourself right now," he ordered in a low, harsh tone. "I am responsible. Not you."

Fresh tears brimmed in her eyes as she stared up at him. "What manner of man are you, to want to pretend this never happened? Get out of my way. I am going to the authorities—"

"I am the authorities, Alice," he whispered emphatically, his eyes shimmering with white-hot intensity.

She searched his face without comprehension.

"Listen to me very closely," he said as softly as the wind. "That woman was a Russian spy. She committed murder under my roof. She killed an American agent in the Grotto. That's why I was questioning her."

"What?"

"I am not a diplomat, Alice. I am a secret agent for the Crown. A spy. And the Grotto is nothing but a front for what we in the Foreign Office call a listening post."

She stared at him shock.

"You wanted the truth. There it is." His silvery eyes were as unreadable as mirrors. "I have now put my life in your hands. If you tell anyone about me, you will jeopardize my safety."

"A spy," she echoed. "You're a spy."

He nodded.

She sank down onto the chair beside the door, staring blankly at the floor as everything came clear to her. "A spy?" She looked at him again, flabbergasted, then studied him as though she were seeing him for the first time.

He crouched down slowly beside her chair. She saw fear darting through the depths of his eyes as he searched her face. "The Russian woman was aiding a dangerous French agent who is even now in London, working against our country. You see? I am not an unfeeling man; it's just that Sophia was aiding the enemy. That's why we are not concerned about her death. When an agent dies on enemy ground, nobody cares. If I had died in France, they would have buried me in an unmarked grave, as well. That's just how it is," he whispered, caressing her thigh as he tried to soothe her shock. "You mustn't blame yourself or worry about what will happen. All that matters is that you are safe."

She gazed at him for a moment, then suddenly pulled him into her arms and held him, closing her eyes tightly. "Oh, my darling." She kissed his cheek. "Thank you for finally telling me," she whispered.

"You aren't angry?"

"No."

"You're not . . . revolted?" he asked.

"Good heavens, why should I be? You are even more extraordinary than I realized." She kissed his hair and felt him shudder in her arms.

He kissed her neck, his shaky exhalation tickling her ear. "I didn't know how you would react. Damien still hasn't forgiven me for my choice of professions," he said bitterly. He looked up at her with his soul in his eyes. "I was afraid that I would lose you, too."

She cupped his jaw and leaned forward, kissing his brow. "My darling, foolish love," she whispered. "You must never fear to tell me the truth." She hugged him again, careful of his wound. "Oh, I can't believe that vicious woman nearly took you away from me. I never saw anything so awful. Thank God you weren't hurt worse."

"I'm all right." He pulled back and stared wonderingly into her eyes. "There isn't much time. Tomorrow morning, I must send you north to Hawkscliffe Hall, my family's ancestral castle in the Lake District, until I've dealt with the situation in London. With a few of my men to guard you, you will be quite safe there."

"What about Gretna Green?"

"We're going to have to postpone it. I'm sorry, love. The situation is critical, and it is my job to catch this man."

"Let me go with you to London, then—"

"Absolutely not. This man is a very disagreeable fellow. That woman was his lover. He will want to avenge her when he realizes she's dead. If he were to find out about us, he might try to harm you or to use you somehow to get to me."

She stared at him in growing dread. "Is he so very ruthless?"

Lucien nodded grimly. "Worse."

"Well, then . . . maybe you shouldn't be the one going after him. You're already hurt. If his mistress did that to you—" She nodded at his wound. "—what will the man himself do? Why don't you send a messenger to the Foreign Office and ask whomever it is that gives you your orders—"

"Lord Castlereagh."

"Ask Lord Castlereagh to assign someone else to the task, because you've already been injured and you're supposed to be getting married? I'm sure there must be other capable agents who can see to this man. That way we can go straight on to Gretna."

"Alice." He smiled wryly at her. "For one thing, Castlereagh is in Vienna; for another, these are my orders. And thirdly—" His expression darkened. "—this is between me and Claude Bardou."

She did not like the cruelty that hardened his face when he mentioned that name. She studied him warily, shaking her head. "I have a bad feeling about this. Look at your side. Look at what almost happened to you tonight. Lucien, as your future wife, I don't think I want you to do this."

"I have to," he said coolly, murder in his eyes. "I *want* to."

"You want to?"

"Yes," he murmured. "I want this man dead."

"Oh? And what if he kills you, instead? What am I to do then?"

He stared at her for a long moment, then shrugged. "I don't know."

"You don't know?" Perhaps she had expected him to put her mind at ease, assure her there was no chance that he would be killed in the line of duty. He offered no such comforting lie.

She got up abruptly from her chair and walked past him across the room, her mind reeling, a cold knot of dread in the pit of her stomach. She rubbed her forehead, trying to absorb it.

"Alice? Are you all right?"

"No, I'm not." She turned around. She fought a sense of rising hysteria. "Lucien, you know what I've been through. I lost my mother, my father, my brother—and now you're telling me there's a good chance that I could lose you, as well? I don't think I can bear it."

He rose warily to his feet and turned, his stare clamped on her.

Tears filled her eyes. "Don't you love me?"

"You know I do. More than anything."

"Then how can you do this to me?"

"Alice, I have a duty. I love my country and I love you."

"But you hate him more."

He looked at her uneasily.

She swallowed hard. "Love or hate, Lucien? You can't have both. Choose."

"Alice, don't be bullheaded—"

"Choose!" she cried, her whole body trembling. "A week ago, you made *me* choose whether Caro or I should go home to Harry. Now it's your turn. Him or me?"

"No more ultimatums, Alice. We made love. You could already be carrying my child—"

"I am like clockwork, Lucien. I have already begun to bleed. Now, choose!"

"Don't do this to me," he whispered.

"I am not going back into mourning again. I'm not dying all my clothes black again, and I am not going to watch another young man's coffin go into the ground. I can't do it, Lucien!"

He let out a furious roar of frustration. "If I don't kill Bardou, he's not going to *give* us any peace, Alice! You have no concept of what this man is capable of! He has to be stopped, and I'm the one to stop him!" His rage charged the air between them like lightning. "We are mortal enemies. Do you understand? If I don't go after him, he'll come after me when he's through making mischief for England. Bardou wants my blood just as much as I want his."

"Oh, my God," she uttered. "Then you must come to Hawkscliffe Hall, as well!"

"Hide from him? The hell I will!"

She flinched. "Then you've made your choice."

"That's right, Alice. I choose revenge!" he flung out, his chest heaving in untamed defiance.

"Then I choose never to see you again," she forced out. She brushed past him and ran out of the room, blinded by tears.

CHAPTER THIRTEEN

A stillness hung upon the gray, misty dawn as Lucien watched his carriage preparing to leave Revell Court with Alice inside, sitting huddled in her cloak. He caught a glimpse of her pale, hurt face as the landau rolled by, but she did not acknowledge him, coldly looking through him as she passed. Her flat gaze twisted the knife in his heart. He could not believe the rash choice she had forced on him, but he refused to accept that he had lost her permanently.

The carriage paused in the courtyard, waiting for the guards to pull back the tall iron gates. Shrugging deeper into his greatcoat, he fought the urge to run after her. He held his ground firmly, his eyes narrowed with guardedness and concentrated intensity.

I'll get her back when it's over.

McLeish saluted him as he rode by on his chestnut gelding. Lucien nodded. He was sending the leather-tough Scotsman and two of his most reliable subordinates to escort Alice to Glenwood Park and to guard her there until his business with Claude Bardou was finished one way or another. He still would have preferred to send her to the more distant and heavily fortified Hawkscliffe Hall, but she had flatly refused to go. After upsetting her so deeply, he felt too guilty to say no. He knew that her beloved home and her Harry were the only things that could comfort her now. Admittedly, he tended toward paranoia. There was probably no reason whatsoever to worry. The only people who even knew she had been with him at Revell Court were the two of them and Caro. The sleepy little Hampshire village of Basingstoke was well enough out of the way that she would be quite safe there, he thought with a sigh, especially with McLeish looking after her.

As the great iron gates of Revell Court creaked open, the coachman flicked the whip over the horses' backs and the carriage was once more in motion. Lucien clenched his jaw and held himself back, swallowing down the lump of emotion in his throat as it bore her away from him.

I will get her back when it's over, he assured himself a second time, *provided, of course, that I live through this.* He had not attempted to soothe her after their awful fight the night before because if he did not survive, it was best to let her hate him. Her anger would brace her for the blow of his demise.

He watched the carriage as it crossed the wooden bridge and climbed the hill out of the valley. Even after it had disappeared, he still stood there in the bleak gray dawn, his chin to his chest, the cold stinging his cheeks, his hands thrust down in his coat pockets. A tremor of contained anger ran the length of his body. He lifted his brooding stare, his expression hardening. The time had come to hunt and kill Bardou.

He was ready. The beast in him was awake and hungry for blood.

* * *

The warm lights gleaming in the windows of home brought tears to Alice's eyes as the landau rolled through the darkness up the drive to Glenwood Park. Her day had been spent dismally staring out the carriage window, nursing her broken heart, with a few stops along the way at coaching inns to break up the tedium of the long ride. Now, at last, she had come home. She could not wait to hold Harry in her arms. The very thought of his smell and his soft little body in her embrace made her chin tremble with threatening tears again, but after all that had happened, at least she still had her beloved home and the people who loved her—Harry, Peg, Nellie, and the others. Never had she been more grateful for their simple comfort.

Wondering what lie Caro had told them to explain her absence, Alice quickly brushed her tears away as Lucien's carriage slowed to a halt in front of the elegant manor house. She had no idea how to explain the presence of McLeish and his two rugged men. The landau had barely stopped when the front door flew open and Peg came rushing out with Nellie and Mitchell a few steps behind. When she alighted from the carriage, they hugged her and greeted her and made much of her.

"Oh, dearie, you've come back to us at last! Thank heavens you're well again! I was so worried! Oh, let me look at you, poor thing." Peg braced Alice by the shoulders and looked into her face by the glow of the carriage lantern. "You still look weak. Have you been able to keep anything down?"

"There's nothing worse than a bad salmon—nothing!" Mitchell said with a grimace.

So, that was Caro's lie, she thought.

"Oh, Miss Alice, can you ever forgive me for leaving you? I begged Her Ladyship to let me stay with you, but she forbade it," Nellie said anxiously. "That place was so strange! But she said if I gave her any cheek I would be dismissed!"

Alice noticed the sharp look that Peg shot Nellie, but did not know what to make of it. "Of course I forgive you, Nellie. I am quite well now. Thank you all so much for worrying about me. It's so good to be home," she choked out, giving Mitchell's arm a squeeze while Peg and Nellie both clung to her. She quickly schooled her composure back into order and turned to Lucien's coachman. "It's too dark to leave now. Please accept our hospitality." She exchanged a meaningful glance with McLeish.

"Thank you, ma'am," the Scotsman said, tipping his hat to her.

"Mitchell, will you be so kind as to show Lord Lucien's servants to their quarters and help them with their horses?"

He bowed and quickly went off to see that McLeish and the others, as well as their horses, were given comfortable accommodations for the night.

"Come now, into the house with you," Peg said in a businesslike tone. "You're barely recovered from one ordeal. I won't have you catchin' the ague next."

"Her Ladyship said there were half a dozen people from Lord Lucien's house party who were laid low from the fish," Nellie said confidentially as they walked back toward the house.

"Yes, er, we were all quite ill," Alice answered, hating herself for lying to her loyal maid and her beloved old nurse, but what choice did she have? She was not about to admit that she had been Lord Lucifer's plaything for the week.

"By the by, we've kept the neighbors at bay," Peg informed her. "Everyone thinks you've been sick in bed here all week with influenza."

"Oh! That's a relief, but I am sorry you had to lie for me."

"We couldn't tell them the truth. It would risk your reputation. Now, there's something in here that should lift your spirits," Peg said with oddly forced cheer as they walked up to the entrance of the house.

"My lambkin?" Alice exclaimed.

"No, dearie—look." Peg held the door open for her.

"What is it?" Alice walked into the brightly lit entrance hall and found it overflowing with six lavish bouquets of flowers. "Oh . . . how beautiful!" After the gray, dreary day, the vibrant colors and the sweet perfume lifted her spirits a bit. There were hothouse roses and orchids, irises, carnations, and delphiniums. "Where did they come from?"

"Your young gentlemen sent them." Peg closed the door, giving her a rueful wink. "You know how those three are always trying to outdo one another to impress you."

"Roger, Freddie, and Tom?" she asked as she took off her cloak.

"Who else? I've been calling it the war of the roses," Peg said with a chuckle. "It appears when they learned of your 'influenza' they were quite beside themselves. A few of your young lady friends also sent flowers—Miss Patterson and the Misses Sheldon from London."

"How kind." Alice's heart clenched at the abundant evidence that she was cared for and loved by so many people. She felt awful for lying to them—or rather, for Caro's lying to them—but it was necessary in order to preserve her reputation and to hide the link between her and Lucien from this Frenchman he was stalking. Perhaps the excuse of illness was not so far from the truth, she thought, for Lucien Knight had infected her blood like a fever.

Nellie took her cloak and hung it on the peg.

"Thanks. It really is wonderful to be home. Nellie, would you mind making tea?"

"Right away!"

"Bring it upstairs when it's ready?" Alice asked. "I'll be either in my room or in the nursery with Harry."

"Oh, dear," Nellie murmured, exchanging a worried look with Peg.

Alice felt her heart stop. "What is it? Is he all right?"

"He's fine, dearie," Peg said, then pursed her lips. "But he isn't here."

Alice stared at her in shock.

"Lady Glenwood has taken him to London."

"Is he all right? Did he need a Town doctor?"

"Nothing like that," Peg soothed, fidgeting with her apron as she always did when she was nervous.

Alice realized she had been so wrapped up in her own heartbreak that she had failed to notice how out of sorts her servants were. "What's happened here?" she cried.

"I'm afraid Her Ladyship found country life, well . . . a trifle dull," Peg said delicately. "It was all I could do to make her wait until he was past the contagion stage."

"Oh, Lord." Alice pressed her hand to her forehead and stared at Peg incredulously. "Do you mean to say that she put that child with full-blown chicken pox through a four-hour carriage ride to London because she was *bored*?"

"Just so, I'm afraid."

"Peg! Why didn't you go with them?" she asked angrily.

"Because she fired me, dearie."

Alice gasped in horror. "*What?*"

"I hope you don't mind that I've been staying on here, waiting for you."

Alice gasped and stared agape at her, utterly appalled. "Fired you?" she sputtered.

Peg nodded, her hurt and indignation eloquent in her serene nod.

"But how? Why?"

"Well, we butted heads for days over the care of the boy. I was able to avert any real disasters, but I'll say it frankly—" she lifted her chin, "—that woman is a blunderer."

"Master Harry was running a fever, and the baroness spanked him for crying," Nellie added. "She said the most awful thing, Miss Alice. She said she would not have Master Harry growing up to be a nancy-boy like his papa.

Alice's jaw dropped. "She said that about my brother?"

"Indeed, she did, dearie," Peg declared. "And when I heard her speaking ill of our poor, dear Master Phillip, I could not hold my tongue. I spoke right out and told them both that Lord Glenwood was a brave man and a hero who died for his country, and I'm afraid, well, then I told the baroness what I thought of her."

Nellie nodded in satisfaction at Peg's words. "You surely did, Mrs. Tate."

"We had quite a row, Lady G and I. That's when

she dismissed me. She took Harry to London the next morning."

Barely able to absorb it all, Alice ran across the room and hugged her nurse. "Peg, I'm so sorry! This is all my fault! Oh, thank you for staying on until I got home to sort this out. I don't know what I would have done if I had come home here and you were gone."

"I couldn't leave," Peg said with sudden tears rising in her eyes. "I am an old woman. I've nowhere else to go—"

"Hush, dearest Nanny Peg." Alice kissed her lined cheek. "You have been the pillar of my life. Glenwood Park is your home just as much as it is mine. You are most assuredly not fired, nor will you ever be. This will not stand." She grasped Peg's pillowlike shoulders gently and gazed at her in determination. "Tomorrow first thing we will go to London and I will personally have it out with Lady Glenwood for this terrible insult she has given you and for her thoughtless cruelty to Harry."

With that, she gave Peg another hug, shutting her eyes tightly against a suffocating wave of guilt. While she had been at Revell Court shamelessly indulging herself in wanton pleasures with Lucien Knight, her sister-in-law had stormed into the tranquil world of Glenwood Park and turned it upside down.

Lucien had warned her of danger if she went to London, but fie on his orders! She was done being his marionette. Nobody else except for Caro even *knew* she had been at his house. This was a risk she was willing to take. In addition to getting Peg's job back, every maternal instinct in her body cried out for her to go to Harry. The poor thing, she thought in desperation. He must be so frightened and alone there in the city without his Nanny Peg or his Aunt Alice to see him through his chicken pox, just strange Town doctors and the cold comfort of the unfeeling baroness. Spanking him for crying! she thought with a shudder.

"She is a fool in her treatment of that boy, but who am I to tell her so?" Peg said with a sniffle.

"Only someone who has been raising up children since before she was born, that's who!" Alice answered, patting her hand. "Please say you will come with me to London tomorrow? I'm sure Harry is lost without you."

"Bless you for saying so, child," Peg whispered, dabbing at her eyes with the corner of her apron. "I should hate not to be needed anymore. Oh, bother!" She quickly sniffled and brushed her hands down her apron, as though sorting herself out. "Tea, then."

"I'll get it," Nellie chimed in.

"Forget the tea. I say we all could do with a brandy," Alice declared, marching over to the liquor cabinet. Somehow she was going to have to sneak away without McLeish and the guards knowing, she mused as she poured them each a small draught. Lucien's men were under orders to keep her at Glenwood Park, but she would not be made a prisoner in her own home. "Here you are."

"I'm sure I couldn't."

"Medicinal—I insist."

"Thank you, Miss Alice," Nellie said shyly.

Alice gave her a bolstering look and clinked her glass against hers. Servants or no, they were the only family she had. "We shall have to send out some supper to Lord Lucien's servants. Do we have any ale for them?"

"Not ale, but we have wine."

"Good," Alice replied with a secretive little smile

rather like Lucien's. She knew just where the laudanum was kept in the household medicine box.

The braw McLeish and his fellows would have a very deep and restful night's sleep.

The thick London fog blurred the feeble glow of the street lamps, floating around Lucien in long, curling streamers as he rode his horse up Pall Mall at a tired walk. The black stallion's shuffling hoofbeats echoed hollowly in the mist. Both man and beast were exhausted.

He had parted ways with Marc and the other young rogues upon entering the city. They had retired to their bachelor lodgings. For his part, Lucien turned right onto St. James's Street presently, bound for Knight House. The stately Palladian mansion on Green Park was the jewel in the family crown. It belonged officially to Robert, his eldest brother, the duke, but the rest of the Knight clan were always welcome there. Lucien and Damien had both been staying there since their return from the war a few months ago. The newlyweds, Robert and Belinda, were still in Vienna, so it wasn't as though the twins were disturbing their connubial bliss. Lucien was most curious to meet Robert's bride. There had been quite a scandal over the duke's marriage, since Belinda had been Robert's courtesan mistress before he asked her to become his duchess. By all accounts, she was a breathtaking beauty.

He sighed, his breath misting in the cold. He had been so eager to show Alice off to his family. Now it would have to wait, but by God, he would get her back. *If she will* take *you back*. His head hurt too badly to consider the possibility that she might not. A short distance down the fashionable avenue, he turned left onto St. James's

Court, where Knight House stood in all its haughty grandeur behind its tall, wrought-iron fence. Lord, he needed a bed. No doubt his wound required fresh dressing, as well. He fully expected to find his bandages soaked through with blood. His side felt like it was on fire. The impact of the stallion's every galloping stride over the day-long ride had strained his twenty stitches, but Lucien had pressed both himself and his horse to the limit; time was of the essence. Unable to eat because of his distress over Alice's fury at him, and having drunk nearly a bottle of whisky over the course of the day to dull the pain of his injury, he was rewarded now with a massive headache. His eyes burned, his heart ached, and his whole body was a bit sore from being in the saddle all day.

Lucien dismounted stiffly and let himself in at the gates, annoyed to find them unlocked. *Bloody Alec,* he thought. His youngest brother was a careless, fashionable rake with a passion for high-stakes gambling. He scowled at the house, seeing the light streaming through the first-floor windows. Already he could hear the noise of some rowdy party in progress. Straitlaced Robert would be most perturbed, he thought as he locked the gate behind him with his copy of the key.

The creaking of the iron gates drew a groom from inside the stable. Lucien handed over the reins to the man and gave his equally exhausted steed a grateful pat on the neck, then dragged himself wearily up the front steps and went in, holding his side in pain under his damp greatcoat. He narrowed his eyes against the sudden brightness of the chandelier as he stepped into the gleaming white marble entrance hall, with its magnificent curved staircase that seemed to float on thin air.

"Good evening, Lord Lucien," Mr. Walsh, the supremely capable butler of Knight House, greeted him, but his polite smile promptly turned into a frown. He passed a worried look over him. "Is there something you require, sir?"

Lucien realized he must look like hell. He dragged his hand wearily through his hair. "Supper, headache powder, hot water for a bath, bandages, and any ointment for cuts that Mrs. Laverty may have stowed away in the medicine box. I have a bit of a scratch."

"I am sorry to hear it, sir. Right away."

"Is that Alec and his friends playing cards?" he asked with a nod toward the dining room as he handed over his greatcoat. In his dull spirits, he could have admittedly used a bit of his little brother's wicked wit and deviltry to cheer him up.

"No, sir, it is Lord Damien and a few officers from the Guards' Club."

"Ah, the heroes of Badajoz," he muttered ironically under his breath. "I'll be in my room."

As he climbed the stairs, each raucous burst of laughter from the dining room made him feel more alone. He went into his room and walked over to the bed without bothering to light a candle. He sat down and rested his throbbing head in his hands. Strange, the past week with Alice had made him forget how empty it made one feel to be alone in the world. Damien's rough-and-tumble camaraderie with his fellow officers brought back Lucien's isolation to him with a cutting edge. He looked at the bed and wondered how he was supposed to sleep in it without Alice in his arms.

Though his emotions were in chaos, hunger had sharpened his mind. Throughout the day's long ride, he had mulled over his plans for how he would go about catching Bardou. There was much to be done, but the hour was late. It would start in the morning.

He lay back in exhaustion and waited in the darkness for the servants to bring his food and the other things he had asked for, and he wondered if right now, somewhere in Hampshire, Alice was hurting as badly as he was.

"Why, Miss Montague!" Mr. Hattersley exclaimed, welcoming her and Peg into the Montague family's elegant London townhouse in Upper Brooke Street the next day. It was early Sunday afternoon. "Oh, bless you, do come in!" The kind-faced butler was a neat little man with a balding head and twinkling blue eyes. "Praise heaven, you are recovered. We were all so worried."

"Thank you, Mr. Hattersley. It's good to see you, too," Alice said warmly.

This morning at dawn, she, Peg, and Nellie had set out for Town, with Mitchell driving the coach—and Lucien's hulking guards sleeping dreamlessly, drugged with laudanum.

"Mrs. Tate," the butler greeted Peg. The two faithful old servants exchanged a look that spoke volumes of mutual commiseration.

"I have come to straighten out all of this nonsense," Alice told him in a lower tone. "Is Her Ladyship at home?"

"Indeed, miss. In the morning room."

"And how is our little patient?"

He smiled. "I am relieved to say Master Harry's spots have begun clearing up."

Alice glanced down the hallway and saw a little blond

head peeping around the corner at her. Her eyes lit up. "Harry?" she asked, taking off her wide-brimmed hat.

He sidled into the doorway, sucking his finger. To her surprise, he was dressed in little boy's clothes rather than the loose, simple gowns in which children of both sexes were customarily dressed until the age of about four years old. He wore miniature trousers, a tiny waistcoat, even a little starched cravat. She had never seen anything so adorable in her life; still, he really was too young for such confining clothes. He hung back.

"Oh, my goodness! Who is that handsome young gentleman?" Alice exclaimed. "That cannot be my wee lambkin. Harry, come and hug me. Have you forgotten me? It's me, Auntie Alice, and look who else is here—your Nanny Peg."

He ran to them. Alice knelt down swiftly and caught him in her arms, hugging him with a lump in her throat. She kissed him gently between two healing red spots on his rose-petal cheek. "I missed you so much," she whispered.

"We were both sick," he told her, making Alice wince inwardly to realize that she was even lying to Harry. She did not know how Lucien could stand it, going around up to his throat in lies, even for the sake of his country.

Harry gave her a sloppy, puppy-dog kiss on her cheek, proudly showed her a few of his scabbed-over chicken pox, then rushed over to hug Peg. "Nana!"

"Good day, Master Harry," Peg greeted him matter-of-factly, as though everything were back to normal. Alice admired the woman's self-possession. When he stretched out his arms, pleading to be picked up, Peg chuckled and lifted him. He clung on around her neck like he would never be pried off. "Now, then, have you been having a nice Town holiday?" she asked him.

As Harry began to chatter about the stray cats that lived in the garden, Peg met Alice's gaze meaningfully. Alice nodded, readier than ever to do battle. She caressed Harry's downy-fine hair.

"I'm going to tell your mama we are here."

The child shot her a strange look at her mention of Lady Glenwood.

"What is it, lambkin?"

He laid his head on Peg's shoulder. "She's a mean lady."

Alice's eyes widened, but she found herself at a loss for how to answer. She glanced at Peg. "Perhaps you and Nellie should take Harry up to the nursery."

Peg nodded shrewdly. The shouting that was soon to come might upset the boy.

"Mrs. Tate, allow me! You cannot carry His Lordship to the third floor," the butler protested.

"Oh, I'm as strong as an old plow horse, Mr. Hattersley," Peg said, stoutly, shooing him away.

"Dear heavens, you shall strain your back!"

Nellie followed them to unpack Alice's things for her stay.

Alice watched them fondly from the bottom of the stairs until they had disappeared from view, then braced herself and walked slowly down the hallway to the morning room. She paused, allowing her simmering rancor to bolster her resolve. She glowered inwardly at the memory of Caro at the Grotto—drunk, disheveled, throwing herself at Lucien. The woman had attacked her, screamed at her, then abandoned her to her fate at Revell Court.

It would be difficult to keep a cool head when Caro

had so thoroughly wronged her and those she loved, but whatever happened, Alice reminded herself, her main objective was to make Caro rehire Peg. That was all. Not only for Peg's sake, but for Harry's. Without bothering to knock, she strode into the morning room, seizing the advantage of surprise.

"Good afternoon, Lady Glenwood."

Reclining on the scroll divan, Caro looked up from her newspaper and quickly masked her shock, narrowing her eyes with a catlike smile. "Well, right on schedule, I see! One week—just as our mutual friend specified." She cast her newspaper aside.

Keeping a firm rein on her temper, Alice turned around and closed the door.

Caro looked quite different, she thought, on her guard. The baroness had abandoned her doll-like curls and instead wore her hair in a sleek, smooth chignon. Her visiting gown exuded modesty and restraint. It was made of mahogany-brown velvet with black piping and a small ruff of ivory-colored lace peeping out from under the long, tight sleeves and around the high neck. Finally, she had begun to act her age, Alice thought; then she realized what the gown signified. Caro had put off her black crape for half mourning. By custom, a widow was to wear black and black only for two full years, but Phillip had only been dead for a little over one year. To Alice, it was the final insult to her brother; Caro could not even pretend to mourn him for the appropriate period.

It was all she could do to bite her tongue on the matter. Phillip would have agreed that what mattered right now was Harry. And Harry needed his nurse. She clasped her hands behind her back and lifted her chin. "I wish to speak to you about Peg Tate."

"How grim you look, my dear. Something's missing . . . hmm." Caro suddenly clapped her hands to her cheeks in mock surprise. "Oh, no! Could it be your virtue? Where have you left your shiny halo?"

Alice stared coldly at her.

Caro trilled a laugh and rose gracefully from the divan. "Let me have a look at you, dear. Our little Goody Two-Shoes is not so good anymore, is she? Don't worry. No one knows what you've been doing—no one but me, that is. Ah, poor little Alice, fallen to earth like her wicked sister-in-law. I can see it in your eyes, but don't fret, I shall never tell. It'll be our little secret, just us girls and Lucien Knight. Tell me, what did you think of it?"

"Of what?" she asked in a low warning tone.

"Fucking," Caro whispered.

Alice bit her tongue to keep from answering in terms she would regret.

"Isn't he magnificent? I love the sound he makes, that primal *growl* when he's on the verge of . . . well, you know," she murmured coyly.

Feeling as though she had just been clearly run through with a rapier, Alice glared at her, her eyes blazing with pain and fury, her cheeks aflame.

"Now, now, what's this?" Oh . . . you little fool," she whispered. "Surely you didn't fall in love with that wolf!"

Alice could not speak. She just stared at her in angry misery.

"But you did, didn't you? Yes, of course you did. You *would.*" Caro rested her hands together suddenly, tilted her head back, and laughed with elegant glee. "Oh, Alice, poor little fool."

Alice's voice was stuck in her throat, choking her. She cast about for something to say to change the subject, for she could not bear another second of this torment. She seized upon another subject to stop herself from breaking down in tears. She would never give her sister-in-law that satisfaction. "I heard that you struck Harry," she said through gritted teeth.

"Oh? That bulldog-faced, old woman has been talking to you, I see. Well, do not concern yourself with my son—he is *my* son, Alice. It is time he learned discipline."

"And you who have never learned it yourself are the one to teach him?" she asked bitterly.

Caro sent her a warning glance over her shoulder as she went to pour a cup of tea from the silver service on the table. "I am, along with a bit of help, perhaps, from the man who may soon become Harry's new step-papa. There is a new man in my life, Alice—oh, such a man! A great, blond, Prussian barbarian. I just might marry him if the fancy takes me; then Harry and I will go to live in Berlin with von Dannecker."

Alice stared at her, paling. "You can't be serious. You can't take Harry away!"

"Don't worry, my dear, you may come, too, if you wish. But don't even think about stealing von Dannecker from me the way you stole Lucien."

Alice dropped her gaze to the carpet, struggling for equilibrium. She forced herself to ignore Caro's wild plans for the moment, concentrating on the main reason for this conformation. "Caro, you must hire back Peg Tate. How could you dismiss her? She has been with our family for twenty-five years, not to mention that Harry adores her. You cannot throw her out on her ear—"

"Yes, I can, Alice, and I can do the same to you if I please. After what you've been through, surely by now you've learned your place. I daresay you've tumbled off your pedestal, hmm?"

Alice's nostrils flared as she drew in another angry inhalation, fighting to check her temper. She lifted her chin, but bit back her retort.

"I have made some changes in your absence," Caro went to. "It's time you acquainted yourself with them." Tea and saucer in hand, the baroness turned and faced her coolly. "I have taken back control of my life and my household. From now on, I am to be treated with the respect that is my due. You and Harry and the old harpy have yet to learn a proper respect for me."

"Usually one's respect must be earned," Alice growled.

"That is just the sort of cheek I refuse to take from you anymore, you little whore!" Caro said, her eyes flaring with malice.

"How dare you?"

"Well, that's what you are, aren't you? I know it. I know what you've done, so don't put on airs with me, or you may remove yourself from my house and be on your way. Don't forget that I can deny you access to Harry."

Alice stared at her, stunned anew. "You wouldn't."

"Try me."

Alice blinked rapidly, trying to absorb this most terrible threat. "What do you want of me?"

"Ah, that is better. You see how much nicer it is when we get along?"

Alice glared at her in loathing.

Caro smiled blandly and sipped her tea. "Now, then.

Our first order of business is for you to put in a few appearances in Society to reassure everyone that you are quite recovered from your bout of influenza. It is essential for women like us to keep up appearances."

Alice fought with herself to hold her tongue over that remark. *I am not like you,* she thought. *No matter what I did with Lucien, I never will be like you.*

"Society is rather thin these days, but there is a concert tonight at Countess Lieven's and a ball at the Argyle Rooms on Friday. You will attend both."

"I can't. It is the French lady's visit," she muttered.

"I see. Very well, you may be excused from the concert tonight, but you *will* go to the ball on Friday with me. You should be quite recovered by then."

"What about Peg?"

With an aloof expression, Caro looked down her nose into her tea, clearly relishing her position of power. "Swear to me that you will forever stay silent on everything that took place at Revell Court, and I will give her a second chance."

Alice studied her in disgust. Clearly, the baroness had realized that if the ton found out that Alice had been Lucien's mistress, and that Caro, her own guardian, had willfully contributed to her downfall and had done nothing to protect her, then both of them would be shunned. It was one matter for Caro to be known as a scandalous adventuress, but quite another to be exposed as a villainess so petty and jealous that she would help to ruin her own maiden sister-in-law. Perhaps Caro did not want her new Prussian lover to know the kind of woman she really was, Alice thought.

"Do you swear?" Caro prodded.

"I have no intention of ever publicly acknowledging

Lucien Knight," Alice replied in a deadened tone. "Before I left, we agreed to treat each other as complete strangers, as though we had never met." The words shot a spasm of pain outward from her heart to her whole body, but she kept her gaze even, her face expressionless.

"Good," Caro replied. "Then it will be our little secret. As a token of good faith, I will allow Mrs. Tate to stay—but I will hold you responsible for keeping that meddling old harpy out of my path. And tell her I demand an apology."

Peg was going to fume at having to humble herself before Lady Glenwood, but for Harry's sake, Alice knew that she would. "Very well."

Caro smiled brightly and smoothed her hair. "Well, then, that wasn't so hard, was it?"

Just then the doorbell rang.

"Ah, that will be von Dannecker. We're going for a drive in Hyde Park." Caro set her teacup down, ran to the mirror that hung over the mantel, and pinched her cheeks to redden them with a girlish blush, then bustled out into the hallway as Mr. Hattersley opened the door.

Alice followed her warily, curious to have a look at the man Caro had threatened could become Harry's stepfather. Von Dannecker was a massive, towering man, maybe even taller than Lucien, and thicker-bodied, with shoulders like granite cliffs. Though his dark clothes were chosen with fashionable reserve, Alice thought wryly that the rugged, weathered brute would have looked more at ease in chain mail. His overly muscular physique seemed to chafe against the severe cut of his tailcoat and the starchy discipline of his austere, white cravat.

"Karl!"

He dwarfed Caro as she sailed over and embraced

him, standing on tiptoe to kiss him on both cheeks, Continental fashion. He had a broad, square face with a wide forehead and a cleft chin; his straw-yellow hair was slicked back flat against his scalp, and he wore a monocle in his right eye.

His monocle suddenly fell, swinging down on its ribbon onto his chest, as he noticed Alice leaning in the doorway of the parlor, while Caro continued fussing over him. When he met her gaze, something in his pale blue eyes made Alice shrink back against the door frame with a faint shudder. He had a thin, cruel mouth; deep hollows under his eyes; and a slight oily gleam on his skin.

"Ah, Karl, that is my sister-in-law, Miss Montague. Alice, this is Baron Karl von Dannecker," Caro said proudly as she slipped her hand through the crook of his arm in a possessive gesture, quite shamelessly caressing his bulging biceps.

Alice nodded to the man. He bowed to her, then looked up toward the stairs as Harry came climbing down them, holding onto each bar of the banister as he descended.

"Auntie! Come and see the kitties in the garden!" the boy cried.

"Coming, Harry! If you'll excuse me." She sketched a curtsy to the couple, then dashed past them, running up to assist Harry on the stairs. She grasped his hand. "You know you are not supposed to walk on the stairs without holding somebody's hand, Harry."

"I saw the kitties out the window. Nanny Peg said we could give them some milk because they're strays."

"Oh, Harry!" Caro called. "Come and greet Lord von Dannecker and give Mama a kiss good-bye." Caro bent down, holding out her arms to the child, putting on a grand show for her lover of what a good mother she was.

Harry's enthusiastic prattle stopped. He looked up dolefully at Alice; she gave him an imperceptible nod. No child was well raised who did not respect his mother, even if the woman was a backstabbing harlot. He heaved a sigh and went dutifully to his mother. Alice's heart clenched at the ginger way he embraced the woman, as though he had been stringently taught never to rumple Mama's hair or her gown.

"What a good boy you are," Caro said, petting his head in a show of lavish affection. "Now give a bow to His Lordship."

Harry barely came up to von Dannecker's knee, but he turned to the man, put his hand on his middle and executed a gentlemanly little bow, then bolted back to Alice. She swung him up in her arms and held him, filled with a strange, protective instinct to shield the child from von Dannecker's unfeeling stare.

There were only six days left until Guy Fawkes Night, and Claude Bardou's preparations were moving along like clockwork. His gun crew had arrived, courtesy of the same Irish fishing boat that had smuggled him into England. His men had brought with them the shiny, bronze-cast cannon—an eighteen-pounder—the well-stocked ammunition chest, and the portable stove for heating hot shot.

This city was going to burn, he thought with a narrow smile. Going out the door with Lady Glenwood, however, he did not like the defiant way her young sister-in-law held his gaze as she picked up the child and braced him against her hip.

Though Miss Montague looked as delicate and demure as any young English gentlewoman, he read a strength of character in her wary blue eyes that gave him pause. Bardou turned away, shrugging off the odd sensation that the girl could somehow see through his charade as a Prussian nobleman. *Absurd.* Eager to escape her cool, blue stare, he escorted Lady Glenwood out to the Stafford's waiting carriage, which he had borrowed.

As soon as they were under way inside the carriage, Caro draped her arms around his neck and kissed him in a more sensual greeting. Bardou had never enjoyed kissing, but he played along willingly enough, for she was highly useful to him. Indeed, she would be the bait with which he would lure Knight away from London on Guy Fawkes Night. Yet, he mused as he kissed her roughly, he sensed there were things Caro was not telling him about her relationship with Lucien Knight. Every time he had skirted the topic of her recent scandal with the Knight twins, she had danced away from the subject with her coy, irritating gaiety.

Bardou had not pressed her too hard because he had not wanted to turn her against him, but as he felt her falling increasingly under his power, he decided to ask again a bit more firmly. He ended the kiss and looked into her lust-glazed eyes. "My darling, you know I am wild for you," he murmured. For a native Frenchman, it was no mean trick to speak English while feigning a Prussian accent.

"Oh, Karl," she purred, running her hands all over his body. "I feel the same for you. You make me feel so alive!"

"You know that I am serious about you, Carolina," he said, stroking her. At the joy that lit her face, he almost felt a twinge of conscience. *What a fool she was.* "But if we are together," he continued sternly, "I must know the substance behind this upsetting gossip about you that greets me everywhere I turn. I will not be made a laughingstock. I must know the truth about what happened between you and those blasted Knight brothers."

She lowered her lashes.

"You almost married Damien Knight, did you not?"

"To me, it was only a flirtation, Karl."

"Is that why you allowed the other one to use you?"

"Lucien Knight did not *use* me!" she retorted, indignation flaring in her eyes. "For your information, he was so desperate to have me that he betrayed his own brother, but I don't mind saying that I quickly bored of him. He was quite hurt. Indeed, he is still furious at me, but what can I say? I lost interest."

"Then, he is in love with you?" he asked, frustrated by the vague sense that she was lying to him. "I only ask in case I should expect trouble from him over you."

She smiled and slipped her arms around him again. "Oh, Karl, how sweet! Would you really protect me from my jealous ex-lovers' advances?"

It was then that he took a canny guess at the lie behind her sugary smile. *Of course.* She was still seeing Lucien Knight behind his back, probably still sleeping with him on the nights that Bardou wasn't with her.

So, that was what she was hiding, he mused. *Why, the bitch thought she was clever, dangling both men.* If Bardou really were von Dannecker, he would have been incensed, but instead he smiled through his guise, happy with his theory that she was still bedding his enemy. It meant that his plan would work perfectly.

"Would you really rescue me if I were a damsel in distress?" she teased, licking her lips in invitation. "Would you protect me, my big, fierce Viking?"

"With life and limb," he vowed, scoffing inwardly at her ignorance. The Vikings had been Norsemen, not Germans.

"Mmm," she murmured, pressing her body against him, kissing him again. His body hardened as she slid her hand down to his crotch, but a thought of Sophia trailed through his mind. She still had not returned, and he was beginning to wonder if his fiery Russian darling had run away.

She wouldn't dare, he assured himself. She had written him a note while en route, chasing Rollo Greene to Lucien Knight's country house, and that was not the behavior of a woman who was about to defect. Nevertheless, that last, small corner of Bardou's soul that still bothered to care about anyone had begun to worry that something had happened to her. There was no other woman like Sophia. She was the only one who had ever understood him, his dark needs. Then he scoffed at his own fearful imaginings. Sophia had always been more than able to take care of herself. He did not doubt that she had succeeded in killing the repulsive American; Sophia always got her man. He knew he could rest assured that she had done her job for him, and that was all that mattered, he thought impatiently.

With that, he put her out of his mind and brought Caro back to the Pulteney Hotel, where he took his enemy's woman like a whore, forcing her to admit between his vengeful thrusts that he was a better lover than Lucien Knight. She did not dare say otherwise, but it pleased him nonetheless.

CHAPTER FOURTEEN

Cloaked in shadows, Lucien watched the glittering ballroom from the dim, high balcony, scanning the crowd below with the brooding patience of a predator stalking its prey. He could not believe that four days had passed. Four days of ceaseless searching and racking his brain to outwit Bardou, and now already it was Friday night. Tomorrow was Guy Fawkes, and he *still* had seen neither hide nor hair of his enemy.

Over the past half week, he had coordinated his defenses with both Bow Street and London's undermanned police force to find Claude Bardou. He had given them a sketch and a verbal description of the big Frenchman, but so far no one had seen him. He had alerted the Horse Guards; ordered security shored up at Westminster Hall and all the more significant buildings and royal dwellings throughout London; and had had the old cellars beneath Parliament searched for explosives, but the premises had been clear. While Bow Street and the constable's men searched the streets and began their torturously slow sweep of the riverside warehouses, Lucien had begun searching for Bardou in Society.

Bardou was no gentleman, but he was probably arrogant enough to think that he could fool the ton for a while if he dressed in the right clothes. It was infuriating. He could feel him here, so close by, just out of sight. That peasant son of a bitch was no doubt laughing up his sleeve at Lucien's desperate efforts to find him. Obviously, he was not going to show himself until he was entirely ready to begin.

Just then, a ripple of excitement moved through the ballroom below. Lucien saw all heads turn curiously toward the entrance; then his jaw dropped as a graceful beauty in white walked in, her chin high, a strand of pearls draped artfully over her strawberry-blond hair.

Alice!

He stared, flabbergasted, transfixed.

What the hell is she doing here? He couldn't believe his eyes. Joy and panic crashed in on him from opposite directions. Oh, God, how he had missed her. *What the hell is she doing in London?*

Caro sidled into the ballroom beside her. The baroness was dressed in a tight black velvet dress, but Alice commanded the room, poised, slender, and cool. With her airy evening gown of white silk wafting sensually against her skin, she was an aloof marble goddess who had just stepped down to life from atop her pedestal. She seemed an entirely different creature than the serious, shy young thing who had ventured into his library last week and had been so easily charmed by a bit of Donne poetry. Now she was a force to be reckoned with. She paused under the grand entrance, surveyed the ballroom with a lofty air of detachment, then glided forward into the ballroom.

Instantly, a swarm of men surrounded her and Caro,

young bucks and dandies and uniformed officers clamoring for her attention, offering their eager gallantries. Seeing this, Lucien's eyes blazed with rage.

"Marcus!" he barked, turning to look for his protégé.

Leaning in the doorway of the stairs that led up to the balcony, the young man strode over to him. Lucien pressed his lips together in a fury beyond words and merely pointed at Alice, giving him a vehement look.

"Oh, bloody hell," Marc said under his breath.

"Get her out of here."

"Consider it done."

Alice was sorry that she had come. She would have much rather been curled up at home staring into the fire or reading a storybook to Harry, but it was necessary to show Society that all was normal—that nothing unusual had happened to her, nothing scandalous, nothing rapturous.

Nothing but influenza. *How fitting,* she thought bitterly, *that she had come back from Lucien's with lies on her tongue.*

She had barely walked into the ballroom when her three longtime suitors—Roger, Freddie, and Tom—came rushing over to greet her and surrounded her, all talking at once. Roger Manners, a serious, high-minded young man with wavy black hair and brown eyes, would make a splendid barrister one day. Freddie Foxham was a dedicated Bond Street Lounger and a tulip of fashion; tonight he wore a purple coat with a cravat so high he could barely turn his head. Tom de Vere, a squire's son, was the largest of the lot, with a loud guffawing laugh and the simple, loyal nature of a hunting dog.

"Who is this prime article?" Tom exploded with a hearty grin.

"Miss Montague, what a splendid recovery you've made. You look ravishing," Roger informed her, kissing her hand with his usual, polite precision.

Freddie merely quizzed her from head to toe through his monocle. "Hmm," he murmured, then pronounced his judgment. "Yes, quite acceptable."

Alice smiled wryly at them. "Thank you for the flowers, all of you."

"Which did you like best?" Tom asked with childlike eagerness.

She laughed. "I couldn't possibly say."

"Come and sit down, Alice. You mustn't tax your strength," Roger ordered, taking charge with a businesslike air as he was wont to do. He grasped her elbow gently and propelled her across the ballroom while Freddie cleared their path by poking people out of the way with the elegant walking stick that he carried with him everywhere.

When they reached the sitting area over by the wall, Tom pulled out a chair for her with an eager flourish. "Your throne, princess!"

"Honestly, you three," she scolded wryly. Her sister-in-law sat down a few feet away, blithely engaged in conversation with her male friends. Alice noticed that Caro's odious brother, Weymouth, was hovering nearby, no doubt come to plague the baroness for another loan. He looked as unkempt and as dazed with drink and opium as ever.

"Tom, old boy, why don't you fetch our gel a bit of punch?" Freddie drawled.

"Right!" Tom said, as though struck with divine inspiration. When he went lumbering off through the crowd to find the punch table, Freddie and Roger sat down on either side of her.

"I'll have you know you gave us quite a scare," Roger told her with a chiding frown.

"Well, I'm quite recovered now."

"Recovered enough to dance with us?" Freddie asked with a lazy grin.

"Perhaps," she answered archly. "That's quite a waistcoat."

"Isn't it, though?"

"Have I missed anything exciting in Town?"

They chatted idly, Roger describing the latest Shakespearean performance of Drury Lane's exciting new star, Edmund Kean; then Freddie tried to top that with a description of the latest equestrian spectacles at Astley's Royal Amphitheatre.

Alice's mind wandered. *What was she to do now that she was no longer a virgin? How was she going to explain that fact to her future husband, or trick him into not noticing? She could marry Tom and dupe him easily enough, but he was such a dear, dumb thing. She could never really love him, and that would be heartless to do to a friend. Worldly-wise Freddie would be the hardest to fool, but perhaps would be the most willing to accept her fallen state philosophically. She had heard a rumor, however, that Freddie had an unusual, perhaps unnaturally close friendship with one of his fellow dandies. After what she had seen in the Grotto, she understood what those rumors implied. Sometimes she felt he had only courted her all this while because he* had *to court some young lady and, deep down, he knew she had no intention of accepting. Ah, well,* she thought. *She adored him anyway as a friend.*

Roger was probably the best choice. No doubt a virgin himself, he might not even notice her missing innocence, for he was so blinded by his devotion to her. He had placed her on the very highest pedestal, for she had always been such a perfect Goody Two-Shoes, she thought cynically.

When Tom returned with her punch, Freddie turned away to greet one of his arrogant, smirking friends, and Roger leaned toward her, murmuring in her ear, "I must speak with you. Alone."

She nodded, wondering what was the matter, when she heard a voice insistently calling her name. "Miss Montague!" She looked up; then her eyes widened as Marc and the rest of Lucien's young hellhounds came striding toward her in a pack.

"Miss Montague! A word with you, if you please."

"Hullo, there," Talbert said. "Don't you look stunning?"

"*Mademoiselle!*" O'Shea chimed in with a bow.

"Well met, my dear Miss Montague! How smart you look this evening," Marc said, his eyes dancing with mischief.

"I say!" Roger snorted as Lucien's rakish protégés gathered around her, crowding her three suitors out.

"Our mutual friend is most displeased to see you here," Marc said under his breath.

"He's here?" she breathed, going motionless. "Where?"

"Watching," Kyle murmured with a sly wink. "Argus of a thousand eyes."

"How is his wound?" she asked quickly, keeping her voice low so her suitors would not hear.

"What do you care?" Marc taunted her.

She glared at him, feeling her cheeks flood with a heated blush. "I don't. Where is the cad? He wouldn't come and talk to me himself?"

"You know full well why."

Alice gave him a sulky look. Marc lifted his gaze up to the gallery above them. She followed his glance discreetly and caught only a flicker of a motion amid the gloomy shadows there, but she saw no one. Lucien had vanished like a cat into the night.

Marc looked at her soberly. "He gave me a message for you. Leave London. Go home to Glenwood Park at once. There is great danger for you here, as you surely know."

"You may give him a message in return for me. He is not my husband. He has no authority over me. I shall do what I please."

"She's got some fight in her yet!" O'Shea said with a grin.

"I say, sirs, this is really quite enough," Roger declared, pushing his way between Kyle and Talbert. "Alice, come with me."

"If you don't mind," Marc started to say to Roger indignantly, when Freddie planted his walking stick squarely on the center of Marc's chest.

"Keep. Your. Distance." He poked Marc backwards a step with great aplomb. "I do not believe you have been properly introduced to the young lady; therefore, you have no right to speak to her."

"Freddie!" Alice exclaimed in shock.

Marc narrowed his eyes in warning. "What are you going to do about it?"

"Not a thing. Why should I wrinkle my clothes when Tom can see to you quite nicely? Sic him, Tom," Freddie said, dusting off his elegant hands.

Marc turned around, and there was big, brawny Tom. Marc's courage appeared to falter by a hair as he tilted his head back to look up at the big young man. Tom's ruddy face darkened with a glower.

Alice drew breath to stop the brawl that seemed imminent, but suddenly Marc swore under his breath and the young men parted, backing out of the way before a looming presence. As they cleared a straight path toward her, Alice blanched and tilted her head back, pinned in the cold, commanding stare of Lucien's identical twin brother.

It was Colonel Lord Damien Knight, the national hero.

He was unmistakable in his crisp scarlet uniform and gold epaulets, white gloves, glittering dress sword. Precisely the same height as Lucien, he towered head and shoulders over the other men, but for some reason he *seemed* more massive than Lucien, imposing in his bearing, inspiring fear and instant submission, while Lucien affected an idle, easy, unthreatening posture, as though not to scare off the prey. Alice stared at him in amazement, astonished by the likeness. As Damien clicked into motion and closed the distance between them, his plumed shako under his arm, she saw that they moved very differently, too. Lucien moved at a languid saunter; Damien advanced head-on at a controlled, rigid march.

It was rather terrifying.

Damien stopped in front of her and cleared his throat. From behind him, another uniformed man hurried out.

The colonel was so broad-shouldered, standing at attention, that the man behind him had not been visible until now. His shock of red hair and elaborate mustachio seemed familiar; then Alice noticed the officer was missing an arm and suddenly realized he was her brother's old friend, Major Jason Sherbrooke.

"Why, Major Sherbrooke!" she exclaimed in surprise.

"Miss Montague, it's been a long time," he said warmly, though he looked rather sheepish. "What a shock it is to see Glenwood's little sister so grown up."

She smiled, but Damien glared at him impatiently.

All the boys watched in varying degrees of trepidation as Major Sherbrooke nodded. "Ahem, Miss Montague, please allow me to present Colonel Lord Damien Knight. My lord, the Honorable Miss Alice Montague."

"How do you do?" she said faintly, curtsying to him.

The boys watched in varying degrees of dismay. A short distance away, Caro sat up, suddenly paying attention. She looked daggers at Alice.

Lord Damien bowed to her. "Miss Montague, will you do me the honor of a dance?"

She heard Caro gasp at his request and looked over at her sister-in-law just as the baroness snapped her mouth shut.

Alice glanced at the colonel suspiciously once more. Lucien had emphasized that neither of them were to tell a soul about their time together at Revell Court, but obviously he had told his twin. How else would Damien know to come looking for her? She had no doubt that the colonel's sole motive in asking her to dance was to repay Lucien in kind for having seduced Caro away from him.

She hesitated, knowing how vulnerable Lucien was

when it came to his celebrated twin. If Lucien was indeed watching from above, he would be incensed.

"I'm not sure it is a good idea," Alice said in a low tone, loath to oppose such an intimidating personage.

"It is a very good idea, Miss Montague," he answered tersely. "I would speak with you." It was an order, not a request. He held out his hand to her, his steely gray eyes full of forceful command.

Well, another overbearing Knight brother! she thought, her nostrils flaring with indignation. On second thought, Lucien deserved some kind of punishment for having chosen to pursue his enemy over her. Let him gnash his teeth over it, she decided.

She gave the stone-faced hero a brilliant smile, rested her gloved hand lightly upon his, and walked with him to the dance floor.

Behind her, the brawl that had seemed on the verge of exploding promptly fizzled out. Her three suitors, Lucien's five young rogues, and even Caro watched in crestfallen silence as Alice and Damien joined the minuet.

"This is a most unexpected honor," Alice remarked.

"I'm rather surprised myself," he replied. "As a rule, I hate dancing, but I had to speak with you."

"Oh?"

She could not fail to notice the many pairs of eyes on her. Women who vied for Lord Damien's attentions watched her jealously, as did Alice's affronted suitors. She only wondered if Lucien was watching. It pained her to glance at his brother, for Damien looked exactly like him, and she missed that devil so much. There were only two small differences that she could discern—Lucien wore his hair a bit longer than Damien's close-cropped style, and Damien's eyes were a deeper shade of gunmetal-gray, while Lucien's were silvery, like the flash of a steel blade.

When the patterns of the minuet partnered them once more, Alice laid her hand on Damien's and slid him a wary look askance as they proceeded through the graceful movements.

He hesitated, attempting friendly conversation. "Lady Glenwood mentioned to me once that you are a great favorite with young Master Harry."

Alice smiled at him in spite of herself. "As he is with me."

"You like children, do you?"

"Most of them," she replied, turning with him. He eyed her with a speculative gleam in his eyes that reminded her entirely of Lucien—and made her ache for that scoundrel.

"How is Harry these days?"

"Recovering from a bout of chicken pox, I'm afraid."

"I am sorry to hear it."

"We must all go through it sometime, I suppose."

"Miss Montague, you must permit me to call on you," Damien said abruptly, gripping her hand with a slightly harder pressure. "We have much to discuss, but this is not the place. May I see you tomorrow?"

"Why?" she asked candidly.

The figures of the dance separated them before he could answer, but she had a fair idea that she knew what he wanted. A single dance for the sake of vexing Lucien was one matter, but his insistence on a private meeting implied something else entirely.

She paled as her mind filled with unbidden imaginings

of Lucien drawling out the tale to his brothers of how he had seduced a virgin and made a wanton of her. Would all the dashing Knight brothers regard her now as fair game?

"You have nothing to fear from me," Damien said quickly, taking in her ashen countenance as the figures of the dance partnered them again.

"Don't I?" she asked coldly, feeling as though Lucien had betrayed her all over again.

"Miss Montague, there is no need for terror. No further harm shall come to you. I give you my word on it. Tomorrow I will explain—"

She wrenched her hand out of his light hold. "No explanation is necessary, my lord. Believe me, I understand perfectly." She pivoted and strode away just as the music ended. Her heart pounded and her legs trembled beneath her as she shoved her way through the crowd. *I have to get out of here.* She could not face her suitors right now. She needed a moment to collect her whirling thoughts. What had she done to her life? What had *he* done to her? Oh, she wanted to throttle that silver-eyed fiend!

Miss Goody Two-Shoes! Sensible Alice! Somehow she had proved to be a bigger fool than Caro.

Hastening out the other side of the ballroom, she ducked out the door to the veranda. The nip of the air was cold, but she walked out to the stone balustrade, determined to clear her head before facing them all again. Worse than her guilty conscience, worse than Lord Damien's suspicious attentions, was knowing that Lucien was here tonight and really had not the slightest intention of acknowledging her. It really was *over*.

She closed her eyes in a wave of pain, then looked

pleadingly at the heavens when she heard the French doors creak open behind her.

"Alice!" Roger's insistent call intruded upon her solitude. "What on earth are you doing? Come in at once! You've been ill—"

She turned around and stared at him, the wind rippling through her gossamer white skirts and lifting tendrils of her hair. He stopped abruptly and let his gaze travel boldly over the length of her. "My God, you're beautiful."

She rolled her eyes and turned away. Resting her hands on the cold stone balustrade, she lifted her chin and searched the dark sky as though the answers she sought might be written in the stars. They were not.

"What did you wish to speak to me about?" she asked wearily.

"Alice . . . are you quite sure you had the influenza?"

She spun to face him, her heart in her throat. "Why do you ask that? What are you implying?"

He furrowed his brow at her snappish tone. "You seem so changed. Maybe it was something more serious, a brain fever. Did you see a proper Town doctor? I'm worried about you. Alice, you know how I feel about you."

She stared at him, taken aback; then she let out an inward groan as she intuited the reason he had wanted to speak to her alone. The man had, after all, asked for her hand in marriage on three separate occasions in the past.

No doubt misreading the desperation in her eyes, he took her hand gently in both of his. "When I saw you walk in tonight looking so beautiful, I knew I couldn't wait anymore. Alice, either marry me or tell me it will never be. This is torture."

"But, my good fellow, young ladies delight in dealing out such torture as this," a deep, silken voice said suddenly from out of the darkness.

Alice nearly shrieked with surprise and whipped her hand out of Roger's light grasp as Lucien came sauntering out of the shadows in all his deadly elegance. His swagger was a touch unsteady as he took a swig from the bottle of burgundy in his grasp. His cravat was askew, his hair rumpled, and to her astonishment, he appeared quite drunk.

"I beg your pardon, sir!" Roger said hotly, his smooth cheeks flushing. "I would like some privacy!"

"I'm sure you would, but I have come as your guardian angel," he said with a slight, tipsy bow.

Alice narrowed her eyes and scowled at him for all she was worth, but her heart was pounding recklessly with the sheer thrill of his presence.

"Are you quite sure you're ready for marriage?" he asked Roger, turning on his dazzling charm. "And are you sure you *really* know her?"

"You drunken lout!" Roger said, his embarrassed blush deepening by the second. "You're the other Knight twin, aren't you?"

"Whatever gave it away?" Lucien asked with an insolent smile.

"I don't care who you are, if you do not hie yourself off this instant, I shall call you out!"

"Roger, you will do no such thing," Alice cried, aghast.

"Do you doubt my skill?" Roger asked her indignantly.

"Of course not. You—you cannot fight this man. He is obviously drunk. It would not be honorable."

"And ladies *so* like honorable men," Lucien drawled.

Roger huffed and grasped her arm. "Come inside, my dear. This cretin has no proper feeling for the tenderness of young ladies' sensibilities."

"Yes, run along, Miss Montague. If you plan on marrying him, you'd best get used to doing as he says," Lucien advised bitterly, his silvery eyes raking her with angry scorn mingled with desire.

"How dare you address her?" Roger barked, releasing her. He stepped in front of her and faced Lucien, who suddenly grabbed him by his lapels and yanked him off his feet.

"You little prick, I've half a mind to throw you through that window," Lucien snarled, casting aside his urbane facade.

"Lucien, no!" Alice cried.

He instantly released Roger, who in turn gave Alice a stunned look. "You know this man?"

It was a moment of truth.

She stared at Roger, unable to speak. What he read in her eyes in that moment, she would never know, but he shook his head in shocked anger, pivoted, and slammed the door behind him as he stalked back inside. She flinched at the bang, then turned to Lucien.

"You *villain*," she spat. "Snake! What are you doing, spying on *me* now?"

"Oh, did I interrupt your new romance, Alice? I'm terribly sorry! How would you have answered if I hadn't interfered? Would you have said yes to his proposal?" he demanded in fury, his aura of drunkenness vanishing at once—another ruse.

She shook her head at him in contempt. "It's none of your affair."

"The hell it is. You're mine. I'm warning you, if you think to marry someone else behind my back, you sign that man's death warrant."

She thrilled to the ferocious possessiveness he displayed, but hid her hungry reaction. "More bloodshed, Lucien? Is that your answer for everything?"

"What are you doing in London? I told you not to come here! Where the hell is McLeish?"

"I don't know where he is, nor do I care. As for what I'm doing, obviously, I am getting on with my life—without you." She shoved away from the balustrade and marched back toward the French doors, but his hand clamped around her arm, yanking her back to him.

"Get your hands off me!"

He pulled her hard against his chest and claimed her mouth in a punishing kiss of scorching want. Her body cared naught for her anger, responding to him with a will of its own, but she fought his black magic, refusing to succumb to his power.

"You still want me," he whispered. "I can feel it."

She pulled back violently in his embrace, planting her hands on his chest to hold him back. "How dare you kiss me?" she hissed, her bosom rising and falling rapidly.

"Maybe you'd rather if Damien did," he snarled. "Are you going to throw yourself at every man you see tonight, or only the ones in my family? Why stop at my brothers? There's always Damien's regiment."

With a cry of rage, she slapped him hard across the face before she could even think.

The low, angry laugh that came bubbling out of him was an animal sound of pain. "Is that all you've got? Hit me again, Alice. Harder."

Her blazing eyes filled with tears at the hurt they both had suffered.

Lucien took in the sight of her tears for a second, then stepped back and with a wild growl, hurled his half-full wine bottle across the broad veranda, shattering it on the stone balustrade, just like he had shattered her heart. The red wine stained the gray stone as it spread and dripped like blood. He turned back to her, his silver eyes glittering with fury and pain.

"Do you think I want it this way?" he whispered harshly. "Do you think I don't dream of you every damned night?"

Then why didn't you choose me? she almost cried out, her heart twisting in her breast, but she bit the words back out of pride and simply glared at him.

"Leave London," he ordered, visibly steeling himself. His eyes glittered, and his angular face was taut.

"I don't have to listen to you. As far as I'm concerned, you don't exist."

"Hate me if you wish, but don't be a fool. It is too dangerous for you to be here."

"Why should I believe you? You're an expert in lies. Maybe you just don't want me getting in the way when you choose your next victim to seduce and abandon."

She saw her cold words strike their mark as he flinched and looked away, then lowered his head and was silent for a long moment.

"I want you out of here," he said gruffly.

"My Lord, I don't give a damn what you want." Pivoting away from him, she stalked toward the French doors, burning too hotly with anger to feel the cold night's chill.

"At least—at least swear to me that you'll stay home tomorrow on Guy Fawkes Night. Alice, I am begging you. That man I told you about—we expect him to make his move tomorrow night. I don't know where. It could be anywhere."

At the weary note of defeat in his voice, she paused and glanced back at him warily. There was a haunted look in his eyes.

"Will you promise me?"

"All right. But there's something I want to know. Whom besides Damien have you told about us?"

"I didn't tell Damien. I didn't tell anyone."

She closed her eyes in vexation. "Yes, you did, Lucien. Just tell me the truth, please, so that I don't have to walk onto any more buried mines."

"I didn't tell anyone," he repeated sharply. "Are you saying he knows?"

"Why else would he seek me out?"

"Because you are the most beautiful woman in the room. By far."

She rolled her eyes and started to open the door.

"Alice."

She shot him a questioning glance over her shoulder, wariness in her eyes. His hands were in the pockets of his black trousers. Moonlight gleamed on his white cravat and along the broad lines of his shoulders, while the night breeze stirred the tousled, wavy locks of his hair. The emotion in his eyes was veiled beneath the sweep of his lashes.

"By far," he repeated wistfully. "I'll get you back, you know."

She stared at him, feeling a lump rise in her throat.

A few soft words, his melting stare, and she was powerless. Even now, she had to hold herself back from running to him and throwing her arms around him. Even after he had seduced her and cast her aside, she had to fight against his magnetic pull upon her soul with all her strength. *No*. By God, she would never be his plaything again. She steeled herself against his haunted stare.

"Stay out of my life," she ordered, opening the door with shaking hands. She hurried back across the ballroom to Caro's side. The baroness was holding court amid her usual band of depraved-looking scoundrels.

"I want to leave," Alice said tersely in her ear. "This is excruciating."

"Oh, all right," Caro answered after a moment's deliberation, fluttering her fan. "Von Dannecker is coming over tonight. I suppose I could use a little time to freshen up before he comes."

"Tonight? It's already half past eleven."

"Yes." Caro slipped her a wicked glance behind her fan. "Don't pay him any mind when you hear him leaving in the morning."

"But you can't have him stay the night with Harry at home, under your roof—"

The baroness rolled her eyes and shrugged off Alice's protest, rising with a lavish smile to say good-bye to her dissolute admirers.

Claude Bardou knew that Lucien Knight had returned to London a few days ago and was tearing the city apart trying to find him. He thought it amusing. He felt very much in control of the game and was enjoying the thrill of his duel of nerves with his old foe. The one thing that worried him was that there was still no sign of Sophia. He had been sure tonight would be the night she would return. He had waited since suppertime in his hotel room, pacing and jittery, smoking a cigar out on the balcony as he searched for her face in the river of people flowing by ceaselessly on Piccadilly. Though he needed her to reappear in order to escape England with him after the deed was done tomorrow night, he refused to worry and focused his mind instead on the last remaining details of his plan. The time was so close.

He had rented a little cottage fifteen miles east of the city. He was taking Caro there in the morning; she would be the bait to lure Lucien Knight away from the city. Meanwhile Bardou would launch his attack. He calculated it would take only about fifteen minutes to carry out the destruction he had in store for London. With church bells thundering and celebratory cannons being fired throughout the city for the annual festival, the drunken, rowdy mob enjoying their stupid English holiday would scarcely realize there was molten fire raining down on them from the sky until it was too late.

Bardou's eyes danced when he imagined the riots there would be in the streets tomorrow night as the stampedes of terrified people fought to flee to safety. There would be no safety for them. His cannon had a range of a thousand yards, and his hardened, veteran gun crew could fire two round-shot a minute. Hot shot was a siege weapon. When one of the furnace-heated cannonballs slammed home, anything wooden that it touched would burst into flames. If it lodged in an enemy's fortress wall, it would smolder for many hours, too hot to be quenched by water. He had seen hot shot doused with water only to burst into flames again minutes after it had been submerged. He mused over his targets. . . . Parliament, of course. The Admiralty, where the war offices were housed. The Bank and the Exchange. The East and West India Docks, whose ships brought the English such a lion's share of their riches. St. James's Palace. Carlton House. . . . So many choices.

When all two dozen of their balls had been fired, as well as a few canisters of shrapnel for good measure, he and his men would flee in separate directions. With London in flames, Bardou would race back out to the cottage for his rendezvous with Knight and finally, at long last, finish the bastard off. He would send a note to Lucien at Knight House advising him when and where to meet him if he wanted to rescue Caro.

Once Knight was dead, it was merely a matter of getting back on the boat and sailing away with his Irish colleagues, who hated England as much as he did. That was why he had to reunite with Sophia now. Tomorrow night, he would have to flee England. If she did not come back soon, they would be separated once more. She should have finished by now. By the time the light died and night descended and still Sophia did not appear, Bardou could no longer escape the sickening certainty that something had happened to her.

He had an empty feeling in the pit of his stomach that he had unwittingly sent her to her death. Rollo Greene could not have killed an assassin of Sophia's expertise, but Lucien Knight could. According to the last message she had sent Bardou, she had been tracking the American to Lucien Knight's country house. What if Knight had captured her? Destroyed her? *What if Knight had won her over to his side?* The thought made his blood run cold. By God, she'd better hope she was dead, for if she had betrayed him, he would kill her himself. He felt his taut self-control dissolving at this possibility.

Damn Knight! He couldn't stand it anymore—this hiding, this stealth! He stalked back in from the balcony and looked around at his hotel room, wild-eyed, his chest heaving, his control hanging by a thread. He was sick of waiting for the right moment, being patient.

All this time, he had been expecting Sophia's imminent return, but Lucien Knight had known she was not coming back. Either he had destroyed her or stolen her. It did not matter so much to Bardou which it was; what mattered was that, once more, Lucien Knight had bested him. He was probably laughing at him. *Bastard!* Something inside of him snapped. With a hellish oath, Bardou picked up the delicate console table by the graceful French balcony doors and smashed it against the wall in rage. To hell with biding his time! Hiding from Lucien Knight was unspeakably degrading. He could not bear it a moment longer. He knew where Knight lived. That arrogant *aristo* son of a bitch did not deserve to live another day. *You thought I gave you pain before. You don't know yet what pain is, my friend.*

He dropped to his knees and reached under his hotel bed, dragging out his leather rifle case. He checked his ammunition and slammed out of his hotel room, his short, blond hair tousled, his clothes askew. Careless, reckless, he stalked across the elegant lobby of the hotel, making no attempt to keep up his charade as von Dannecker. The discreet rifle case hung from his grasp like an odd-shaped portmanteau. A few minutes later, he went tearing out of the hotel livery stable in Stafford's carriage, leaving the groom behind and handling the reins himself.

The drive was not long. Bardou had learned that the ducal family's chief residence in Town was the imposing Palladian mansion on Green Park, Knight House. Behind a high, black, wrought-iron fence with wicked spikes atop it, the lawn was neat and green. Bardou noticed half a dozen guard dogs trotting around the premises as he drove by slowly. The mansion's towering white facade rose in haughty austerity, gleaming in the moonlight. Passing the property, Bardou slapped the reins over the horses' rumps and drove around the block into Green Park.

The park was deserted, so he drove right up onto the grass, pulling the carriage into the cover of a coppice of small trees. The chilly wind whispered through the bedraggled autumn branches, but Bardou's eyes glittered with anticipation as his scanning stare homed in on the veranda on the back of the house.

Lucien Knight was sitting there smoking a cigar, all at his leisure, his booted heels propped up on the stone balustrade. Hatred pulsed through Bardou at the sight of his enemy. The single lantern by the door provided all the illumination he needed for a clear shot. At approximately 150 yards, he was well within firing range, but far enough away that the dogs did not pick up his scent and sound the alarm at his presence. He walked away from the carriage, crouched down behind the trunk of a large tree, and opened the case. Working in quick, efficient silence, he assembled his Jäger rifle, glancing up repeatedly to make sure that Knight did not go inside. The long silver bayonet gleamed where it lay in the open case, but

Bardou did not need it. He dropped the prepared cartridge into the muzzle and rammed it down in simmering violence. Then he crept down onto his belly, braced his elbows on the cold ground, and took aim. *Enjoy your cigar,* mon ami. *It will be your last.*

His heart pounded with anticipation. Sweat beaded on his forehead. His finger curled over the trigger.

All of a sudden, the veranda door flew open and the other Knight twin came out with a drink in hand. Bardou furrowed his brow.

He stared at one, then the other, unable to tell them apart. They were dressed the same, both rid of their coats and cravats at the end of the night, their waistcoats unbuttoned, white shirtsleeves rolled up. Whichever one of them was the colonel, he was not wearing his scarlet uniform jacket.

Which damned one of them was Lucien? he thought furiously. To be sure, he would have been almost as happy to kill the war hero, but there was one problem. Though he knew he could hit one of the brothers, he had no doubt that the second he fired, the other one would be over that fence and after him with all those dogs in the blink of an eye. It would jeopardize the beautiful mission he had so carefully planned.

He filled his lungs with a deep breath of the cold night air, then mentally cursed as he lowered his head. This was too easy a death for that English bastard anyway, he thought, rubbing his forehead in agitation. He wanted Knight alive so that the man could see the devastation of London after Guy Fawkes Night, see what he had failed to avert. Then Knight would know that even if Napoleon's armies had lost the war, Bardou had won the private battle between the two of them.

The chill in the air brought him back to his senses until he had his emotions tightly under control once more.

He was no amateur. He would follow his plan and not risk making a mistake out of hot-tempered impulse. When he had Lucien Knight in his power, he would find out exactly what the man had done to Sophia and punish him for it.

He made a mental note to save one of his cannonballs to obliterate Knight House and everyone in it, then pushed up silently from the ground, picked up his weapon's leather case, and returned to the carriage, his rifle propped on his shoulder.

Lucien was on the verge of giving up. He did not know where else to look or what more to try. Failing all else, his main concern had been addressed—Alice had agreed to stay at home on Guy Fawkes Night. The stubborn chit should have stayed safely tucked away at Hawkscliffe Hall or at least in Hampshire, but she refused to leave London and when it came down to it, he had no real authority over her.

Standing at the balustrade with the night wind rippling through his hair, Lucien gazed out at the night-clad grounds of Green Park. He thought he detected a distant flicker of movement in the shadows, but he shrugged it off, too obsessed with his thoughts of Alice to pay much attention. He took a drink of his brandy, then glanced over his shoulder at Damien, who slid him a wary look in return, sitting there idly smoking his cigar.

Lucien eyed his brother half hostilely, uncertain of how to proceed. One way or another, he would warn Damien away from his woman, but he had to broach the subject cautiously. Alice had claimed that Damien knew about the two of them. Lucien couldn't see how. Despite her refusal to believe him, he had not told his brother anything. If Damien indeed knew, Lucien knew that he had gone after Alice simply to get back at him for seducing Caro. That had to be the reason. *To be sure, you ass,* he scoffed at himself, *it could have nothing to do with the fact that she was the most exquisite woman in the room.* The knowledge filled him with misery and jealous, burning frustration. All those young bucks crowding around her had been infuriating enough, but if Damien was serious in his pursuit of Alice, Lucien thought he might as well hang himself.

Surely she realized that she could hope for no better revenge on him than to accept Damien as a suitor, he thought bleakly. If she wanted to hurt him—and he did not blame her, if she did—then she already held the perfect weapon in her delicate, artist's hands.

"I trust you enjoyed the evening," Damien remarked, his voice a deep, ironic drawl.

Lucien turned as Damien let out a stream of smoke, looking rather pleased with himself.

"Noticed you actually stood up to dance tonight," Lucien said smoothly, masking his resentment.

"Couldn't resist," he answered. "Did you see the girl I met? Beautiful."

"Very," he agreed through gritted teeth. He felt his face flush with anger.

"How's Caro?" Damien asked innocently. "Ah, but I reckon it didn't work out between the two of you, since she's been seen all over town with that Prussian ape."

"I don't give a damn about her," Lucien said in a warning tone, holding his stare.

"Or any woman, eh, brother?" Damien stood and sauntered over to him, stopping mere inches away from him. "Not really. You never really care about anyone, do you? Except yourself."

Lucien gazed insolently at him. *I do not need this right now.*

"You have done a terrible thing," Damien said, his voice barely louder than the low night breeze, though its undertone was steel. "Nothing you've done to date has equaled the dishonor with which you have treated that girl, Lucien. You took a gently bred virgin, seduced her, then cast her aside as though she were a whore. I am ashamed of you."

"How did you find out?"

Damien stared at him. "Is that all you have to say? How did I find out? Caro told me, if you must know. She came here one night last week to throw herself at me again, and when I asked her to leave, she told me about you and Miss Montague. She threw it in my face about what a pack of 'scoundrels' we Knight brothers are."

"That sounds like Caro, all right."

"Lucien, what were you thinking? Miss Montague is a baron's daughter, a gentlewoman. You would shame not only her, but yourself and our family with your flagrant immorality."

"Damien." He sighed, pinching the bridge of his nose as he struggled for patience.

"How you plan to live with yourself is your own affair, but I wanted you to know that I am going to take care of this situation. As usual, it falls to me to clean up your mess."

He suddenly stopped. "Take care of it?"

"I am seeing Miss Montague tomorrow," Damien

replied in a grim tone of resolve. "I am going to ask her to marry me."

Lucien stared at him, shocked to the core; then flames of fury sprang to life in his eyes. "Don't. You. Dare," he whispered.

"Then do what honor requires."

"I can't," he nearly wailed.

"Well, I can," Damien said, then roughly brushed past him and stalked into the house.

Lucien stood there paralyzed, his mind reeling, his heart pounding. How appallingly easy it was to imagine them together—the war hero and Goody Two-Shoes! What a match! Damien wanted heirs; Alice longed for a brood of children to dote upon. How like his honor-bound brother to take matters into his own hands.

Lucien ran his hand through his hair, then clasped the back of his neck and closed his eyes, hating himself. He had never felt like more of a failure. *Alice might have said no to that lad's proposal, but what woman in her right mind would refuse the great Damien Knight, soon to become the earl of Winterley?* he thought bitterly. *He might as well accept it. She would be better off with Damien anyway. Damien could make her a countess. Lucien couldn't do that. Damien was admired, respected. She would never have to be ashamed of him and would never need to beg him not to play such dangerous games.* If Claude Bardou ended up killing Lucien, at least he could rest in peace knowing that Damien was taking care of Alice. *It was for the best,* he told himself, a lump of despair rising in his throat. *Whatever she had loved about him, she could have in his twin brother. Damien was just like him, after all.*

Without the flaws.

* * *

Alice had long since arrived home, retired to her chamber, and gone to bed, but she could not fall asleep for worrying about Lucien. She prayed feverishly to God to keep him safe. At last, just when she had started to doze off, she was lurched back to wakefulness by the noise of von Dannecker and Caro passing in the hallway outside her door on their way to the baroness's bedchamber.

"What's wrong, darling?" she heard Caro murmur. "You look so grim."

She could not make out von Dannecker's mumbled reply as they moved on. But it was not long before she began to hear Caro's muffled laughter through the wall, the murmurs of love play, and then the groaning.

Alice pulled her pillow over her head in vexation, trying to drown out the sounds, but the couple grew louder, their moans ever more feverish, until her own memories tortured her, making her body burn for the only man she had ever known, ever wanted: her seducer, that hateful, silver-eyed fiend that she loved. Agonized with missing him, she threw off the covers, pulled on her dressing gown, and tiptoed up to the nursery to check on Harry.

He was fast asleep when she glided silently into his room. He looked so peaceful, slumbering on his back, a beam of moonlight falling across his cherubic face. Gazing down at him, trembling in the night's chill, tears filled her eyes.

Lambkin, you're all I have left.

The floorboards creaked when she shifted her weight. She almost wanted him to wake up so she wouldn't have to be so alone. She stifled the urge to pet his downy head, picking up his cotton-stuffed toy dog instead. She hugged it to her as she stared down at him, crystalline tears streaming down her face in the moonlight. She lowered her head and hugged the toy harder, careful to keep her heartbroken sobs silent while every atom of her body and her heart screamed for Lucien.

CHAPTER FIFTEEN

The next morning, Alice sat on a bench in Hyde Park, bundled up in her pelisse, scarf, and gloves, sketching the bleak lines of the trees. She had told Lucien that she would not go out on Guy Fawkes Night, but she hadn't made any promises about the daytime. Shortly after dawn, she had been awakened by von Dannecker's clumping footfalls as he left Caro's bedchamber. Alice supposed she should be grateful that he had not stayed for breakfast.

With a bit of a headache from crying herself to sleep the night before, she glanced over her shoulder in irritation at the workmen pounding their hammers. They were putting the finishing touches on the dais where the dignitaries would give their speech tonight before the fireworks display was set alight. Alice had never much cared for the holiday of Guy Fawkes Night. It was a noisy, chaotic, rather coarse festival day that always made her fret over the precarious mix of cavorting drunkards and blazing bonfires.

She squinted against the overcast glare and continued with her drawing. It comforted her. The sky was a tumbling sea of tall gray clouds with sharp silver edges; here and there, the sun poked through in fanlike rays. The trees' rich autumn leaves had long since fallen and scattered away upon the wind, leaving them bare, scraggly stalks against the pewter sky.

Nellie had ambled down to the muddy bank of the Serpentine, her sewing basket draped over her forearm. Alice knew that her withdrawn attitude was making her maid uneasy, but she could not stir even a shred of cheer. She just sat brooding, idly sketching the trees, her hand moving across the page with a will of its own, shading here, adding detail there. Suddenly the dull, thudding cadence of hoofbeats broke into her thoughts.

She looked up, then let out a small gasp as a tall, imposing, wonderfully familiar horseman came riding toward her on a large white steed. Her heart leaped with instant recognition and she sat up straight, but as he came closer, she made out the scarlet uniform beneath his greatcoat and slumped again on the bench, mocking her own pitiful hopes.

It was the other one. *Lord, hadn't she made it perfectly clear last night that she would not welcome his advances?*

Damien reined his tall white horse in before her and swept off his plumed shako, giving her a curt nod in greeting. "Miss Montague. Harry's nurse told me I might find you here."

She heaved a sigh as he dismounted with an athletic leap and strode toward her, hesitating a little when he noticed her dull stare. He looked so much like Lucien that she felt a pang at the sight of him.

"I realize you do not wish to speak with me, but you must hear me out," he said.

"Must I?" she murmured rather cynically. This was a man accustomed to giving orders and being unquestioningly obeyed, she thought. At his overbearing tone, Nellie came over and stood by her protectively. Alice nodded to her. “It’s all right.” With a faint look of distress, Nellie backed off to a respectful distance but stayed near enough for propriety. “Very well.” Alice sighed, gesturing toward the bench. “You may join me.”

The colonel sat down beside her and searched her face with a penetrating stare.

Though his face was weathered and hard, he had the saddest eyes she had ever seen.

“Miss Montague, I will come straight to the point.”

No, she thought wryly, *this was definitely not Lucien.*

“I am aware of the unpardonable way my brother has behaved toward you. I know what happened, and I know you are not to blame for what befell you. It is entirely his fault. He knows better.” He shook his head with a look of contained fury. “When Caro told me—”

“Caro told you?” she interrupted.

“Yes.”

“Oh.” She was taken aback to realize that Lucien had been telling the truth last night. He had not boasted to anyone about his conquest of her.

“I cannot help but feel somewhat responsible for my brother’s actions.”

“Not at all, my lord,” she murmured, even as she recalled Mr. Whitby’s assertion that Damien had appointed himself his brother’s keeper years ago.

“Nevertheless, I mean to ensure that no further harm comes to you,” he said soberly. “I shall not allow my brother to dishonor our family name or you. The reason I wished to see you was, uh—” He cleared his throat; then his words rushed at her like a veritable cavalry charge riding to her rescue. “I have come to offer you the protection of my name—to make you my wife if you will have me. You will not go unprotected after what my brother has done to you. I will make it right. As for the past, as I said, I'm well aware that it wasn't your fault. My stature in society is such that this . . . mishap . . . need never come back to haunt you."

She stared at him, astonished by his offer when she had thought so ill of him. She lowered her gaze, humbled and chastened by his chivalry. Though his speech was well rehearsed, she found the big warrior's uneasiness entirely endearing.

While he waited for her reply, Alice took a brief mental glance at the possibility that he was offering. The man was a godsend, in truth. She would not have to explain her lack of virginity, nor would she be blamed for it. He was a national hero with a sterling reputation, a man known for his courage and integrity. As his wife, she would be a countess, a respected member of Society—and better still, a wife and mother. But slowly, Alice laid her hand on his forearm and gazed wistfully into his deep gray eyes.

"What a dear, decent man you are. Please accept my deepest thanks. Though I am honored beyond words by your generosity, I cannot accept."

He furrowed his brow. "Why?"

"I'm in love with your brother," she confessed softly.

He frowned. "Miss Montague, do not be foolish. Men and women marry every day without love. You will be ruined, and I need a wife anyway. I am offering you a lifeline. I advise you to take it."

"It would hurt him too much."

"So what if it does?" he asked, scowling just like Lucien. "How can you harbor any tenderness for a man who seduced you without a qualm and then abandoned you?"

"I *love* him," she said more determinedly. "He has hurt me, yes, but I don't want to punish him or take revenge on him. What happened between us was not *all* his doing, after all. He wooed me, but it was I who surrendered. I was the fool who gave him my heart."

"And now he has broken it," he said in a hard tone, studying her.

She lowered her gaze. "I apologize for my rudeness to you last night at the ball. I feared you had less than honorable intentions."

"Understandable. Do not trouble yourself. Unlike my brother, I am quite thick-skinned, and as he would claim, thick-headed to match." He cracked a rueful smile as he rose and handed her his calling card. "I realize this must be a difficult time for you. If you reconsider over the next few days and wish to change your mind, you can reach me at Knight House on Green Park. My offer stands." He gave her a curt bow, then marched back to his horse, pulling on his hat. Gathering the reins, he swung up into the saddle and tipped her a vague salute, then reeled his white horse around and cantered off across the drab green field.

Alice watched him ride away and hoped she had not made a huge mistake.

"You *idiots*!"

Lucien's bellow carried through the halls of the Bow Street justice offices. *He had officially reached his wit's end,* he thought. He turned away from the huddle of bewildered French immigrants, emigrés, and tourists waiting behind bars in the holding cell and glared at the Bow Street Runners who had detained them. Even the duke of

Devonshire's haughty French chef had been taken captive. Marc and the others stood around waiting to assist, shifting their weight uneasily while Lucien vented his temper on the Bow Street officers.

"How many times are we going to go through this? I told you Bardou is a big man—bigger than me, blond haired—look at these men! This is what you bring me? Have you even looked at the sketch I made up?"

"Yes, we have. My lads are doing their best, but the fact is, you're the only one who has ever laid eyes on this man," their captain protested while the Runners stood around, their hands on their hips, eyeing him sullenly.

"If this is your best, it's not good enough," Lucien clipped out. "People are going to die if this man is not found. God damn it! Release them."

As the harassed Frenchmen were freed and sent on their way, Lucien brushed off the Runners and stalked out, his young associates marching in a tight V behind him. He pushed open the doors and paced restlessly on the pavement, his hands in his pockets. He racked his brain, to no avail, and somehow restrained himself from punching the brick wall beside him. The day had come—it was three in the afternoon of Guy Fawkes—yet somehow on the paramount day when he should have been deducing Claude Bardou's plot, all he could do was obsess over finding out what Alice's answer had been to Damien.

Bloody hell, if he were Damien, Bardou would have already been captured, thrown in the Tower, and executed, he thought in vicious self-contempt.

"You didn't have to bite their heads off," Marc muttered to him as he paced by. "Now they're going to be even less cooperative."

"Does it still bloody matter?" he said. "It's too late. We've already failed."

"Don't say that! You can't give up hope yet."

Lucien knew he was right, but his mood was frayed and raw after having slept a total of ten minutes the night before. He rubbed his forehead. "They're incompetent."

"Yes, but the captain had a point. Frankly, your drawing is terrible." Marc grimaced wryly. "You can draw topographical maps with marvelous precision, my lord, I'll give you that, but your sketch of Bardou—well, it barely looks human."

Lucien ran his hand impatiently through his hair. "It's no "Mona Lisa," but how can any idiot confuse a fair-haired man of forty who's over six feet tall with a little five-foot chef? They are *dunces*!"

"You're the only one of us who has ever seen this man, my lord. Clearly, we need to unite you with someone who specializes in portrait drawings," Talbert said.

"Miss Montague could do it," Kyle said under his breath.

"I don't want to hear it. I will not have her involved," Lucien warned.

"Sir, people are going to die. You said it yourself!"

"And she will not be one of them," he answered darkly.

"Now that we know she's in Town, anyway, we might as well make use of her talents. She's good at faces," Jenkins argued.

"He's right," Marc insisted. "If three dozen of the constable's watchmen and Runners and we ourselves have seen neither hide nor hair of Bardou, obviously, he is nowhere nearby. Where, then, is the danger in your simply going to her and asking her to help us? We will stand guard outside her house to ensure her safety, if you wish. All you have to do is describe Bardou's face and let her draw it. She could be our only hope!"

"What makes you think she'll help?" Lucien bit back. "I am not exactly in her good graces."

"She would never refuse, knowing people's lives depended on it," O'Shea said sagely.

"Isn't it the perfect excuse to go see her?" Talbert asked with a grin.

Scowling, Lucien turned away, but his heart had begun pounding at the mere thought of seeing her. Simply being near her strengthened him, and today he needed all the help he could get. The lads were right. She *was* talented at portrait work. He had seen that for himself. And God knew he was dying to find out what her answer had been to Damien.

He let out a huff full of bravado. "Oh, very well. I can't believe I'm letting you little bastards talk me into this."

"Do you know where she lives?"

"Could get there blindfolded."

"Did he just blush?" Talbert asked Marc as Lucien strode over to his black stallion and swung up into the saddle.

"I heard that," he retorted.

A short while later, he dismounted in front of the Montagues' townhouse in Upper Brooke Street. Leaving his horse with his men, he strode up to the front door, braced himself, and knocked. God's blood, he was as nervous as a youth—dry-mouthed, his pulse racing, his heart thumping in a state of jealous, tortured love. The minute or two that he waited on her doorstep felt like an eternity. He took his fob watch out of his waistcoat. Twenty past three. He snapped it shut again and tucked it back into his pocket just as a pleasant-looking little butler with a well-polished bald head answered.

"Good afternoon, sir. May I help you?"

"Er, good afternoon," Lucien forced out brightly as he fidgeted with his riding crop. "I am here to see—" He swallowed hard. "—Miss Montague."

"Whom shall I say is calling, sir?"

"Lord Lucien Knight."

The butler's amiable face instantly turned severe; his posture stiffened. Lucien realized in dismay that the good servant obviously recognized his name from his earlier adventures with the baroness.

"Begging your pardon, my lord," the butler said, lifting his chin to a haughty angle. "Did I understand you correctly? You wish to see Lady Glenwood?"

"No, you impertinent flea. Miss Montague, please," he repeated, his face coloring with—*was it shame for his past behavior*? he thought. *Good God, what was happening to him?* He was as bewildered as a snake that had begun to shed its skin.

"One moment." Glaring with affront, the butler shut the door in his face.

This did not look promising. He turned away, tapping his riding crop against his leg with jittery impatience. What if she refused to see him?

Suddenly, out of the corner of his eye, he noticed a flutter of motion in the window as the curtain moved. He looked over quickly, but whoever had been peering out at him had vanished. He narrowed his eyes. Was the chit planning on hiding from him, pretending she wasn't at home, perhaps?

Watching the window a moment longer, however, he lifted his eyebrows as a small, downy-blond head appeared. Young Master Harry must have climbed up onto a piece of furniture, for presently, he peeped out the window at Lucien, looking altogether pleased with himself. Lucien smiled slowly, charmed by the tot's sparkling, china-blue eyes and babyish grin.

When Lucien bowed to the tot, Harry ducked out of sight. Lucien frowned. A second later, the toddler looked out at him again, playing peekaboo. Lucien laughed softly and decided to rob Miss Montague of the chance to evade him. He opened the front door and poked his head in, bringing Alice's whispered, worried exchange with the butler to an abrupt halt. They were standing in the entrance hall.

"—Am I to tell him you are not at home?"

"Lucien!" she forced out, her eyes widening. Then her cheeks blazed. "Oh, Lord! You cannot just walk into someone's house!"

"Really, sir!" the butler scolded, but Lucien stared only at her.

"Hullo," he said hopefully, gazing at her with his penitent heart in his eyes.

She braced her hands on her slim waist. "*What* are you doing here?"

God, she looked adorable. She was clad in a loose-fitting morning gown covered by a pretty, frilled house apron, her luxurious hair flowing long and unbound over her shoulders in a most fetching state of dishabille. This was his beloved as he remembered her best, not the terrifyingly beautiful goddess in white from the ballroom the night before.

Before he could gather his wits to launch into his request for her drawing skills, Harry came charging out of the front parlor to investigate. He hurled himself up against Alice, cushioned by the softness of her skirts.

She wrapped her arm around his small shoulders with an automatic gesture, steadying him. Half hiding behind his lovely young aunt, Harry stuck his finger in his mouth and studied Lucien from a wary distance in intense curiosity.

Lucien gazed back at them. The sight of the woman and child together, both staring at him, moved him on some deep inner plane that he had never known existed. Moving carefully, he closed the front door behind him and slowly lowered himself to a crouched position a few feet away from Alice and the boy.

"Hullo, Master Harry. My name is Lord Lucien."

"Um, we have kitties in our garden. They're *strays*," Harry said proudly.

"Aren't you lucky," he said with a soft laugh. "I only have dogs in my garden. Big, ugly ones."

Harry's eyebrows shot up, and he took his finger out of his mouth. "I have a dog at home in the country. She's a country dog. She catches wabbits!"

Lucien grinned and glanced up at Alice. His smile faded when he saw the tears in her eyes. Holding fast onto Harry's little shoulders, she looked away and petted his head.

"Harry, I brought you something. I heard you had the chicken pox, and I thought this might cheer you up." Reaching into his pocket, he pulled out a small triangular bar of quartz and held it up before the child's wonder-filled eyes. "It's called a prism. Did you ever see one of these before?"

The boy's whole body turned as he shook his head, his finger in his mouth.

"Come here. I'll show you how it works." He rested his knee on the floor and offered Harry his other hand. The boy came to him trustingly. Lucien slipped his arm around the child and held the prism up to the golden ray of late-day sun that streamed through the crescent-shaped window above the door. "It just looks like plain glass, doesn't it? But when you tilt it . . . Do you see?" Lucien pointed to the refracted array of colors cascading onto the marble floor.

"Colors!" Harry gasped. He reached for the prism and pulled it into his grasp, staring at it. "How did you do that?" He began shaking it.

"You have to hold it up to the light and tilt it until they come out again."

"It's a wainbow," Harry said reverently, then gave him a look of perplexity.

"Do you know your colors?" he asked.

"Wed, green, blue, yellow," he recited proudly.

"Zounds, you know them all!" he said in vast admiration, then smiled at Alice. "Did you teach him that?"

She sniffled and nodded, watching them with her arms folded tightly across her chest. Harry giggled, snuggling up to Lucien and studying him at close range. Lucien gazed at him for a long moment, easily able to see why Alice was so devoted to the child. He was clever, likable, and irresistibly cute. Though the dark-haired, dark-eyed Caro was his mother, Harry had the Montagues' fair coloring and blue eyes. Lucien gave his little nose a pinch.

"Why don't you go show your aunt how the prism works?"

He ran over to Alice. "Look, it's a prison!"

"Prism, Harry. Prism, not prison." She bent down and helped him hold the prism just so, making the light bend and the colors appear. "Pretty!" she cooed to him. "Tell Lord Lucien thank you."

"Thank you!" he yelled.

"You're welcome," Lucien said in amusement.

After another moment, Alice sent Harry back to his nurse with a kiss. "Mr. Hattersley, would you kindly take him back to Peg?" she asked when the butler reappeared in answer to her summons.

"Indeed, Miss. Master Harry, if you please."

"Bye-bye!" Harry called, waving to Lucien as the butler carried him up the steps.

Lucien waved back. "Good-bye, Harry."

He and Alice were left standing together in the entrance hall in awkward silence. Lucien had a feeling that if Harry had not taken to him, she would have thrown him out already.

"He's a charming little scamp."

"Yes." She put her hands in her apron pockets and shifted her weight onto her other foot. "What do you want?"

"I, er, need to borrow your talents."

She lifted her eyebrows with an aloof, questioning look.

"The man I've been trying to locate—well, the lads were hoping you might be willing to make a sketch of his face based on my description. If we can get an accurate drawing of him, maybe the Bow Street Runners or the constable's men will have more luck finding him."

"I see. You came for a favor. After the way you've treated me."

"It's not so much for me! He's a very dangerous man.

He's at large. We're running out of time. . . ." His voice trailed off in dismay.

With a sigh, she turned around and walked away, going down the corridor. "Just let me get my charcoals."

His heart soared. "Thank you."

She waved him off with a rude gesture and disappeared into a room at the end of the hallway. While she went to fetch her sketchbook and charcoals, Lucien stepped back outside and dispatched Marc and the other lads to various posts around the first floor of the terrace house to keep watch for any sign of trouble. When he went back inside, Alice was standing at the end of the corridor. She beckoned to him, then let him into the morning room and sat down on a Windsor chair by the oak worktable, tucking her feet under her chair.

She rested her sketchbook on her lap and waited, a stub of charcoal in her hand, then looked up, still bristling at him a bit. "Did you want something to drink?"

"No, thanks."

"Then let's get this over with."

"Right." He paced, restless with her nearness. "The subject is male, French, about forty years old."

"Describe the shape of his face. Round, square?"

"Rectangular, I suppose, with a cleft chin."

"We're not at the chin yet."

"Well, pardon me," he retorted, stung by her snippy tone.

She tilted her head and drew a deep breath. "We'll be working from the top down," she explained in a more civil manner. "How would you describe his forehead?"

"Wide. Thick eyebrows. Deep hollows under the eyes."

Her hand moved with swift, light grace over the page,

making a few preliminary lines. The only sound was the soft, wispy scraping of her charcoal feathering over the page. "What sort of nose does he have?"

"Big and ugly. Like a potato," he muttered.

"A potato?" she asked quizzically.

He shrugged.

"Right." She chewed her lip in concentration as she worked, unaware that Lucien was gazing at her with his heart in his eyes.

She looked up and noticed his forlorn stare before he could hide it. They gazed at each other for a long moment.

"Alice?" he whispered.

Her mouth trembled. "Yes?"

"I think—there's something I have to tell you." He felt physically ill at the prospect before him, but he knew he was going to lose her if he didn't say what needed to be said.

"What is it?"

He lowered his head, then walked with measured paces to the door of the morning room, and shut it. Unable to meet her gaze, he closed his eyes and willed himself to be done with it. "I would not have chosen this over you unless I had a very good reason." He swallowed hard. His heart was pounding recklessly. He took a deep breath. "Last spring I was captured in France by this man and his associates. I was held as their prisoner for five weeks before I managed to escape. Under torture—"

"Torture?" she asked sharply.

He brought his chin up and forced himself to meet her stricken stare from across the room. "Of course," he said with far more self-possession than he felt. "Every agent knows that torture and execution are distinct possibilities if one is captured."

Turning pale with shock, she looked down at the half-completed sketch. "This man *tortured* you?"

"He did his job. He did it well. I broke, Alice." He shook his head slowly. "I finally revealed the name of one of my associates, Patrick Kelley. He was a fine man, a mentor of mine. I couldn't take it anymore. I didn't even know what I was saying. When I regained my senses, I was too late. Bardou had already gone. He hunted Kelley down and killed him on the strength of my information." He clenched his fists at his sides, shuddering. "I was weak. I am as responsible for my friend's death as though I'd cut his throat myself. That is why I, and I alone, must kill Bardou."

"Oh, Lucien," she whispered.

"I couldn't tell you before. I didn't want you to know I was afraid," he said, barely audibly.

She put her sketch pad aside and held out her arms to him. "Come to me."

He crossed the room on legs that trembled beneath him and knelt down before her chair. He stared into her eyes, trying anxiously to read her reaction, desperate to see if she still could respect him after his weakness, his terrible betrayal of his friend.

Tears flooded her eyes. She shook her head and pulled him into her arms. She stroked his hair, kissed his face, overwhelmed him with her gentleness. The pain that he had kept neatly coiled and tucked away inside of him for so long began to unfurl and to swell like wet ropes, like the binds that had chafed his wrists raw for so long in that French cellar.

His eyes burned with anguish as he laid his head on

her lap. She bent over him, holding him in tender strength. He kept his head down, burying his face in her long golden hair as it spilled over him.

"It's all right," she whispered, caressing his back. "Tell me what happened."

His throat was so tightly constricted he could barely breathe, but he forced himself to obey her. She deserved that from him. "I've never told anyone before. Not Damien, not even Castlereagh. Bardou was in charge of the operation. They caught me in Paris, lured me into an alley by using a young girl. I heard her screaming. I thought someone was being attacked. When I went into the alley to try to help, I was struck over the head, blindfolded. They threw me into a carriage and drove. I don't know where exactly it was." He paused, forcing himself to tell her the full, ugly truth. He realized he was shaking, his hold on himself becoming frayed, as though the ropes were about to break. He labored inwardly to free himself.

"For the next five weeks, I was locked in a cold, clammy cellar without light, just enough food and water to keep me alive. The thirst was terrible. They beat me. Starved me. They held me down and pulled two of my damned teeth out when I wouldn't talk. Threatened to rape me, threatened to castrate me, threatened every damned thing. They wanted me to turn traitor, but I resisted." He drew an unsteady breath while Alice watched every nuance of tormented emotion that flitted across his face. "I think I must have gone a little mad for a while afterwards," he forced out. "I don't remember much about the few weeks that followed. I wound up in a monastery just over the Spanish border where I received medical attention. There were some *guerrilleros* under a priest called Padre Garcia. They were using the monastery as their headquarters. It had been fortified since the days of the Moors. Garcia and his men brought me back to Wellington's headquarters."

"How did you manage to escape your captors?"

"I finally killed one of them when he came to look in on me. I took his weapon and fought my way out. I killed every one of them," he said grimly, "except Bardou. He had already left to hunt down Patrick Kelley."

They were both silent for a long moment.

"Oh, Alice," he said in a kind of spiritual exhaustion, "I've given all I have to give to this war since I was twenty-six years old. I've given what even Damien would not give—my good name; I knew what I was getting into, but everyone thinks I'm a blackguard and that is hard."

She touched his face in wordless empathy. He pressed his cheek into her hand, but could not bring himself to meet her gaze.

Abruptly, without warning, more words came tumbling out of him in a rush, devoid of his usual silver-tongued eloquence. "I never even wanted to go to the war! I should've been a doctor. I wanted to use the gifts God gave me to heal people, not to kill them, but my first loyalty was to my brother. Always my brother. I gave away my future for him. I damned myself for him because he was the only friend I ever really had, and now he won't even acknowledge me. I can't bear for him to take you away from me, as well. You don't understand how alone I am. If you don't love me—" He cut his words off and lowered his head hating himself. He felt himself crumbling, finally, unable to avoid or ignore for one second longer the view down into his shattered soul.

He cast about inwardly for his Machiavellian control, but it was nowhere to be found. By God, if she had agreed to wed Damien, so be it. He fought himself, teetering on the edge of despair. *Don't cry in front of her. Don't cry in front of Alice. For God's sake, for once in your life, don't be a little fucking weakling—*

But when she lifted his chin with a gentle touch, there were tears of anguish burning in his eyes. "I'm sorry," he choked out, startled. "I'm sorry I'm weak. I'm sorry I'm a failure. I'm sorry I'm not as good as—"

"Don't. Don't you dare say it," she warned him, tears rising in her eyes, as well. She shook her head fiercely. "It is not true, not *one* word of it."

Lucien stared pleadingly at her. "I know he came here today. I know he asked for your hand. What did you say, Alice? Please tell me."

"What do you think I said?" she asked with a look of gentle reproach.

He shook his head. "I just don't know."

"Lucien." She curled her fingers around his trembling hands on her lap, gazing intensely at him. "Your brother is a good man, but he's not you. I said no. I could never love anyone but you, and I told him so."

"You did?" he choked out, staring at her, overwhelmed by the youthful sincerity in her blue eyes.

At her simple nod, a shudder racked him and slowly he lowered his head all the way to her lap. He clung to her, unworthy as he was, and then he broke down. He covered her beautiful, artist's hands in kisses and hot, stinging tears. "Save me," he whispered. "My beloved, my beautiful friend. You're the only thing that's ever really gone right in my life."

She held him in her embrace for a long moment, nuzzling his ear as she bent over his back and stroked him lovingly. "Lucien, my warlock, my enchanter, you *are* a healer. You've healed me."

He lifted his shattered gaze and stared at her, lost. "Now let me heal you," she whispered.

He closed his eyes in silent desperation. Gently caressing his face, she kissed his eyelids and his cheeks.

"I love you," she murmured again and again. He held very still, drawing the words in deeply to the innermost recesses of his being. When her silken lips grazed his coaxingly, he claimed her mouth in a kiss full trembling urgency.

Her arms went around him; her warm, wet mouth opened hungrily to welcome him. He stroked her tongue with his own and cupped her breast through her gown, then tore his lips away from hers after a moment, his heart pounding wildly, his eyes glittering with fevered desire.

"I need you."

"Yes," she said, her voice faint and breathless as she reached down and stroked his hardness. "I'm yours, Lucien. Yours to take. Take my love. Take me."

With a groan of soul-deep gratitude, he kissed her again and rose to his feet, lifting her in his arms. He carried her over to the sturdy mahogany table and laid her on it, pushing the silver tea service off to the side.

"God, I've missed you," he breathed, slipping her skirts up over her thighs. "Your body, your laughter, your smile. You don't know how much I need you."

"Lucien, hurry," she wimpered, arching hungrily against him, plucking at his falls. Her eyes were hazy with longing, oceans of love to quench the fires of his damnation.

"You're so beautiful," he whispered helplessly, moved. When he stroked her core, she was already hot and wet.

She freed him from his trousers with trembling hands, then let out a soft moan of satisfaction as he pressed deep inside her, taking her there on the table with frantic, jittery urgency, both of them still fully clothed. Gripping her creamy-smooth buttocks, he cradled her body from the hard surface of the table, kissing her throat while she writhed under him. He nuzzled his way down her chest and sucked on her swollen nipples until she let out a sharp cry of pleasure, wrapping her legs around his hips.

"Oh! You drive me mad," she panted.

"Shh," he murmured with a possessive smile, laying his finger over her lips as her sounds of sensual delight grew louder. She licked the finger with which he had tried to silence her, then sucked it. He watched her in lust, taking her more forcefully. Turning her head to the side, she bit her lip to stifle her moans, but her body arched desperately under him as his hips plunged between her silken thighs. "Lucien—"

"Yes, angel. *Now.*"

She went rigid, her face etched with need. Lucien could not hold back a second longer. He clenched his jaw to keep from crying out with release as his expert control dissolved. Each burst of his climax seemed to come slamming out from the depths of his being, until he collapsed on her in panting, mindless bliss.

He remained inside of her, staring at her as she held him, stroking his hair. The quiet within him was profound. Everything suddenly seemed so clear.

"I love you," he whispered at length.

She slid him a roguish glance, her voice sated and scratchy as a cat's purr. "You certainly do." But then her gaze sobered. Rolling onto her side, she leaned on her elbow and studied him deeply. "This man, Bardou," she said in cool-nerved calm. "Can you beat him?"

"If I have your love, I feel I can do anything," he whispered.

"Then go with my blessing and kill this man, Lucien. He deserves to die for what he's done to you. I would kill him myself if it were in my power, but the task is yours. End this," she commanded, staring at him like some fierce, young queen, righteous fury blazing in the indigo depths of her eyes. "Do it for our future. Our children. Do it and come home to me."

The angelic intensity in her eyes sent chills down his spine, as though she had just endowed him with divine protection, supernatural power. He gazed at her in awe. "I love you more than life itself. I am yours, Alice."

She cupped his cheek and drew him to her once more, kissing him with trembling passion. "Let's finish our task, then. I'll complete that drawing for you and we shall drag this monster out of the shadows."

He lifted her hand to his lips. "Thank you," he whispered, holding her gaze meaningfully.

She gave him a smile full of womanly courage, then they both hastened to put themselves back into more respectable order. Lucien tucked in his shirt, feeling like a new man, then, in amusement, used his monogrammed handkerchief to polish away the charming imprint of her bottom left behind on the shiny mahogany table.

Unaware of his discreet tidying up, Alice cleared her throat, smoothed her hair, and marched back to her chair, picking up her sketch pad.

Lucien wanted nothing but to curl up in bed with her for the rest of the day, but he went and stood beside her, playing with her hair and answering her questions to the best of his ability as she quizzed him on more details of Bardou's face.

He was taken aback by the likeness that began to emerge on the page.

"That's very close. The eyes are a little too close together, and you can make the jaw a bit more rounded. Also, he has an oily quality to his skin. Is there any way that you can bring that out?"

But she just sat there, staring down at the picture, not responding.

Lucien glanced at her and suddenly noticed that she had turned quite pale. "Alice, are you all right?"

"Lucien—I know this man."

"*What?*"

She looked up at him with panic in her eyes. "This is Karl von Dannecker, Caro's new beau. I'm sure it's him, but he's not French—isn't he Prussian? Lucien, he is going to be here any minute!"

Alice had never before seen Lucien turn quite that shade of sickly pale.

"He's been here? In this house?" he clipped out. "While you were here? And Harry?"

"He's spent the past few nights here with Caro."

He let out the foulest curse under his breath that she had ever heard, pivoted away from her, and was already marching toward the door.

"Lucien!"

"Get the baby ready; get your coat on. You're leaving. I'm sending you to where you'll be safe. Fetch Caro as well. She'll have to leave with you. Tell the servants to move to the back of the house and stay down. I don't want anybody making a sound, do you understand? Marc! Kyle!" he bellowed down the hallway, then turned back to her, his expression black with ire. "Do you know what time he's coming?"

She glanced at the mantel clock. "In ten minutes. She expects him at four," she stammered. "She is supposed to go away with him somewhere for the weekend."

Lucien cursed under his breath and started to walk away again.

"What are you going to do?"

"Arrest him. Kill him, with any luck," he added, glancing toward the front door.

"I belong by your side. Let me help."

"Hell, no. I'll try to avoid bloodshed here in your house, but the courts will hang him either way. You!" Lucien called to the startled Mr. Hattersley, who had hurried out at the sound of all the yelling. "Have the carriage made ready for Miss Montague. Marc," he said as the young man strode into the room. "Bardou's on his way here. He's tracked me through Lady Glenwood. We're going to ambush him when he walks in the door. I want Alice and Harry and the baroness out of here. Take them to Knight House and tell Damien they have to be protected. I'm entrusting them to him. You will help him."

"Yes, sir."

"Talbert!"

"Here, sir!"

"Can you play a butler?"

"Most assuredly, my lord," the slight-framed young showman answered with a grin.

"Good. We need Bardou to step into the entrance hall where we can trap him rather than letting him run away."

"I understand perfectly. I'll go find a uniform."

"Kyle!"

"Yes, sir!"

"Make sure our horses are well out of sight when Bardou drives up to the house. If he gets away somehow, we'll need to be ready to ride in a trice."

"Yes, my lord."

"Jenkins, O'Shea, check your weapons. You'll cover me when I attack him. I suppose we ought to take him alive in case he's got accomplices at large in the city. Alice, what are you waiting for?" he barked, noticing her still standing there in bewilderment. "Do as I told you!"

"But, Lucien, Caro's not going to listen to me!"

"Make her listen! Now, go!"

Frightened into obedience, she ran up to the nursery to get Harry. Her hands shook as she put his shoes and coat on him and told Peg Tate that she must come with them to Knight House. With an outward show of calm while her heart pounded with fright, Alice shepherded the old woman, the child, Nellie, and the rest of the household staff to the back of the house and gave them Lucien's instructions, hushing them; then she went back up to get Caro. She braced herself as she knocked briskly on the door of Caro's bedchamber, because she knew her sister-in-law was going to give her trouble. She could hear the baroness humming to herself in her room.

"Caro!" Alice opened the door.

She was clad only in her negligee with a velvet dressing gown over it, harrying her beleaguered maid as the long-suffering servant carried an armful of the baroness's gowns from the armoire to the bed.

"What do you want, Alice?" Caro asked in a lofty tone. "You can see I'm very busy. Von Dannecker will be here in a few minutes."

"That's what I have come to talk to you about. Alone."

With an irked look, Caro dismissed her maid. Alice cast about for words. God, she did not want to be the one to have to tell Caro this. "Caro, von Dannecker is not what he appears. He is some sort of criminal," she said, being purposely vague. "Lucien Knight is downstairs—"

"Lucien?" she exclaimed, straightening up from smoothing the gowns on the bed. She braced her hands on her waist and looked at Alice in confusion.

"Lucien is going to take von Dannecker into custody."

She wrinkled her nose in confusion. "*What?*"

"Caro, there may be shooting. We have to get out of here right now. This is very serious. We are all in danger. Hurry up and put something on. Lucien is sending us to Knight House until it's over."

Caro stared at her uncertainly for a moment, then burst out laughing. "That devil! He never tires of his little pranks, does he? Well, you just run along and tell that silver-eyed fiend to wait for me downstairs. I will talk to him in a moment, and we shall see what mischief he is up to now; but first I have to get dressed."

"Caro, this is no prank," Alice exclaimed in exasperation. "Lucien is not what you think." She hesitated, for she had promised never to tell anyone his true occupation, but under the circumstances, he would understand. "Lucien is a secret agent for the Crown, and von Dannecker is a French spy. His real name is Claude Bardou."

"A spy?" she scoffed.

"Even if you don't believe me, we can discuss it later.

Just throw on some clothes and come with me and Harry to Knight House. I am begging you."

"Knight House! Well, I am not about to go to the duke of Hawkscliffe's mansion in my dressing gown," she snapped, but her face had turned white and her movements were jerky as she pulled off her banyan and quickly began to dress.

Alice let out a private sigh of relief. "Come down to the kitchen as soon as you are dressed. I have Harry and the staff already gathered there. The grooms are readying the carriage for us even now."

Caro gave her an insolent nod, simmering fury in her dark eyes. As she withdrew from her sumptuous chamber, Alice heard the baroness muttering indignantly under her breath. "This is absurd! That devil—thinks he can come into my house and start ordering everyone around. . . ."

Alice rolled her eyes at her sister-in-law's temperamental ways, but at least she had succeeded in getting her cooperation. She picked the hem of her skirts up and ran back down the steps. She saw Lucien standing in the entrance hall. He cocked his pistol and looked up as Alice came hurrying down the stairs.

"Where's Caro?" he asked in a grim tone. The brooding wrath in his eyes sent a shudder of dread through her.

"Coming. She's not happy, but she'll cooperate."

"Good."

Before leaving the entrance hall, Alice ran over to Lucien and embraced him. Standing on her tiptoes, she kissed his cheek. When their gazes met, she made no effort to conceal the tenderness and worry in her eyes. "Be careful," she whispered.

He nodded tautly and looked away, his jaw clenched. "Alice, I'm so sorry for everything. If I'm killed . . ."

She captured his chiseled face between her hands and stared fiercely into his eyes. "Don't you dare say that to me. You come home to me. I will be waiting." She swallowed hard. "I love you."

A flicker of anguish passed fleetingly through the crystalline depths of his soulful eyes. He lowered his lashes, turned his face, and kissed her palm. "Go and hide with the others," he murmured roughly.

She nodded and released him, striding back to the kitchen while he returned to his men. Before closing the kitchen door behind her, she looked down the hallway at him one last time. His face was beautiful, savage, and as wrathfully remote as an avenging archangel's. His eyes gleamed like diamonds set in burnished silver. The sun flashed on the pistol that he pulled out from under his waistcoat as he moved with a predator's grace through the entrance hall, ordering the younger men into position.

He took his place beside the door, pressing his back up against the wall.

Oh, God, this could not be happening, she thought. Spies and arrests in her very home! Shaken, she shut the door and took her place with the others. Each minute dragged interminably. Where was Caro? What was taking her so long? she thought. Just then, Mr. Hattersley slipped into the kitchen through the garden door.

"Mitchell is harnessing the team, miss. It will be ready in just a few minutes."

"Good."

Marc suddenly strode into the kitchen where they all were gathered. He put his finger to his lips and waved

Alice down behind the heavy wooden worktable, which the men had turned onto its side to serve as a barricade.

"Are we leaving?" Alice whispered.

"Too late," Marc replied.

"Silent, now. He and Ethan Stafford just pulled up."

"But Caro—!"

"It's too late. She's still upstairs. She should be fine as long as she stays up there."

"Perhaps I should get the door," Mr. Hattersley said in distress.

"They'll answer it," Marc said grimly.

Peg met Alice's eyes grimly. The bewildered old woman was huddled with Nellie and the terrified young scullery maid behind the chopping block. Marc drew his pistol and positioned his body protectively in front of Alice and Harry.

Harry began fussing, disliking the atmosphere of tension. "Where my mama?"

"Keep him quiet," Marc murmured.

Alice cupped the baby's downy head against her chest. "Shh."

"We play hide-and-seek?" Harry whispered.

"Yes, now hush. Put your head down, lambkin."

He giggled and nestled his head under the crook of her chin. She wondered if the child could hear her heart pounding, but he grew quiet and still in her arms, playing the game. She closed her eyes and shielded him in fierce protectiveness, only wishing she could shield Lucien as well. All too vividly, she remembered the wound on his side, which she had stitched up that last night at Revell Court. *Please, God, keep him safe.*

She flicked her eyes open at the sound of a hard knock

that came from the direction of the entrance hall. Then she held her breath at the creaking sound of the front door opening.

CHAPTER SIXTEEN

The day had come at last.

A moment earlier, Claude Bardou had jumped down from the carriage while Ethan held the reins. Bardou walked up to Caro's front door, feeling strong. The previous night, he had slept peacefully after rutting with the baroness for the last time. Today he was taking her to the cottage where he would use her as the bait to lure Lucien Knight away from London. She had no idea, of course. She thought he was taking her away for a romantic escape, just the two of them.

Fool, he thought. After leaving her this morning, he had checked on his gun crew one last time and had made sure that his fieldpiece was ready for action, that the kegs of gunpowder were of the proper mixture, that there was plenty of coal and wood to fuel the portable stove. The ammunition would have to sit in the blazing furnace for hours in advance to make it hot enough to wield its full destructive power. Napoleon would have been proud of him, he mused. His planning had been meticulous, he had not allowed his small-minded American moneymen to deter him, and everything was in order. By this time tomorrow, he would be on a ship bound for the Italian coast to see what he could do to help Fouché get the emperor out of captivity on Elba.

In his buoyant mood, he started to whistle a few notes of the "Marseillese" as he lifted his hand to knock on the door, but quickly caught himself before his patriotism showed through. Lord, he would be glad to be done playing the tedious von Dannecker.

When the door opened, Bardou instantly went on his guard. A different butler. Young. Blond hair slicked back, well-turned cravat, smooth and neat.

"Good afternoon, sir. May I help you?"

"Where is the usual butler?" he asked cautiously.

"It's Mr. Hattersley's day off, sir. I am Talbert, the under-butler. May I be of assistance?"

"I am Lord von Dannecker. I am here to fetch Lady Glenwood."

"Ah, yes, of course, my lord. Would you care to wait inside for Her Ladyship?" He opened the door wider and stood aside with a smile of bland politeness.

Bardou gave him a wary look and stepped into the entrance hall; then the world exploded into fireworks before his eyes as a shattering blow hit him in the side of the head. He crashed against the door, falling, too stunned to reach for his weapon, completely ambushed; then Lucien Knight was standing over him, pointing a loaded pistol right between his eyes.

Bardou's dizzied gaze zigzagged from the muzzle of the gun to the murderous silver eyes pinning him in a stare full of white-hot hatred. "*Bonjour*, Monsieur Bardou," Knight said, his lips curving into a bitter smile. "What a pleasant surprise to see you again."

He started to get up, but Knight punched him across

the face, just as Bardou had so often punched him. Bardou cursed after the thunderous blow, which was followed by a kick in the ribs. He balled up on the floor, sprawled against the door. He looked up at his former captive, suddenly afraid. His heart pounded; his chest heaved. He touched the blood that he felt trickling from the corner of his mouth.

"Get up," Knight ground out.

Bardou realized the restraint his enemy was using. He climbed cautiously to his feet and looked around at Knight's men, all of whom tracked him with their pistols.

"Step away from the door," Knight ordered.

Bardou gritted his teeth, hatred churning in his belly and flaming in his eyes, but he obeyed. The young "butler" slammed the door behind him, and Knight stepped closer, resting the muzzle of his gun against Bardou's temple.

"Jenkins, shackle him. Don't move, Bardou, or this bullet is going into your brain."

Bardou's mind swam. He could not let them put shackles on him or he was doomed. As the seconds ticked by and the young man cautiously came toward him with the wrist irons in his grasp, Bardou struggled to decide which of them to attack. There were four besides Knight. Even the "butler" was holding a gun on him. Bardou stood there fuming, his chest heaving. He refused to accept that he was caught. He glared in warning at the young man who had been ordered to shackle him, when suddenly, his salvation came walking down the staircase.

"Karl! Lucien! What is the meaning of this?" Caro demanded in shock, several steps from the bottom.

"Caro, stay back," Knight warned through gritted teeth.

"My lady, help me!" Bardou panted. "Call off your jealous fool before he pulls the trigger!"

"Lucien, have you gone mad? Put your weapons down, all of you! There is a child in this house. I will not have guns drawn here." Bardou stared at her, his heart pounding with renewed hope as she came rushing down the steps.

"Stay back," Knight ordered her as she ran toward them. "Caro, no!" Knight roared, throwing up his hand to ward her off, but he was too late.

Bardou shot out his hand and grabbed her by her hair, yanking her toward him. She shrieked as she stumbled against him, but he whipped out his pistol before any of them could stop him and put the gun to her head.

Caro screamed.

"Stay back or she dies," he warned with a wolfish grin.

"Karl! You're hurting me!"

"Shut up," he growled at her.

"Bardou, let her go," Knight said in deadly quiet. "This is between you and me."

"And Sophia, too, yes? I'll see you tonight, old friend," he threatened softly, then kicked the door open and dragged Caro out to the waiting carriage. "Wake up, Stafford!" he bellowed.

Sitting in the driver's seat of his fast drag-carriage, Stafford turned around in question. His face went ashen when he saw that Bardou had taken Lady Glenwood hostage. "What on earth—"

"Shut up and drive!"

"Von Dannecker—"

"Don't question me!" he roared. "Do as I say unless you want us both to hang! You're in too deep to back out now, so just bloody *drive*!"

He clapped his hand over Caro's mouth when she drew breath to scream. She fought and clawed at him every step of the way, but he was relentless, hauling her out the door, down the front steps, and across the pavement toward the waiting carriage. Her feet barely touched the ground as he hefted her like a rag doll in his grasp, but he didn't take his eyes off Lucien Knight and his men as they followed him like a pack of salivating dogs closing in on a stag at bay.

"Stay back or I'll shoot the bitch!" he yelled, sweat beading his forehead. Wrenching open the carriage door with one hand, Bardou backed in, pulling Caro in after him. Stafford whipped the four-horse team, and the drag tore off down the quiet, residential street.

"Which way should I go?" Stafford asked.

"Head east. Weave your way toward the river and try to lose them in the City if you can, then take the Ratcliffe Highway. You claim you're a good driver. Let's see how good you really are."

"All right," Stafford said grimly, his expression hardening with resolve. He brought down his whip on the horses' backs and the drag shot ahead, zooming down Brooke Street. Crossing Grosvenor Square, they swerved around slower traffic in the road, scattering pedestrians out of their path. Bardou looked out the window and saw Lucien on a large, black horse, riding hard after them with his men, in hot pursuit. Bardou knew how to slow them down. Right in the middle of Grosvenor Square, he took aim and shot at Knight from out the carriage window. The bullet went wide, but the shot had the calculated effect. Though it did not discourage Knight and his men, he saw their furious looks. They slowed a bit, letting Stafford's carriage widen its lead on them rather than risk an exchange of gunfire in the midst of city streets crowded with civilians.

Their lead increased as Stafford veered the drag into a sharp right turn onto Bond Street. They went thundering past gigs, wagons, and a mail coach, pounding down the busy main artery of the fashionable shopping district. Bardou's pulse was racing with glee as he took another glance out the window. Caro was crying, her face ashen with fright, her cosmetics smearing down her cheeks. She held onto the leather hand strap for dear life.

"Von Dannecker, what is going on?" she wailed.

"My name is Bardou, and you are my hostage," he said coldly. "Your lover took my woman from me. Now I take his woman in return. But never fear, he will come to save you, and when he does, he will die."

"He is not my lover!" she cried as the carriage took another jarring turn.

He scoffed at her lie.

"It's true! I mean nothing to him!"

"He is following," he pointed out. He took another glance out the carriage window and grinned. "Keep going, Stafford! You are doing well. We're losing them."

"Von Dannecker—Bardou—you must let me go. You've made a mistake," she insisted, wiping her tears; then she let out another yelp as the carriage rocked up onto two wheels, tearing around the corner at Piccadilly, then crashed back down onto all four and kept going.

"What mistake?" he growled.

"Lucien Knight was never in love with me! It's my sister-in-law he's mad for—Alice!"

"What is this you say?" he asked dangerously, recalling the moody allure of the young blue-eyed blond.

She was, like Lucien Knight himself, a mysterious creature of quiet elegance. "You told me he was so desperate to have you that he stole you away from his brother."

"Well, yes, that's what I told you, but that is not what happened. Alice is the one who captivated him, not me! Last week she didn't have influenza, as we told everyone. She spent the week at his house. She is his lover—his mistress! I was merely covering up for her."

He narrowed his eyes. "You're lying."

"No! I lied before, I admit it—I wanted to make you jealous, and I didn't want you to notice her, only me. But this is the truth!"

"You lied to me?" he snarled, incredulous as he realized that she had fooled him. She was useless to him. It was the little blond that he needed.

"I had to! Now you have to let me go, don't you see? It's Alice that you want!"

"You deceitful bitch! You wasted my time!" He backhanded her hard across the face.

She flew back against the squabs with a shriek as they lurched onto the Strand, but rather than easing his tension, hitting her only whetted his appetite. He picked her up and slapped her again. "Go on, cry, useless bitch. Cry all you want."

"Von Dannecker!" Stafford yelled from up on the driver's seat. "What are you doing to her? Stop it!"

With blood trickling from the corner of her mouth, Caro blubbered in terrorized self-pity at Stafford's attempt to interfere.

"You're right, Mr. Stafford," Bardou murmured. "It's time to silence her lying tongue. Good-bye, Lady Glenwood," he whispered, leaning toward her.

"No—no! Get away from me—"

Her protest ended in a sudden choking sound as he grasped her throat, a snarl fixed on his face. She clawed at him, gagging and slowly turning blue as he strangled her with one hand, his grip unrelenting, his stare as cold as stone, until after a minute or two, her struggles ended. He dropped her then, and looked at her crumpled body in contempt.

"Whore," he whispered.

Less than ten lengths behind, Lucien and his men chased the drag as it thundered down the Strand and into Fleet Street. A world away from Mayfair's elegant avenues, the noisy, mercantile city was a medieval maze of narrow, crowded, zigzagging streets. Lucien yelled to his men as Stafford veered right at New Bridge. Immediately upon rounding the corner, a cold, November wind rushed up from the broad river ahead, riffling through his hair. Ahead, the Thames was dull pewter, busy with boats of all shapes and sizes moving upriver and down, their white sails bowed. New Bridge Street bustled with wagons and vendors taking their goods to Fleet Market, just up the road behind him, but the working day was ending early and there was a holiday atmosphere in the air. Everywhere people were starting to get ready for the Guy Fawkes Night celebrations. At this time of year, night came early. Already the sun had begun to set.

Lucien narrowed his eyes against the gritty, blowing wind, then cursed, signaling his horse just in time to jump a vegetable seller's wheelbarrow that nosed out of a side alley without warning into his path. The vendor yelped as the black stallion arced gracefully over the cart; then he cursed Lucien as the horse landed neatly on the pavement and raced on.

Stafford did not cross the imposing Blackfriars Bridge that spanned the Thames straight ahead, Lucien saw, but instead made another reeling, right-hand turn onto Earl Street, which became Upper Thames. Lined with industrial wharves and yards, various workers' halls and the occasional brewery, Upper Thames hugged the curves of the river. They passed the waterworks and London Bridge, where Upper Thames turned into Lower Thames and things got decidedly seedier. Stafford made a sharp, unexpected left turn by St. Dunstan's workhouse and suddenly disappeared.

"Damn!" Lucien whispered, his heart pounding. He scanned the buildings and licked his dry lips, feeling them becoming chapped in the wind. Kyle and the others reined in and looked at him in question. "Spread out," Lucien ordered in a low tone. "We'll box him in. Whoever sees him first, yell for the rest of us. Lady Glenwood's life depends on us, lads."

He hoped they were not already too late.

They nodded grimly and rode off in separate directions to close off the area, but Lucien urged his horse into the deserted alleyway. Suddenly, down a dark, garbage-strewn lane adjoining the alley, he saw Stafford's drag flash by.

Bardou leaped out of the moving carriage and ducked into the gloom of one of the dilapidated building's overhanging eaves. Lucien's eyes flared. Dimly aware of Kyle's shout some distance away as the lads spotted the carriage, he made a split-second decision, biting back the shout on the tip of his tongue.

Bardou's move was a ruse designed to make Lucien and his men chase the empty carriage when Bardou had already escaped. Ethan Stafford probably didn't even know that the Frenchman was no longer in the carriage.

Let the bastard believe he has made a clean escape, Lucien thought, his heart pounding. Sophia had warned him that Bardou had explosives stored in a warehouse by the river. Lucien had a strong suspicion that Bardou was headed for his lair. Lucien decided to follow him alone because if he shouted to his men, Bardou would be alerted that he was still being followed and thus would not go to his headquarters where the explosives were stored.

At the same time, he realized with sickening certainty that Bardou would not have abandoned a usable hostage. It could only mean that Caro was already dead. *Oh, God,* he thought, slammed by the realization that he was too late.

He drove his heels into his horse's sides and started after Bardou, only to rein in a few paces later. Stealth was impossible with the horse under him. Its clopping hoofbeats echoed too loudly throughout these quiet back alleys. They would alert Bardou to his presence; besides, Bardou would surely dart indoors soon at one of the riverside warehouses.

While his men chased Stafford's carriage back toward London Bridge, Lucien slid down off his horse and stole after Bardou on foot. He steeled himself against the realization that he was leaving his proud, loyal steed unattended in a rookery of thieves, but all that mattered was getting Bardou. With rage in his heart, his pistol in his grasp, and his nemesis in his clear line of fire, the only thing that stopped him from shooting Bardou in the back was the knowledge that the man might have other accomplices besides Ethan Stafford, who might still carry out his plot even if Bardou himself were killed. The only way to eradicate the threat completely was to find Bardou's headquarters and learn his plans.

Then and only then, Lucien promised himself blackly, he would blow the bastard's head off. As he gave chase, his heart thundered with blood lust that was not tempered even by the sight of St. Dunstan's weightless Gothic bell tower and serene religious statues as Bardou ran into the church. Lucien noticed Bardou's slight limp as he raced in after him. The Frenchman seemed to favor his right leg. Inside the ancient stone walls of the church, a few old ladies were dusting the pews and chatting in low tones. Unnoticed, Lucien glided silently through the gloom of the church; Bardou exited on the other side of the nave.

Plunging outdoors once more into the noise of the city and the cold overcast afternoon, Lucien trailed Bardou as the man ran down St. Dunstan's Hill and back to Lower Thames Street. To his surprise, the son of a bitch backtracked to Blackfriars Bridge and crossed it on foot.

So, he's not working out of the City, he realized in surprise. *No wonder the constables' sweep of the riverside warehouses turned up nothing. He's working out of Southwark or Lambeth, on the other side of the river.*

Lucien trailed him as he reached the south shore of the Thames and made his way down Albion Street, making a quick right turn onto Upper Ground Street, which soon turned into Narrow Wall Street. Everywhere, the wheels of industry were turning, getting in their last hour of production before the holiday. The smells of the fishing docks and the various factories clustered in the area filled the cold autumn air. Bardou pressed on with a purposeful stride, his limp becoming more pronounced as their walk dragged on. He passed the old Barge Brewery, the cloth manufactory, the iron foundry. Lucien shadowed him through the busy timber yards until, at last, Bardou hurried toward a dilapidated brick warehouse that sat alone, overgrown with weeds, at the river's edge. Though it looked abandoned, there was smoke rising from the chimney.

Keeping to the shadows of the high fence that surrounded the adjoining timber yard, Lucien glided closer, studying the situation as dusk fell. A rifleman stood guard at both of the warehouse's corners that were visible from his standpoint. Bardou returned their salutes as he ducked furtively into the building.

Lucien could only assume that there were men posted on the other two corners, as well, but he doubted there were many more inside. On enemy ground, a wise agent winnowed his forces down to the smallest number of the most highly skilled men he could acquire. Lucien was very interested to know what was inside that warehouse, but first he had to get rid of the guards.

Mayhem glittered in his eyes and the siren's call of revenge sang in his blood as he holstered his pistol and slid his dagger out of its sheath with a soft whisper of metal. He clung to the fence's shadow, then moved from cover to cover, inching closer like a lion in the grass. His heart thundering, he used the cast-off chunks of factory machinery strewn here and there—a great capstan from some long-rotted hulk, a broken-down wagon, a pile of bricks—to conceal his approach. He picked up a handful of pebbles as he crept into striking distance.

A few moments later, the first guard turned in the direction of a small, suspicious sound. When he turned his back, Lucien materialized behind him, grabbed the man from behind, clamping his hand over his mouth, and cut his throat without a noise. Almost with a kind of elegance, he set the body down silently, thrusting it well out of view, then faded back into the shadows of the building's edge. Rage chanted through his spirit like his minions in the Grotto at their most intoxicated, their most ecstatic, even as he struggled to hold Alice's love in his heart, fueling him to justice, not the cruelty that his hatred would prescribe.

In under five minutes, the second guard met a similar fate, but as Lucien stalked up behind the third, the man turned and saw him.

The guard let out a yell as Lucien knocked the rifle out of his hands. The fourth shouted from fifty yards away. Lucien yanked the disarmed guard in front of him just as the fourth guard fired his rifle. The bullet struck the hefty Frenchman instead of him. Lucien dropped the third man, smoothly pulled out one of his pair of Manton pistols, and took aim before the fourth guard could reload. He saw the man's eyes widen in dread, frozen in his sights; then he pulled the trigger.

Mere seconds had passed. The fourth guard was still twitching in the dust as Lucien drew his second pistol, stalked up to the door of the warehouse, and kicked it open, nearly throwing it off its rusty hinges. As it flung open, he came face-to-face with Bardou, a mere six or seven feet between them. Apparently, the Frenchman had been rushing toward the door to investigate the sound of gunfire outside. Bardou froze as Lucien brought up his pistol and leveled it at him.

"Give my regards to the devil."

"Don't shoot, Argus! Look!" Bardou raised his hands

in a gesture of surrender, but nodded toward the barrels stacked just behind him.

Lucien's gaze flicked to the white letter A painted on each barrel. Top quality gunpowder. The explosives Sophia had warned him about, he realized.

His glance swept the warehouse, freezing in shock on the cannon with its nose pointed out the window. It was aimed straight across the river at Parliament. No wonder he hadn't found any explosives planted in Westminster Hall. Bardou had planned on launching his attack from here. He saw the portable stove thrust into the large industrial hearth, throwing off heat that made the whole warehouse uncomfortably warm. *Good God,* he realized in horror, *Bardou had been preparing hot shot.*

"If you pull that trigger, we both die," Bardou warned. "All it takes is one spark."

"Move away from the barrels."

He laughed softly, shaking his head. "I think not."

"Come away from those barrels and *fight me*, you coward!" Lucien roared.

"Coward?"

"You hid behind Caro the same way you're trying to shield yourself with those barrels. Maybe you don't dare, now that I'm no longer in chains."

"Well, maybe you had better pull that trigger and kill us both, Argus, because I know now about your little mistress, Alice Montague." Bardou smiled as Lucien's face drained of color. "Such a tender young beauty. I hope she fights me when I take her. I hope she cries. In fact, I'll make sure that she does."

Blind rage overwhelmed Lucien. With hellfire burning in his eyes, he tossed his pistol aside, well out of Bardou's reach. He did not need it to kill the son of a bitch. He wanted to do it with his bare hands. Lucien charged him, slamming Bardou back bodily into the stacked barrels of gunpowder, which crashed down all around them, some splitting and puffing up clouds of black powder that hung in the air like soot and covered both men in a fine, metallic dust. Lucien hauled back and smashed his fist into Bardou's jaw.

They fought savagely, pummeling each other with blood in their eyes. Lucien was impervious to the punches he took until Bardou's fist slammed into his stitches. He let out a harsh cry of pain and doubled over, failing to block Bardou's next blow to his head. It knocked him to the ground. He coughed, inhaling a bit of the gunpowder that puffed up around him as he fell.

With a brutish grunt, Bardou heaved one of the barrels of gunpowder up and held it aloft over Lucien, who shook his head clear just in time to react. Recalling Bardou's limp, he kicked him in the right knee with shattering force. Bardou let out a roar of pain and dropped the barrel. Lucien rolled out of the way as the barrel crashed to the floor and broke open.

Cursing over his injured leg, Bardou ran off at a crippled hobble out of the warehouse, pausing only long enough to grab a sleek leather rifle case. *He was escaping!* Lucien searched frantically through the deep layer of black powder, trying to find his cast-off pistol. Once the Frenchman left the vicinity of the gunpowder, Lucien could safely fire at him. Failing to find his pistol quickly enough, he dragged himself up and ran doggedly after Bardou. When he flung out of the warehouse, he looked around, then saw Bardou climbing into a rowboat at the water's edge. Beyond, the fiery sunset faded into the western horizon.

"Bardou!" he bellowed.

As Lucien ran after him, Bardou untied the boat from the post and pushed away from the small wooden dock with an oar. Lucien took a running leap off the dock and landed with a crash on top of Bardou in the boat as the current of the Thames began moving them along at an ever-quickening pace.

Lucien whipped out his dagger and slashed at Bardou, but the Frenchman blocked the arc of his knife with the oar, then grasped Lucien's wrist. They struggled and Lucien let out a furious curse, dropping his dagger over the side into the rushing river when Bardou bashed his wrist on the metal oarlock, then knocked him back with a blow from the oar.

"Now you die," Bardou snarled. Falling atop him, he wrapped his big hands around Lucien's throat and began strangling him, choking the life out of him.

With each vain attempt to pull air into his lungs, Lucien felt his awareness sliding back into an ancient panic. *Can't . . . breathe.* The terror of his childhood asthma attacks came flooding back to him, a deeply ingrained fear against which he had no defense. He pummeled Bardou's stomach and clawed at his face until the little boat pitched wildly with their struggles. He started to throw Bardou off and in the next heartbeat, fell over the side. Before he knew what had happened to him, he was underwater, sucked down under a current so frigid it shocked him. He nearly drowned himself with the impulse to gasp for air now that the viselike grip had been removed from his throat. For that instant, he didn't care that Bardou was escaping. All that mattered was getting air into his lungs. The cold, murky Thames tumbled him in a somersault, but he righted himself and pulled upward against the weight of his waterlogged boots and clothes.

He shot to the surface, gasping and choking for breath. As he wiped the water out of his eyes, drinking in great lungfuls of air, he saw Bardou rowing swiftly with the current.

"You haven't begun to suffer, Knight!" Bardou shouted over the water at him. "Just wait till I kill Alice Montague!"

"No!" he choked out. "God damn it!" Though his strength was spent, pure rage fueled Lucien's strokes as he swam back to the docks against the sweeping pull of the current. Bruised and bleeding, shivering with the wintry cold, his clothes and hair dripping with greasy Thames water, he felt nothing but volcanic fury as he grasped the ladder on the dock and pulled himself out of the river. He scrambled up onto the dock and ran through the warehouse yard, past the strewn bodies of the guards and the industrial refuse, making his way back out to Narrow Wall Street.

With the sky darkening in autumn's early twilight, people were already milling about in the streets, waving their Guy Fawkes torches, singing their songs, and drinking their ale. In the distance, the revelers had already begun to set off crackers and Roman candles, but some children darted in front of Lucien, chanting, *"Guy, guy, guy! Stick him up on high! Hang him on a lamppost and leave him there to die!"*

He dodged around them, his pulse thundering in his ears as he raced toward Westminster Bridge. He heard the first celebratory cannons being fired from the direction of the royal parks. Their booming report reverberated in his chest, taking him back in a flash to his army days and the wild rage of battle. His mind was crisply clear, and he realized that he would never get to Alice first on foot.

Pounding up to the well-trafficked bridge, his waterlogged boots slogging with every stride, he stepped into the road in front of a dandy on a tall gray horse. The spooked gray reared up, but Lucien seized the reins and laid hold of the bridle.

"Get down," he ordered the rider in a deadly tone.

"What is the meaning of this? Remove your hands from my—whoa!" the man cried as Lucien pulled him down out of the saddle, leaving him in a heap on the bridge. "Thief! Stop thief!"

Lucien swung up into the saddle and rode, urging the nervous gray into a gallop. He flew past the other traffic on the bridge as the first burst of the holiday fireworks climbed into the sky over the river and exploded in a hail of blue, red, and green, followed by another in resplendent orange and yellow. He glanced at the water. By their colorful illumination, he searched the river's glittering surface for Bardou's rowboat and let out a sharp curse as he spied the big Frenchman already climbing out of the boat onto the wharf by Craven Street. Bardou knew that Lucien trusted his twin brother above all men, thus, could easily deduce that he had sent Alice to be protected by Damien at Knight House. It was reasonable for Bardou at least to check there, since Knight House was so close. Bardou need only take Cockspur Street to Pall Mall; from there it was practically a straight shot to the mansion. Lucien urged the gray on at breakneck speed, flying past the elegant wrought-iron lamps on the bridge. *Too many streets lay between him and Alice,* he thought, his face set in grim frustration. His only hope of arriving before Bardou was to cut through St. James's Park, where the fire festival was under way.

CHAPTER SEVENTEEN

While Peg kept Harry entertained on the floor with a quiet game of spillikins, and the formidable Lord Damien paced back to the window, keeping guard in stony silence, Alice sat with Weymouth on the couch in the elegant drawing room of Knight House, trying to console him.

"How can she be gone? Oh, my sweet, beautiful sister. How could anyone hurt her?"

Alice rubbed his bony arm in wordless sorrow. Her own eyes were red-rimmed from crying, but she wished that the unkempt viscount would get himself under control before he upset Harry. She had received the terrible news of Caro's murder about an hour ago. She had feared this outcome from the moment she had heard Bardou take her sister-in-law hostage back at the house in Upper Brooke Street. Though she had long had premonitions of disaster for Caro, it still came as a horrible shock. As soon as she had regained her composure, she had sent for Weymouth as Caro's next of kin.

Unfortunately, the opium clouding the viscount's wits made it all the more difficult for him to absorb the shocking news. If only for once he were not intoxicated. As Weymouth went on sobbing uncontrollably, Alice was tempted to shake him. He was taking the blow worse than Harry had, but in truth, she admitted, the three-year-old had no comprehension of what death meant. Perhaps this was a blessing.

Fighting tears, Alice had explained to Harry that Mama had gone to live in heaven with Papa and the angels. Harry seemed to think that it was just another occasion of the baroness leaving him again. As long as Harry had his Nanny Peg and his Aunt Alice, he seemed content, at least for now. Though Alice was trying to be strong for Harry and for the pitiful Lord Weymouth, she could barely keep control of her emotions with Lucien still missing.

An hour ago, at about five o'clock, Kyle, Talbert, and the others had returned to Knight House in defeat. They had explained to her how they had quickly caught up with Ethan Stafford's fleeing carriage and how they had found Caro murdered inside. Bardou had escaped. They had handed Stafford over to the constable. For Alice, somehow, even worse than hearing the news of Caro's murder was the sight of Kyle leading Lucien's black horse in through the gates of Knight House, riderless. Kyle had told her that they had become separated from Lucien somewhere in the East End. Now that she had seen the unfeeling cruelty of which Bardou was capable, the fact that the Frenchman and Lucien were both missing made her blood feel like ice in her veins.

The lads had gone back out to look for him in the area where they had found his horse. This time Marc had joined them, abandoning his orders, since a man with Damien's years of combat experience surely did not need any help protecting Alice. And yet, ever since the Guy

Fawkes fireworks had begun exploding through the night sky, she had noticed that Damien had started to seem . . . strange. He seemed to be on edge, pacing restlessly. Alice noticed that he jumped each time the salute cannons boomed in the distance. She could not account for it. If anyone were used to the sound of cannonfire, she thought, surely it would be the battle-hardened colonel.

When she looked at him again, she could see the tension bristling in the broad lines of his shoulders. When another cannon roared in the distance, he flinched.

"Damien?"

He turned to her abruptly, as though she had startled him.

A shudder ran through him. When he glanced at her, the look in his gray eyes was ferocious, yet miles away. His face was quite pale and streaming with sweat.

She stood up and took a step toward him. "Damien, are you all right?"

He cast about as though confused for a second.

She moved toward him. "Maybe you'd better sit down."

"No—I—I'm—fine. Would you excuse me," he mumbled, then stalked out of the room.

Harry waved cheerfully. "Bye-bye, Lucien!"

Alice glanced from Damien's retreating back to her nephew. Unable to quite absorb the concept that the twins were two separate men, Harry could not figure out why this "Lucien" seemed so remote and unwilling to play with him, unlike the friendly man who had given him the prism back at the townhouse. As Alice glanced in the direction Damien had gone, she still was not convinced that he was well.

"Weymouth, would you excuse me?"

"Harry will keep me company," he said with a sniffle. "Come to Uncle Weymouth, Harry."

Alice hurried out of the drawing room while Weymouth went on trying to get Harry's attention. *Damien had looked feverish,* she thought as she marched down the corridor to the gleaming entrance hall. She hoped he had not fallen ill. When she reached the entrance hall, she saw Damien standing midway up the stairs. He was just standing there staring at the ground, his back to her. He looked so unsteady that she thought he was on the verge of passing out with fever, so she started to run up the steps after him to try to stop him from falling. Hearing her footfalls, he suddenly spun around with lightning speed.

"Stay back!" he snarled. He was wild-eyed, panting. He had a large knife in his hand and was holding it with a white-knuckled grasp.

Alice froze with a gasp.

They stared at each other. She did not dare move. The creature she saw in his eyes was not the same stoic, controlled colonel who had proposed to her in Hyde Park.

"Damien? What's wrong?" she asked, her heart in her throat. She began inching back down the steps as though backing away from a wild animal.

Another cannon boomed in the distance, and his glance darted in the direction from which the sound had come. His face was taut with fierce concentration.

"Less than a mile off. Look sharp, boots. Pull up camp. They'll be here in minutes."

"Who will?" she asked faintly, paling at the glittering madness in his eyes.

"Boney's coming. He's just over that rise." He pointed up the staircase with his knife, then laid his finger over his lips. "Don't make a sound. We've got to get the artillery in place."

Before Alice could react, he glided up the stairs, keeping low.

She stood stock-still, her hand clapped over her mouth in shock. *Oh, my God.*

For a long moment, she just stood there, not knowing what to do; then she jumped with fright as a loud banging reached her from somewhere upstairs. It sounded as though the colonel was barricading himself into one of the upper rooms. Her heart pounding in dread, Alice rushed down the stairs and began frantically searching the mansion for Mr. Walsh, the unflappable butler of Knight House. Surely he would know what was to be done. She glanced into the duke's elegant library at the end of the hallway, when suddenly, Peg screamed her name.

"Miss Montague! Lord Damien! Stop him! Stop him!"

Alice picked up her skirts and ran back to the entrance hall, where Peg was standing beside the open door, pointing. "He took him! Hurry! I tried to stop him; he's taken Harry—"

"Bardou?" Alice cried.

"No, Weymouth!"

As she rushed out into the cold night, she could already hear Harry crying.

"Weymouth!" Alice screamed in rage, racing after him. "What do you think you're doing?"

Clutching Harry in his arms, the viscount started to step up into his waiting carriage, but Alice barreled over to him and fought him, trying to take Harry from him.

"Get your hands off him!" she ordered through gritted teeth, trying to be heard above Harry's wailing screams and the booming fireworks. The bonfires and torches lit up the rowdy festival in the adjoining park, throwing a dim glow upon the austere face of Knight House. "Don't cry, Harry—"

"Auntie!" The child got hold of her hair and would not let go, but Weymouth yanked Harry's hands down.

"Give him back to me!" Alice shouted.

"I'm taking him, Alice! It is in Caro's will. *I* am Harry's legal guardian."

She stared at him, aghast. She had not thought that far in advance, but she realized he was right.

For a moment, she was so stunned by the realization, she did not know what to do. Weymouth refused to listen to her, and she had no legal grounds to stand on. "But—you can't! You can't take him, Weymouth! He barely knows you, he's terrified, and you don't know the first thing about caring for a child!"

"No, I don't, so would you please tell his nurse to stop dawdling and come with us? She will look after him."

"Weymouth, you are not taking that child! You are an opium eater and a drunkard! Now, give him back to me or I will call the constable!"

"He is *my* ward. I'm the one who can call the constable on you," he muttered, turning to put Harry into the carriage.

"Noooo!" Harry wailed, reaching for her. He began throwing a hysterical tantrum, screaming and thrashing.

With all her might, Alice reached for him again, but Weymouth turned around in sudden fury and shoved her hard. She stumbled backward and tripped on the hem of her gown, falling onto her backside on the graveled drive.

"Have you no feelings?" Weymouth cried, glaring down at her. "I lost my sister today! Harry is the one little piece of her that I have left! Now, if you'll excuse us, I'm going home and I'm taking Harry with me."

She started to get up, cursing at him, when a flicker of motion in the corner of her eye caught her attention. She turned and glanced toward Green Park—and then her blood ran cold.

Von Dannecker—or rather, Bardou—was standing just on the other side of the wrought-iron fence, peering through the bars at her, with Green Park at his back. Alice froze, paralyzed. Her stare locked with his. She ceased hearing the sounds of the festival; time stopped. Bardou brought up a rifle and smoothly aimed it at her.

Her eyes widened as a rider on a white horse came streaking out of the park as though he had burst out of the roaring bonfire itself.

Lucien!

He leaped off the galloping horse onto Bardou, tackling the big man to the ground. The rifle went off, the bullet zooming high up into the trees where it startled a hidden flock of roosting birds. They fluttered up out of the branches with indignant cries.

Still clutching Harry tightly in his arms, Weymouth let out a shocked oath and went over to see what was happening, but Alice stood rooted to her spot, watching their fight, all of her awareness focused on Lucien. He had told her it would be a struggle to the death, and she saw now what that meant.

They fought like two wild predators, rolling over the pavement, Lucien slamming Bardou against the ground. The Guy Fawkes illuminations gave her only glimpses of their faces, casting both men—snarling, feral—in a primal glow of firelight, molded by shadow. Neither seemed to feel the blows each rained on the other; both seemed unaware of anything else around them. Their concentration was total. Lucien pinned Bardou to the ground, punching him again and again in the face, then Bardou reached up and grasped Lucien's throat, starting to strangle him. Lucien reached toward Bardou's open rifle case, feeling about with his hand while the Frenchman kept squeezing the life out of him.

When Lucien suddenly lifted his hand from the rifle case, he was grasping a ten-inch steel bayonet. Alice gasped as Lucien's arm plunged. He drove the bayonet straight downward like a spike into Bardou's heart.

She was still holding her breath when the big Frenchman's hand slithered down from Lucien's throat and fell limply onto the pavement.

He was dead.

Lucien wiped his brow and rose, leaving the bayonet sticking out of Bardou's chest. For a second, he stood over the body, looking down at it, his chest heaving; then he lifted his gleaming, silvery stare and looked at Alice.

She let out a cry that was half a sob and ran to the gate, fumbling to let him in. She could hardly see through her tears. The moment he stepped through, he caught her up hard in his arms and held her tightly, cupping her head against his chest.

She sobbed incoherently and held him for all she was worth.

"Shh," he whispered. "It's all right now."

She could hear his heart still pounding from his exertions. "You're alive," she choked out, looking up at him. "You're all wet."

He kissed her forehead, then caught her face between his hands and stared at her, his fierce, primal victory blazing in his eyes.

She pulled him down to kiss her, and she didn't care who saw. He was alive and he had saved her life. She ended the kiss, her hands shaking with the aftermath of shock as she clung to his lapels.

"Lucien, you have to stop Weymouth! He's trying to take Harry away!"

"Oh, is he?" He glanced at the scrawny viscount, released her, and began stalking slowly toward Weymouth. His black, threatening glower made the untidy little man blanch.

"Well, er, you know—it was just a thought. There you are. I'm sure he'll be in excellent hands here." Weymouth quickly thrust Harry back into Alice's arms.

"Lambkin," she whispered, holding him tightly.

Weymouth cast Lucien a look of terror, backing away toward his carriage. He let out a nervous little laugh. "Perhaps I'm not the, er, best guardian for Harry at this . . . time. Of course, my name is on the will, but if Harry would be happier—that is, I'm sure I only want what is—" He glanced at Bardou's crumpled body, then at Lucien again and gulped. "—best for my little nephew. I'll drop by and check on him—"

"Leave," Lucien growled.

"Love to!" Weymouth sprang up into his carriage and rapped nervously for his driver.

Alice hugged Harry to her, calming him. As Weymouth's carriage rolled out of the gates, Lucien turned to her and stared at her and Harry for a moment with a quiet, solid possessiveness. Alice returned his gaze in mute adoration and bottomless thanks. *Defeating Bardou might have been the harder task, but for getting Harry back from Weymouth for her, he would eternally be her hero,* she thought. He walked over to them and embraced her and Harry together. He kissed her forehead; then he kissed Harry's forehead and whispered, "Don't cry, child."

"He can't help it," Alice started to say apologetically. Weymouth had scared the wits out of the boy, trying to steal him away, but to her surprise, Harry stopped crying abruptly at Lucien's gentle words.

Harry blinked and turned to Lucien, his finger in his mouth. Alice watched in wonder as Harry held out his arms to Lucien, wordlessly asking to be held.

"I'm all wet, Harry."

The boy started fussing again and reached for Lucien more insistently. Lucien's gray eyes mist briefly as he relented, taking Harry into his arms with obliging care. "There's a brave little fellow," he murmured, his voice gruff with emotion.

"Come inside," Alice whispered, tears of love shining in her eyes for both the boy and the man.

Lucien slipped his other arm around her shoulders. Together, their arms around each other, they walked back toward the warmly lit portico and went into the house.

Then Alice turned to him in worry. "Lucien, I almost forgot—there's something wrong with Damien. He's upstairs. You have to help him."

He had been fondly nuzzling Harry's temple, but at her words, he stopped and turned to her with a look of concern, handing the child back to her. "What's happened?"

"I'm not sure. All the fireworks and cannons seemed to confuse his wits. I'm fairly sure he thought he was back at the war."

Lucien stared at her. With a nod, he started to go into the house when a sudden clattering of hoofbeats sounded from the street behind them.

"Lord Lucien!"

"There he is!"

"My lord, you're alive!" Marc and the other young rogues came riding up to the gates and swung down from their horses.

Lucien waved to them, but she knew he was anxious to go to Damien. "Tell them to see to Bardou and to notify the constable. Marc knows the procedure."

Alice nodded. He leaned down and kissed her cheek, then went inside and climbed the stairs to see if he could help his brother. She followed him as far as the entrance hall, bringing Harry in from the cold night air. Her nephew had settled down to quiet sniffles, resting his head on her shoulder. She rubbed his back as she waited for the young men to join them. Peg walked over to her and caressed Harry's head, then glanced into her eyes.

"Bad salmon, eh?" Peg asked softly, giving her a chiding look.

Her eyes widened in sudden alarm, and a scarlet blush filled her cheeks; but when Peg smiled knowingly, tears misting her eyes, Alice broke into a smile from ear to ear.

"Oh, Peg, I love him so much," she choked out. "I couldn't help it!"

"Dearie," Peg scolded, laughing softly. The old woman embraced her and Harry both in her motherly arms. "I thought you'd never find the right one."

With victory and the jittery aftermath of rage still coursing through his veins, Lucien walked down the dim corridor to Damien's room. Bruised, bleeding, miserably cold and wet though he was, he felt none of it. He'd be sore tomorrow, no doubt, but for now, his aches and pains were entirely cancelled out by the exhilaration of his savage triumph. He did not want to think about how close that had been.

The terror he had felt when he had seen Bardou take aim at Alice would haunt him for the rest of his days. By the grace of God, he had arrived in time to save her. He knew that she and Harry both belonged to him now, and he was ready for it.

It was only his poor, battle-scarred brother that worried him. He knocked softly on Damien's door. "Demon, it's me. Let me in."

When no reply came, Lucien tried the door. It wasn't locked. He opened it cautiously and looked in.

The room was dark. The only light came from the window, where the cold, wintry moonlight angled in, outlining his brother's silhouette in silver. Damien was sitting on the floor, leaning against the wall, his elbows resting on his bent knees as he held his head in his hands. There was a pistol lying on the floor beside him. Lucien felt his blood run cold at the sight of it. Damien didn't move or respond when he walked in and closed the door behind him. He took a few cautious steps into the room. Even when he picked up the gun and unloaded it, his brother still didn't react.

"Are you all right?"

Damien didn't look up, but when he spoke his voice was low and gravelly, quietly racked with pain. "I'm losing my mind."

Lucien crouched down slowly beside him and studied him.

"What the hell is happening to me? You're smarter than me, Lucien. Tell me what to do, because I'm lost."

"Perhaps I should call the physician—"

"No. What for? To give me laudanum to calm me? Already tried it. Doesn't work. It merely fills my brain with even worse visions than I'm already having. *Jesus.*" He leaned his head back against the wall and closed his eyes with a look of exhaustion.

"How long has this been going on?" Lucien asked.

"A while." Damien was silent for a moment. "I swear I can see the face of every soldier I ever lost, and they want to know why I got to come home and they didn't. Why I get a title and the nation's thanks when all they got was a grave in the dust of Spain."

Lucien swallowed hard, shaken by his brother's words.

Damien looked at him starkly, dried tears staining his rugged cheeks in the moonlight. "Do me a favor. If I do go completely lunatic, put me out of my misery. You'd do that for me, wouldn't you? I don't care how. Poison me; shoot me; just don't put me in an asylum, because they really can't cure you, and I don't want people coming to look at me for their amusement, laughing at me. Anything but that."

"Shh." Lucien cut him off, putting his arm around him in a brotherly half hug. He held him like that for a long moment, his mind going back to when they were children and Damien would comfort him after the terror of one of his asthma attacks.

He leaned his head against Damien's and willed him to be all right. "You're not going mad. It's just going to take you some time to get used to civilian life again. Lord, Demon, you were in nearly every major action that was fought. You can't expect to come out of that entirely unscathed. It will pass."

"I hope you're right."

"Do you want me to send for some of the chaps from your regiment? Sherbrooke? He's always good for a drink."

"God, no. I don't want them to see me like this." Damien let out a low sigh. "What the hell am I supposed to do?" he asked in a stoic tone deadened by despair. "I've served my purpose, and now it's done. There's only one thing I know how to do anymore, and that's kill."

Lucien sat down on the floor next to him, watching his face in worry. "Maybe you should get away from London for a while. Go somewhere peaceful. Perhaps a few weeks up at Hawkscliffe Hall would help clear your head."

"Before I hurt someone, you mean?" He dragged his eyes open and looked at Lucien with a cynical smile. "Don't worry; I'll be all right. It's passed now. I just need to get laid," he added wryly. "Good night for it. I'm sure the girls are out in full force, ready for business."

"Are you sure that's a good idea?"

"Works better than the bloody laudanum." He climbed to his feet and stood up straight, shrugging the tension out of his shoulders.

As Lucien rose stiffly, as well, he could almost see Damien donning his mental armor, becoming once more the famed colonel, proud as ever, totally in control of himself and the world around him, as though none of this had ever happened. It saddened him, but at least Damien seemed to be feeling stable again. Damien opened the window and inhaled a few breaths of the chilly night air. He avoided Lucien's gaze. "Please tell Miss Montague I am sorry for frightening her."

"No apology necessary. Alice merely wants you to be well, as do I." Lucien shook his head. "God, Damien, don't take out your sidearm when you're in this state. You scared the hell out of me. I'm your twin brother. I should have realized something was wrong. Usually I don't even need to be in the same country as you to know how you're doing, but here we are, both in London, living under the same bloody roof, and I had no idea."

"I didn't want you to know."

"Because you're angry at me?"

"I'm not angry at you."

"What?" Lucien demanded. "You've been treating me like a bloody leper."

Damien's glance swung to him. "Yes, because I just wanted to ignore this—problem—and I knew you wouldn't let me. Nobody can hide any damned thing from you. It's vexing."

"Do you mean to say you're not bitter toward me for leaving the army?" he exclaimed.

"No, Lucien. I was glad you left. If you would've gotten killed, like so many of our friends . . ." His words trailed off, grief hanging upon the air between them.

Lucien's voice was quiet, thunderstruck. He shook his head dazedly. "I thought you hated my choice of professions."

"Part of me dislikes it. It's a dirty job, but as Wellington says, a necessary one. I couldn't do it, I freely admit that. I don't have the skill. I tell you, Lucien, I had to respect you for following your conscience after Badajoz. That took bottom."

"You son of a bitch," Lucien said, laughing quietly in amazement. "You had me utterly fooled."

"Did I? Well, that's something." Damien's wistful smile faded. "I suppose the charade's over now."

"Well, don't worry. I keep a secret pretty well. But listen to me. You've got to quit worrying about your men and take care of yourself for a while. You're not indestructible, contrary to popular opinion. There's no shame in it."

"The hell there's not. You're not the one going mad. By the way," he said, changing the subject, "I do hope you've come to your senses about marrying Alice. You're a fortunate man to have found someone so loyal. She is pure sterling. Turned down my offer, you know. She told me in no uncertain terms that she's in love with you."

Lucien grinned as he sauntered to the door. "So I've heard, so I've heard! I assure you, the sentiment is most ardently mutual, and marry her I shall—which reminds me. Will you stand as my groomsman?"

Damien cast him a wry look. "If you don't mind having a lunatic in your wedding party, I'd be honored."

Lucien paused in the doorway and gave him a look of reassurance. "We're all a *little* mad, my friend. Keeps life interesting. If you need anything, you know where to find me."

"Thanks," he said softly.

Lucien nodded and left the room. He walked down the corridor to his bedroom, savoring his victory. When he opened the door, he found his dim chamber glowing intimately with candles. The bed had been turned down, and Alice was waiting for him over by the smoldering fireplace, scantily clad in her thin cotton chemise. Her glorious hair cascaded over her shoulders as she bent down, swirling her hand in the steaming bathing tub, which she must have had prepared for him, he realized, while he was talking with Damien.

Ah, it was good to be a man, he thought, casting her a devilish smile as he pushed the door shut soundly behind him—and locked it. "Well, well, what a pleasant surprise."

"I think I shocked your butler when I asked him to show me to your room," she said, blushing prettily as she dried her hand on her hip. "I tried to explain we are engaged, but he looked, well, doubtful."

"Did he?" He just stared at her, feeling his very soul well with love as she padded toward him, barefooted. He loved her eyes; he loved her smile; he loved her pale, slender arms. He loved her dainty ankles, skimmed by the hem of her chemise. He loved her gliding walk and the way her long, thick hair swung around her waist as she hurried toward him. God help him, he was her slave.

He lowered his chin, mute with adoration, as she came to stand before him. Laying hold of his still-damp lapels, she lifted up onto her tiptoes and kissed his lips, then passed a wifely, assessing gaze over him, her Chartres-blue eyes full of youthful earnestness. It made him smile faintly.

"How are you?" she asked soberly.

"Wet."

"So you are. What did you do? Fall in the river?"

"Something like that."

"Come." She took his hand and pulled him toward the bed, then pushed him down to sit on the edge of it, nudged in between his thighs, and began undressing him.

"How efficient you are, my lady."

"I want you out of these wet clothes and into that hot bath before you catch cold."

"Only if you'll join me."

She smiled at him as she unbuttoned his sodden waistcoat, blushing prettily. "I don't see why not. Peg put Harry to bed, so you have me all to yourself."

"That, Miss Montague," he said, smiling as he pulled her into his arms and deftly tumbled her onto the bed, "is my definition of heaven."

EPILOGUE

They were married two weeks later by special license in the village church at Basingstoke with a grand reception afterward at Glenwood Park. Alice's mantua-maker had hastened to fashion her exquisite blush-satin bridal gown, while Lucien had searched for the most obscenely large diamond he could find for her ring. This had permitted time for Their Graces of Hawkscliffe to return from Vienna along with Lady Jacinda and Miss Carlisle. Now the Knight family, with the exception of the black sheep, Lord Jack, was gathered in the crowded, cheerfully noisy drawing room at Glenwood Park.

Alice was enchanted with her new brothers- and sisters-in-law.

The handsome duke, Robert, and his ravishing bride, Bel, had announced that they expected a blessed event in the spring. Alice found Robert, the patriarch of the family, a bit intimidating, though it was clear that he doted shamelessly on his wife. She had adored the witty, down-to-earth Bel from the moment the woman had hugged her in greeting and called her "sister."

Lucien's maiden sister, Lady Jacinda, was a beautiful, vivacious imp with apple cheeks and a cloud of golden curls. Though she would not make her debut until next year, to Alice's eye, the seventeen-year-old had already mastered the finer points of flirting and had quickly enchanted all five of Lucien's young rogues, who had also been invited to the wedding. Lady Jacinda's shy, serious, and dignified companion, Miss Carlisle, stood by the wall, ready to lend a moment's hand wherever she was needed, but Alice distinctly noticed Miss Carlisle staring with a look of helpless, painful infatuation at the golden Lord Alec, the youngest of the Knight brothers, who was not yet thirty. Alec was a fashionable rake with a teasing manner toward those he liked, the hauteur of a prince toward those he did not, and the looks of an Adonis—which got him anything in the world that he desired.

As for Damien, one short week ago he had been made the earl of Winterley, awarded a manor house and a thousand acres in Berkshire. He had stood proudly at the front of the church as Lucien's groomsman, but he still seemed restless. Alice worried for him.

On the other side of the room, she was presently engrossed in a conversation with Bel and some of the genteel neighbor ladies about everything having to do with babies. Since neither woman had a sister or a mother living, Alice shared the young duchess's excitement wholeheartedly over her first pregnancy. At great length, they discussed nursery arrangements, possible names, whether or not to use a wet nurse, when to wean a child, and how many they wanted to have.

Just then, Harry came tearing through the drawing room chasing the kitten that Lucien had finally persuaded Alice to let the boy adopt from among the strays in the garden behind the townhouse. The child's big, satin bow tie flopped under his chin as he gave chase, but the kitten fled toward the couch and scrambled up Mr. Whitby's leg. The old man yelped, drawing Lucien's attention at once.

Elegantly attired in his dove-gray morning coat with long tails, the bridegroom turned from laughing with his brothers just in time to stop the kitten from scrambling any farther up the old man's person. He picked the kitten up by the scruff of its neck and turned to Harry, who hopped around impatiently, begging to have his kitten back.

Harry let out a peal of laughter, however, when Lord Alec picked him up and tossed him in the air, then held him upside down, to Harry's vast hilarity, and deposited him gently on the couch behind them. Harry scrambled upright and ran back to Alec, begging to be thrown in the air again.

"How nice to see you've finally found a friend of your own august maturity, Alec," Robert said drily.

Alec's grin was undaunted, though the guests standing around them had a jovial laugh at his expense. Lucien, however, had caught Alice's eye. They exchanged a gaze from across the room that set her soul on fire. He slid a furtive glance toward the door, then raised his eyebrow discreetly in question. She sent him a sly, answering wink.

A moment later, she made a polite excuse to Bel and the other ladies who were standing nearby chatting with them, and stole off to meet the rogue in secret.

Turn the page for
a sneak peak at the next
thrilling Gaelen Foley novel

Turn the page for
a sneak peak at the next
thrilling Gaelen Foley novel,

Lord of Ice.

The story of Damien Knight unfolds . . .

CHAPTER ONE

Berkshire

With a hard-eyed stare, Damien Knight, the earl of Winterley, swung the long-handled axe up over his head and slammed it down with savage force, cleanly splitting the upright log down the middle. The sharp crack of the blow ripped across the snow-frosted field like a gunshot, rousing the squabbling blackbirds that fed upon the frozen stubbled cornstalks. His movements were smooth, his mind blissfully blank as he threw down the axe, adjusted one of his thick leather gloves, and picked up the splintered halves of wood, stacking them on the fortresslike pile that had grown over the past weeks to looming proportions, as though no amount of fuel could build a fire capable of warming him. Positioning the next log on the tree stump that served as his chopping block, he dealt it, in turn, a death blow.

He repeated this ritual again and again, concentrating intensely on the task, allowing it to absorb his tattered mind, until suddenly, in the nearby field, he noticed that something had caught his stallion's attention.

His white warhorse was his only companion in this place. The stallion had been idly pawing through the frost, nibbling at whatever bits of grazing it could find, but now it lifted its head and pricked up its elegantly tapered ears toward the drive. Damien wiped the sweat off his brow with the back of his arm, rested his other hand on the axe's handle, and squinted against the white glare of the mid-December day, following his horse's stare.

The stallion let out a belligerent whinny and raced toward the fence, its ivory tail streaming out like a battle pennant. He watched the animal for a moment in simple pleasure. It must have been a month since Zeus had worn a saddle. Both of them were reverting back to a state of nature, he thought, scratching the short, rough, black beard that had grown in on his jaw. Without surprise, only a dim flicker of distress, he watched as his identical twin brother, Lord Lucien Knight, came cantering up the drive astride his fine black Andalusian.

Zeus raced alongside them on the opposite side of the fence, trumpeting challenges to the black for encroaching upon his territory. Fortunately, Lucien was too skilled a rider to lose control of his mount.

Damien dropped his chin almost to his chest and let out a sigh that misted on the crisp, cold air. He supposed his brother had come to check up on him.

He did not fancy the notion of anyone seeing him like this, but at least with his keenly perceptive twin, he did not have to pretend that he was right in the head.

Lucien and his bride of three weeks, Alice, were living in Hampshire, a two-hour ride from Damien's ramshackle manor house, newly bestowed on him by Parliament along with his title. Not that he knew much about being an earl. His new rank seemed merely to have made him the servant of the bloody politicians. Picking up his last split logs and adding them to the woodpile, he cast an uncertain glance toward the run-down, overgrown mansion they had given him. Constructed of white-gray limestone, Bayley House, circa 1760, was modeled on a classical Greek temple with a triangular pediment atop four mighty columns. Damien thought it looked like a mausoleum.

It felt like one inside, too, sprawling hectares of empty floor bereft of furniture, cold enough to preserve a corpse. He half fancied the place was infested with ghosts, but he knew too well that it was only he who was haunted. He had neither the gold nor the energy to see the house brought back to life and properly appointed, nor did he particularly care. Spartan that he was, he did not require luxury.

Upon arriving here in November shortly after Guy Fawkes Night, he had set up camp and had been bivouacking near the fireplace in what had once been the drawing room. His fellow officers from the regiment—what few survivors there were—had scattered and returned to their families, but at least he was still surrounded by his equipment, all sixty pounds of which he had carried on his back for hundreds of miles on marches through Portugal and Spain. It comforted him: his trusty tent; his scuffed and battered tin mess kit and wooden canteen; his greatcoat for a blanket; his haversack for a pillow; a bit of cheese, biscuit, and sausage to sustain him; a few cigars. A soldier needed little else in life, except, of course, for liquor and whores, but Damien had given these up in an earnest effort to mend his fractured wits through the ascetic life.

'Sblood, though, he missed the lasses a hundred times more than the gin, he thought with a wistful sigh. Lucien could have his refined lady wife; Damien preferred low, bawdy wenches who knew how to handle a soldier. The mere thought of a soft, willing female roused his body's starved needs, but he ignored his agonized craving for release, coolly setting the axe out of the way as his brother approached. He could not risk anything that might upset his precarious equilibrium.

Snow flew up from under the black's prancing hoofs as Lucien reined in, vibrant and pink-cheeked with the cold, his silvery eyes sparkling with the aura of the newlywed. He sat back in the saddle for a moment, rested his right fist on his hip, and shook his head, looking Damien over in sardonic amusement. "Oh, my poor, dear brother," he said with a lordly chuckle.

"What?" Damien growled, scowling a bit.

"How charmingly rustic. You look like some hermit woodsman. Lancelot, maybe, after he became a monk."

Damien snorted. "So, she let you out from under the cat's paw for a few hours, eh? When's your curfew?"

"Only long enough for my sweet lady to remember afresh how desperately she adores me. When I return—" He flashed a wicked smile. "—the welcome home ought to be worth it." His luxurious black wool greatcoat whirled out behind him as he dismounted with an agile movement. Smart and elegant, full of Diplomatic Corps finesse, Lucien reached into his coat and presented Damien with a newspaper as he strode toward him. "I thought you might like to see what is going on in the world."

"Napoleon still under guard on Elba?"

"Of course."

"That's all I need to know."

"Well, burn it for fuel, then, though you certainly seem well supplied in that particular. Planning on burning a witch?" Lucien looked askance at the giant woodpile.

Damien regarded him wryly and accepted yesterday's copy of the *London Times* without further argument.

Lucien passed a shrewd glance over his face. "How goes it, Brother?" he asked more softly.

Damien shrugged and turned away, abashed by his concern. "It's quiet here. I like it."

"And?" Lucien waited for him to report on his mental condition, but Damien dodged the unspoken inquiry, avoiding his twin's penetrating stare.

"Needs work, of course, this old place. Fences to be mended. We'll plant barley there"—he pointed to the fields—"oats there, wheat over there, in the spring." *If it ever comes,* he thought.

"God, grant me patience. Do not be deliberately obtuse, please. I didn't ask how your house is. I want to know how you're doing. Has there been any repeat of—"

"No," he cut him off, flashing him a warning look. He had no desire to be reminded of his hellish delirium—or bout of madness or whatever the devil it had been—on Guy Fawkes Night. He hated even thinking about it. The booming of the festival cannons and exploding fireworks had played a kind of trick on his mind, deluding him into thinking he was back at the war. For a full five or six minutes, he had lost track of reality, a horrifying state of affairs for a man so highly trained to kill.

When he thought of how easily he could have hurt someone, it made his blood run cold. He had exiled himself here since that night and did not intend to show his face in Society again until he had somehow cured himself, was no longer a threat to the very people he had sacrificed his innocence to protect, and had become once more the ironclad military hero the world expected him to be.

He noticed Lucien studying him, reading him in his all-too-knowing way, those silvery eyes flashing with formidable intelligence. "Still having nightmares?"

Damien just looked at him.

He did not want to admit it, but the ghastly dreams of

blood and destruction were even more frequent now, as though his addled brain could not unburden itself of its poisons fast enough. The rage in him was a frozen river like the ice-encrusted Thames that wrapped around his property. He knew it was there, but the strangest thing was he could not quite . . . feel it. He could not feel much of anything. Six years of combat—of ignoring terror, horror, and heartbreak—had that effect on a man, he supposed.

"You really shouldn't be alone at a time like this," Lucien said gently.

"Yes, I should, and you know why." Avoiding his brother's scrutiny, he shoved some of the wood into a neater pile, then dusted a few stray bits of bark off his buff-leather trousers.

"At least you're still coming to London for Christmas with the family, I trust?"

He nodded firmly. "I'll be there." As long as the too-jolly prince regent could restrain himself from sponsoring another irritating fireworks show for the city, Damien saw little reason to worry. Christmas was a holy, tranquil night; it was New Year's Eve that tended to be raucous, accompanied by the usual rowdiness, noise, and explosives. He would return to his sanctuary at Bayley House by then. "Do you want something to drink?" he offered, belatedly remembering hospitality.

"No, thanks." Lucien slipped his hands into the pockets of his greatcoat and looked away, squinting toward the horizon. He seemed to hesitate. "There is . . . actually another reason I'm here, Damien. The truth is . . . ah, hell," he whispered, shutting his eyes. "I really don't know how to tell you this."

Damien looked over, taken aback by Lucien's stark tone. A prickle of dread ran down his spine as his gaze took in his brother's paling face and anguished stare. "Jesus, Lucien, what is it?" Abandoning the woodpile, Damien walked over to him, drawing off his gloves. "What's happened? The family—"

"No, we're all fine," he said quickly, then lowered his head and spoke with difficulty. "I was in London on business earlier in the week when I heard. The news is all over Town. I'm so damned sorry, Damien." Steeling himself, he lifted his head and looked into his eyes. "Sherbrooke's dead. He was murdered Wednesday night."

"*What?*" He felt his stomach plummet with nauseating swiftness, but could only stare at his brother without comprehension.

"Apparently there was a robbery. The intruder shot him in the chest. I came as soon as I heard." Lucien gazed at him in distress. "I know—God, I know—you're in no condition to hear this, but I didn't want you to find out some other way."

Damien felt the air leave his lungs in a whoosh. "Are you sure?" he forced out.

Lucien gave a pained nod.

"Oh, God." He turned and walked a few paces away, then stopped, blank with shock. He dragged his hand through his hair and just stood there, at a loss, staring at the bleak horizon and the winter-bare trees of the cherry orchard on the ridge, black and gnarled, and the cold glint of the frozen river. The sun had gone behind the clouds, and where there had been bright sparkles on the snow, now there was only a white, unforgiving glare.

There was a very long silence.

Behind him, he heard Lucien's black stallion snort and paw the ground in princely impatience. His brother murmured softly, quieting the animal, while Damien fought in silence to absorb the blow without falling to his knees in sheer despair. He had thought they were safe now. The war was over. How could he have forgotten that death, the ultimate victor, marched on?

He spun around abruptly, wrath darkening his face. "Do they know who did it?"

"No. Bow Street is still investigating. They suspect any number of known thieves in the area. I've taken the liberty of sending a few of my young associates to inquire into the matter."

"Thank you." He looked away, trembling, his face hard and expressionless, but even he was shocked by how quickly he adapted to the news. To be sure, this was an old routine by now, the death of a friend, he thought in deep, welling bitterness. There were courtesies to be carried out, rituals to be observed. Duties to be fulfilled. He clung to them for his sanity's sake.

His men would need him. As their colonel, it fell to him to set the example of conduct, discipline, manly self-control. They still depended on him, as they had on the battlefield, to stand firm against the chaos and disequilibrium they all felt. Half a decade of their lives had passed in a roaring, blood-spattered flash of horror, and suddenly, here they were, dazed to find themselves in tranquil old England again, blooded savages thrown back into Society, where they must be gentlemen again. *By God, I have been selfish,* he thought, closing his eyes and damning himself for leaving them, coming out here to lick his wounds. If he had stayed in London, if he had looked after Sherbrooke better . . . *I should have been there.*

He bowed his head, agonized by the thought. Clearly, he had tarried in solitude long enough.

When he lifted his head again, his eyes were as cold and

gray as stone, and when he spoke, his voice was the controlled, deadened monotone of a seasoned commander. "I will be needed in London for the burial, I presume. He was not close to his family."

Lucien passed an uneasy glance over his face, trying to read him. "There's something else." He reached into his waistcoat and took out a folded piece of paper, handing it to him. "Sherbrooke's solicitor has already tried to contact you. I told him I would deliver this. It seems Jason named you guardian of his ward."

"Damn, I had forgotten," he murmured, taking the letter. He cracked the seal and unfolded it with a private shudder to recall the conversation after the Battle of Albuera when Sherbrooke, half dead from saber wounds, his right arm gone, had begged him to accept the guardianship of his little orphaned niece if he didn't survive. Damien had reassured him that, of course, he would.

With a wave of loss that he quickly tamped down, he remembered how Sherbrooke used to buy souvenirs for the little girl, sending bits of Spanish lace and beads back to England for her from every town they conquered. Gaudy, colorful scarves, little dolls, satin slippers.

What the devil was her name again? He skimmed the solicitor's letter. *Yardley School, Warwickshire . . .*

He had never seen the child, but he knew she was the bastard daughter of Sherbrooke's deceased eldest brother, Viscount Hubert, by his mistress, who had been some sort of actress. Before Albuera, Sherbrooke had spoken often of the lively child, reading her earnest, little-girl letters aloud, to the hilarity of the officers at the mess, but after being maimed, he seemed to forget all about her, withdrawing into himself, drinking ever more heavily.

Ah, yes, he thought, scanning down the page. That was it.

Miranda.

Just like the girl in Shakespeare's *The Tempest*. A deuced fanciful name for an English schoolgirl, he thought with a stern frown. No doubt it was the actress's doing. He supposed the chit was fourteen or fifteen by now—or had she passed that age years ago? he wondered with a sudden flicker of uneasiness. He brushed it aside. Folding the solicitor's letter, he tucked it into his breast pocket.

Duty had a galvanizing effect on him. For a man of action, he had felt cut adrift since his regiment had been dissolved at the close of the war. He rolled up his emotions and tucked them away as quickly as a piquet could pull up camp and march. For the first time in weeks, he had some direction. After all, his demons could not haunt him when his mind was fixed on helping other people—his men, his new ward. He would hurry to London, arrange the memorial service for Jason, and steady his men after this difficult blow. With Lucien's background in espionage for the Foreign Office, the two of them would help Bow Street however they could in the effort to find the person who had done this; then Damien would ride to Warwickshire to break the news in person to the girl about her uncle's death.

Damn, he thought bleakly. That would be the hardest part. He would rather rushed a fortified line of French earthworks than face a female's tears, no matter her age, but it had to be done.

He looked hollowly at Lucien, the silver-tongued, multilingual diplomat-spy. "How do you tell a little girl who watched her parents drown that the only person left in the world who loved her is dead?"

Lucien winced and shook his head. "Gently, my friend. Very, very gently."

"Jesus," Damien whispered, then looked away and let out sharp curse under his breath. For Sherbrooke's sake, he vowed to give the girl the best of everything, even if it meant foregoing the purchase of the broodmares with which he had planned on starting his racing stock in the spring—his dream, such as it was.

Above all, he would find out who had done this.

"I'll go with you to London if you wish," Lucien offered, watching him closely.

"Thanks, but give me a moment," he muttered, scratching his scruffy jaw with a barren sigh. "I've got to shave."

Ready or not, it was time to face the world.

Lord of Ice
Gaelen Foley

Damien Knight, the earl of Winterley, is proud, aloof, and tormented by memories of war.

Though living in seclusion, he is named guardian to a fellow officer's ward. Instead of the young homeless waif he was expecting, however, Miranda FitzHubert is a stunning, passionate beauty who invades his sanctuary and forces him back into society. Struggling to maintain honour and self-control, Damien now faces an ever greater threat: desire.

A bold, free spirit, Miranda has witnessed the darkest depths of Damien's soul – and has seen his desperate need for love. But before she can thaw his unyielding heart, she must endure a terrifying nightmare of her own . . .

***Lord of Ice* is a historical romance set in the Regency period and is part of Gaelen Goley's award-winning and bestselling *Knights Miscellany* series.**